RAVAGES OF HONOR

RAVAGES OF HONOR

CONQUEST

MONALISA FOSTER

For all who serve.

ACKNOWLEDGMENTS

My profound thanks to ...

Imogen Keeper, Miranda Honfleur, Zeta Lordes, Scott Bell, and all the other writers who offered critiques and helped me figure out just how much I had to learn.

Dean Wesley Smith, whose invaluable classes and mentorship allowed me to hone my skills and hold on to my sanity.

Kacey Ezell, who pegged exactly what was wrong and helped me figure out how to make it right.

Cathe Smith, for her help with filling in all the biological stuff. Without her help, the genetic handwavium in this story would have been puny. Instead, it stands strong.

Justin Watson, who underpromised and over-delivered.

Tom Kratman, who thought enough of me to call me friend and was there when the haters were wearing me down.

Most of all, I must thank my husband, who not only provided me with the freedom to pursue this dream, but spent countless hours listening to me talk about my process (aka crazy writer talk), always told me the truth (including "this sucks") and is always there for me.

CHAPTER ONE

*I*t had been more than a decade since Syteria had breathed the sweet air of Kappa, the world where she'd been born. High above her, Rho—Kappa's larger planetary sister, with its brilliant polar caps, its milky, white clouds swirling across deep, blue oceans—dominated the sky. To Syteria, it still looked like a vast, malevolent eye, despite all its beauty. A beauty that washed out the hauntingly familiar stars struggling to make their presence known.

A leaden weight, as heavy as her tactical vest's armor plating, took form in her belly. Her grip on the rifle tightened, each deliberate breath bringing it closer as if it were some talisman.

Syteria had been paired with Mara, a trusted *eniseri* veteran. Age lines and scars crisscrossed the older woman's face. Her dark hair, clipped close to the scalp like Syteria's own, was covered almost entirely by her helmet. Mara's gloved hands rested lightly on her rifle. A soft wind stirred the leaves on the trees above them, sending shadows into play across her confident face.

They knelt at the edge of a clearing, in the cover and concealment of a downed tree, awaiting the order to advance on the lone shack with its pitiful column of smoke.

A stone well fronted an animal corral. The lowing of the beasts within, the odor of manure, the tinkle of bells worn by the animals in case they got lost, all poked at her memory. Syteria had been born and raised in a place not so unlike this one.

She closed her eyes as flashes of her past surfaced: running barefoot through leaves; watching Rho rise and set; holding a soft, downy hatchling in her hands.

Syteria shook her head and opened her eyes, darting a glance at Mara, checking to see if she'd somehow given something away. But Mara was watching the shack.

To keep her hand from drifting up to the monitoring collar, Syteria tightened her grip on her rifle's stock. Maybe the collar would attribute the change in her breathing and body chemistry to nerves, to this being her first time. Maybe the Matrons who were monitoring this mission were too busy to notice.

A jolt of pain traveled up to pierce her temple. She winced, gritting her teeth.

Others might get a pass. They didn't have her history of disobedience, her willingness to endure round after round of exhaustion, pain, and deprivation. Others willingly took the mind-altering drugs that poisoned the soul and stripped them of individuality. For whatever reason, they didn't work as well on Syteria, a fact for which she was grateful, despite the price.

Another jolt coursed up and down her spine. She would have screamed, but the collar took her voice. It would not be returned until it echoed in unison with all the others.

She mouthed the required words: I am *eniseri*. I will obey.

Closing her eyes, she repeated the words again and again. The tightening muscles felt like they might tear each other apart. Pain radiated from her heart. She could no longer breathe. The muscles in her chest had stopped working.

I am eniseri. *I will obey.*

Oh please, stop. Let this end. She sent that thought, that prayer not to the Matrons, not to Rho's ruling Matriarchs, but to the Kappan deity whose name she couldn't even remember.

Syteria didn't care how it ended. Dead on the grass was as good as any other option. Better perhaps. But in all these years, the Matrons had not granted her that escape. Only the well-behaved *eniseri* that were monitored less closely managed to take their own lives.

The pain stopped as if someone had flipped a switch.

It'd be a while before they'd use the collar again. Recovery from pain scrambled the signals. Until they returned to baseline, Syteria could enjoy a bit of autonomy. Or at least the illusion of it, for whatever that was worth.

Trembling, she dragged a gloved hand across her mouth and tugged the water tube forward. The sip of water refused to make its way down. She spat it onto the already wet ground beside her and sat back, waiting for the shaking to subside.

"Your first culling?" Mara asked, her first words to Syteria. The hours since their initial introduction aboard the Rhoan drop-ship had been filled with the uneasy silence of untrusting strangers.

Syteria nodded.

A chilling gaze swept over her as Mara's lip curled into a sneer. "Just remember why you're here."

How could Syteria forget? She was an instrument, a means to wage war against her own people.

"Adults are your priority targets," Mara reminded her. "Take them out first. Let the children run. Remember, we want them to run."

She remembered. Every day and night, every time she had to do any of the vile, vicious things required of her. Syteria would never forget the mask of streaked greens and browns, the harsh sneering face under a helmet masked with leaves. Ten years ago, an *eniseri* had appeared out of the forest to snatch her.

Her twelve-year-old self had screamed and kicked and bitten, earning the first of many "therapies." And now the Matrons expected her to take just-orphaned Kappan children and make them forget who and what they were. All so they could replenish the dwindling numbers in the *eniseri* crèches.

Eniseri numbers must've dwindled unexpectedly. Why else would the Matrons drop them off only in pairs?

Obey. Obey and live.

3

The life of an *eniseri* was better than death. There were worse fates than life as an interchangeable cog in the Rhoan machine. A machine that ran on the inviolable, infallible triumvirate of the Matriarchy: Unity. Uniformity. Stability.

Syteria took another sip, forestalling the urge to retch. The water, body-warm and stale, slid down her throat more easily this time.

"What's Control waiting for?" she asked, her voice soft and uncertain.

Mara gave her a look that asked, *What kind of idiot are you?* or perhaps, *You're going to get us both killed.* Mara shrugged the question off, gaze darting to the shack.

Not even a breath of wind stirred.

"Last year one of them got me," Mara said in that toneless voice of an *eniseri* veteran. "If they're armed, they're a target. Understand?"

"I understand."

"Don't let them get near you." A hard edge cut through Mara's tone. It matched the look in the older woman's eyes.

Syteria had seen that edge before—in the eyes of the Matrons. Mara, was close, very close, to becoming one of *them*. Perhaps as close as one mission, *this* mission.

"They're feral little beasts," Mara added.

Heartbeats crashed in Syteria's ears, accompanied by a rush of cold that seeped bone-deep.

"Feral beasts," Syteria echoed. "I'll be careful."

Without these "feral beasts" the Rhoans would have to do their own fighting and dying. The Kappans were physically and emotionally better suited to fighting. Less to the dying, though, which made their use a double-edged sword. Without their technological advantage, the Rhoans never would have gained control of the Kappans.

Lying awake at night, Syteria's mind had endlessly played with the question: What if the Kappans could advance enough to neutralize the Rhoans' technological edge?

The collar vibrated in warning.

Follow orders. Obey.

The mantra echoed in the back of her mind, drowning out the bird

4

and insect calls filling the night. Rho had risen to its zenith. A silent drone circled overhead. Over her earpiece, the comm chatter slowed to a trickle, then died, leaving only the lull of static.

Syteria shifted, easing back onto one knee.

The shack was no more than a dark shadow. Its column of smoke had thinned, gray tendrils turning to vapors. It was so quiet she could make out the drip from a leaking bucket hitting the distant well-water below.

Syteria wet her lips and whispered, "How did the 'feral beast' get you?"

"One of the little monsters had a knife," Mara said. "Plunged it into my leg, right between the plates and into my thigh." There was an edge of anger there, a tiny bit of it.

"What did you do?"

"Put a bullet in its brain," Mara said, speaking as though it was something she did every day, something that didn't haunt her at night.

How had Mara erased her true self? Like all *eniseri*, she'd been born on Kappa. How long had it taken to turn her into this monster? How many missions like this one, culling her own people? How much therapy? The questions died, unspoken. The scars on Syteria's body were a testament to the severity with which such talk was punished.

"What if I'm wrong?" Syteria asked. "What if I kill a female?"

Mara reached for her spare magazine and flipped it so the ammunition nestled inside could be seen in the threadbare light.

"All our rounds are lethal, see? That means the Matrons don't care." Mara reseated the magazine in its pouch, shifted to a more comfortable position, and flashed a white smile. "This makes it easier for us. We don't have to risk injury, or worry about collateral damage. You'll see. Easy."

"Easy."

The word fouled Syteria's mouth. Once more, she reached for the water tube dangling off her shoulder and sipped. Even as it went down, the water failed to clear her revulsion. One bullet was all that it would take to end Mara's life. But the Rhoans had taken precautions. A rifle aimed at an *eniseri* wouldn't fire.

"Once the adults and older children are dead," Mara said, "we'll round up the rest and worry about separating the males from the females."

Syteria nodded. It was a kindness, really—for the Matriarchy was, by their own definition, kind. It had little use for males of any race and no use for Kappan males. They were too aggressive, too hard to control. Unpredictable too. She'd seen what had happened to the few Kappan males the Rhoans had brought back. Seen enough to know her brothers hadn't been one of the unfortunates that had been captured.

And then she'd forgotten what she'd seen, buried it deep and kept it hidden, lest it weaken her. The collar buzzed, vibrating against her bones, sending pulses in quick succession to stab and claw at her conscience and her body.

She would dispense, quick, merciful kindness. She would follow orders.

Adrenaline flooded her body until she became as taut as a bowstring held too long at draw. She trembled, craving and fearing release.

Release came over the earpiece as a mix of orders and expletives. It was followed by the boom of a low-yield diversionary device that hit the shack's meager roof. It didn't demolish the structure, but it did make its walls shake and the roof planks splinter.

A child's cry joined another and quickly died. That the children were still alive was a given. It wasn't like the Kappans to kill their own outright, not even to deny them to the Rhoans. Every *eniseri* was proof of that.

Kappans fought viciously to save their offspring. Many fought to the end. It's what made each culling so dangerous.

The airborne drone painted the clearing with its searchlight. Mara moved up and took point. Syteria followed, coming to rest behind the thickest tree trunk she could find.

They waited.

"Here they come," Mara said, her voice tight. "Cover me."

Syteria raised her rifle and thumbed the safety. She obediently put

6

the center of the reticle on the shack door, right on the point where an adult's center of mass would be.

Mara advanced, boots crunching the twigs and leaves beneath.

The shack door opened with a slow, deliberate swing, but no one emerged.

"Hold. I want them out in the open," Mara said, her whisper carrying in the crisp, night air.

The stirrup and limbs of a crossbow preceded a rough, unkempt male as he crouch-walked into the open and turned towards them.

Syteria lowered her scope's reticle until it framed a bearded face.

Breath caught in her chest. Blood froze in her veins. Muscles locked in place.

She knew him.

The crossbow twanged and an arrow cut through the air.

The wet sound of flesh parting for the arrowhead was followed by the gurgle of blood caught in an unyielding throat. A sack of flesh and bone that had once responded to the name of Mara, dropped. The twitching and gurgling of Mara's life faded, joining the unnatural silence that hung like a fog.

He looked up. Long, dirty hair fell back to reveal a determined face illuminated by the drone's light.

They had been apart longer than they had been together, Syteria and her brother. But it *was* him. She was certain. They shared the same rare coloring, green eyes and chestnut hair, and whenever she looked in the contraband mirror in the *eniseri* barracks, the features that stared back at her reflected him more than not.

His name—Aviel—formed on her lips without sound.

He ducked back into the shack.

The door swung open again. Aviel's back was to her as he shielded a pregnant female who was herding two small children towards the other side of the clearing. He looked up at the circling drone. An unarmed observer, it posed no immediate threat.

Would Aviel know that?

Syteria ran towards them, heart pounding, rifle held low. If he was alive, maybe the rest of her family was too. She'd forgotten their faces,

7

their voices, their names. But something remained, like a scent in the air, that, if followed, led to the source.

She stumbled as the Matrons ordered her to kill the adults, their harsh voices buzzing in her ear.

Just short of the clearing, she ducked behind a tree, dug her gloved hands into the thick foliage, and bit down on a scream as she closed her eyes and pressed her face into the rough bark. There was only so much pain they could make her feel until her body simply shut down on its own. She waited for darkness to swallow her, to render her useless to them.

But it didn't come.

Her rifle had swung to a stop at her side, its weight suddenly too burdensome to bear. She dropped the loaded magazine and cleared the chamber, tossing both into a thicket. She did the same with the spares. Then she released the buckle and the strap fell away. Numb fingers dropped the harness rig from across her chest. Whatever the Matrons did to compel her obedience now would be wasted.

Unarmed, she posed no threat to *her* people, or her family.

Syteria worked the clasp at her chin, took the helmet off, and dropped it. Next, she yanked the earpiece, placed it atop a rock, and crushed it under her heel. A wind had risen, whipping about her, tumbling the pieces of broken tech into the soil.

Aviel had stopped on the other side of the well. The woman and children huddled behind him. He spoke, but the wind snatched his words before they could reach Syteria.

She would not reveal herself, nor plead for the chance to join them.

After what the Rhoans had done to her body, her brother would not recognize her anyway. The homing beacon in her collar and the tracking implant in her body still posed a threat. By following them, by joining them, she would only doom them to her own fate.

Vision smearing, she bolted in the opposite direction.

An *eniseri* gone rogue would entice the drone to pursue her instead. A traitor was the worthier target, someone to be made an example of, someone to break.

She ran, stumbled, fell. Without hesitation, she pushed herself up and ran again, fueled by the return of something she had believed lost forever, something she'd surrendered, something that had been extracted from her unwilling self, something that had no value to the Rhoans—her honor.

The air rushing past her whispered with her grandfather's voice, *There is no greater love…*

She swiped at the branches blocking her way. Uncaring, she plunged through darkness, ducking and weaving through the thinning trees.

There is no greater love…

The drone passed overhead, floating like a specter above the treetops.

How much time she'd bought Aviel, or if it was enough to let him and his escape what was to come, she didn't know.

It had to be enough.

Syteria stumbled out into a field gone fallow and almost made it across. Between one step and another pain bloomed at the base of her spine and took her legs out from underneath her. She rolled onto her back, chest heaving. Copper and iron spilled over lips stretched into a smile.

An honorable death at last.

Tears filled her eyes as Rho's malevolent light went grey. Her breaths rattled like a rusty chain about to snap.

And then there was no more light.

And no more pain.

THE SMACK of her skull against metal blurred Syteria's vision. Blood dripped down from her nose, salty and thick. It stuck to and soured in the back of her throat.

The Matrons who'd captured her must have given her something after she'd fallen. She could barely breathe. She needed to swallow, to blink, but couldn't. They had placed her on her back, under a dull grey ceiling. Blurred images passed in and out of her field of vision, casting shadows. Her eyes watered, filling slowly and then emptying, all without sensation.

Whispers rose, distorted at first, then sharpening. Whatever had paralyzed her muscles hadn't affected her hearing.

"It's perfectly safe, Compeer Captain," a female voice said. Its contralto pitch betrayed it as the voice of an older Matron. "Just keep her sedated once the paralytic wears off."

A backlit silhouette came to stand over Syteria. Her eyes wouldn't focus enough to bring in fine details. The lack of height betrayed a Rhoan male.

"We are not soldiers," the captain said. He backed out of Syteria's field of vision. "This cell was built to hold zoo specimens, not Kappans, and definitely not *eniseri* gone rogue. Can't we have a Matron for our safety?"

"I have none to spare, Compeer. I am very sorry," she said, making no effort to hide her contempt.

While the Rhoan Matriarchs terrified the Matrons, the Rhoan males did not. Smaller and weaker than Rhoan females, they were the opposite of Kappan males. The Matriarchs had bred aggression out of most of them. They were meek and passive. The captain would've never questioned a Rhoan female the way he had the Matron, even with fear driving him.

"You expect us to tend to this dangerous traitor ourselves?" His tone clearly said that the Rhoan language did not have the proper words to express the disgust that the act of tending implied. "Why not just execute her here and now?"

Execution. Not re-education. Not re-conditioning. If the Matrons hadn't known of her ties to Aviel and his family when they'd sent her in, they would surely have figured them out by now. And if they'd captured him—them—then the torment of watching Aviel and his family share her fate awaited. Perhaps that's why she was still alive. Syteria's heart beat painfully in her chest.

"Her execution must be a public spectacle," the Matron said. "One that every *eniseri* must witness. It's the perfect example for the Kappan females we are bringing back with us. They will see how disobedience and treason are dealt with and it will make them easier to control. More of them will survive the transition from Kappan to *eniseri*."

The captain's silhouette came back into view and leaned closer.

Syteria could not get her eyes to focus no matter how hard she tried. She'd rather have all the pain and agony in the world than this helplessness.

"Then use one of your own transports," the captain insisted, pulling away and turning to face the Matron.

"We are not done with the culling," the Matron said. "It could be days. The Matriarchs want her on Rho now. I'm sorry, Compeer. I have my orders."

She moved away.

Reflex must've taken over: Syteria's throat spasmed, ejecting blood and sputum. Her lungs burned.

"It would be unfortunate if you allowed her to drown in her own blood, Compeer Captain," the Matron's departing voice said.

Shadows shifted with the Rhoan captain's movements. He gave Syteria's head a nudge, turning it so the blood could run out of her mouth. Thudding footsteps were followed by the sound of grating metal.

Bars sliced the light in the telltale pattern of a cell. She must be aboard a Rhoan vessel, one used to bring specimens from Kappa back to Rho. Syteria had helped unload such ships before. Their holds were full of tools and artifacts collected to assess how fast the Kappans were advancing. She'd never been this far inside one though.

The roar of vibrations she could not feel filled her ears. Shifting gravity tugged at her stomach as the ship took off.

Syteria gasped her last breath of Kappan air. It was bittersweet as it faded to be replaced by the drier, sanitized air of the transport's reserves.

As the ship shuddered around her, sensation fell into place bit by bit. First, the pain from the jolt to her back, the one that had caused her to stumble and fall. Then the tightness around her wrists and ankles. The weight of the collar. The cold of the metal surface to which they had strapped her seeped in through her bare scalp.

Light faded to total darkness. Sparks danced in her vision, an illusion as her brain compensated for the lack of light. She'd experienced the sensation once before, when she'd been punished with days in a sensory deprivation tank. In it she'd floated in water fouled by her own waste. It had eaten at her skin, leaving it raw. Once the Matrons pulled her out, she'd oozed with open sores for days, despite being hosed down with antiseptic.

The floating sensation confusing her ears was unlike the buoyancy of the sensory deprivation tank. This was something else, a weightlessness, like she was falling in place, despite being held fast to the table by the restraints.

Syteria worked her throat to call out, but no sounds emerged. The collar was still in place, stealing her voice. Its warning buzz was almost lost as she was pulled down against the table. Gravity's pull mimicked the weight of another person perched atop her chest. It increased two-fold. Then three.

The ship was under acceleration, but not the kind she'd come to expect, not even from the faster, more maneuverable *eniseri* transports.

Weight increased beyond what she'd ever experienced before. The sparks behind her closed eyelids flashed like a swarm of lightning bugs. Gravity shifts pushed the flesh on her face to one side, then another.

Gradually, that pull eased.

Syteria lifted her head. Panicked screams drifted through the bulkheads. A change in acceleration pulled her to the left, the cuffs tearing at her as the ship rolled, then pitched.

Gravity changed again accompanied by the groan of metal. Lights flickered on, blinding her, then cut back to darkness. The red of emergency lighting came up, revealing the tube inserted into her arm. She was still wearing her uniform. Kappan mud still clung to her boots.

She groaned. Her muscles responded, testing the restraints.

Her cell spun with her, tugging at the tie-down points, sending the fluid in the sedation bag sloshing. Weightlessness returned and the fluid coalesced into spheres floating within the confines of the bag.

Acceleration battered her about. She slipped in and out of consciousness, waking to panicked screams and the tearing of metal.

How long had it been?

Unbearable dryness parched her throat. The empty sedation bag had come off its hook. It floated over her, then crashed to the floor, yanking the needle out of her arm.

A great light swelled like a star gone nova. Syteria squeezed her eyes against it lest it sear her into blindness. Still, the light persisted. Klaxons blared in her ears. When they stopped, a ringing replaced them. She gasped at air gone thin, tugging viciously against the restraints.

She wasn't going to die like this, like some sacrifice bound to an altar, waiting for the death blow.

Putting her remaining strength into the motion, she pulled against the metal cuff around her left wrist. Pain radiated from her hand as skin and tendons tore, as the cuff's unyielding metal squeezed down on delicate bones cracking one, then another, then a third.

It wasn't pain that took her. Not this time. It was something else, something strange, something she'd never felt before, and hoped never to feel again. Even in the cell's dimness, reality appeared to fracture. A fissure here. A fissure there, sparkling with a million tiny stars shifting in color from red to blue and back again.

I'm hallucinating.

She had to be. It was the only explanation.

Acceleration returned with a vengeance. It squeezed at her until her vision tunneled, until she could no longer feel the pain of her left hand. Acceleration held her on a precipice between oblivion and consciousness, between light and dark, between death and life.

Her mind fought its way out of numbing shadows, towards the pain of reality.

She would not die this way.

She wouldn't.

CHAPTER TWO

*P*aired chimes announced the last half hour of the day. They bounced off the fifty metres of wood-paneled bulkhead at Darien's back as he stood, eyes closed, barely breathing. He focused on the *Edlyn's* bells. Their vibrations caressed the skin of his bare torso as they traveled around him. Most of them met their end in front of him, against the swordhall's viewscreen.

The weaker bounce-backs betrayed the presence of the support struts reinforcing the viewscreen from below his feet all the way up to the deck four metres above. Those very struts would transform into an armored physical barrier that would shield the spartan chamber against anything that might penetrate the energy field surrounding the capital ship.

The field's pulses harmonized at the edge of his perception, bringing with them other harmonies from the *Edlyn's* gravitic genera-tors, her inertial inhibitors, the electromagnetic fields that flowed through her like lifeblood. All those minuscule disturbances swirled around his bare feet and up his legs, dampened slightly by the weight of the traditional *hakama* wrapped around his hips.

Taking a deep breath, he brought his left hand to rest on the scab-bard of his sword.

Darien opened his eyes.

Thousands of stars pricked the darkness of open space. Three-quarters of the *Edlyn's* long axis, six-hundred-kilometres of hull stretched before him. Half of that length defined his ship's short axis, but most of it remained out of sight, below this deck.

He gave the scabbard a precise twist. The polish of its jet-black lacquer caught the starlight as he put his right hand around the braid-wrapped hilt. He drew the curved blade for a horizontal cut. It sliced air perfumed by wood, metal, and oil.

The second pair of chimes echoed softly, like a ghost whispering warnings of midnight's approach. He moved across the wooden surface. With a two-handed grip, he raised the killing sword for a vertical cut. It sang its way down.

Each step, each cut, each pivot, sent the billowing, ebony pleats of the *hakama* swirling around him.

The last lone chime brought him to a halt and filled the moment with the reminder that only another half-hour and two more days stood between him and freedom. Between the *Edlyn's* crew and their freedom.

He advanced once more, crisscrossing the swordhall. The lunges and thrusts drove the air before him, stirring the silk House banners above. A golden hawk against indigo waves swung above him. Next to it, a pair of silver cranes faced each other on an emerald field set into gentle motion. A third banner, that of his own House, the one with a crimson wolf howling into an eternal night, swayed in time with the first two.

Darien sped up. The swordhall's viewscreen and surrounding bulkheads blurred past him as his feet drummed out an inhuman pace, keeping time with the sword's cutting song.

His father should've taken the *Edlyn* away from him. Instead, she was being wasted on a punishment detail and a disgraced, half-breed heir.

Lord Dobromil had sent them to the farthest reaches of his domain —their border with the Imperium.

All because Darien had defied not only orders, but tradition. He'd challenged the Imperium's authority by refusing to return escaped imperial slaves to their master. He'd done so, expecting to bear the consequences on his own. He'd thought that his *donai* would be protected by their fealty oaths. He'd believed that his human crew would be protected by their status as chattel. He'd been wrong.

It was why they—his humans, his oath-sworn *donai*—were all here at the edge of Dobromil space, doing penance.

Fortunately, his father's fondness for tradition hadn't extended to executing his crew, so there was that small mercy at least.

He would've been spared of course. His father only had one heir, and proper *donai* heirs—even half-breed ones—were too valuable to waste. *They* were given a chance to regain their honor. After a proper penance, of course.

A proper *donai* heir, a proper penance.

Proper, traditional, just like this swordhall with its wood-paneled bulkheads, its silken banners, its ancient swords and the duty and honor that came with them.

Darien came to a stop in front of four, life-size portraits, each one rendered in oil by a master artist's hand. Framed in woodgrain metal, four generations of House Dobromil's rulers adorned the wood-paneled bulkhead.

His ancestors looked every bit the genetically engineered soldiers they had been. Whether adorned in traditional robes, formal dress, or ship fatigues, they stood with a nobility of bearing that made them seem larger than life. He'd been born too late to know any of the first three except as the legends they'd become. How much of them, of what they were, truly flowed in *his* veins?

He wrapped his palm around the scabbard's mouth and quickly drew the sword's spine along his forearm and wrist. The weight of its hurried caress was as tender as the finger of a teasing lover. He slid the sword's tip into the scabbard slowly, deliberately, an act of will as well as good form.

The blade's collar clicked into place as Darien lingered in front of his father's likeness.

Strong and defined, his father's features seemed fashioned from granite. Dark brows sloped downwards in a brooding expression. A perpetual seriousness drew hard lines across his face, right down his straight nose to his strong jaw.

At first glance, the *donai* looked like oversized humans. It was the points of their ears, their layered amber irises and the gold of the pupils underneath that gave them away.

That older mirror image of himself, that promise and threat of destiny, held Darien's gaze as though the man himself was present. He had inherited most of his father's physical traits—the height, the dark hair—and more importantly, most of his father's genetic augmentations. Most, but not all.

Not with a human mother. A fact for which he was, often, grateful. She'd gifted him with a lighter tone of skin. It was the only cosmetic trait he could attribute to her. For good, or ill, he'd also inherited her disproportionate sense for the most tenuous of values—the drive to do the right thing, even at great cost.

It was exactly that, what his human mother would have called the willingness to do the right thing, what his *donai* father called honor, that had led him here.

Honor, or at least his interpretation of it, was why the *Edlyn* and the imperial ship that had been sent to keep an eye on him had been playing a six-month-long game of cat-and-mouse, mirroring each other's movements across this region of space.

Darien now knew his imperial counterpart well enough to exchange meaningless pleasantries while pretending that they were somehow counting coup.

All in service to a greater political game in which he was an unwilling participant. This was how Lord Dobromil had decided to punish his heir. Not by handing him over as the emperor had demanded, not by allowing the Imperium to extract its penance directly. No, Lord Dobromil had found a way to make it appear as if he bowed to the emperor's will, making Darien as close to a hostage as possible without turning him over to his political rivals.

It is restitution. A way to save face. Nothing more.

How many times had he told himself this over the endless months? How many times had he told himself that it had been worth it?

But, the political game was almost over.

Darien's real challenge—sealing the rift between himself and his father, a rift that time had widened into a chasm—was about to begin.

Just two more days.

Again, he drew his sword.

Dozens of precision strokes loosened a strand of hair from the bundle of his shoulder-length queue. Warmth flooded his muscles as he completed the kata.

With a one-handed grip, he raised the sword and brought it down in a sweeping, circular motion designed to clear its blood-groove. Nothing dripped to the floor. There was no tang of salt and copper and iron.

If only he could cleanse his honor, his name, with a flick of the wrist.

If only he could return home as easily as the blade that slipped into its scabbard.

If only he could untangle the mess he'd made as readily as he undid the ties that held the scabbard to his belt.

He returned the sword to its rack and bowed to it. Tradition again. It had him in its grasp, flowing from one generation to the next. Its power was waiting to take him, to serve him, to be wielded by him.

He straightened, raising his gaze to a distant silhouette, a shape too symmetrical to be anything but a ship, floating against the beauty of the stars. The ship belonged to Darien's imperial counterpart, one Commander Doregan Valteri. A contemporary of his father, Valteri was probably looking forward to the end of this game as much as Darien was.

Only one-hundredth the size of the *Edlyn*, Valteri's ship was formidable for a cruiser, but had never been meant to be anything but an insult. The emperor was using it to tell the rest of his vassal houses that he didn't consider the *Edlyn*'s presence here to be anything more than an annoyance.

A swirl of light formed around the silhouette of Valteri's ship.

The sweat-soaked hairs on the back of Darien's neck rose. His heart pounded in his chest, the coursing adrenaline activating his visual augmentations. A pair of *donai* irises swirled into place over his pupils, expanding his vision into both the ultraviolet and infrared range.

He sucked in a sharp breath and held it as a burst of energy split the fabric of space. A boiling mass like a forming thundercloud bloomed. Spectral plumes of energy and matter pulsed like a beacon, like a heart spiking and then beating out its last.

For an instant there was no more motion, no more heat or light or radiation, as if the whole universe had stopped to take a breath.

A streak of light tore through the fabric of the universe and raced right into the deep, dark heart of imperial space.

THE CONTOURS OF EMPTY, midnight-quiet passageways blurred past Darien. His bare feet struck the metal decking with a steady rhythm.

The hardened heart of the *Edlyn*, her bridge, irised opened before him, the brushed metal leaves pulling away smoothly.

He entered at the command deck, an oval ring that bisected the bridge and wrapped itself around the main holographic display. House Dobromil's wolf's head sigil floated in one holographic corner, representing the *Edlyn*. The closest star burned bright at the other end, separated by dozens of icons indicating the last known location of imperial ships. A lone communications array orbited the star, high above the system's ecliptic.

The system's only rocky planet, a world known as Thertore was surrounded by two layers of icons spread out like points on a sphere. The twenty-four satellites in synchronous orbit made up the planet's active defenses. A second constellation of twenty-four warning buoys formed a larger shell farther out.

An imperial-green icon in the shape of a dragon identified Valteri's ship. It was the only imperial asset close enough for real-time data.

Flickering pin-pricks of light surrounded the icon, tumbling wildly away from it, showing the tracks made by debris.

Darien took a deliberate breath, waiting for the data to correct itself, to once again pick up Valteri's codes, to re-tag his ship's icon. Instead, the debris tracks multiplied and not one of them squawked a distress call or a life-pod's transponder.

He looked away, casting his gaze downward. Below the command deck, staggered layers of consoles surrounded the main display. Haptic interfaces and holographic projections wrapped the console operators in streaming ribbons of data.

The urgency of a hundred questions stood poised and ready to be launched at the bridge crew. His rising pulse pushed at his augmentations, as if seeing the ship's data feeds with *donai* vision would help him interpret things differently.

The patter of lightweight, hurried footsteps approached from behind. The familiar scent accompanying them halted his questions. Commander Drea Bomani, the *Edlyn's* captain—denied that rank only because she was human—was running towards him. A tell-tale cloud of mint and honey trailed her as she sealed the top of her uniform and worked the clasps at her throat. The black ship fatigues with their red trim set off a braid of long blonde hair streaked with grey, an affectation she maintained for command dignity. She pulled the braid off her shoulder and gave it a twist. Deft fingers worked it into a bun at the back of her neck.

Her blue gaze met his. A barely raised pale brow offered silent commentary on his appearance. She strode right past him and displaced the officer of the watch from the command station.

Within the main hologram, a new icon appeared. It flickered as it voraciously consumed the distance between the *Edlyn* and Thertore's star.

"Unknown craft, unknown craft," Comms was saying, his voice rising above the chatter of the bridge, "This is the Royal Serigalan Navy Ship *Edlyn*. Identify yourself."

Bomani worked the holograms that had popped up around her with efficient, decisive motions. Darien came up behind her and settled just outside what humans considered an appropriate personal space.

Eyes intent on the displays in front of her, Bomani reported, "My lord, we detected anomalous readings just prior to the appearance of the intruder."

"And Valteri's ship?" Darien asked.

"Destroyed."

His gaze flickered to the washed-out icon and the multiplying debris tracks. Valteri's ship had not survived, and neither had any of his crew. To be snuffed out like that as if they had been swatted out of existence for no reason...

Frowning, he leaned over Bomani's shoulder, seeking clues in the data and image streams. But there was nothing in either the numbers or the icons to give Valteri and his crew's deaths meaning, to give them some small measure of purpose.

"How?" Darien asked.

"Collision," she said.

Darien frowned. "Show me."

A new image formed between them. That of a wedge-shaped ship unlike anything he'd ever seen. Its markings bore no semblance to imperial script or House sigils.

The static image was replaced by a looped recording, one that showed the alien ship winking into existence an instant before it plowed through Valteri's cruiser. The alien ship emerged from the resulting sphere of boiling plasma with no signs of impact or damage. Tendrils of ionized gas swirled and dissipated as it hurtled deeper into imperial space.

Darien put his hands around the hologram and slowed the looped recording with a compressing gesture.

Bomani's pale forehead wrinkled as the frames slowed. He reversed the image flow and stopped at a frame where the haze that surrounded the alien's hull could be clearly seen. The haze tapered out to a point ahead of the alien's bow and flared out at its stern, cradling the craft in an oversized grip. Cradling it like a hand holding a precious seed.

Bomani noticed it too, a small gasp the only sign that she'd missed it the first time.

Anything that could survive collision with an imperial craft's shielding could be the key to a formidable weapon. Indeed, it could be the key to more than weapons.

Darien wanted it—the ship itself if possible—a closer look if not.

"How has the Imperium responded?" he asked.

"No response. No contacts," Bomani said as she isolated the confirming data. "All imperial defenses appear to be inactive."

Darien looked up at the main tactical display. Along the alien ship's trajectory, the imperial icons faded from their bright, solid green, to a pale, ghostly gray. Their status markers were changing as well, flashing either "unknown" or "undetermined" for everything from ident codes to vector and acceleration numbers.

Bomani cleared her throat.

"My lord, I believe we're seeing a catastrophic failure of the Imperium's systems—manned craft, drones, buoys—everything."

"Have *our* systems been affected?" he asked.

"No," Bomani said, her tone betraying surprise and just a hint of disbelief.

He called up tactical logs. They bloomed around him, verifying that Valteri's ship had attempted no communication, issued no challenge. No weapons had been fired. Valteri had been taken by surprise, unaware of any threat. Had Darien not seen it with his own eyes, he wouldn't have believed it.

He swiped the reports out of existence and brought up the record of the alien craft's first appearance. The wedge-shaped ship had no armaments, no arrays for generating manifolds to effect superluminal speed, nothing to explain how it had emerged unharmed from a collision that had obliterated an imperial craft ten times its size.

None of the data explained the intruder's sheer velocity.

If anything, its control surfaces suggested a transport designed primarily to maneuver within atmospheres, not travel through deep space and certainly not at such speeds.

Curiosity clawed at Darien, digging its talons into a part of him he thought he'd shut away. The mysterious haze around the ship, the way it had burst forth from that tear in space all became part of a puzzle he desperately needed to piece together.

"Have they made any course corrections?" he asked.

"None," Bomani answered. "Engines are off-line. Blackbody re-radiation indicates life support systems operating within human parameters."

"So it's not some unmanned test vehicle, then." Darien took a deep breath. It didn't take *donai* enhancements to scent the apprehension building up around him. "That certainly complicates things."

"What are you thinking?" she asked, eyes narrowing.

His fingers swept across her console, activating additional sensors. He pushed the output to the main display.

The *Edlyn's* projections placed the alien ship on a collision course with Thertore. By imperial fiat the small planet was forbidden. It was the local imperial squadron's job to prevent unauthorized landings, protect Thertore's secrets, and ensure that nothing left the planet alive.

Bomani turned towards Comms. "Warn them!"

"Unknown craft, unknown craft, collision alert. Immediate course change, any direction."

Instinct rose within Darien, bringing to surface a visceral reaction, as though an enemy was present.

Thertore's secrets were not entirely unknown. With no imperial ships to stop it, that alien craft was about to crash on the emperor's breeding ground—a place for experimental life deemed too dangerous to develop elsewhere.

Despite Comms' warning, the alien craft's trajectory remained unchanged.

"Can you tell if they're receiving?" Darien asked.

"There are no outgoing signals, no active sensors of any kind," Comms replied.

No, there wouldn't be.

An alien ship that shared their comm frequencies and language would be an anomaly indeed.

Darien's hands tightened into fists.

"I know what you're thinking," Bomani said sotto voce. "But we can't fire into imperial space, not even as a warning."

Plots synchronized, showing the ship's projected path alongside a countdown to impact. Green gave way to amber until crimson dominated the image.

"And it wouldn't do any good," she added.

She was right of course. He'd waited too long. Perhaps if he'd given the order to fire a warning shot into their path when he'd entered the bridge—

The *Edlyn's* gravitational sensors came to life, confirming a surface impact. The alien ship's icon disappeared.

Darien bared his teeth. It was over.

Thertore and the space around it, the so-called exclusion zone, were forbidden to them. He'd have to be content with recordings and logged telemetry. It would give him something to speculate about on the long trip home.

Failure lingered thick in the air, tainting it.

"Let it go," Bomani subvocalized.

He dipped his head slightly and opened his fists. She was right. There was nothing here worth risking another incident with the Imper—

A distress beacon pierced the background noise with shrill electromagnetic pleas.

"Scramble a rescue ship," Darien said. "Make sure Palleton knows *exactly* where he's taking his men."

Bomani cleared her throat. "My lord, a word?"

"Commander, I know what you're going to say." He turned to leave, refusing her implied invitation for a private chat in the captain's ready room.

Undeterred by his long strides, Bomani's following steps echoed, insisting.

He pivoted to face her, wishing that she wasn't so unaffected by his towering height, his status, his title. But if she were, she wouldn't be here.

"You have nothing at stake," she said, still speaking for him alone.

"The Imperium will see anything you do now as provocation."

"We do not ignore distress calls because they're politically inconvenient, Commander."

She leaned in, a sour look on her face.

"What makes you think it's a distress call? I've never heard a distress call of this kind." Her chin rose defiantly.

He tilted his head at the weak attempt to deter him. "In your experience, surface impacts at those speeds are followed by what? Greetings and salutations?"

She took a deep breath. "The Imperium has mirrored our every move for months. Don't you find it odd that there has been no imperial response? *None at all.*"

Her scolding demeanor, her tone all silently said, *I've been your teacher far longer than I've been your flag captain.* There might have even been a "young man" in there to punctuate the whole thing.

"I am aware, Commander," he said. "How do *you* interpret this lack of response?"

"As a trap. As their last chance to make you blunder."

He bristled, shoulders tightening.

It was a remote possibility, one heavy with consequences: another political nightmare for House Dobromil, one his father would not welcome; further evidence of his unsuitability as heir, a recurring theme that would plague him for the rest of his life; the resumption of open hostilities between the Imperium and his House that would result in loss of life, power, and territory.

But the ship had survived a collision with a shielded imperial craft. More than survived it. It had torn Valteri's ship to shreds. According to their sensors, it had caused imperial warning buoys to fail as it passed them, by no means an unremarkable feat. Everything he had seen said the odds were in the alien craft's favor.

However, Bomani was right: sacrificing an unknown number of alien lives would cost him nothing. It wounded only his honor and self-respect, tenuous things of far more value to his kind than to…humans.

"It has to be a trap," Bomani said.

25

He bared his teeth. Thankfully the growl that was building in his chest remained there.

"Hardly, Commander. I'm sure they'll have many other opportunities to make me blunder and none will require the sacrifice of imperial lives and ships. Or the challenge of conjuring an alien-looking craft for the occasion."

"Trap or not," Bomani said far too calmly, "it will cost the Imperium nothing, politically or otherwise, to destroy any ship that lands on Thertore. You, my lord, are sending your men to their deaths."

" 'Catastrophic failure of all imperial systems.' Those are your words, Commander. Are you revising your report?"

The throbbing of a small muscle around her mouth was the only sign of the sneer she was suppressing. Her heart raced, its roar suddenly deafening in his *donai* hearing.

"No," she said. It was clipped and full of rebuke.

He acknowledged it with a tight smile. Her argument did have a modicum of merit even if her solution did not. And he had an answer for her. One she would not like.

"We have a duty to render aid to all distress calls," he said. "And if it's a trap, it is for me, not my men. They won't destroy a rescue ship if I'm aboard. Have my gear brought to the hangar."

Despite the twitch at the corner of her mouth, she held his gaze for an instant before acknowledging his command with a reluctant nod. Bomani wouldn't defy his direct order—not while on the command deck. He took shameless advantage of her adherence to protocol, knowing that she'd follow him into hell but save the reproof for a private moment after their arrival.

Bomani marched past the tactical and weapons control stations. She stopped at the communication console, gently tapping Comms' shoulder, bringing his ongoing attempts to contact the Imperium to a halt.

"Send out a priority communique to any surviving imperial ships," she said. Despite her pained expression, her voice had lost none of its calm.

"Inform them that we are answering the distress call originating on

26

Thertore," she added, "and that Lord Dobromil's heir is aboard the rescue ship."

Across the expanse of consoles, Bomani's gaze rose to meet Darien's.

"Two days. You couldn't give me *two* more days," she said so quietly that he doubted that even Comms had heard her.

Darien dipped his head in way of apology. Words would've been pointless. Her human hearing wouldn't have caught them anyway.

CHAPTER THREE

The flesh of Syteria's swollen left hand puckered above and below the metal cuff.

The compartment's tilt told her that they must have crashed. The Rhoans had muted the warning klaxons. Emergency lighting washed everything in a crimson sheen. Footsteps approached. The compartment door slid aside and two Rhoans ducked in and slammed the emergency lock into place.

They backed away from the pounding that followed. Pounding that left bulges in the metal.

Androgynous faces turned her way, their eyes filled with panic. Their green-grey robes were stained with what looked like blood. The taller of the two limped towards Syteria's cage and slid the door aside.

The shorter Rhoan followed and grabbed the taller one by the elbow, pulling it back.

"Are you crazy?" the short one asked.

"One monster to fight another," the taller one replied.

The world shimmered around Syteria as though they had passed through a veil. The sensation made her skin crawl. The Rhoans felt it too. They looked up and around as if expecting something to materialize out of thin air.

The taller Rhoan moved closer and released the cuffs from Syteria's ankles and wrists. She rolled off the table just as the ship lurched. The motion sent the Rhoans into the far corner and Syteria into the table.

A long blade pierced the compartment door and the Rhoans screamed. They scrambled up, tangling themselves in their robes and ran for the next compartment.

The tall one stopped and looked back at her. "Kill it, *eniseri*. Protect us."

They passed through the door. The familiar click of a lock engaging made a small sound full of finality.

How very...Rhoan. Syteria shook her head with disgust. What did they expect her to do? Strangle whatever that was with her bare hands?

At least they'd freed her.

Cradling her hand against her chest, she turned to face the other door.

The tear in the hull widened, parting for saber-like claws. A reptilian creature poked its head through, sniffing. The head alone was twice as large as any human's.

The creature pulled its head back and for a moment there was an eerie silence. Syteria looked around for something to use as a weapon, but the compartment was bare. There was only the metal table, bolted into the floor, and the cage itself. The pole that had held the sedation bag was made of polymer and held in place by a clamp. Syteria released the clamp, grabbed the pole, and held it up in her right hand.

The creature shouldered its way through the opening.

She backed away, as far as she could, holding up the meager pole as the creature straightened. Its height pushed it up against the ceiling. It sniffed the air, folding its forelimbs so it could use them to move on all fours. Its gaze swept to her as it paused to neatly slice through the bars. Pieces of metal dropped to the deck, clattering and rolling towards the door through which the Rhoans had escaped.

The creature's slitted pupils dilated. Its head tilted, almost like it was considering what to do next. Plates of armor-like hide covered its torso. Its joints were protected by smaller, pliable scales. Despite its reptilian markings, it reminded her of some impossibly giant ape. She'd never seen anything like it. Not on Kappa. Not on Rho.

Heart in her throat, Syteria pushed the realization aside and waited. She might be able to jab one of its eyes out. But not without allowing it close enough to use those sabers. Its reach was three times the length of her own.

Screams echoed from the adjoining compartment. Thuds followed. The creature crouched and leapt towards the door the Rhoans had taken, raised both of its forelimbs, and made two diagonal slices.

Syteria sprinted the other way, through the damaged bulkhead. A piece of jagged metal sliced through her uniform and caught her thigh.

She ran through pools of blood, past disemboweled Rhoans and monsters hunched down to feast on still-living prey. Into passageways of darkness she went, not knowing if they held safety or death.

She knew there would be no weapons. Not aboard a Rhoan ship. She needed to get to the lower decks, the cargo holds. It was there that Kappan artifacts would be stored. Anything would do. A spear. A long gun. Anything to extend her reach. She'd even settle for a scythe. It would do better than her bare hands.

The first cargo hold was empty. Approaching noises drove her down to the next level. Her boots pounded the decking, betraying her, a signal that prey was in flight, but she had no choice.

The next cargo hold beckoned. She pulled the door open and stepped in. Frantic, she moved down a row of Kappan artifacts. Carriages, the hull of a primitive aircraft, something that might have been a steam engine, but nothing useful.

She retraced her path. Thuds told her that at least two—maybe more—creatures were close.

Syteria grabbed crates and tore the lids off, one after the other. A short metal probe with a sharp end stuck up out of the packing in the last crate. She threw the polymer stick aside. The metal probe was a comforting weight in her hand. She tucked it inside her jacket.

In her frenzy, she almost ran past the three elongated cylinders of a flame-thrower. A long, tangled up hose trailed from the device.

She grabbed the carrier strap, but couldn't lift it onto her back one-handed. Instead, she dragged the flame-thrower forward and dropped to her knees to untangle the hose. Someone had wrapped aged leather around portions of the shaft. The firing mechanism and nozzle looked clear. Ignoring the telltale blood stains on the firing handle, she faced the oncoming pounding and primed the firing mechanism.

The creature entered cautiously, its muzzle red with Rhoan blood. A strand of bowel swung out from the side of its jaw.

As she stood, Syteria pressed down on the firing handle. Fuel squirted out in a wet stream. Panic rose in her chest as the beast lunged at her, saber-claws held high.

Squeezing the firing handle, she raised the nozzle and flame fountained outward, engulfing the creature. It fell back, its screech echoing.

As the creature rolled around, she doused it with fire. Not until it stopped moving, until it was a scorched carcass, did she ease up.

Gulping for air, she strained to lift the cylinders again but failed. She'd have to stand her ground. And so she did, as another creature came at her, and then another. When the flame went out she was staring into a monster's face.

One of its saber-claws went through her abdomen, setting it afire. It held her there, lifting her up off her toes as it used its other forelimb to stab her again and again.

Jaws closed in, tilting, going for her throat.

Syteria grabbed the metal probe from inside her jacket and thrust it into the creature's open maw. Her hands sizzled, burning as the creature's drool touched her skin. With one final burst of energy she drove the probe in farther, pushing it into its brain.

The creature collapsed atop her and she burned. She closed her eyes against the searing liquid. Her screams echoed as the drool dissolved her eyelids and ate her eyes.

Crushed beneath the monster's weight, her life ebbed away. She welcomed the release, embraced the scorching sting of it, reveling in the knowledge that she'd exacted a toll for her life.

And that she was, finally, free.

CHAPTER FOUR

*I*nside the *Edlyn's* main hangar, combat drop-ships squatted on the main deck like giant beasts with wings wrapped and tucked tightly along bulky hulls. Even in slumber, their bodies bristled with arrays of closed gun- and missile-ports. However, their bellies were empty of both cargo and troops.

The Imperium was bound to take exception to their heavy weapons, maneuverability, and speed, even though they were no match for Thertore's planetary defenses.

Darien passed between them, under the shadows cast by enormous engines. On the far side of the hangar, a lightly armed rescue ship—a small, box-like craft—waited, prepped and ready. Its size alone halved the number of *donai* he would've preferred to take along for a landing on Thertore. The ship had none of the authority it would need to project if they were challenged, even if its sole intent was to broadcast that they had come only to render aid.

Palleton's powerhouse body blocked the ramp as he waited at the rescue ship's base. Age lines separated eyebrows the color of iron. Framing the points of his ears, his clipped gray hair resembled a pelt more than anything else. Amber *donai* eyes shone with excitement in a face so dark that it rivaled the black of his ship fatigues.

"My lord, you do know what's down there," Palleton said, the timbre of his voice cresting with the revving engines.

"Why do you think I'm bringing you along?" Darien asked as he closed the gap between them.

Palleton quirked an eyebrow and revealed the pearly white of prominent *donai* cuspids. "Does that mean we get to destroy some of the emperor's 'creations'?"

"Should they interfere with our attempts to apprehend the intruders on behalf of the Imperium, most definitely." That was the official version he would give in his report. It had the virtue of being true.

Palleton's understanding smile was as cold as ice.

Darien jogged up the ramp, Palleton at his heels. Inside the rescue ship's cargo area ten *donai* snapped to attention. Like Palleton, their hair was clipped short, some to the scalp. The gold of their pupils shone with excitement even as they stood motionless in ship fatigues and boots. Darien graced them with a cursory inspection, confident in Palleton's thoroughness.

Familiar vibrations flowed along the deck as Darien ordered them to stand at ease. They settled into the waiting harnesses as the pilot announced the completion of flight preparations.

Darien climbed the ladder that connected the cargo bay to the mid-deck, then continued forward to the cockpit. He brushed up against the hull's tight proportions and took a seat behind the pilot. Lieutenant Ghedi, a human of middle age, commanded the shuttle fleet. Apparently, Bomani had roused the most experienced pilot for this mission.

As Ghedi finished his flight prep, the distress beacon's steady plea continued to pierce the Imperium's inexplicable silence. Surviving imperial ships should've responded by now, even if only with an acknowledgment that they had things under control. Ghedi's co-pilot reduced the volume on the *Edlyn's* unanswered hails.

The rescue shuttle floated out of the hangar to linger alongside the *Edlyn*. It waited for the leviathan to open a hole in her shields. Ghedi cleared the opening and plunged along their new vector.

Darien shifted for a better view of the images hovering above the main console. A cascade of color turned crimson and then black, spreading outward through this region of space until only the far edges of Thertore's system showed signs of activity.

Bomani had been correct. They were seeing a collapse of the Imperium's assets in the region. Within that collapse, a narrow window of opportunity emerged, one Darien would use to full advantage.

"Under my authority as Lord Dobromil's proxy," he said, "I invoke The Duty to Render Aid. You are authorized to enter imperial space."

The shuttle accelerated. Inertia pushed at them, pinning them, then easing off as the inhibitors caught up. With a *donai* crew, they could've moved so much faster. An imperial ship would've sacrificed any humans aboard, taking advantage of full speed. But while Darien was racing time, he wasn't racing an imperial ship, or running his command as one.

Their proximity alarm made a shrill, discordant sound. Ghedi slowed, breath catching, beads of sweat glistening atop the steady hand working the throttle. His intent but surprised gaze bounced from sensors to viewscreen and back.

"A warning buoy," Darien said. "Dead center."

It was clear in *his* vision. The buoy's blistered hull contorted in the grip of an intermittent darkness. The enhanced *donai* rods and cones in his eyes changed form, extending the range of his vision. That darkness was like a tunnel, an ethereal one that narrowed into the distance as it reached out toward Thertore. The tunnel's surface...flickered. There was no other way to describe it. The buoy had been caught in that surface, part of it embedded and unable to break free. It gave off no electromagnetic signals, no power signatures, nothing, as if all of its energy had been sucked dry.

Darien had never seen anything like it. "What are you reading on that?"

"Nothing on any of our instruments," Ghedi said, disbelief coloring his tone. "What are you seeing, my lord?"

If he had the buoy brought aboard, examined, maybe—

No. He didn't know what he was really looking at and he was not going to risk his ship and men. Perhaps later, he could indulge his curiosity, but for now...

"Resume course. Pick it up on the way back."

Ghedi gave the buoy a wide berth.

Thertore's star grew, luminous against the star-flecked pitch of the Void. Darien sat back, letting the inertia hold him. Caution was warranted. So was their reduced speed. He didn't want to become part of the "catastrophic failure" that had taken out Valteri's ship and the buoy.

"My lord," Ghedi said over his shoulder, "you have a tight-beam transmission from the *Edlyn*. Encrypted."

"I'll take it above."

Darien extricated himself from the confines of the cockpit.

He reached the top deck as Bomani's image coalesced in front of him. He passed through the hologram and settled onto the larger of two berths.

"We've received an imperial response," Bomani said, venom in her voice.

When Bomani allowed her disdain to seep past the mask of her profession, it was definitely time to take notice.

"All is not well in the Imperium, I take it," he said, raising an eyebrow.

"They've dispatched 'replacements' for the manned craft they lost." The slight quaver in her voice said that she considered the imperial response woefully inadequate.

"How long before they get here?"

"Three days," she said, her expression tightening. "Furthermore, we are explicitly forbidden to respond to *any* distress calls, even those originating from imperial craft."

Newfound compassion for imperials from Bomani of all people? When had she started caring so much for the emperor's *donai*?

"Have we received imperial distress calls?" he asked. "Do we have any indication that anyone is still alive?"

"No. Nothing." Her expression soured further.

Darien propped his elbows on his knees. The reason for the Imperium's silence, their strange but explicit orders, made sense only if they no longer had forces in the system, which meant—

"My lord, I must advise you to return at once." Stilted. Flat. So unlike Bomani. But, paying lip service to protocol was part of her job.

"Thank you, Commander. I understand."

"If the orbital defenses are active…"

"We are no match for them. I know."

"I can move the *Edlyn* into position, provide you with—"

"No."

"Darien, don't make me fall on my sword." There was a pleading edge to her tone, one he couldn't indulge.

"I give you my word," he said. "We won't engage planetary defenses."

It was an easy promise to make. He had no reason to think Thertore's orbital platforms had survived.

"Give me your word that I won't need to explain your 'detainment,' or your corpse, to your father." It was half demand, half plea.

"The emperor can summon me for aid and counsel at any time and I must obey; he need not 'detain' me."

"Yes, my lord." Her image faded; her displeasure lingered. Even without her physical presence, he could almost smell it.

The easy, prudent choice was to obey the Imperium's orders, turn around, and in two days, set a course for home. Proper. Obedient. A good little vassal, just following orders.

The right thing to do was to render aid. Every spacefarer accepted that obligation. To one's own. To one's enemy. To any and all unknowns. Any *donai* who failed to do so blemished not only his own honor, but that of his House. The emperor knew this. And so did whatever imperial lackey had issued those orders in his name.

The lackey also knew that the distress call gave Darien a legal justification to land on Thertore.

There was something on Thertore, something beyond the open secret everyone pretended wasn't there. Something that the emperor did not want House Dobromil to know about.

~

DARIEN STOOD and rolled his shoulders, loosening the tension that had crept into his neck. Bomani's plea about not making her fall on her sword still echoed in his ears. Would she bring the *Edlyn* into imperial space just to save him? The answer was an unequivocal yes.

It would be up to him to make sure she wouldn't need to.

He stepped out of the *hakama* and set it onto the berth he'd just vacated.

Beside him, the components of his armor waited. The cylindrical container attached to the main chest plate clicked free at his touch. With a twist, he broke the seal and poured the viscous black gel onto the deck at his feet.

It flowed around his heels and toes like a living thing. He lifted each foot in turn, allowing the gel to cover his soles. The nanites that made up the gel oozed up his naked body. Some would form biometric arrays and interfaces; others, a second skin.

He held his queue off his neck. Its ridiculous length, required by the peerage, was forever getting in his way. He'd already defied tradition by cutting it down to a practical length. It would be nothing to shorten it further.

Darien eyed his knife—still in its armored sheath on the thigh plate in front of him—as the gel molded around the rigid planes of his stubbled jawline. The knife's nanometer edge would make short work of the damned queue.

No.

He'd grown past such petty defiances. Oh, yes. Grown right past them to truly monumental ones like this dubious rescue mission.

As the gel gloved his hands, he let the queue settle back on his neck. He stretched and flexed his muscles, testing the integrity of his new skin.

With the ease of acquired habit he donned the armored segments of the exoskeleton: chest, back and shoulder plates; gauntlets, thigh plates, and boots. Each component integrated, shifting form to fit.

The satisfaction of becoming more than a human shade, of being *donai*, flowed through him.

Darien returned to the cockpit, tucking his helmet under one arm.

His suit had added just enough height and bulk to make it impossible to wedge himself into the seat behind the flight crew, forcing him to loom over them like a wingless gargoyle. He grabbed onto a handhold.

"Passive sensors show no active defenses," Ghedi reported. "Thertore's defensive grid seems to be down."

"Active sweep," Darien ordered.

A casual glide of Ghedi's fingers across one of the interfaces and a moment filled with trepidation was all that it took to confirm. Ghedi gave Darien an expectant look.

There was no satisfaction in being right. Instinct argued for further caution, for retreat, for return with a larger force with more firepower.

Instinct be damned.

He'd set them down this path because at the end of it all he saw a prize that his House could use to cast off the emperor's yoke. The prize was worth the risk.

"Proceed," Darien said.

"Yes, my lord."

Anticipation, fear, and surprise oozed out of Ghedi's pores. He exchanged a brief look with his copilot who drew in a shaky breath as he faced forward, his posture stiff like a marionette's. The co-pilot's ensign tabs covered a fluttering pulse and Darien had to look away as his vision shifted.

The humans looked like prey. They smelled like prey. But they were crew, not prey. Darien backed away despite the opposing push of acceleration. All these months aboard the *Edlyn*, surrounded by so many humans had done little to suppress his prey-drive. And he shouldn't have expected it to. He'd not taken them into danger. Drills and simulations aboard the *Edlyn* didn't quite evoke the same responses. If he was having this reaction, so would the other *donai*. After this was over, he'd have to remedy that.

He ran his thumb under his nose, making it an all-too-human gesture. An itch. Nothing more. Nothing to worry about. He wasn't a threat. They were not prey.

Primed by the fear-scent, his *donai* vision persisted, so he aimed it at the cockpit's viewscreen. He saw nothing like the twisting, intermittent darkness that had caught that warning buoy.

The shuttle passed through Thertore's planetary defense grid without challenge, without so much as a stray signal. Even the automated recording that should've been squawking a warning was silent.

Below them, Thertore largest continent revealed a vast crater, its fresh edges bleeding a raging inferno. Swirls of grey obscured the terrain as stratospheric winds carried ash across its surface. Turbulence and static gave birth to bursts of lightning that lanced downward, igniting the landscape.

"Tell me that's not the crash site," Darien said. Nothing could've survived *that* impact.

"It's not, my lord. Telemetry places the distress beacon on the other side of the planet."

Holograms popped up, giving them a clearer, sensor-enhanced image of what lay below all the ash. Despite the crater's size, its features suggested not impact, but a massive underground detonation.

At least one intelligence report had speculated that the research facility on Thertore did not adhere to standards for zoological studies. The facility was too fortified, even for the breeding and study of creatures like the genetically engineered *grierugon*.

"Distress beacon located," Ghedi narrated for the official record. "No imperial contacts."

He angled the shuttle towards the beacon.

Their descent into Thertore's atmosphere remained unchallenged. The crater lagged behind them as they crossed continents at sub-orbital speeds and broke through clouds still free of ash. For the time being, the winds were in their favor.

The alien ship rested within a deep furrow carved into a grass-covered plain. It had scraped the edge of an isolated rock formation rising abruptly from the plain. The rock formation had forced the ship to veer slightly to the left where it had spun to a stop, cushioned by the soil and vegetation it had driven in front of it.

The cockpit's sensors showed no immediate threats, no approaching lifeforms. Portions of the crashed ship flickered red within the holographic display as though the sensors were struggling to remain locked on it. Its distress call remained strong, however.

"Land as close to it as you can," Darien said.

The shuttle traced another spiral around the wrecked alien ship before touching down.

The alien ship's clean lines and symmetries were gone. It was broken and battered—a lifeless derelict that would never rise again. It made no sense. This same ship had torn through a shielded imperial vessel like a blade through paper. Its passage through the system had rendered imperial defenses inert. Its trajectory had brought it in at an angle that had allowed it to skim the surface, cushioning the impact.

The *donai* emerged from the shuttle in pairs, leapfrogging each other as they made their way to the alien ship. Half of them spread out, creating a perimeter. Palleton led the rest towards the wreckage as a fog rose to shroud it.

"Stand by to take off," Darien said as he exited the cockpit.

He returned to the lower deck, pulled a rifle off the rack, loaded it, and slung it over his shoulder. On his way down the ramp, he donned his helmet. Its smooth, anonymizing surface didn't bear any markings or betray the presence of its sensors.

Blue icons identifying his *donai* flowed across the helmet's interior. A distant bolt of lightning overloaded its upper right quadrant. It flickered before returning to normal.

On the horizon, a shelf cloud was forming, threatening a storm. Rumbling preceded a gust of wind and a seismic tremor revealed fissures hidden by the thick ground cover. Multiple warnings sounded. With an angry flick of his head he muted them all.

At a steady pace that belied his desire to catch up with his *donai*, he approached the wreck. Thick, opaque smoke boiled from a tear in the hull. His suit warned of toxins.

A heat signature, fading to ambient, betrayed the presence of a *grierugon* carcass blocking his way. Despite its *donai*-sized body, the ape-like creature had a short, reptilian snout. The scales that covered it merged into a mottled brown and green pattern. Saber-like claws protruded from its forelimbs. Its hide was thick, some of it resembling plating. Red, orange, and yellow pigment sacks stood up like pustules on parts of a crest that started just above the sloping brows and snaked down its curved torso. Well-muscled legs terminated on wide paws. Based on its size, this had to have been a small specimen, possibly a juvenile.

There were no scorch marks or entry wounds from *donai* weapons and no injuries. At least, not that he could see. His helmet's analysis confirmed his conclusion. The command interface had not logged any fire from the other *donai*, only their sparse, calm chatter as they made their way into the wreck.

Darien reached for the drool seeping from the *grierugon's* slack jaw. His suit flashed a warning. As his fingers neared the dark brown secretions, the suit's protective routines sent a mild shock into his hand.

Ignoring the intensifying shocks, he dipped a cautious fingertip into the drool. The ichorous fluid had no effect on his armor, but it etched the exposed underlying layer. Amid a flurry of scolding tones, nanites were dispatched to repair the damage.

"My lord," Ghedi said over the comm, "a group of large lifeforms are heading this way."

Darien straightened and pivoted to scan the area. His suit's limited sensors detected nothing.

"How many? How long?" Darien asked.

"I count at least twenty, with more following. At present speed, first contact estimated in fifteen minutes. I can buy you some time if we take off and engage them."

Once they returned, House Dobromil would have to share this mission's logs with the Imperium. Destroying more of the creatures than absolutely necessary could be seen an act of sabotage. It would add to a growing list of "violations" that would no doubt be used against him. A defense of necessity would only go so far. No point in adding to that tally without dire need.

"I want you on the ground in case we find survivors," Darien said.

"Yes, my lord."

Darien side-stepped the carcass and raced towards the tear in the wreck's hull, following the trail logged by his *donai*.

Just like the warning buoy, sections of the hull shimmered with an unusual phosphorescence his helmet couldn't identify. It made the affected area appear ethereal.

Under his hand, however, the hull seemed solid enough.

Damaged adaptive camouflage or an optical illusion? Or perhaps a sensor ghost.

Taking off the helmet was the only way to make sure it wasn't something fooling his equipment, but even he was unwilling to risk the unidentified toxins.

He was hard to kill, not immortal.

According to the data feed, six of his *donai* were inside, exploring the wreck.

He focused on the tear in the hull, tasking his helmet sensors to perform an enhanced analysis that came back as inconclusive. There was no way to tell if the hull had succumbed to the stresses of impact or the *grierugon's* saber-like claws.

"My lord, an unknown number of *grierugon* have made it inside," Palleton reported. A data stream from his *donai's* helmets merged with his own, creating a partial map of the ship's interior. It showed additional points of entry from the other side of the wreck.

"Survivors?" Darien asked.

"Not sure. One." Palleton paused. "Maybe."

"I need detailed scans of the ship," Darien said. "Find and salvage the data core, whatever you can manage. And I want at least one intact *grierugon* specimen."

Even with his father and the Imperium three breaths away from war, he could not—would not—pass up the opportunity to gain valuable intelligence. Some among the peerage believed that the emperor was breeding the *grierugon* as weapons.

Darien needed to be cautious, however. He was still required to discharge his duty as a vassal of the Imperium, first by rescuing any survivors, second by turning over whatever data they salvaged from the ship. Both parties would just have to pretend no duplicate data sets existed, even as they both lived with the truth.

He stepped through the hull breach and into a dimly lit cargo hold. The helmet adjusted for the low light. The hold's meager contents were strewn about. The layouts and telemetry from his *donai's* suits continued to merge with his own. He used the data to guide him to the alien ship's bridge.

A corrosive liquid, another unidentified substance, dripping from a broken conduit derailed his first attempt. His helmet presented him with another path.

The design of the bridge—compact, with just one seat—reminded him more of pleasure craft's cockpit than anything else. The pilot lay recumbent in the lone seat. Foam from lips turned blue by death trailed a path down his pale, smooth cheek. Vacant eyes stared at the hull above, their dark color matching the black of his skullcap.

Chief Aeson, their *donai* medic, stood over the corpse, working a handheld scanner.

"Dead a while, my lord. Dead before the crash. Poison."

Darien's helmet received the data from Aeson's scanner. The poison was a substance easily neutralized by a *donai's* nanites.

"Human," Darien said, unable to keep surprise out of his voice. The pilot had been small, even for a human.

"Yes, my lord."

"This was suicide?"

"There are no signs of forced ingestion." Aeson indicated the corpse's hands. They were set in rigor, clutching an empty vial.

"The others?"

Aeson led Darien out of the cockpit and into a passageway littered with bodies. Four had followed the pilot's example. Similar in dress and size, their bodies were mostly intact. The *grierugon* were apparently uninterested in cold remains.

Further down the gruesome passage, the other corpses, however, showed signs of predation.

"I believe *they* were alive," Aeson said with the detachment of an experienced combat medic. His voice remained steady and clinical as he assessed cause of death for the record and pointed to sanguine patterns clinging to the bulkheads. "See the aortic spray, here and here. No signs of struggle though, and they're warmer than the others."

"What?"

"The aortic sprays, my lord."

Darien shook his head. "No signs of struggle. You're certain?"

"Yes, my lord." It came without hesitation and with absolute certainty.

"These 'people' didn't even fight for their own lives?" Darien swallowed the sour bile clawing its way up his throat.

"They did not," Aeson said with the same unwavering certainty.

Behind the opacity of the helmet, Darien knew he would find *donai* stoicism. And perhaps indifference. The humans' lack of struggle surprised him, but not Aeson.

"We're almost done with the survey scans," Palleton's voice intruded. "A primitive data core has been located and we're retriev—"

"*Any* survivors?" Darien asked.

"No, my lord."

"Weapons?" Just how had this ship, so fragile after all, and these people, who'd chosen suicide, who'd not even defended themselves, managed to destroy Valteri's ship?

"This ship is unarmed." Palleton's tone was clipped, sharp.

Darien bared his teeth. He needed answers. Answers only a survivor could give him. Not just to justify the risk but to explain why these people hadn't fought. When cornered, even the most docile humans fought.

"I *need* a survivor."

Silence. Darien imagined the raised eyebrows and quiet indignation that Palleton reserved for those occasions when his pupil-turned-commander was being unreasonable.

"Acknowledged," Palleton said. "Moving aft to sections unexplored."

"My lord," Ghedi's strained voice interjected. "You have about five minutes, maybe less."

"Understood."

Aeson had knelt to examine another intact body. It was covered in blood. A single slash had cut from shoulder to abdomen revealing breasts that could have belonged to a young man or an undeveloped woman. But, the lines on its face betrayed someone closer to middle age.

"Did this one struggle? Fight?" Darien asked.

"No, my lord."

"You're certain?"

Aeson's helmet swept bright beams right over the bulkheads and the corpse. "No defensive wounds. I'm certain."

Darien's helmet lit up with icons showing incoming threats. The alien ship's hull dampened the distant sound of *donai* weapons responding.

"Palleton, we're out of—"

"Reporting a survivor."

The expletive caught in Darien's throat.

With Aeson close behind, Darien raced into the ship's depths towards Palleton's locator beacon. Several decks below, Palleton was standing over a scorched *grierugon* carcass.

Underneath the charred remains, the torn body of the survivor sprawled in a pool of blood. Aeson knelt and a pale blue diagnostic beam sprouted from the top of his helmet. From a pouch on his belt, he deployed a pair of medical rovers, each a sphere about the size of a human fist. They hovered over the survivor, caressing mangled limbs with their own beams.

Darien and Palleton heaved the *grierugon* carcass aside, giving Aeson better access.

The *grierugon's* caustic secretions had burned off the survivor's face, exposing frothy, failing attempts to draw breath. A bald head was covered in blood and gore. Unlike the others, this one wasn't wrapped in robes. Something more like a uniform, perhaps one made up of mottled greens and browns had been pierced and shredded by *grierugon's* saber-claw.

Darien drew in a hesitant breath.

This was what he'd wanted, what he'd needed: one dubious life

45

that had just become an acceptable tribute to their honor, to their—to his—defiance of imperial orders.

Blood fountained out of the survivor's straining throat. Aeson directed the rovers to staunch blood flow. He tore off the thick, band of metal around the survivor's neck and created an airway. The band landed in the expanding pool of blood fed by all those stab wounds.

Darien stepped back. "What do you need?"

"Time. I have a life-pod en route."

"We can give you ten minutes." It was all the time Darien could justify, or promise, with any degree of certainty.

Aeson nodded, the pace of his work intensifying as he prepped the body for transport.

"Palleton, let's buy the man some time."

CHAPTER FIVE

The *Edlyn* was on her way home to Serigala.

Obedient to the last set of confirmed orders, the ones given by his father, Darien had waited the two days required to fulfill his penance, and then set out at top speed. During those two days, they had received no distress calls, no signals of any kind. Thertore and the exclusion zone around it had remained as silent as the graveyard it had become.

There was even a remote chance that the Imperium remained unaware of their landing on Thertore. Bomani had said that it would take the Imperium at least three days to respond. The *Edlyn* had a one-day lead. Darien intended to make the most of it.

Eventually the Imperium would find the downed alien craft, or whatever remained of it, as well as the creatures he and his men had killed. It had been a slaughter.

The *grierugon* had none of the rumored regenerative abilities that would've been required of a species designed as a weapon. Despite their size, speed, and ferocity, they had turned out to be little more than beasts—deadly to unarmed humans, a challenge to the *donai*—but nothing worth making the planet forbidden. The emperor was either behind in their development or House Dobromil's intelligence was wrong. Only time, and more information, would tell.

His trophy, the human they'd recovered, the survivor that might hold the key to how imperial defenses had been so easily breached, how Thertore had been wounded, was in the infirmary. It was the only place aboard the *Edlyn* where Darien's word was not law, where his presence was tolerated—or endured as a nuisance—depending on the whims of a human.

The infirmary had seen little use during their mission. Two days ago, Darien had laid something barely alive in the hands of Galen Karamat, House Dobromil's Court Physician.

Hands clasped smartly behind his back, Darien roamed the periphery of Galen's lab. Consoles and panels idled, their austere metal surfaces glowing with a muted, pearlescent quality. Whenever he leaned in close enough to activate them, they sprouted control surfaces. He stepped back so they could reassume their default appearance.

On his second circuit, he paused to examine a set of new rovers. The small spheres floated up and out of their cradles, circling him, their blue, pencil-thin beams seeking an injury to justify their activation. Finding none, the temperamental little machines re-nested with indignant beeps.

"You're hovering," Galen said without turning from his work.

A gray tunic with a high collar, more like their formal uniforms than the fatigues worn by most of the crew, framed the older, stocky human. Galen sat at the controls of the lab's biomedical reconstruction unit, viewing something remotely through a layered set of floating nano-optic filters. Using minuscule twisting motions, he worked the haptic interfaces, focusing and controlling the remote lenses.

"I recall a time when you encouraged me to take an interest in your work," Darien said.

He strolled past Galen to the center of the lab and stood at the foot of the reconstruction unit. Part of its canopy had receded, making it look more like a cradle than the sarcophagus it otherwise resembled. Within, a body was wrapped in a blue shroud. Streaks of light flashed across the shroud's surface, a sign of Galen's continuing endeavors.

"Is that what you're taking an interest in?" Galen asked. "My work."

Darien dismissed the waspish tone with a smile.

It was not unusual for Galen to ignore everyone and everything around him. He'd at least graced Darien with a verbal response instead of silence or an inattentive grunt.

Lingering over the survivor, Darien waved the rest of the canopy aside. It retracted like petals yielding to reveal the pistil of a flower.

Chestnut curls crowned a face hidden by a mask that ebbed and flowed, but never revealed.

"This isn't the human we rescued," Darien said.

"I must be getting old." Galen looked around absently, patting at his pockets with emphasis. "Have I misplaced a patient?"

Darien smirked. Mocking him into leaving was a tried-and-true tactic, one to which he wasn't about to succumb.

"The man we rescued had no hair," Darien argued. He swept the chestnut mass out over the cradling edges of the reconstruction unit. It spilled over like silk and cascaded halfway to the deck.

Galen returned to manipulating controls. "Rapid hair growth is normal for systemic repairs of this scope. *You* wanted immediate results. She can cut it when she wakes."

"*She?*"

Darien blinked. Even with how mangled the survivor's body had been, he would have—he should have—noticed such an obvious trait.

His memory insisted Galen was wrong. Darien peeled back the shroud. It revealed an elegant neck, a toned shoulder, but refused to part farther, denying his curiosity.

The shroud reformed over the parts he'd exposed.

He took hold of a silken strand of hair, coiling it around his finger. The razor-sharp tips of his fingernails cut through, separating a lock of hair.

"Yes, *she*," Galen said, his tone distant, distracted.

Darien raised the silken bundle to his nose. It had only the barest hint of pheromone, but it was definitely female. Scent. To his kind it was like sight was to humans.

"She has the most interesting biochemistry…" Galen was saying.

"Interesting how?"

"Someone altered it."

"Someone?" Darien edged closer. "Why 'someone'?"

"I've never seen such sophisticated biochemical changes alongside such crude, token attempts at physical repairs," Galen said. He swept the nano-optics from where they floated and set them aside.

With a clipped hand gesture, he launched a barrage of holograms at Darien. The images showed specialized nano-molecular machines at work. They had spread throughout the woman's body. Some were reattaching newly grown tissue. Others connected nerve fibers and repaired viable flesh.

It didn't take a medic, or even a physician, to see the truth behind Galen's assessment. Darien had seen such damage among those unfortunate enough to belong to *donai* Houses that denied their humans even the most rudimentary nanotech. Humans required nanites tailored specifically for their cells, and with how easily and prolifically humans bred, their numbers were not in short supply.

"Perhaps her people advanced in one field at the expense of another," Darien said.

"I can't be certain," Galen said, rubbing his chin thoughtfully, "not with all the damage, but I think there's more to it. I doubt she consented to any of the changes."

More images formed to show the legions of nanites engaging in molecular repairs.

"I don't understand," Darien admitted.

"Her neuronal structures indicate torture…" Galen said, his voice tapering off, losing its clinical detachment.

Darien waited for the rest, knowing it wouldn't come.

Galen was far too familiar with the Imperium's methods. The old physician's right hand strayed to his collar in an all-too-familiar gesture he always tried to hide. Tried and failed.

Darien waited for Galen's hand to stop shaking, for his heart rate to go back to normal. "But you don't know."

"*Know* is a strong word in here," Galen said.

"What do you *know* then?"

Galen raised a silvered brow. "There was extensive physical damage from her encounter with those creatures. It took remarkable will to live through that, Darien. Truly remarkable."

"You're impressed," Darien said.

Darien had known Galen all his life, and could count on one hand the number of times the physician had been impressed, by anything, or anyone.

"I'm sure she'll appreciate the compliment when she wakes," Darien said. He cleared his throat. "When will that be?"

"Soon. She's burning through my sedatives faster than I'd anticipated. I don't dare try anything more potent. My last attempt had unforeseen results."

Darien cocked his head. Galen was not prone to mistakes and took them as a personal insult from the universe.

"Is she human?" It was easier to ask for confirmation than tempt himself with a closer examination.

"Yes." Galen shifted in his seat and resumed working.

Like a vine curling for purchase, the silken tendril of chestnut hair remained wrapped around Darien's finger. Its luster shone against the pearl-black of his fingernails.

Galen might be impressed with her "remarkable" will to live, but he hadn't seen her people's willingness to take poison rather than fight. The *grierugon* had probably been injured by something on the ship. Dripping acid came to mind. Injured, the creature had probably survived long enough to die while trying to kill her.

The survivor had been lucky, that's all.

"How...fortunate," Darien whispered.

"Does that mean you want me to continue, or not?" A harsh, unamused look framed Galen's question.

Darien worked the tendril between his thumb and forefinger. "I need answers."

"I take it you haven't reviewed the internal surveillance from her ship." Galen manipulated controls. "Perhaps these would help."

A new barrage of silent, crude, flat images circled Darien.

A whimpering human scrambling under a console, only to be pulled out by an ankle. The *grierugon* regarded its prey for a second, tilting its massive head and sniffing. The human's bladder released as the creature's nostrils closed the gap. It sampled the scent before opening the abdomen with a saber-claw. The human lived long enough to watch its own insides be swallowed and savored.

Darien dismissed the hologram.

Other images flew at him. They showed an enraged *grierugon* slashing through bulkheads, exposing ill-disguised hiding places, and feasting on the contents.

One by one, Darien dismissed them.

Finally, an image of *her* appeared. Tenacious, she struggled to control a stream of flame from a tool re-tasked as a weapon, its size as much of a challenge as the *grierugon* it dispatched before it ran dry.

He winced as saber claws found their target again and again.

Jaws gaped in anticipation of tearing into her throat.

Beneath a mask of grime and blood, her eyes promised a heavy toll for her life. With a desperate burst of energy, she drove a sharpened probe into the *grierugon's* open maw, pushing it into its brain.

It collapsed on top of its slayer. Poison dripped from the *grierugon's* slack jaw and melted her face. Another one of the creatures lumbered by. Sniffing and scenting only one of its own dead it moved out of view.

The image of the dead *grierugon* atop the dying survivor flickered and froze.

"The emperor drew the line at making them cannibals," Galen said. "Ironic, is it not? It saved her life."

Darien didn't find it ironic at all. Beasts, even ones designed as weapons, stopping mid-battle to eat their own, wouldn't be desirable at all. But then again, they'd exhibited no behaviors to make him think they were meant to fight in any cohesive way. It reinforced his theory that they'd probably run into prototypes.

Galen restarted the recording as though making Darien watch them all again was necessary, as though every frame wasn't already committed to memory, as though it would somehow matter enough to elicit whatever emotional reaction the physician wanted from him.

Darien turned his back to the images and approached the reconstruction unit. Galen followed, crossing the chamber to stand at his side.

"Your survivor—this *human*—killed that *grierugon* without a single proper weapon," Galen said. "That's quite a prize you've secured for the emperor, my lord."

On the images Galen had shown him, Darien had caught only the briefest glimpse of the woman's face: she had dark eyes, deep pools jeweled with green.

"Well worth the risk you took..." Galen continued.

The taunting derision in Galen's voice faded as Darien caressed the chestnut tendril with his thumb.

"...a shrewd *political* move," Galen said.

CHAPTER SIX

$\mathcal{C}$ommander Drea Bomani had been sitting in the captain's chair too long, and the bridge had been far too quiet. The imperial border and Thertore's exclusion zone were all behind them and they were about to go through the nearest transit-point.

The transit-point—a "surface" in space not unlike the "disk" created by two soap bubbles where they touched—was rendered as a silver ring in the main holographic display. It was tagged with its exit coordinates, a system they would cross to get to the next transit-point.

She shifted her weight and worked the interfaces at her fingertips. An updated time-to-transit estimate popped up. She swept it away and pursed her lips.

Had they had support ships, like a capital ship should, their route to Serigala would be unencumbered by the need to go only through transit points large enough for a ship the size of a small moon. Several dilation ships always traveled with capital ships so they could suck energy from a nearby star, dump it into a transit-point and widen it enough for the larger ships to go through. During war, the need was justified, for once a transit-point was dilated, it became unstable for a time. The maneuver stranded the dilation ship on the wrong side, often for the enemy to destroy.

She rubbed away the frown that had settled between her brows. *We're not at war.*

Still, she would've felt better having one, or several, dilation ships at her side, just in case. She understood the reasons why Lord Dobromil hadn't authorized any support ships and dilation ships in particular. To deploy a whole fleet on this cursed detail would've sent a different message—not one of penance for his wayward heir, but a show of power. Drea would have preferred the latter. She had argued for it only to have her words fall on deaf ears.

She sighed. It was almost over. The penance, the kowtowing to imperial demands, the required political posturing for which she had nothing but disdain.

And more importantly, the heir she had sworn to protect, was safe. She'd never been happier to be wrong: about the exclusion zone, about Thertore.

Although the rescued human bore no imperial marks, Drea had been less than happy with Darien's decision to bring a potential imperial spy aboard. A small part of her hoped that Galen would fail. That warm corpse they'd brought back was hardly worth the trouble it would, no doubt, bring.

At first, she'd approved of Darien's decision to wait the required two days. She'd hoped that the Imperium would show, force his hand, and that he'd actually discharge his duty as a vassal acting on the Imperium's behalf. It turned her stomach, the thought of turning anyone over to the Imperium, but doing so would've proved that Darien had indeed learned his lesson. It would have made him less of a target for imperial attentions in the future.

But the Imperium had not shown. She still didn't share in Darien's belief that the ship and its crew were of alien origin. Decades of experience told her that this situation was a trap baited with an intriguing lure.

Providing protection to escaping humans had compromised Darien's honor in the first place.

No matter how much she ruminated on her attempt to stop Darien, she could not come up with an argument that would have worked. She sighed in resignation and summoned a holographic report from her console.

The drones she'd dispatched along their border with the Imperium had returned. Their data dumps waited on her attention. The drones' small size let them travel through far more transit-points and she'd deployed them to the extent of their range, as far into imperial territory as she'd dared. Fewer than half had returned, a better percentage than she'd expected. Either the imperials were busy with other things, or their systems were still down. She accessed the drones' long-range telemetry and fed the data to the main display.

Much to her surprise, the exclusion zone remained inert. No imperial rescue ships had been detected. The orbital defenses around Thertore were still quite dead. No ships pursued.

It was incomplete data, hours to days old, depending on the route the drone had taken. Her desire for a complete, real-time picture remained unfulfilled. Perhaps someday, someone would figure out a way to make interstellar communication instantaneous. For now, she had to make do with what she had, and take comfort in knowing that everyone else shared in this limitation.

She drummed her fingers on the arm of her chair.

No imperial contacts.

No anomalies.

Dead calm, one might call it.

The yawn she'd been holding, escaped. She hid it behind a well-timed stretch.

Enough.

Time to run some drills. At least if she had someone to evaluate, she'd have something interesting to do, keep her thoughts from wandering to things she could not change. She checked the duty roster. It was Lieutenant Laleo's turn to trade in his position as Comms for a chance to demonstrate his ability to command, even if all he'd be doing was making sure the ship remained on course.

"Lieuten—"

An alarm drowned her out, jolting her attention back up to the main display. Navigational data auto-populated the hologram: their position, well outside imperial space, vectoring hard for the transit-point; the Imperium's inert communications array, well within. Cryptic bursts of static flared and faded. They were painted as layered waves and nodes atop the navigational rendering.

"Kill that transmission!" Drea shouted, rising out of her chair.

"Unable to comply," Comms said as he stabbed at the holographic controls around him. "Activating jamming protocols."

"Source?"

"Tracers are active," Ops reported. Ops' tactical station was awash in so many holographic layers that Drea could barely make out Lieutenant Exton's silhouette.

Drea held her breath. They were close to being out of range for that type of signal. It was faint, almost an echo, but it was clearly aimed at the communications array inside the exclusion zone. If the array had repaired itself, if the signal reached the array, it would be relayed by drone, via transit-point, back to Kanavar, the Imperium's seat of power.

If, if, if…

Conflicting data flowed around her. The source of the transmission was inside the *Edlyn*, but she was a capital ship, one heavily shielded against unauthorized transmission.

It could only mean one thing: there was a hole in their security.

"Shut down all our communications," Drea said.

"Deactivating," Comms confirmed.

The signal faded, then died, leaving only log entries as evidence of its temporal existence.

THE PILOT'S harness tightened around Owyn Tolek's spare frame as his one-man infiltrator decelerated. The jolt sent a lock of pearl-white hair forward, right into his eyes. He swept it out of the way as he sighed in frustration.

He had at his disposal, access and override codes for everything the Imperium had ever created, the authority to speak with the emperor's own voice if necessary, and a network of spies and informants so vast that it dwarfed the population of some minor Houses. And still, he had fallen prey to the limitations of the transit-point system.

In the simplest of terms, he was late.

His infiltrator had been designed to outrun most other ships, but its acceleration and maneuverability were only an advantage outside of a transit-point.

He'd jumped through several such points in order to travel from Kanavar to Thertore. However, each of those transit-points had been separated by the need to traverse normal space. Even with the inertial inhibitors, even with his *donai* ability to withstand gravitational forces, there was a limit to how much time he could make up for, given the late start.

When he'd emerged from the transit-point into Thertore's system, the last thing he'd expected to find was one of the *Edlyn's* shuttles heading for the planet. He'd known the *Edlyn* had been deployed along their border, but the emperor had sent Valteri's cruiser to keep Dobromil's crew distracted.

It had been a calculated risk, conducting the wormhole generator's pre-test with the *Edlyn* so close, but the emperor's most loyal scientists had assured him that the pre-test was too limited to draw attention. The real test—actually generating a wormhole—was to await his arrival and the *Edlyn's* departure.

As soon as Tolek had emerged from the transit-point, he'd realized that something had gone horribly wrong and sent drones back to Kanavar, requesting additional ships. He'd also sent out an imperial order, forbidding the *Edlyn* to respond to any distress calls, but they had ignored him.

He could've turned around, gone back through the transit-point and sent for help. But he hadn't. If there was one thing he could count on with House Dobromil, it was their over-developed sense of honor.

They could've launched their own ships to overtake and destroy him. Without other imperial ships in the vicinity, with the entire defense network down, no one would've known. He and his ship would be just another cloud of debris orbiting Thertore's star. No one would've been able to dispute a version of events that had him and his ship falling prey to whatever had destroyed everything else the Imperium had in the system.

But Dobromil's heir hadn't pressed his advantage. There had been a part of Tolek that would've enjoyed seeing House Dobromil shed some of its precious honor.

Nevertheless, the emperor would not take House Dobromil's intrusion lightly. The infiltrator's sensors had evidence of the shuttle's landing, its trajectory, and the fact that the *Edlyn* had received Tolek's order, even if it had not been acknowledged.

Tolek settled his infiltrator into orbit around Thertore.

Additional haptic interfaces came to life under his hands. With a few quick taps, he pinged the orbital defenses. A hologram formed, floating in front of him, showing their positions. They were all there, yet he received no response. He pinged them again, this time with an initialization code. Still nothing.

From the images around him, it was easy to see that they were intact. They should've repaired themselves by now, at least enough to respond.

A hologram of Thertore wrapped in a dark cloud appeared on the cockpit's eggshell-like interior. Thertore glowed with dozens of hotspots indicating erupting volcanoes. According to the sensors, quakes were tearing the planet's crust apart. The research station had drawn most of the power for its experimental generator from the planet's molten core. Apparently, its destruction had affected the tectonic stability of the planet far more than any of its designers had anticipated.

The distress beacon that had led the *Edlyn's* shuttle to the surface was still active. He plotted a course towards the same coordinates.

Flanked by indigo streaks of lightning, he plunged through thick clouds. Turbulence hit the infiltrator, nudging him off course, again and again. He broke through the lowest cloud layer, streaking over the land too fast to catch glimpse of anything more than the red smudges of lava flows. He didn't need to see the specifics to know that Thertore was in the grip of a mass-extinction event.

His hands tightened around the ship's controls as he circled the remains of the downed craft. The caustic atmosphere was eating away at the crashed ship's hull. His sensors swept the deteriorating remains.

No wonder House Dobromil had risked a landing. The ship was unlike anything he, or his database, had ever seen. Its hull was giving off an unusual energy reading, one that kept confusing his ship's sensors.

His heart rate increased for an instant before he got it under control. It had worked. That was the only explanation. The wormhole generator's pre-test had worked far better than expected. Either that or someone had exceeded their authority, gone to the next phase.

He took his ship closer. Despite the buffeting winds, he hovered above the crash site and deployed drones. Alongside the alien craft, the spherical drones looked like mere insects drawn in by the scent of carrion.

They entered the ship and beamed back images of what looked like human and *grierugon* skeletons.

Tolek tapped his fingers on the armrest. Curiosity about the alien ship gnawed at him. His armored bio-mechanical suit would protect him from the caustic atmosphere, but its sensors were no better than those of the drones.

The ground beneath the alien ship split with a roar. Its weight shifted, opening another tear along its hull. If the transports he'd sent for didn't get here soon, there wouldn't be much left to bring back to Kanavar, but his infiltrator wasn't built to lift and tow even that deteriorating wreck.

He let out a frustrated breath, wishing he'd anticipated this. He should have anticipated it. It was part of his job. There had been a dissenting voice, a lone one, that had warned them that this could happen. Like most dissenting voices, it had been ignored.

As Tolek made for orbit Thertore tore at him with greedy hands, as though its death throes yearned for his company. Once safely out its clutches, he programmed and deployed a satellite to monitor and record the rest of Thertore's demise.

The emperor was not going to be happy. Not about losing Thertore.

Not about House Dobromil landing here. Not about what they had seen or how much they had, no doubt, learned.

Tolek adjusted his course, heading for the communications array orbiting above the star's ecliptic. To his surprise, it hadn't been as affected as the rest of Thertore's defense systems, and it had been quietly repairing itself. Its position and distance from Thertore seemed to have given it some protection. All the planetary defenses in the exclusion zone, along with the research station, would have sent their data to the array, right up until they had failed. From that information, he would reconstruct events and determine exactly what had happened.

He nudged his ship into position and established a physical connection with the array. His infiltrator channeled additional power into the structure. A few hours later, he was still monitoring its progress, re-prioritizing its repairs, when a faint signal, a stream of data from Dobromil space hit the array.

Tolek smiled.

CHAPTER SEVEN

*D*arien's strides consumed the tiled pathway that bisected his flag cabin. It led him back to his desk. Upon its stygian surface an imperial missive rested.

It had been written on a scroll, delivered by courier, and placed in Darien's own hands. The malachite-green canister that had protected the scroll from prying eyes lay beside it, its biometric seal opened by Darien's touch.

He traced the beveled edge of the desk with impatient fingers and pivoted on his heel to cover familiar ground one more time.

A set of couches, the kind with supple reddish-brown leather that embraced you like the welcoming arms of a long-lost friend, faced each other in the wide, open space between the tiled pathway and the refreshment alcove. The low table between the couches waited too, under gold-rimmed crystal stemware and the type of wine preferred by his still-absent guest.

Back and forth Darien paced, booted heels clicking against the smooth dark tiles. In those odd moments when he stopped for no reason he could understand, he caught reflections of a troubled face that looked far too much like his own one moment, and nothing like his the next. He tugged on the left sleeve of his ship fatigues like a new cadet nervous about his first inspection.

On impulse, he snatched up the missive, rolling it tight into his fist, and tucked it behind his back. It was already burned into his memory, and would remain so, for as long as he lived, like a scar that would never heal.

The doors parted and Galen strode in, a puzzled frown wrinkling his brow. He was still in his uniform as though he'd come straight from the infirmary, despite the late hour. Without breaking his pace, Darien passed him the imperial missive.

Galen unrolled the scroll and casually propped himself against the desk.

Darien turned back to the viewscreen. The imperial courier's ship was a bloom of light against the Void as it entered the transit-point leading to Kanavar, Emperor Thán Kabrin's seat of power.

Hands still clasped behind his back where they could do no damage, Darien glanced over his shoulder to check Galen's progress. The physician was reading the missive with deliberate care, his gaze moving slowly over each line.

Darien relaxed one muscle at a time, starting with the ones in his neck and working his way down. He ran through his calming routine twice and started a third.

Finally, Galen crossed the cabin to pour himself a glass of wine. He sank into the couch across the room and leaned back, frown lines deepening and read the missive again.

Darien stifled a groan. There was no hurrying the old man, no value in prompting him. He resumed his pacing.

Galen cleared his throat.

"Why do you want to save her life?" Galen asked.

Darien halted mid-stride and jerked around, summoning as much incredulity as he could.

Galen's frown was gone, his face a blank mask suggesting nothing but interested detachment. No concern about how the emperor had found out they had a survivor aboard. Nothing about the compromise in their security and communications. No commentary on the absurdity of the emperor's conclusion. Just a straight path to the one question Darien didn't want to answer.

Very well. He was prepared. Detachment was a familiar enough cloak for him as well.

"There are things we need to know. Orbital mechanics suggests the devastation on Thertore coincided with her ship's appearance, not their crash. *They* are being blamed for the destruction of all imperial assets in the exclusion zone, even though their ship never veered off course between the time it appeared and the time it crashed."

They. The word stung his mouth. There was no they; there was only a she. One scapegoat destined to bear the burden of injuring imperial pride, a burden worsened by Darien's actions.

"Ah, I see," Galen said, rolling the missive closed as he raised a skeptical eyebrow. He propped his elbow on the armrest, sliding into a relaxed position.

It was a tactic of false ease, one so easily recognized that Galen should've known better than to try it on him. Nevertheless, Darien braced himself.

"Your interest," Galen said, "is in the technology that destroyed the imperial craft. No problem. Once she's conscious, one dose, maybe two, of the right psycho-active agent, and the mystery will be solved. If not, the emperor's own interrogators will extract the necessary information."

Galen's hand formed into a fist, betraying his struggle not to adjust his collar. The apprehension escaping his pores clouded the air. For a man who'd spent his entire life in servitude to the *donai*, who knew *donai* physiology better than anyone else alive, he should have known better than to play this game. But old habits died hard, and perhaps even more so for humans, for they all did this, this little dance of trying to hide what they felt, of projecting calm when they stank of fear and anxiety.

"Remember why you entered the exclusion zone," Galen said. "Why you landed on Thertore: to protect the Imperium's interests." His voice faltered only on the penultimate word.

"I did my duty."

"Then continue doing it." Galen took a sip of wine. "Or do you still doubt the worth of your prize?"

"She is not my prize."

"No, she's not. She's the emperor's. *His* personal property. *His* prize. That is how Thán Kabrin in all of his imperial majesty will see this. It is how the Imperial Court will see it. Your father as well."

Galen's eyes narrowed, his gaze burning through Darien like a weapon.

"My lord, I see the path you want to take and it's not the one you set us on. Before you go any farther, consider Kabrin's response to the challenge you'd be making to his primacy."

I did. I am.

"What will the emperor do to—with—her?" Darien asked.

"For an intrusion into imperial space, loss of all imperial assets in the exclusion zone, including those creatures—"

"That was my doing, not theirs." *Not hers*, Darien had almost said.

"Yes, true. Then let's factor in the loss of face, the failures that allowed a subordinate House to land on Thertore, to rescue intrud—"

"—apprehend, Galen."

Galen waved his hand dismissively. "Does 'apprehending' involve ignoring orders?"

Darien fixed his jaw in stubborn silence as Galen set his glass down with emphasis. For years, the defiant banter bordering on insubordination between Galen and his father had been a source of great amusement and awe; both had waned once Darien had become a part of the exchanges.

Galen was not only a beloved retainer, but his father's most valued advisor—someone too valuable to send on a punishment detail. Darien understood the reasons, the real reasons, behind Galen's presence not only on his ship, but in this very moment.

Galen was testing him.

"Illegal orders," Darien said. "I responded to a distress call and apprehended the surviving intruder. If the *grierugon* had torn her apart, the emperor would have no one to blame. Or interrogate."

Galen ran his finger along the rim of the wine glass, circling it once and again.

"So, it's guilt then." Galen's tone was gentle, conveying no insult.

"Guilt for what?"

"For placing her at the tender mercies of the Imperium."

Darien denied the charge with silence.

Guilt was useless, a human emotion, one in which *donai* did not indulge. The humans who'd created the *donai* had denied it to them so it wouldn't blunt their usefulness. Galen's gentle tone was a reminder that because Darien's mother had been human, he would not be judged for indulging his humanity.

All he had to do was acknowledge it.

"You know what Kabrin will do," Galen finally said, his voice hollow yet full of emotion at the same time, as though a host of ghosts spoke with him.

Darien tightened his hands into fists. His fingernails drew minute beads of blood. They healed without a trace, a reminder that he was, first and foremost, *donai*.

"I would prefer not to draw my House into an all-out conflict with the Imperium," Darien said.

At best, this was a half-truth. Conflict was his preference; it was the reason for his existence. This innate desire was his blind spot, his awareness of it a virtue at times, a burden at others.

He waited for Galen to point out that any conflict with the Imperium could be avoided—all he had to do was sacrifice a woman he'd never met, never spoken to, a woman whose name he didn't even know. Never need know.

Instead, Galen's silence piqued Darien's curiosity. It was unlike Galen to miss the opportunity to point out such an obvious solution. Something else, something subtle, something Darien had missed was in play.

Darien crossed the room and poured himself a glass of wine. It was a symbolic gesture: *donai* were unaffected by alcohol. Its consumption was ceremonial, part of an effort to appear human.

"Can you tell me anything about where she might be from?" Darien asked. "A lost seed colony, perhaps?"

"A lost seed colony *would* explain why she's human."

"And her injuries?"

"Injuries?" Galen said, mocking the word and its meaning as though taking some offense to its very use. "You put a warm corpse in stasis and presented it to me with a challenge: Here, Galen, fix this. As if she were just like any number of injured animals you found on the palace grounds."

Darien smiled at the memories evoked by Galen's false modesty. "Not *just* a challenge. Confidence. You saved them all."

"This is not an injured wolf cub you can keep," Galen said. "This woman would make a very dangerous pet."

Darien flinched. "I don't want a pet."

A sip of wine failed to clear the revulsion brought on by the idea of a human familiar. It was not an unknown practice among some *donai*.

"What do you want?" Galen asked.

"An answer," Darien said. A perfect answer. One that didn't require any sort of sacrifice.

Galen leaned forward, resting his elbows on his knees as he steepled his fingers.

"Stab wounds—more than I cared to count. I had to clone a new set of eyes for her. Incredible stuff, those *grierugon* secretions. Vile."

House Dobromil's Court physician, a man who had seen every kind of wound, every atrocity that could be perpetrated on a body—human or *donai*—shuddered, reaching for more wine, then took a long sip and indulged in an even longer silence.

"How fortunate for the emperor," Galen finally said. "He'll have a perfectly healthy human to interrogate."

Darien had seen Galen's compassion compromise his clinical detachment at times, but he'd never seen it degrade into callousness. Tenacious as ever, Galen was still testing him, reminding him, perhaps hoping that there was still a small part inside him that was human, that could be guilted.

He resumed his pacing, although without its initial fervor.

"We've analyzed the data recovered from her ship," Darien said. Objective data. Facts. They were so much clearer. And cleaner.

"There's nothing to indicate their route," he continued, "or their point of origin. Enough of their data core was intact for some linguistic analysis. I'm told we have enough for a language matrix. At least we'll be able to talk to her."

"Yes, that will be useful." Galen raised his glass high. "Welcome to the Imperium. A death sentence awaits you for exposing the emperor's weakness. What kind of execution would you prefer? Choose carefully—"

"Enough."

Darien gave Galen his back. Facing the viewscreen gave him a glimpse into the vastness under House Dobromil's protection. A vastness whose full measure he dared not tally. He feared failing under its burden.

"I don't have a lot of time," Darien said. "These demands mean that our security is compromised, that Kabrin has people on my ship. That is the bigger threat, the one we should be focusing on, because this will not end with a courier.

"The emperor will send other ships, pursue and engage us in our own territory, force my House into a conflict we cannot win. I need your help."

Galen's reflection rubbed at the tension between its eyes and scrubbed its hand through its grey hair. Setting the wine glass aside, Galen cleared his throat. He stood and produced a curt bow to Darien's back.

"My lord, there is a way, one where no one—not even the emperor —will be able to touch her."

The casual words, cloaked in formality, meant—

No.

It was a path Darien would've never thought of, could never consider.

Darien whirled. He crushed the wine glass in the cradle of his hand. Its shards raced a cascade of blood and wine to the floor.

"Do not mock me," he said, a tremor creeping into the warning.

There was only one basis for laying claim to another *donai's* property—a pregnancy.

Darien's augmentations activated. He could truly see now, see the heat emanating from Galen's form, the energy trails of blood racing through his veins. Galen's vital organs glowed, revealing targets— heart, lungs, brain. The predator Darien was knew them all and could end Galen's life with one motion. Quickly and mercifully. Or painfully, lingeringly, like Galen deserved.

It was the steady thrum of Galen's heart beating in stark contrast to his own that brought back some semblance of control.

"I will not." Three words, distorted by a visceral ache brought on by Galen's stab at his honor. While in his custody, the prisoner was under his protection, whether she was the emperor's property or not.

Darien envied Galen's calm, the courage behind it, envied him more than he could've thought possible.

"Crashing in imperial territory makes her Kabrin's property," Galen said. "But your rights to your own progeny would free her, make her yours. Once you claim her, not even the emperor can interfere. The other Houses won't tolerate it."

Such resolve was something to be admired, Darien told himself.

"This is the only way, Darien. You know it."

Human apprehension no longer permeated the air. Galen was enjoying himself. There was triumph and pride in his voice. It was a rare and dangerous pleasure to provoke the *donai*, one few humans indulged and fewer survived.

This is what loyalty looks like. It allows him to revel in provoking me, but it is still loyalty.

Darien turned away, closing his eyes as he leaned his forehead against the chill of the viewscreen. He examined his hand and removed two slivers of glass still embedded in his palm. A residual glow generated by his nanites flared before they disappeared below the surface.

Two more breaths and his vision shifted back to its limited human range. He straightened, folding his hands behind his back.

"Galen, exactly how does a prisoner, a human from a world

69

unknown to us, one who doesn't even speak our language or know our ways, become pregnant after a few days in my custody?"

"How, will not matter to the Imperium." Galen's voice was cold, speaking hard truth without emotion.

"It matters to me."

"You need never touch her. She doesn't even need to know."

"And when there is no child?" Darien asked.

"Human-*donai* pregnancies are almost as prone to failure as *donai* ones. A miscarriage is far more likely than a child."

Such a clinical answer. As if Galen could hide behind it. Perhaps a human could. Darien did not, however, have such a luxury. This went beyond the philosophies of things like honor and the legalities of orders.

"You want me to lie to the emperor," Darien said.

"Yes."

The ease with which Galen said it caught Darien off guard. How could one who had such painful intimacy with the emperor and his methods even entertain such an idea? Did Galen really find himself with so little to lose?

"My lord, I have served your House for many decades. I've watched the Imperial Court play its games. Kabrin will see this sudden claim as a positive. He's never sanctioned your father's practices towards us humans. House Dobromil's treatment of us as free men, in practice if not in law, has been a thorn in Kabrin's side for as long as I can remember.

"Kabrin will look at this claim you find so abhorrent, as a move by you towards him, not as a black mark on your honor. He will look forward to having you ascend your father's throne."

Darien could disagree with none of it, but humans didn't understand what it meant to be *donai*. Among other things it meant that abusing the sanctity of a claim—no matter its good intentions—would jeopardize his ability to lead the other *donai*. There was more to inheriting his father's throne than the fortune of his birth.

"How will I stand in front of my father again? You would have me explain that my lies to the emperor are somehow less dishonorable than betraying someone under my protection?"

"I would have you stand in front of your father, having saved her life. That is what you asked for: her life. First, when you pulled her from the wreckage of that ship, and again when you decided she deserved a better fate than what awaits her on Kanavar."

"I've made no such decision," Darien said.

"Haven't you? Have you ordered Bomani to change course? Are we on our way back to Thertore? To Kanavar?"

Darien's silence lengthened, stretched, and finally reached its limit.

"There has to be another way," Darien said, staring down at his freshly healed hand. "One that doesn't involve deceiving and dishonoring my father, my House.

"One that doesn't dishonor me.

"One that doesn't dishonor her."

TWO-OH-FOUR TRAILED the imperial courier at a distance sufficient enough for it to remain undetected. Its sensors dutifully recorded the phase shift that transitioned the courier out of Dobromil space.

Within its shell, Two-oh-four created three copies of its telemetry, loaded each into three of twelve pods resting within in its core, and launched them.

Pod One vectored for the *Edlyn*, while Pod Two and Pod Three headed for the other transit points in the system. Once through, Pods Two and Three would take separate routes to Serigala, House Dobromil's seat of power.

With the pods well on their way, Two-oh-four crept toward the transit point, comparing the tracks of nearby resources—asteroids, comets, gaseous and rocky planets. With nine pods to spare, it had no reason to seek out the additional raw materials for the molecular assemblers residing in its belly. Nevertheless, it obeyed its protocols and took inventory.

Two-oh-four hit the churning waves surrounding the transit point and rode the gradients around the disk just close enough to remain on this side. Cloaking itself in the warped space, it drew power from the resulting "friction" on its hull.

Hidden, it lay in wait like a spider awaiting a disturbance in its web.

CHAPTER EIGHT

*T*he doors closed behind Bomani and Palleton as they exited Darien's flag cabin. The latest progress reports continued to flow across the dark surface of his desk.

His people were no closer to an explanation for the alien craft's appearance. Bomani was no closer to the source of the unauthorized transmission, or an explanation for how the Imperium had pinpointed their location well enough to send a courier. Darien was no closer to an honorable solution that wouldn't challenge the emperor than he'd been when he'd rejected Galen's plan.

He plucked a report mid-stream and flicked it upward. The hologram formed above the desk, splitting into charts and diagrams of the alien ship and the haunting images of slaughter. He dismissed all but one: the survivor making her stand. His repeated queries about her status had met only vagueness.

There was a deliberate pattern, one that set Galen's responses apart from the norm. It was in this pattern that he saw Galen's thinly veiled reprimand.

Darien left the images floating as he exited and made his way to the infirmary. Once there, he passed three physicians in retreat, their disapproving backward glances and rigid postures betraying professional indignation. They nodded in cursory recognition of his rank, but offered no explanation as they fled Galen's lab.

A mournful cry filled the infirmary.

The hairs on the back of his neck rose. He lengthened his stride as habit guided his hand to the grip of his sidearm.

As he entered Galen's lab, a sterilizing force field snared him, halting him mid-stride and bathing him in blue light. He struggled against it, bristling at the confinement. He fought back a snarl as he turned his head, looking for the source of those cries.

Galen stood over the survivor, oblivious to or ignoring Darien's presence.

"It's not working," Galen said, speaking to someone in the gallery above.

The angle and the fluctuating light of the force field distorted Darien's view of the figure, but the silhouette resembled Galen's eldest daughter.

The voice drifting from the gallery said, "Another moment, my lord."

"Anasera," Darien said, "is this really necessary?"

"Of course," she said, the smoothness of her lilting tone confirming the dubious nature of her actions.

Another lament echoed through the chamber, but training and habit held him in place, kept him from mustering the strength needed to break through. Seconds ticked by as the field did its work. Seconds became minutes that stoked his irritation.

Galen made soothing sounds, directing them at the semi-conscious survivor. She was struggling, thwarting Galen's attempts to calm her. A flock of spherical rovers floated above her, their beams tracing a synchronized pattern.

"Anasera," Darien warned, drawing out her name. The force field finally released him just as he was about to break protocol.

He rushed forward.

Long, thick lashes fluttered beneath arched eyebrows. Aristocratic cheekbones emphasized an exquisite beauty. Her scent was unique, exotic. The outline of her body beckoned beneath its sheath, inviting him to reach out and remove the offending garment.

It was the sight of her exposed neck, tilted in a gesture of submission—a gesture heavy with meaning and intent to the non-human side of him—that evoked the picture of her under him, spiraling to heights of ecstasy as he drove himself into her. The intensity of that image stopped him dead in his tracks and robbed him of breath.

Galen pinned him with a knowing glare.

"You shouldn't be in here," Galen said.

Darien's lip curled as he bared his teeth.

Galen ignored him and looked up at the gallery. "Put her all the way back under and *go*."

Darien caught a glimpse of reluctance from Anasera as she nodded and withdrew. He dodged the rovers as they zoomed past his head like a flight in precision formation.

From the head of the reconstruction unit, a dormant bubble rose from its cradle. It unfurled and crowned the woman in shimmering light. Her arched back dropped, robbing Darien of the sight of tautly outlined breasts straining against sheer fabric. His gaze followed the cascade of straining muscles as they surrendered.

He stepped closer. The sides of the reconstruction unit rose, preparing to embrace her again. He blocked the canopy with his hands and swept one strand of hair from her face, then another, trailing his finger along her cheek and across full lips. Her face was softer and finer than the surveillance from her ship had suggested.

Were the jewels of her eyes as brilliant as his memory insisted?

Galen cleared his throat.

"She's in pain," Darien said.

"Yes."

"She's in a lot of pain."

"I don't need a *donai's* sense of smell to tell me that," Galen snapped. "I know how much pain she's in."

"Help her." The accusation that Galen wasn't doing enough hung silently between them.

"I am *helping* her."

"Do more." Darien wanted to recall his words as soon as he'd given them form.

"Why?" Galen asked, temper rising. "So those imperial butchers can tear her apart again? Finish the *grierugon's* work? Draw it out so Thán Kabrin can enjoy the spectacle?"

Darien had witnessed the emperor do all those things and stood mute under his judgmental glance. A glance that accused him of weakness and sentiment.

"If you're going to send her to that kind of death anyway..." Galen's voice faded, his tone deferential and wounded. "She deserves a painless death."

The walls of the lab blurred around him as Darien's hands closed around Galen's throat. He smacked him up against a wall and held him there.

As Galen struggled for breath, Darien waited for his augmented vision to show him the exact moment when Galen needed to breathe. When it did, he relaxed his grip, granted Galen breath, and met his gaze across the length of his reach.

Eyes full of rebellion, Galen dangled from his grasp, his smile defiant in a crimson face.

I'm being provoked. Tested. Again.

It didn't matter. He had every reason to demonstrate the limit of his tolerance.

Galen clawed at Darien's hands, his feeble human nails too weak to damage *donai* skin. Darien tightened his grip enough to encourage Galen to yield. He bent his elbows and leaned into Galen's face.

"If she dies, you die," he whispered, his words rumbling. He'd had his fill of being tested, of having the moral dilemma he'd created out of his sense of duty and honor, used against him. "Do you understand?"

Galen nodded, but triumph, not fear, played across his face.

Darien let him go.

Galen found his balance and caught his breath. Heaving, gulping, he stood as if he remained undefeated.

Darien headed towards the door. He stopped just short of it and spoke over his shoulder. "I will do what I can to buy her more time."

"You'll need to do more than that. You"—Galen dared through gasping breaths, his voice strained and hoarse—"cannot satisfy your honor and save her life...

"You're going to have to choose."

THE FLUSH of adrenaline coursing through Galen's body dissipated with Darien's departure. He eased into a seat as Anasera rushed into the lab, eyes wide, olive skin paling.

How much had she seen?

At least she'd had the good sense not to interfere. Her presence might've tempered Darien's reaction and hindered Galen's intent.

"Why do you so enjoy poking the bear?" she asked, as she grappled with his tunic's collar, vanquished its hold, and then attacked the shirt underneath. "Well, the wolf, anyway."

A sharp jolt of pain accompanied the clearing of his throat.

"He asked for my help," Galen said. "I'm providing it."

He winced at the sound of his own voice. The damage was worse than he'd expected.

Anasera shot him an incredulous look, one she'd borrowed from her mother.

"Can you do it without risking your life?" she asked.

"I have nothing to fear from Darien Dayasagar. Of this I am certain."

"This," she said, jabbing his neck hard enough to make him wince, "says otherwise."

He tugged at his collar again and cringed, more at the memories the pain evoked than the pain itself. Over the years, he'd paid dearly for indulgences no other human enjoyed—autonomy and a domain of his own—even if sometimes the boundaries blurred. As long as he remained in House Dobromil's territory, he was as close to a free human as existed; he had a home, a family, friends, a purpose and a cause. He had freedom and responsibilities, power and duty.

Anasera summoned a rover. It floated silently toward them. Galen waved it away.

"Leave it. I want him to have to look at it."

She crossed her arms. "Why?"

He waited for her foot to stop tapping. It didn't.

"A lesson," he said, hoping she'd find him merely flippant.

He did not want to delve into the symbolism of the lesson he'd just imparted. Galen's bruised throat would remind Darien how close he'd come to emulating the "imperial temper." Darien knew some of the intimate details of Galen's experience with the emperor, but Anasera did not. He meant to keep it that way.

"*You* never learn," she said. "Why do you expect him to?"

"Because I'm still alive."

She shook her head and brushed away dark strands of hair that had escaped the tight braid crowning her head.

He smiled, hoping to quell her anxiety.

One of the *Edlyn's* communications officers entered the compartment just as Galen was about to offer her a more reassuring answer. The lanky man's ever-present slouch and aimless gaze made him seem perpetually lost. A small box was tucked under his arm.

"Can I help you, Lieutenant Laleo?" Galen asked as he fidgeted with his loosened collar again.

His attempt to close the collar called unwanted attention to the contusions that were no doubt purpling his neck.

Laleo's eyes widened; he looked away.

Galen closed the clasps at his throat. He made a small sound to cue Laleo. The effort sharpened his pain.

"Sir," Laleo said, "I have your translation devices."

He presented the small box, opening it to reveal four metallic disks, each the size of a pearl. He set the box down on the console at Galen's elbow and strayed over to the patient.

"She looks human," Laleo said, his shoulders rounding further.

"She *is* human. What did you expect?" Anasera asked as she held one of the translators up to the light.

Galen picked up one of its duplicates and rolled its unexpectedly heavy weight around between his fingers. The dull gray sheen hinted at industrial purpose rather than decoration.

"Someone fierce," Laleo said as he leaned over the patient, making the most of his opportunity to scrutinize the alien intruder.

What other rumors, besides ferocity, had his patient inspired?

Galen held up one of the translators. "Is it a complete matrix?"

Laleo fidgeted and said, "Oh," as he tugged at his tunic, then his sleeve, as if the answer was somewhere inside.

Could Galen get Bomani to order Laleo in for some tests? It wasn't just the unmilitary slouch that bothered Galen. The jerky movements to which Laleo was prone didn't inspire confidence in the abilities of a bridge officer, even a newly minted one. If it was neurological, it would be an easy enough fix.

"No, sir," Laleo finally said, apparently finding the answer. "Cryptology wants a stab at her."

Unfazed by Anasera's flinch and shake of the head, Laleo continued, "Preferably as soon as she wakes, to help them fill in the gaps. They could only match about a third of our language. Common Kanthlos, that is. Not High Kanthlos. Almost none to High, I believe."

"Is that enough to let us talk to her?" Anasera asked.

"Mostly," Laleo said. "Contextual interpretations will be a problem, at least at first. But basic conversations should be doable. Once calibrated, it'll even cancel out the foreign words. To us, it'll seem like she's speaking Kanthlos—the common aspects of it. To her, it'll sound like we're speaking Rhoan."

"Rhoan?" Galen asked.

"Yes, sir. That's what they call themselves. Their home world is known as Rho."

The monitors spiked. Galen walked over to his patient as Anasera settled behind a console. She frowned and shot Galen an accusing glare.

He'd kept his patient under too long. Anasera had wanted to wake her days ago. He'd pulled rank, citing the most creative and obscure medical reasons that his decades of experience could conjure.

Galen stood over the woman, whose closed eyelids twitched as her eyes jerked back and forth, fighting the induced sleep paralysis.

Laleo joined him, standing a bit too close for comfort as he peered curiously at the woman.

"I would suggest some precautions, sir, before you wake her," Laleo said. "The Rhoan ship's data designates her as prisoner DRD4."

"A prisoner? Are you sure?" Anasera asked.

Laleo shrugged. "As certain as we are of anything, given the gaps in the surveillance. That's why Linguistics would also like a stab at her when she—"

"Yes, yes," Galen said, impatiently making a shooing motion that encouraged Laleo to leave.

"Have I said—"

"Out!"

Laleo's eyes widened. His mouth gaped.

"Thank you, Lieutenant," Anasera said. "We're grateful for the translators. We'll let you know as soon as our patient is ready to talk with Linguistics."

He offered her a hesitant bow and slouched his way out.

Galen activated a console and called up the records from the Rhoan ship. He scrolled through the images until he found the time point showing Chief Aeson ripping a collar—one that looked very much like that of a slave—off his patient's throat. Anasera looked at the image over his shoulder.

"You said you found evidence of torture," she said.

"Yes," he said, hand straying to his tunic's collar before he realized it.

"Bomani thinks she's an imperial spy," Anasera said. "She will insist on an interrogation."

"She can insist all she wants," Galen said. "Her authority does not extend into my domain. There will be no interrogations, not as long as she remains my patient."

"Is there any chance that Bomani is right?"

"I've been trying to match her genetic code to all known human sources. If our ancestors and her ancestors ever encountered each other, it was over three thousand generations ago."

"Three thousand generations," Anasera said, her voice colored with disbelief. "That precedes our own recorded history. No wonder that ship looked so alien."

"It's a poor estimate. A variable one as well."

"It's not like you to guess."

His lips twisted in a wry smile. "Oh, believe me, I'd rather have a more precise number. I just haven't been able to produce one. Perhaps once we return to Serigala, I can dig into Dobromil's more extensive archives and send out some queries to allied Houses."

"And rouse unnecessary suspicions?" she asked.

He shrugged. "I'm known for making unusual requests and for my eccentricities. And Lord Dobromil is known for indulging me."

Anasera tapped her foot, brow furrowing. "You can't phrase your query as information about generations. The length of a human generation varies too much, even now. You'd have to specify it as the length of time that human women are fertile, and that would raise suspicions."

He nodded. He'd considered this too. On some planets where humans had technology, most girls became fertile in their early teens. On others, years later. There were worlds where humans lived out their natural life spans. Others where nanites extended it. And there were worlds where they saw early deaths in middle age, long before their reproductive years were over. It had been so under the *donai's* creators and continued under the Imperium.

"Is this why I didn't see any of this in your notes?" she finally asked.

"Yes. You can see where it might pique the interest of the wrong people, given my so-called reputation."

"Perhaps if I made the queries."

"Your association with me is too close," he said.

"Then we'll need to bring in someone else. Someone we can trust but who won't immediately raise suspicions."

"We need to know how the emperor is playing this. If he admits to an alien ship appearing out of nowhere…"

"We need to return to Serigala," she said, "get updated intelligence."

"In his communique to Darien, Kabrin cast her as an invader, a threat."

"That doesn't mean he'll cast her as such to the Court. And the only 'threat' she might pose"—she worked the console—"is her immune system."

He scoffed. "I updated her immune system while she was still in stasis in the life-pod."

Anasera made more queries, the skeptical look on her face firmly in place.

"And destroyed anything that might be a threat to us," he added.

"Are you sure no one...what did they call themselves?"

"Rhoans."

"Are you sure no other Rhoans survived?" she asked. "They *could* pose a threat to the humans in the Imperium."

"I went over the mission logs very carefully. If any Rhoans did survive the *grierugon*, I doubt they survived Thertore. The atmosphere had already turned caustic enough to eat away at her ship's hull."

"Good," she said. "Then we have an advantage. One we must retain."

He gave her a little smile. There was a part of him that wanted to bring her in on his plan, enlist her help in convincing Darien to claim the woman. But he remained silent. Bringing Anasera into the treason that a false claim entailed would endanger her life and reputation. His need to protect his daughter outweighed his desire to save the woman's life.

That task fell, properly, on Darien's shoulders. And it was one he would leave in its proper place.

CHAPTER NINE

*D*rea's stomach did a little flip as the lift capsule came to a stop. The doors pulled away to reveal one of the semi-cylindrical tunnels that served as passageways in the *Edlyn's* lower decks. Amber light from the honeycombed ceiling moved with her. Her breath plumed in the cold air.

Shadowy figures stirred at the end, bare-headed *donai* in otherwise full armor, their weapons at low-ready. They waited on her just outside the spherical chamber that housed the *Edlyn's* communications array.

The *donai* parted for Drea with acknowledging nods.

Inside the spherical chamber, dark, inert spikes and spires jutted inward from all angles, like blackened teeth in a cavernous mouth. Palleton stood over one of his warrant officers, a *donai* named Kell, who was down on one knee at the edge of the tunnel just outside the chamber. Reflected light from his instruments pulsed off his armor.

Kell turned his signature shaved head to acknowledge her with a nod. Odd man. He proudly sported a scarred jawline as evidence of having saved Lord Dobromil's life. The actual injury had healed within hours of the event but he'd had a special set of nanites designed to recreate the scar. It gave him a sinister, villainous look, very much in contrast to his personality.

She inched forward as the *donai* closed in to loom over her. She suppressed a sigh—nothing like a passageway full of *donai* to make a human feel even smaller.

"What do you see?" she asked Kell. It wasn't often she wished for *donai* augmentations.

He pointed at one of the larger spires within the array. She crouched behind him, sighting along Kell's extended arm. There was nothing there.

"Here you go, Commander." Palleton passed her a handheld scanner that resembled a sheet of opaque glass.

Drea used both hands to raise the device so she could look through it. A ghost of a heat image rastered across the surface and lingered for an instant.

"The mass, sitting on that node," Palleton said, "is made up of shielded nanites. They're leaking residual heat."

Huddled together, the molecular machines' heat signature looked every bit a cluster of malignancy and ill intent. Drea blew out a breath and tightened her grip on the scanner.

"Are they multiplying?" she asked as she stood.

"Not at this time," Kell said, lowering his arm.

"Why can't the *Edlyn* detect them?" she asked.

"Their shielding is *very* good," Kell said. "Better than anything I've ever seen."

Better than anything he'd seen most likely meant imperial technology. It was possible another House was involved, but, given the timing, she was prone to think it was the Imperium. She ran through a mental list of Dobromil's rivals and enemies. An enemy would share, or sell, the breakthrough for such tech with the Imperium to gain favor. A rival, maybe; maybe not.

Reverse engineering the nanites would give House Dobromil insight not only into the technological advances, but would also allow them to procure evidence of the Imperium's spying. She hated the way *donai* House politics played into everything.

"How long have they been here?" she asked.

"Can't tell. Maybe if we deprocess them…" Kell said.

"Have to catch them first," Palleton grumbled, shifting his weight to get a better view down into the array. As his layered pupils expanded and contracted, the unhappy look already there intensified.

Drea used the scanner again, but could see nothing, not even the heat that had been present before.

"What are they doing?" she asked.

"Right now, they're intermittently leaking heat," Kell answered. "Our communications array has been idle, cooling. They can no longer dump their residual heat into the array's sink. However, as soon as we start using the array again, they'll be impossible to detect."

"Are they a threat?" she asked.

"Anything we don't control or understand is a threat, Commander," Palleton opined.

"Can you catch them without destroying them?" she asked.

Kell shrugged. "These types of invasive nanites tend to self-destruct, sometimes spectacularly."

"How spectacularly? Enough to harm the *Edlyn*?" Drea asked.

"Not in such small numbers, Commander," Kell said.

"And if there are others?" Palleton asked. "More of them?"

"The destruction of one colony could trigger others to self-destruct or go inert," Kell said. "There's only one way to find out."

"How long will it take to sweep the ship?" Drea asked Palleton, as she handed back the scanner.

An amused eyebrow quirked. "The *entire* ship?"

Drea was willing to turn even a ship the size of the *Edlyn* inside out. She toyed with the idea of making it an order just to see how long it would take. It was certain to wipe that amusement off Palleton's face.

"It'd be easier if we had fewer people aboard," Kell said. "We can turn off life support rotating through sections and decks. Once it's cool enough the heat leaks through the shielding. In a vacuum, they'll have nowhere to dump their heat."

Drea wrinkled her nose. "So, once we start using comms again, we won't know what they're doing, or how they're doing it. Is that correct?"

"Yes, ma'am."

"And there could be more of them. We just can't detect them as long as our life support is active."

"So it would seem," Kell said.

"Could they take refuge in areas where we still have life support?"

"We have no reason to think their mobility is limited."

She glared at the array.

"Can you contain them within this space?" she asked.

"I don't think so," Kell said. "They got in somehow, through our shielding, our sensor sweeps, our containment protocols."

"Can you fry them?"

"Yes, ma'am. With the right kind of radiation, but that will destroy comms as well."

Politics or not, her responsibility was to the ship and the crew. Without evidence, they couldn't prove that the Imperium had violated their agreement. She thanked an entire pantheon of gods and titans that she need not weigh in the machinations of the Imperial Court. Being human did have its own distinct advantages.

"Make sure our secondary array is clean," she said. "Then fry them."

THE ODDITY of blinking tugged at the edge of Syteria's consciousness, as if the sensation belonged to someone else. The center of her vision cleared, bringing the room into focus: a glowing ceiling, one without lights, like the inside of a giant pearl, smooth and without source; the subtle rhythm of biomonitors; the faint scent of antiseptic.

Taxed by the increasing brightness, her eyes strained to adjust. Tears welled. She shielded them with unbound hands. They moved with the stiffness of long disuse, but the burns were gone. Not a single scar remained.

She flexed her fingers to make sure they were her own.

The cradling surfaces around her receded. She turned on her side and faced seamless, curving walls.

The platform underneath her moved. She shifted as it reformed around her, gliding softly into a reclined position and lowering under her legs.

Despite her racing heart, she felt blood drain from her face. There were rumors that the Matriarchs had such places of healing. That they could even do miraculous things, if they chose.

But why would the Rhoans leave her unbound? Perhaps because there was nothing within reach, nothing to use as a weapon. And no door.

All rooms have doors. This one's just hidden.

The beeping of biomonitors matched the staccato beat of her heart and the platform stopped, as if some controlling entity had become aware of her fear.

Anchoring her hands along the platform's edge, she pulled her shoulders forward. The motion was too easy, too light. She felt off-balance.

No collar.

She dared not reach for her neck and swallowed hard instead. The collar's oppressive weight wasn't there.

She swallowed again. The familiar tightness *was* gone.

She skimmed her torso for the betraying biomonitor leads, but found none.

Instead, Syteria found the contours of a body that wasn't her own.

The biomonitor's tones spiked. She froze, clutching the unfamiliar gown. What would she find if she parted the soft, pale-blue fabric? She lowered shaking hands and gulped forced breaths until the betraying tones steadied.

With agonizing slowness, she lowered one bare foot to the floor. Then the other. Her legs held as the floor warmed under her bare feet.

A cautious step forward, followed by a second. The third step brought her closer to the wall. The effort of those three steps sapped her strength. Her knees gave way.

She reached out to brace herself, finding support with both hands against a smooth surface. It shimmered, transforming into a mirror.

A whimper escaped Syteria's throat and for a moment she didn't think she could stop another, so she looked away and squeezed her eyes shut until they hurt.

That reflection was a delusion. A mirage. A hallucination.

That image, that woman, had never existed. Could never exist. The Matriarchs had made sure. It was dangerous to hope, believe, or think otherwise.

Bile rose, bubbling and burning in anticipation of having to admit she'd conjured such an image, that her heresy existed even in her dreams. Whatever *this* was, it had to be a dream, or a nightmare. The kind that tricked you into thinking you were awake and wouldn't let you rouse even as it got worse and worse.

She feared what was to come, for the worst torment surely awaited, that of Aviel and his family, his children, used against her.

A sob welled up in her chest, building to excruciating pressure.

Biomonitors spiked again. She clamped her hands over her ears, gritting her teeth, expecting Matrons to burst through the door at any second.

Seconds turned to minutes. The minutes multiplied and she lowered tired arms to the sound of her rasping, trembling breaths.

That simple task, the drawing of breath, became her shield. It eased the piercing, grievous ache and cleared her mind. Reason intruded, stoked in no small measure by a childish hope that she wasn't dreaming, that the Matriarchs were wrong and her spirit had not been eternally condemned to the torment reserved for heretics and deniers.

Syteria opened her eyes, forced them to remain so, and challenged the reflection before her.

The last time her hair had been longer than a finger's width, she'd been ten years old. The childhood curls had softened, tamed. They were gathered in a coil behind her neck. She reached up and found a clasp that gave way to her touch. Her hair unfurled like a silken flag, cascading down past her shoulder, her elbow, all the way down to her hips.

She gasped. And so did the reflection. The reflection *was* hers.

No, no, please, n—

Around her, alien words spoken by a familiar voice, were followed by, "Do you like it?" in Rhoan coming from behind her ear.

She spun around and backed into the mirror.

The familiar voice belonged to a male. He had her grandfather's wavy, iron-gray hair, but his eyes were more gray than blue. He wore a reassuring smile and stood with the same proud Kappan posture. His tunic, trousers, and boots all suggested a uniform, but one unlike any she'd seen before. Unlike Rhoan males, he didn't slouch in an attempt to reduce his height or make himself appear less threatening.

The biomonitors that kept pace with her racing heart faded into the background. The Rhoans had used her childhood memories against her before, promised to return her to her people, and to reunite her with her family. And for years, she'd believed them.

And then, by chance, she'd seen what the Rhoans did to Kappan males, the few they allowed to live. The Rhoans had become adept at reducing them to pale imitations of themselves until the men could bear it no more and ended their own lives or provoked the *eniseri* into killing them.

"Do you 'understand me?' " the male asked. The alien and Rhoan words overlapped. He touched his neck at the juncture just below his ear as he turned his head to reveal a smooth, metal disk.

Syteria cautiously explored the same space behind her own right ear. The device had to be Rhoan. This had to be just another level of Rhoan deceit.

"Don't be afraid. You're safe."

The soothing words merged, more refined now, all in Rhoan.

Adrenaline surged—Rhoan, even spoken by this male—was still Rhoan.

The entryway that framed him beckoned.

"Where am I?" It came out a broken whisper, betraying weakness and long neglect.

"Safe. You're safe. What is your name?"

She pushed herself off the mirror and stumbled past him.

He caught her easily.

Despite his size—he was bigger than any Rhoan male—he made no attempt to hold her, allowing her to push him away with ease. It surprised her, costing her a moment of hesitation. She backed away, floundered through the entryway and fell hard as her legs caught in the gown.

She strained to push herself off the floor. It took effort to stand, as if gravity itself had somehow increased.

Impossible. I'm just tired, weak.

She untangled herself, ran, and emerged into an open space, a pearl-white mausoleum filled with dozens of enormous coffins.

Her feet tangled underneath her once again.

Syteria staggered, regaining a precarious balance. She caught a glimpse of the male as he slowly followed. Another door materialized and she charged through, ignoring both his pleas and warnings.

A veil of blue light as unyielding as any wall caught her in its grasp and held her despite her struggles, cocooning her.

He came up to her slowly, forehead wrinkling.

"Please," he said. "Let me help you."

"Where am I?" Her voice cracked, turning her demand into a frail, breathy plea.

"You're safe. What is your name?"

"Syteria Kainda."

The sound of the forbidden patronymic had a bittersweet flavor, one she'd almost forgotten. It had escaped, unbidden, but elicited no reaction. She ceased her struggles. A Rhoan would've recoiled at the name, at her daring to speak it, much less claim it.

Instead, he smiled.

She held herself in place, no longer overcome by the urge to run.

"Syteria," he repeated. He gave her a curt nod and a shallow bow. "I am Galen."

The veil of light around her faded, yielding under her splayed hands, loosening its grip gradually as though it knew how close she was to falling again.

"Where am I?"

"Aboard the Ed-Lynne."

She frowned.

"What's an Ed-Lynne?"

"A ship. A spaceship." He made an uncertain frown of his own. "You're aboard a ship."

Syteria tilted her head back. The ceiling above her soared, emitting a soft glow. Galleries ringed the chamber, two and three high on some sides. Giant oblong items nestled in dedicated spaces above the galleries like clutches of eggs.

She had never seen a Rhoan ship like this, but that didn't mean it wasn't one. Memories rushed back at her: the Rhoan crew, panicking; the drugged haze that kept her sedated, fading.

The creatures...

Claws piercing her body...

"The monsters?" she asked, her ragged voice shaking as she lowered her gaze back to his.

"Dead. You killed it."

There was a hint of something she might have once called admiration.

"The Rhoans?" she asked.

"I'm sorry"—he spoke hesitantly—"but, you are the only survivor."

TWO-OH-FOUR SKIMMED the edges of the transit point, riding the outer-most spiral to bleed off accumulated heat. It could absorb no more power, and, had it been able to feel anything, it would've felt like a bloated tick.

It ran some calculations and modeled the results of the best choices: whether or not to remain in place; to top off the raw materials from sources within the system; or return to the *Edlyn*.

It was considering the last, refining the model further with its data about imperial response times, source allocations, distances, and transit routes, when the prow of a ship lanced through the transit point, "stretching" the "disk" as it punched through.

A wake tugged at the gravitic spiral Two-oh-four was cooling off in.

As the rest of the emerging ship pushed through, Two-oh-four accelerated and gave itself a realistic tumble that simulated a random piece of debris. It kept its active sensors off, feeding the telemetry and images to its remaining pods before launching the entire batch.

As soon as the pods launched, the imperial ship knew of their—and Two-oh-four's—existence.

Two-oh-four had no armaments, no defenses, but it did have a fully-charged shield and the ability to move very quickly. It intercepted the weapons launched at the pods. It saved four of the nine before its shields failed and it became just another cloud of interstellar dust.

CHAPTER TEN

*T*he mirror had become Syteria's enemy. That one anonymous panel, nestled among so many had been mocking her one moment, beckoning the next.

Alone, she sat cross-legged on the floor, far from the elevated platform that behaved like a living thing intent on smothering her in its embrace. She stared at the panel, safe from the revelations it held—revelations that were both threat and promise.

Resting her elbows on her knees, she leaned forward. Her hands looked nothing like she remembered. Smooth, pale skin denied the memory of scorched flesh melting under Rhoan brands. This softness had never been etched by acid or marred by blood. It had never endured biting cold or burning friction.

Being *eniseri* had prepared her for death, and prepared her well. She had no illusions about how painful the transition could be.

Nothing had prepared her for surviving it, much less for emerging from it whole—whole and unblemished.

Enough.

Syteria stood and stopped in front of the panel. All it would take to bring the mirror to life was a touch—a touch and an act of will. She opened the fist she'd made and thrust her arm out, placing her palm on the panel's smooth, hard surface and snatching it back as if it would brand her.

Her bare feet protruded from beneath the floor-length garment. She dug her fingers into the soft fabric that yielded in her hands like liquid, and raised it.

She pivoted one leg, then the other, for a better view. All the scars were gone, as was the tug and weakness of damaged tissue, the ache of mending bones. On some level she had known this, for she'd run. But still, the technology, the skill for such flawlessness...

Astonishing.

She walked the fabric into her grasp. Up it went, revealing her thighs. There should have been a scar. The one she'd earned while fleeing the compartment on the Rhoan ship, the one owed to the monster who'd given into the instinct all predators had to pursue the weak before expending energy on hardier prey.

She ran her hand over where the scar should have been. Her thigh was as flawless as her hands.

Syteria took a deep breath and let it out slowly, trembling, torn between accepting what she saw and what could not be.

The gathered fabric dropped as her grip on it loosened. A set of ties, delicate ribbons arranged in a diagonal from shoulder to hip, held the garment together. Anticipation and fear throbbed in her chest.

She pulled on the tie at her shoulder. It dangled, swaying gently with her breathing as her trembling hands worked each of them in turn. She released them all, vanquishing their hold on the garment and allowing it to fall open.

The pristine condition of her body did not shock her.

Its shape did. Flared hips, a tapered waist, and full, useless breasts refuted years of forced equalization.

While her body had never reached the Rhoan ideal, defying their ongoing attempts to change her, it now assumed a forbidden form— that of a Kappan woman. Years of painful Rhoan manipulation designed to force her into an androgynous mold had been reversed as if by magic.

How? Why? She grappled with a spiraling fear that she'd fallen into madness. As the chamber spun around her she placed her palms against the panel and closed her eyes until she no longer felt like she was falling.

She retied the ribbons with fingers suddenly too clumsy for their work and leaned into the mirror as she traced her right brow; even her childhood scar was gone. Feminine softness had been restored to her cheeks and lips, altering the proportions of her face. Her jawline, her brow line, no longer looked like they belonged to her brother.

She took a step back, blinking away the moisture gathering in her eyes, certain that if she started, she'd cry herself into exhaustion. The panel turned opaque. Almost at once, the urge to look again overtook her, railing against all logic and good sense.

A soft, intentional sound—polite, reserved—made her turn. Galen had returned.

"Can it be undone?" Syteria asked, the question rushing out on its own, spoken in a voice not quite her own.

"Can what be undone?"

"This." She swept her hand down the length of her body.

"This is your true biological form, is it not?" The tone was flat, professional, but the wounded look in his eyes belied the detachment he was projecting.

It was her true form, the one she would have grown into had the Rhoans not taken her. So why did it feel like she was trapped in another's body?

"Don't you like it?" he asked.

She blinked at the non-sequitur. Was he actually asking for her preference? No one had asked what she liked since she'd lost her grandfather.

Syteria ached with the desire to trust this stranger. It shuddered in her chest, sending tendrils of false hope poking at her soul, reawakening memories the Rhoans had forced her to bury.

Safety. Love. Trust. She hungered for them, a woman starved. And like any starving creature, prone to being fooled, tricked, and used, she needed to be cautious. She could not trust, much less love or allow herself to believe in any foolish notion of safety.

"I must get back," she said. "If I return looking like this—"

She stopped herself.

Until she was sure that he was not the Matriarchy's puppet there was no reason to explain that Rhoans punished all who dared exhibit any sexual dimorphism.

And if all of this was the Matriarchy's doing, if the Rhoans were behind this, there was only one reason for it: to use her against her own people.

But they would not succeed. The Kappans were not fools. Her people would reject her for being an outsider, no matter how much she looked like one of them. Lost and isolated, she belonged nowhere, would be welcomed by no one.

"Why—" Fear silenced her. She wrung her hands.

Why did you do this to me, she wanted to ask, but it might lead him to ask questions of his own. Questions she didn't want to answer.

Cautiously, uncertain of the word she wanted, she ventured, "What nation?"

"Nation?" he asked, a curious tilt to his head. Then his eyes brightened, as if an answer had come to him.

Perhaps his translation device was more than it seemed. Perhaps hers was as well. Driven by a sudden urge to yank it away and toss it across the room, she touched the device behind her ear.

"You are in the *Donai* Imperium," he said.

The Rhoan translation echoed in her ear, the penultimate word as alien as the ones that left Galen's mouth. She'd never heard of a place called "*Donai*."

Perhaps she should have used planet instead. Rho was a unified planet. All nations had merged under the Matriarchy long ago.

Meanwhile, Kappa had been reduced to a primitive state. There was no semblance of anything like a nation on Kappa. Only isolated homesteads, small villages and nomadic tribes remained.

Unless this ship...

Galen had said she was aboard a ship.

It couldn't be.

No life, no sapient life, existed outside the Rho-Kappa binary.

She wrapped her arms around her body as if she could shield herself from the discovery that she was wrong.

Galen made a small, aborted motion towards her.

She recoiled.

He looked like he didn't know what to do with his hands. They ended up clasped behind his back.

"Where is this Imperium?" she asked.

His deliberate strides as he crossed the room to another panel were achingly familiar: no jerky, wasted Rhoan motions; no gaze downcast in submission; no stoop.

He activated the surface of one of the dozen panels around them and manipulated the holographic images and symbols that appeared. The chamber darkened.

A spiral galaxy materialized around her.

Syteria gasped, stifling the voiced delight with her hands.

Images of stars and nebulae appeared, floating, filling the room, awakening memories of nights spend under a starry sky. Braced against the cold by a blanket she had rested in her grandfather's embrace. His smoldering pipe would release an intoxicating scent and turn his voice to gravel. He would name the stars and point out the shapes they made. His voice, like the smoke from that worn pipe, would wrap around her, lull her to sleep.

Awed by the magnificent display, she inhaled deeply. She spun towards the center of the chamber, keenly aware and yet unashamed of how closely she must resemble an awed child.

Markers appeared. Layer upon layer of information brought her back to the problems of the present.

Galen's smile remained indulgent. Ever patient, he gave her a wide berth when he walked around the perimeter of the projection. He stopped by a segment crowded with sigils. His hands hovered, embracing a region.

"This is the *Donai* Imperium," he said indicating the holographic region bracketed by his hands.

He pushed the holographic region out towards her.

The cloud and its swarm of pulsating stars obeyed his command.

Reoriented, the Imperium floated between them, its amorphous shape engulfing a quarter of the galaxy.

He pointed to a tiny swatch of space, rendered in green. Slowly, he expanded the region, magnifying the border between green and red.

"This is the imperial exclusion zone," he said, tracing part of the border. "We are two weeks out from where your ship crashed—here." He pointed to a star system inside the green boundary.

Two weeks—an utterly meaningless span of time. The little device behind her ear was just presenting the words its programming had picked as the best match.

Two weeks out meant nothing. Her own recovery argued for a much longer time span. She loosened a strand of hair from the bundle tied together at the nape of her neck and rolled it between her fingers. Its length alone suggested years. Many years. Perhaps a decade.

The Rhoan ship could not have traveled for a decade. Designed exclusively for hops between the planets of the Rho-Kappa binary, it couldn't have had enough air or fuel for a decade. Even an *eniseri* as lowly as she knew that.

"Can you tell me what happened?" Galen asked, his gentle voice heavy with concern.

Syteria wrapped her arms around her torso. Raw, undefined emotions—for a Kappa that may or may not still exist, for everything and everyone she'd ever known—stronger than anything she'd felt in a long time, threatened to overwhelm her. She pushed her fears aside, denied them form and substance, and buried them as deep as she could. She tucked the strand of hair back into its place.

Curiosity played across Galen's face, but he didn't insist on an answer. Instead, he restored the galactic expanse to its entirety.

"Can you tell me where Rho is?"

Her heart raced as if doing so would it to escape the question. "What do you know of Rho?"

"We recovered some of the data from your ship, deciphered part of your language." He tapped the little device by his ear as evidence. "We know you call your home world Rho, but little else. We can't determine where Rho is from the data we have."

Did he really expect her to pick a star and point at it?

For an instant she entertained a fantasy, one where she was free from the Rhoans, the Matriarchy, the *eniseri*, forever. One where she was out of their reach, free to start over—a true rebirth.

"Rho is the larger of a binary planet," she said, "separated from a single white star by three smaller planets with no satellites."

Changes propagated through the hologram until only single white stars remained.

"Four gas giants are part of the solar system,"she added.

Stars faded once more, until only a scattered few remained. Her heart raced at the prospect of finding some marker, some sense of where she'd washed ashore.

"The gas giant closest to our star has a unique system of rings; the plane of the rings is perpendicular to the plane of its orbit."

The galaxy went dark. Only the outlines of Galen's Imperium remained.

"Our data may be incomplete," he said, placating. He dissolved the hologram and returned the room to its former brightness.

"The translation may not be refined enough—"

His reasoning echoed hollow. So, a decade wasn't as unreasonable as she'd thought.

"—I'm sure we have better maps, more accurate maps."

He reached out for her, caught himself as she flinched away, and stepped back.

Syteria's entire universe collapsed to a lone truth, a singularity: *I am alone.*

"There are others," Galen was saying, "with more expertise and better data...I'm sure my master will arrange—"

Her sense of loss battled with something else, something visceral. *I am free.*

Loss surged, swelled, and burst.

But Aviel is not.

Even if he and his family had escaped, it was a temporary freedom, a matter of time. Would he have survived another decade? And if it took just as long to return? To a Kappan, two decades were a lifetime.

What little she'd been taught as *eniseri*, about the universe and its size, all said that a decade was too short a time. However the Rhoan ship had survived, however it had made this voyage…hundreds or thousands of years could have passed.

Galen caught her as her knees gave way.

"I'm sorry," he whispered when she pulled away.

His hands were firm around her shoulders, steadily raising her.

Syteria folded herself into his embrace, hands tucked into her chest as his arms wrapped around her.

She pushed him away, more violently than she'd intended, certain that his touch would make the *eniseri* she was lash out…

And kill him.

THE WOMAN KNEELING before Owyn Tolek, had been beautiful once. He knew this from her file. It had included an image of her in her youth. Her hair had been that odd color called auburn, her eyes a light brown, not quite the amber of the *donai*, but maybe a shade or two darker.

If she'd had any hair left, it would've probably been gray, or even white with age, unlike his which had been engineered to be pearl-white so his nanites could change its color. And she'd probably worn it longer than he wore his, as was custom among the humans. Ironically, human custom was also why he wore his that way, despite his place in the *donai* hierarchy not warranting the length.

Having the emperor's special dispensation meant he could bask in the envy of his *donai* brethren without providing an explanation. It didn't take them long to figure out why he was allowed the length, and then their envy would turn to fear and the false deference that came with it. The fear, he enjoyed. The false deference had become an acquired taste, one he often wondered if he'd miss should it ever cease.

He'd asked the guards to clean her up and dress her before bringing her before him. The loose two-piece set—a long-sleeved tunic hanging over baggy trousers—was made of coarse fabric, threadbare in spots, stained and mended, and probably the cleanest thing she'd been allowed to wear in the five months since she'd been sent here.

Her skin sagged, bruised and purpling, everywhere that it was exposed—her hands, her feet, the neck bent before him. House Kabrin's brand was like ink against the pale skin at the base of her skull.

The cell itself was pristine, like a surgery, bathed in antiseptic and the glare of scalding lights. Immaculate and utterly empty, the drain in the floor had been placed there more as a reminder as to what this room was used for than the need for such a primitive means of getting rid of bodily fluids.

"You are Luuedei Kennen," he said. It was a formality. Her name was part of the brand on her scalp, easily seen as he shifted his vision to the ultraviolet.

She looked up with far less caution than she should have. They did that sometimes, when they thought they were near the end, when they hoped that this was the last day of their suffering, when they believed they had nothing more to lose.

He stood before her in Kabrin colors, green on black, and because he wanted to appear as unthreatening as possible, unarmed. A look of disbelief flowed across her face as she shook her head and looked back down.

"You're not real," she said, with the hoarse ragged whisper that of someone who'd spent more time screaming than talking.

He could hardly blame her. He did not look like most *donai*. He was a bit of an anomaly, not quite a one-off, but part of a small batch that some human creator, some scientist like her, had cooked up to see if it could be done. As far as he knew, he was the last one still living.

Smaller than the *donai* standard, he could pass for human—a tall one. Or a young *donai*, someone who hadn't quite grown into the majesty of his genetic mold. But for most, it was the eyes that threw them—the odd combination of silver and gold irises below the amber one.

He drew back the amber iris—the one that most resembled a human's. Then closed the silver one and changed it to black. He lost a bit of the enhanced spectrum when he did that, but his vision was still better than a human's. Auburn flowed into the pearly strands at his shoulders as he squatted down in front of her.

" 'Sire, I beseech you to delay this test,' " Tolek said, drawing Luuedei's own words from memory and mimicking her voice. " 'With all due respect to my esteemed colleagues, my calculations show that they are wrong, that they are ignoring key criteria that should not be dismissed.' "

She looked up again, eyes clouded with tears. She raised a frail arm. Her hands were blistered, her fingers bent. Someone had broken them and they'd healed wrong. They came into contact with House Kabrin's sigil, the one on his chest.

Had she dreamt of this? Of someone sent to save her from this awful fate, from work and punishment designed to break her, body and soul.

He smiled. Without elongated cuspids, with the length of his hair covering the tips of his ears, he knew just how human he looked. When he'd first mastered this transformation, he'd smashed the mirror in disgust. He'd thought himself cursed and condemned. The old emperor, Thán Kabrin's father, had been the first *donai* who appreciated his uniqueness enough to reward him. He had gone from barely tolerated outcast to a valued member of the emperor's inner circle.

"You were right, Luuedei," he whispered using his own voice. "Out of all of them, *you* were right."

She sat back on her heels, hands rising to cover her face. She sobbed into them, the salt of her tears drifting in the air for an instant before the lingering antiseptic overpowered it. Tolek waited patiently for her to finish.

"Are they all dead?" she asked.

"Yes, Luuedei. They are."

She placed a splayed hand by the drain and pushed up. Her bones creaked with the motion. He rose with her and inclined his head a fraction. It was just enough to be considered a sign of respect.

She blinked her eyes clear and struggled to hold herself straight. There was a hint there now, of what she had once been—a scientist bold enough to stand against consensus and protest directly to the emperor himself.

"And now you want my help," she said, strength displacing the hopelessness in her voice.

"The emperor sent me himself. For you. He will see that your health is restored. Put you in charge of rebuilding his wormhole generator. Give you anything you desire. "

"Anything I desire?"

"Anything you desire." Anything within the emperor's power, Thán Kabrin had said.

"I want every guard who raped me, crucified," she said.

"Done."

CHAPTER ELEVEN

A grierugon carcass was laid out in the center of Galen's isolation lab. The hemispherical compartment had layers of diamond-hard transparent walls, augmented force fields, and an armored shell of the same material as the *Edlyn's* outer hull.

Darien stood over the *grierugon* carcass, suffering through Galen's didactic ramblings and a stench strong enough to defeat both the low temperature and the specimen's stasis field.

Nyree Tero, the *Edlyn's* intelligence officer and the only female *donai* in his command, stood across from him, breathing through her mouth, her efforts creating small puffs in the chilled air. Her augmentations matched not just her male counterparts' musculature, bone density, and enhancements, but a sense of smell that put Darien's to shame.

He gave her a sympathetic look and whispered, "Almost there, Major."

I hope.

She nodded, eyes watering, but she remained silent and attentive. Subtly, she raised her left hand to cradle her nose between thumb and forefinger.

"Forget the technical details of the alien ship," Galen said. "*This* is the remarkable piece of engineering." He reached through the sterile field to peel back layers of tissue with the flourish of a master chef.

Tero's mien soured, and she swallowed, long and hard, the thick corded muscles in her neck rising prominently through an almost non-existent layer of fat. A green tinge swept her paling skin. Carnage was familiar, to all of them, but there was something obscene about the surgical precision of the dissection, the sterility of it all.

"I'm glad you're pleased, Galen," Darien said as he wrinkled his nose and scratched his upper lip. "Was it worth the risk?"

Galen looked up and around, as if suddenly aware of their discomfort. He activated a force field that obscured the specimen from sight.

Darien made a strong exhale, clearing the lingering scent.

Tero held her breath for a few heartbeats.

"Thank you," she whispered.

Galen gave her a sheepish grin and brought up a holographic image of the specimen.

"I found no pathogens, no malicious nanites, nothing to warrant a 'quarantine' of Thertore. However, everything about these creatures is deliberate. I may even know the designer. Surprised he's still alive, actually.

Galen tugged at his collar. "Are you sure their surveillance was down?"

"Yes," Darien said. "Even active surveillance would only show us taking one life pod into the wreck and bringing one out. One survivor, one life pod."

"What did you do with its tracer tag?" Tero asked with a voice that had regained its contralto strength.

"Threw it into a pool of caustic liquid leaking from the alien ship. If the imperials recover it, they should conclude that the creature was overcome and consumed."

"Well done, Darien," Galen said.

The corner of Darien's mouth lifted at the implied pat on the head.

"So, what did you find?" Darien asked.

"I've confirmed that your imperial cousin's arrogance is without bounds."

"You'll have to be more specific. We are speaking of Thán Kabrin."

"The initial reports about their claws were right," Galen said. "The material is almost a biological analogue to our outer hulls."

"Almost?" Tero asked.

"An intermittent step. A prototype, as it were. Once perfected, it would tear right through *donai* armor. If these things get off Thertore…" Galen flicked Tero a questioning gaze that obviously invited her to finish his statement.

She remained silent. A microscopic bead of sweat—one too small for Galen to see—at the edge of the shorn cap of black hair, betrayed her. The reaction told Darien that she was not certain, but didn't want to admit to it. Not with a human—even Galen—in the room, anyway.

"The Imperial Court was assured of all necessary precautions," Darien said. "The *grierugon* would remain on Thertore. They'll never be used against the *donai*."

"They're animals, aren't they?" Tero asked. "Low on the sapience scale."

"As though that would make any difference," Galen said, echoing Darien's own thoughts.

"This one's brain suggests low sapience," Galen was saying, "but the emperor tolerates nothing that doesn't bring him an advantage."

Galen's gaze drew distant. He winced and reached for his neck, then aborted the gesture. Darien knew how dearly Galen had paid for his insight into the emperor's thinking. He was not about to ignore his expert assessment.

"How does he intend to use them?" Galen asked. "This specimen has no regenerative ability and without some method of control, why even create them?"

"Perhaps the emperor's intent is to overwhelm," Tero said. A frown distorted her calm, pondering features.

"How long does it take to breed these things?" she asked.

Galen shrugged. "They're hermaphrodites, so each one is a potential bearer of young. That can be an advantage or a liability."

"It takes a quarter of a century to bring each of us to full maturity, to fighting strength," Tero said.

"A quarter century and a lot of resources, and given your dwindling numbers..." Galen said. "A few more generations of inbreeding, and humans and *donai* won't be the same species anymore. Even with your regenerative abilities, your lifespan, the *donai* are in a demographic death spiral."

"Not our doing," Darien reminded him. "We didn't bring ourselves into existence."

Galen flushed, deep and dark, right up to the tips of his ears. "Yes, quite. Sorry."

"You were saying something about arrogance," Darien prompted.

"The designers implanted a failsafe into this *grierugon*," Galen said as he magnified a minuscule region between the holographic creature's eyes. It glowed a false, pale, blue.

Darien reached out, expanded the hologram to its limit until they could see the details of the biological circuitry of the implant.

Tero's smile was predatory. Her eyes shone. "We must get this to Serigala."

"I agree," Darien said. Failsafes implied a fear of losing control. "How soon can you be ready, Major?"

"At once, my lord."

"I haven't completed my examination," Galen said, his crestfallen look resembling that of a child denied the excitement of a new toy.

"Doctor, you're welcome to join me," Tero said. "You, me, the *grierugon*—my transport can accommodate the three of us. It'll be very...cozy."

Galen flushed red again. His face contorted like he was about to sputter nonsensically.

"The failsafe. How does it work?" Darien asked.

"I still need to figure that out." Galen cleared his throat. "Your cryptologists are useless when it comes to organic components. I need a specialist."

"Figure it out. Soon," Darien said as he turned to leave.

Tero followed.

Darien stopped at the isolation lab's threshold, turned back, and with a smile, added, "And Galen, well done!"

Galen snorted as he waved them off and returned to work.

"Soon," he mumbled. "Of course he wants it soon. Boy has no patience."

His voice trailed behind the *donai*, fading as he added, "Never had. Never will."

∾

DREA QUIRKED AN EYEBROW AT PALLETON. He'd propped his feet up on her desk, crossed his arms, closed his eyes, and thrown his head back. Underneath him, the chair groaned, taxed by his size.

Even with the chamber presence taking into account that *donai* were bound to use the same furniture as the humans, he simply exceeded parameters. He was big, even for an elder *donai*, one of the few remaining originals created by the Ryhmans. She made a note directing the *Edlyn* to expand the parameters and propagate them throughout the ship, and wondered why she hadn't thought of it earlier.

Because he rarely parked himself in her day cabin, that's why. For someone who resembled a wall, he rarely idled.

She waited for the next puff of air, that nuanced huff Palleton used in place of actual speech—along with grunts for emphasis. It came, right on time.

Drea smiled.

"What are you smiling at?" he grumbled.

Gooseflesh rose along her arms. Even after all these decades the *donai* ability to track her reactions was unnerving. What had that smile changed? Her breathing, her scent, her heart rate?

Envy stabbed at her again. The practical, soldierly way he rested and conserved energy instead of wasting it came to him too easily.

They didn't sleep. They could go without rest for days. As far as she'd been able to determine, their only weakness was their need for fuel. Watching a growing *donai* eat was like watching a black hole suck everything down into its depths. Getting in their way when they were healing, when their reserves were low from the process, was only slightly less dangerous than challenging one of them to a fight.

"Just seeing if you're awake," she said, teasing.

Drea manipulated the data stream flowing across the surface of her desk and ran it through a variety of algorithms. The manual process was slow, much slower than what the *Edlyn* could perform, but sometimes, it was more about the art than the science. And sometimes it was about the human need to do something, whether it made sense to or not.

The bug hunt, as Palleton and his men called it, had yielded a single spectacular explosion that took out their primary communications array and little else.

Despite checking beforehand, the malicious nanites had made their way into the secondary array. Whenever they primed it, unauthorized transmissions plagued them.

Every time they'd thought their location compromised, Darien had ordered a course change. It had resulted in passing through far more transit points than they'd planned, and it was taking them farther and farther away from their destination, delaying their return to Serigala.

Her gut told her they were being followed, despite the course changes, despite the *Edlyn's* countermeasures, despite everything that everyone in Comms was telling her.

"Aha!" she said, pushing the image that had resulted from her models and calculations into a hologram between them.

Palleton opened one eye. "You call that evidence?"

The blurry smudge at the extreme of their sensor range was barely worthy of being called an image. He was being generous. He closed the eye, resuming his pretense at sleep.

"I call that a sensor ghost," she said and ran additional calculations, playing off several other models.

Opening his eyes, Palleton unfurled and dropped his feet to the deck, making the chair creak again. He leaned forward, studying the blurs. They never looked at the holograms or displays with their enhanced vision. There was simply nothing extra for them to see. The holograms had been designed for human eyes, a pre-Imperium historical artifact that had never been remedied.

Drea painted some overlays atop the blurs as she fit acceleration curves to launch points and ran simulations.

His frown deepened.

"The bugs are aiming the transmissions as if they know something is following us and along what vector," he said.

Drea nodded.

"They're receiving," she said, "not just transmitting. Receiving something we're not able to detect."

"We either have a more serious bug problem than we thought..."

"Or we have someone aboard, relaying instructions," she finished for him.

CHAPTER TWELVE

*A*s his back hit the reinforced wood floor of the sparring gym, the landing knocked the air from Darien's lungs. It was followed by the distinct sound of unyielding skull against unyielding surface.

Palleton's left knee bore down on the hollow of Darien's throat, denying him breath. The dark, sweat-covered face sported a triumphant, savage grin. Darien's right arm was underneath him, trapped at a painful angle. Palleton's right foot crushed his left hand so he couldn't even tap out.

Not only was the elder *donai* faster and stronger, but he had no reservations about beating his liege lord to a bloody pulp to reinforce a lesson when needed. Today's lesson was about the perils of letting one's guard down while one's mind wandered.

"Had enough?" Palleton asked, breathing without strain.

Light footsteps approached.

Bomani's grinning face came into view to linger above Darien's head. She bent at the waist, hands folded smartly behind her back as if she were conducting an inspection of the cadet corps. Her long golden braid slid over her shoulder and dangled tauntingly above him.

"There's still a lot of defiance in those eyes, Palleton," she said. "No contrition at all."

Darien found purchase with his feet.

"Don't." Palleton's voice was a low, warning rumble. "Keep those legs grounded or I'll break them as well. That would mean a trip to the infirmary, my lord. It would be such a shame if you required Galen's services today."

Well struck.

Darien scowled in the forced silence. He held Palleton's gaze, maintaining what little dignity he still had.

"I believe the match goes to Palleton," Bomani said, self-satisfaction gleaming in her eyes.

Apparently, it was no small pleasure to watch Palleton best him and probably an even greater pleasure to see Palleton's comment get under his skin. She withheld the release signal a second longer and smiled.

Red and black whorls swam in Darien's vision. Oxygen rushed back into his lungs, quenching, then stoking the fiery pain. With a groan, he rolled onto his side, drew his legs up and coughed. Blood bubbled into his mouth.

Bomani knelt by his shoulder, taunting him with a hand towel. It swayed like a sadistic pendulum off the end of her finger.

"Your shoulder is dislocated," Palleton said. "You know the drill."

Darien nodded, grimacing, still unable to speak. Muscles tightening in anticipation, he rolled onto his back again.

Palleton placed a foot in Darien's armpit and grasped his wrist with both hands.

"Ready?"

Before Darien could nod, Palleton pulled. The steady tension stretched Darien's screaming shoulder muscles. His throat worked, the unhealed damage preventing any sound. The shoulder refused to reseat itself which meant that Palleton was tempering his strength, catering to the limitations of Darien's mixed heritage. The pain was bad enough, but his drawn-out weakness on display was unbearable.

"What do you intend to do about the imperial ship pursuing us?" Bomani asked.

Darien exhaled, grateful for Bomani's distraction.

"How long"—a spasm in his chest made him cough—"before we have to"—a jolt of pain slurred the words—"accommodate imperial guests?"

"Based on their last position and vector," she said, "a matter of days. Maybe as few as two. How fast do you intend to run?"

Darien gave her a sharp look. They both knew that it was only a matter of time before the smaller imperial ships overtook the *Edlyn*.

"That's what I thought," Bomani said.

She stepped over him and looked at Palleton. "Let me try. At least we know *I* won't be able to pull his arm off and beat him with it."

Palleton laughed and increased the tension by a fraction. The shoulder set with an audible pop. Awash in pain, Darien groaned and rolled to his side again.

"Let the nanites do their work," Palleton said. "Don't move it until they're done, or I *will* tear it off and beat you with it."

Darien nodded reluctant thanks as Palleton walked off to reorder the disarrayed gym.

"What are you trying to do?" Bomani asked. "We cannot evade the Imperium forever. We need to change course, head back home, or at least deeper into our own territory. Then we'd have reinforcements."

"I'm"—his chest and throat constricted, then spasmed—"buying time."

She dabbed at his forehead and cleared sweat-soaked hair from his eyes.

"I don't understand," she said.

Darien flexed his left hand, verifying that it had healed, and propped himself up on his elbow. Another jolt of pain reminded him that Palleton and the sparring phantoms had done more than break his bones. One of the phantoms—humanoid analogues designed to simulate either humans or *donai*—had sacrificed itself to score a hit to his abdomen.

"I'm buying time for Galen…" he said, the words sliding from his healing voice box more smoothly now. "For Galen's patient."

Palleton woke one of the defunct phantoms and ordered it to its alcove. Battle damage made the featureless phantom appear even less human. Its cohorts lay strewn about, dismembered, broken reminders of their unarmed combat simulation.

"Galen should never have allowed her to wake," Bomani said.

"Say what you mean, Commander." He coughed, clearing out residue. "It would've been better if I'd left her to die."

Bomani's callousness was a practical reminder that his refusal to turn the survivor over to the emperor was endangering the *Edlyn* and everyone aboard. There was nothing personal in it, at least not as far as he could tell. Protecting the ship was her responsibility. And his.

Sighing, he tested the flexibility in his right shoulder and was rewarded with a dull ache. He snatched Bomani's towel and wiped his face clean, taking his time, waiting for the cutting, scratching pain in his throat to fade.

"Any progress on"—another cough and spasm—"finding out whom we need to thank for informing the emperor of her survival?"

Bomani's spine went rigid. "No, my lord. Nothing."

He knew she blamed herself for the hole in their security, the unexplained transmissions. The emperor's missive demanding possession of the survivor had been too specific, too detailed to be mere conjecture.

"We have a spy onboard," he said. "The ships pursuing us are confirmation, nothing more. We must, therefore, act accordingly."

"Not just a spy, a traitor," Bomani said, bitterness threading her voice.

"Can you pinpoint the source if he transmits again?"

"Now that we know what to look for, yes."

The radiating pain from his abdomen was fading, allowing Darien to sit up. He rested his arms on his knees. The blooms of microscopic heat coursing along his forearms warned that the nanites were still at work.

"Recommendations?" he asked.

"We need to reveal valuable information. Something this spy won't think is a ruse."

"Such as?"

"Make him, or her," she said, "think we had something to do with whatever happened to Valteri's ship."

"That would not further the peace my father desires."

"Neither does protecting this survivor. Yet you persist. Why?"

He made to rise.

The motion drew Palleton's punishing glare, a look perfected over many decades at the expense of countless students, including Darien's own father.

He settled back down. He could sit for a few moments longer.

"What would you have me do, Commander?"

"Give them the survivor," she said as if it was the most obvious thing in the world.

"Then we'd be giving up the only proof that Thertore is more than just a breeding ground for animals of dubious tactical value," he said.

Bomani's gaze narrowed. "How is she proof?"

"We've never encountered anything like her ship before. It was unarmed yet it destroyed Valteri's ship. And it was far too primitive to account for anything that happened on, or to, Thertore. We determined that easily enough from our cursory inspection of the ship."

"So how do you explain what happened?"

He quelled a shrug just in time to avoid a jolt of pain and rubbed at his reseated shoulder instead.

"My *beloved* imperial cousin has a penchant not only for playing god, but for believing himself infallible. Protecting a new weapon with a 'quarantine' of 'dangerous lifeforms' sounds just like the kind of subterfuge in which he'd indulge. Whatever caused the devastation on Thertore was created at Kabrin's order. I'm certain."

"Why would the emperor destroy one of his own planets?" she asked.

"He wouldn't," Darien said. "Perhaps something went wrong."

Bomani's mouth opened as if to speak, then snapped shut. He'd caught her off-guard.

She pursed her lips, her gaze wandering to the other side of the gym where Palleton had finished matching phantom limbs and heads to phantom bodies. He was setting them all into their alcoves to mend. He returned to stand in front of Darien and looked him up and down.

Darien would never get used to the strange sensation of having another *donai* peer into his body. He could hide nothing; not his pain, not his weakness. His failures were a work laid bare to Palleton's scrutiny.

"Well?" Darien demanded.

"You'll do," Palleton said, offering him a hand up.

Grimacing only a little, Darien grabbed Palleton's forearm and stood.

Palleton turned to Bomani. "He's all yours, Commander."

"Thank you, Colonel."

She crossed her arms and looked at Darien, nodding with a tight expression.

"What do I do if he falls over?" she called to Palleton's retreating back. "He's too heavy and too stubborn to move."

Darien crossed the gym and waved his healing hand in front of a panel. It withdrew to reveal a pitcher and a glass filled with nanite-infused water. He raised the glowing liquid to his mouth and swallowed. The fire in his lungs died. The pain in his body waned. He poured himself a second glass and drained it in two gulps.

"How did the Rhoan ship get here?" Bomani asked.

"Kabrin brought it here."

"Why? It's useless if it's as primitive, as defenseless as you say—"

"I don't think that bringing it here was his real intent."

Her brows drew together, an unspoken question.

"I think," Darien continued, "that these Rhoans just happened to be in the wrong place at the wrong time."

"A lot of unknowns, Darien. You need to confirm this before you take too many actions based on *assumptions*. Have you asked her? The survivor."

"No," he said, the denial sharper than he'd intended.

She raised a pale, golden eyebrow. "Do you intend to?"

"Yes." *Eventually.*

"Why so reluctant? It's unlike you."

"I have my reasons."

He couldn't explain something he didn't understand himself.
Silence lingered, filling the space between them.

"Reasons you don't intend to share with me?"

Darien shook his head.

"Very well," she said, "but I need to know if those reasons, whatever they are, have anything to do with Galen's request for all our
highly classified navigational data."

"I believe so."

"Are you going to send her back to where she came from?" she
asked, frustration in her voice.

"It would be an elegant solution, would it not?"

"Elegant, yes; possible, no," she said, offering him a tit-for-tat
smile.

"And why is that?"

"Because the planetary system she described as her point of origin
doesn't exist, at least not in any regions familiar to us. Short of creating
your own wormhole to a part of the galaxy we know nothing about,
you'll find no elegant solutions."

His hand tightened around the glass he was holding and for a
moment he thought he would shatter it as well. Shame crawled over his
skin, wrapped itself tight around him, and settled like a cloak he
couldn't cast aside.

"Galen thinks a claim is the only way I can prevent the emperor
from taking her."

Bomani drew a deep breath. She let it out very slowly.

He dared not look at her. Whatever outward demeanor she was
projecting for his sake would be shattered by his enhanced vision. He
didn't trust himself not to use it.

"A claim?"

As if she'd misheard. As if granting him the opportunity to retract
it. As if doing so would matter.

"Yes," he said. "Falsely invoking the only mechanism that allows
me to take the emperor's property without his consent *is* treason. For

me and anyone who aids me. But, it saves her life, allows her to remain under House Dobromil's protection, under *our* laws."

Her quiet contemplation drew his gaze. She wasn't wearing the appalled look he'd expected.

"Only if they found out," she said, her voice echoing with the knowledge that unlike *donai*, human traitors rarely enjoyed a quick death, but her expression held no sarcasm, no mockery.

"When did you stop hating us, Drea?"

She cocked her head, reflecting his scrutiny.

"When I realized that," she said, pausing as if she were choosing her words ever so carefully, "humans had more freedoms under House Dobromil than anywhere else in the Imperium, even in the rebellious Outer Regions."

She glanced at the floor, hesitant. "When your father gave me my freedom."

Darien had known Bomani for as long as he could remember. Her answer still surprised him. His vision shifted, allowing him to read her, an unashamed voyeur to her honesty.

"Yet you stayed," he said gently. "Why?"

"Because I haven't stopped hating the *donai*. I just learned to channel my hate to those who deserve it."

"Like those who would take a woman against her will."

Concern played across her face. "You have never taken advantage of your position, never mistreated a human."

"I have." He flexed his hand. "I can still feel Galen struggling in my grasp, still taste the power I had over his life. It was... intoxicating."

She touched his cheek, her gaze seeking and capturing his as he towered over her.

"But you find it revolting, even as you yearn for it. Like your father, you are *donai*, but you are not *lūsus nātūrae*...not the jest or whim of nature that you could be, not the monster you imagine yourself to be. I've seen you refuse that easy path even when it serves you."

"Drea, I can't separate my reputation, my public face from my personal honor."

"You can."

She sighed.

"You must," she added. "It's an imperfect solution, an effort to make virtue out of necessity. There is a certain type of honor in that, is there not?"

CHAPTER THIRTEEN

*S*yteria's vision blurred. Rubbing didn't ease the burn, only seemed to make it worse. She pinched the bridge of her nose and sighed, shutting everything out: the smooth, pearlescent walls with their annoying tendency to react and interact; the consoles that Galen and his staff used to make her feel like a specimen in a petrie-dish; the caging bio-bed; the dozen other things in the infirmary she didn't know the names of.

Galen was right—this was an impossible task.

The *Edlyn's* astrophysical catalog had information on tens of thousands of star systems. One of them had to be Rho-Kappa. If she could only find it, then perhaps, somehow, she could go back. Surely Galen's people, with all their miraculous knowledge and technology could find a way. They would have to. They had no reason to hold her. And if they did, then what?

Escape. Run. Make it on her own.

The *eniseri* were never trained as pilots, or navigators, never given access to the top levels of Rhoan technology, but she could learn. However, she had to know where she was going.

Kneading her aching neck muscles with one hand, she resumed her search. She manipulated the interface floating around her as she stood in the middle of the compartment, surrounded by holographic projections.

Even on Kappa, she'd seen photographs of nearby star systems. Her ancestors had taken those images using powerful telescopes built before the Rhoans had bombed Kappa back into primitivism.

Tap, tap, tap—three more images down; thousands to go.

The compartment lights brightened.

Anasera swept in, arms loaded with a pair of red boxes. She stepped right through the washed-out holograms and set the boxes atop one of the flat, raised surfaces protruding from the bio-bed. She let out a very loud and satisfied sigh.

"Holograms off," Anasera said.

The holograms and the interface controlling them both faded.

Anasera was bristling with energy. She was practically rocking on her heels as she stood expectantly with a hand resting gently atop the boxes. The gesture clearly said, *You can't ignore this.*

They'd had battles of will before. There was no doubt, they were about to battle again.

"What's this?" Syteria asked.

"I'd like to prove to you that we are *not* an elaborate Rhoan trick."

There was a part of Syteria that had accepted this. And another that had not.

They warred within her, surfacing in moments like this, moments filled with trepidation, with fear, that she could take no more of this strange new world. It was so much more complicated than she could've ever imagined.

"Something in those boxes will convince me?" Syteria asked.

"No," Anasera said, crossing the distance between them, "but I didn't think you'd want to walk around the ship in what we call"—the translator beeped out an error tone—"wear."

Anasera leaned in conspiratorially, one palm bracketing the side of her mouth. "I'm told it's not a popular look."

She eyed Syteria's garment.

"My father has written orders. You," she said, poking Syteria's shoulder, "are to get out of the infirmary and get some fresh air."

121

But we're on a ship…

The tightness plaguing Syteria's shoulders and neck rose to her face. At her side, her hands formed into fists and the roar of blood pounded in her ears.

"If your medical technology didn't convince me, then what makes Galen think the rest of your technology will?"

Lips pursing, Anasera crossed her arms. "Still holding on to the delusion that we are Rhoan agents?"

When Syteria didn't answer, Anasera's eyes went wide and soft. She reached out to touch her again but stopped just short of doing so. Syteria pretended that she hadn't flinched again.

"I thought you'd accepted that we weren't your enemy."

"I've reconsidered," Syteria said.

"No you haven't. I see it in your eyes. You just don't want to do as you're told."

Syteria wasn't going to deny it. Doing so would only lead to another lengthy discussion about why, a conversation that did not need yet another take.

Anasera sighed. "Well, the man in charge has decreed, *you* are to tour the ship and then I'm to take you to your new quarters."

Syteria raised her chin, a petty defiance meant to distract from how hard she was clenching her hands.

"Quarters?"

"You can't hide in the infirmary forever."

"I'm not hiding." *Am I?*

"Please," Anasera said, running her hands over the boxes. "It's only clothing."

Syteria remained firmly rooted in place, straining to breathe past the heaviness that had settled on her chest.

After seeing what the other females here wore, she'd come to appreciate her infirmary gown for its true and sole virtue—its tent-like design hid everything. It had become her armor.

Now Anasera wanted to take it away. Throbbing pain reminded her that she'd clenched her jaw too hard again.

She eyed the boxes as Anasera opened them. Her pulse quickened despite the depth of her breathing.

The large box contained clothing; the small one, a pair of soft-soled boots. Neither looked particularly threatening as Anasera laid them out on the bio-bed.

Syteria approached with caution and skimmed the delicate fabric with trembling fingers.

"Why green?" she asked. She'd never seen a fabric of such vibrant color.

"Your eyes. They're unique, did you know that? Are jade-colored eyes common on Rho?"

Syteria shook her head. "I've never met a Rhoan with eyes like mine. My brother was—is—the only other person I knew—know—with eyes of jade."

Anasera reached into the larger box and pulled out two delicate pieces of flesh-toned fabric. The material was too sheer to provide any coverage and although the cut was somewhat familiar, Syteria couldn't think why anyone would waste such finery for what was meant to be a utilitarian piece of cloth.

She cast a questioning glance in Anasera's direction.

Anasera smiled. "Allow me."

Syteria surrendered to her new role as mannequin. At least, that's what it felt like. She had to rely on Anasera to move her stiff limbs around and through the openings.

When Anasera stood back, grinning, it was as if dressing Syteria had been the singular achievement of her day.

"Perfect," Anasera declared.

The high praise was directed at the long, sinuous, green "skirt" that flowed with a grace all its own. Something Anasera had named a "bodice" hugged her torso with perfectly matching color.

By what standard was the clothing being judged? For Syteria, its most redeeming quality was that it completely hid the sheer scraps of cloth underneath.

Syteria rubbed the silken green fabric between uncertain fingers. "Do you have something less...feminizing?"

Anasera's questioning gaze swept over her.

Syteria held her breath, regretting giving her an opening for the questions that were obviously forming behind those inquisitive, dark eyes.

"Hmm," Anasera mused. "Perhaps another time. Sit."

She opened several drawers and returned with a variety of implements.

Syteria backed up, her gaze fixed on the strange objects. She bumped up against the bio-bed and sat, as much out of obedience as out of necessity. Her legs were shaking too much for her to trust them to bear her weight. She anchored her hands around the rim of the bio-bed as Anasera moved behind her.

When Anasera touched and stroked her hair, Syteria did not flinch. It helped that Anasera moved very slowly, describing her intentions with light-hearted, incessant babble, naming each implement and demonstrating its function as she worked Syteria's hair into something translated as a "loose plait."

It was an act of will, but Syteria closed her eyes, focusing on the rhythm of the tugging motions. They lulled her into the depths of memory.

Pipe smoke. Sunshine. A light breeze.

Her brother running around, turning cartwheels, teasing her about her hair. Asking their grandfather to make sure the braids were tight so they wouldn't come undone when he and his friends tugged them.

Grandfather scolding him, promising retribution for such rude behavior.

A whispered apology in her ear: *Your mother was much better at this. I'm sorry, sweet girl. This is the best I can do.*

She'd turned to smile up at him, reassure him that it was fine, but the sun's glare stole his face. All she could recall was his voice, his hands. Thick, gnarled fingers. Bruised fingernails torn painfully short. Others missing altogether.

Rough, tanned skin. Scars.

"You do look lovely," Anasera said.

Syteria opened her eyes and immediately closed them, turning away from the mirror Anasera was holding in her hand.

They'd done this before too. Anasera insisting that she look at herself; Syteria adamantly refusing.

"Are you sure?" Anasera asked.

Moisture had seeped between Syteria's lashes. "I'm sure."

She didn't open her eyes until Anasera was done with the boots, barely aware of what was involved in putting them on. She'd figure out how to take them off later, once she got through whatever ordeal Anasera had planned.

Retracing the panicked route she'd taken when her first and only instinct had been to run, she followed Anasera into the infirmary's main arena.

That first night, she'd have paid almost any price to step over that threshold. Today she'd have paid almost any price not to. She'd fallen into the trappings of safe familiarity. Unable to release the painful pressure that had built up in her chest, she hesitated.

Eyes closed, she took that necessary first step, over the threshold, onto a balcony...out into sunlight.

HUNDREDS OF BALCONIES sprouted from dozens of tiers that enclosed the area below like a giant amphitheater. At the far end, across a great expanse, a mountain soared into clouds. Waterfalls fed a lake. Streams and brooks snaked through woodland tracts.

"Impossible," Syteria whispered, raising her hand to shade her eyes.

"Not impossible at all," Anasera said proudly. "The sun and clouds are holograms. The mountain is a façade, but everything else is real."

A breeze caressed Syteria's cheek, reaching up to loosen tendrils of hair with ethereal fingers. The fresh, crisp air held a promise of rain. Gusts shepherded a tide of pink and red blossoms toward them. She plucked one from the air before the petals fell into a swirl to settle around her feet. Its scent was light and sweet; its texture, silken. This was no hologram.

As she glanced over her shoulder, an I-told-you-so grin split

Anasera's face. She towed Syteria down a sweeping staircase to the parkland below.

Syteria's boots sank into soft grass. Fresh, earthy tones mingled with the perfumed breeze. A button-sized insect armored in red and black scurried out of her way before taking flight. She squatted and dug her fingers deep into the soil. It gave way, yielding under her touch to stain her skin with a dark, rich green. She raised a handful to her nose, inhaling deeply. Familiar and alien at the same time, it was mustier than Kappan soil.

"How big is this ship?" she asked as she let the soil and grass fall back to the ground.

"You wouldn't believe me if I told you."

Anasera was right of course. Even with her own eyes telling her how big this parkland alone was, Syteria was having trouble imagining the sheer size of the system that must be in place to make it possible.

"Want to see more?" Anasera asked.

Syteria nodded. The stubborn reluctance that had almost prevented her from experiencing such wonder was gone.

Anasera led her to a bridge spanning a sparkling stream. Syteria veered off to dip her hand in. It's cold water caressed her fingers. Tiny arrows of color darted by, leaving bubbles in their wake.

"Fish?" she asked.

Anasera's grin widened as she nodded.

Syteria stood and reluctantly wiped her dripping hands on her dress. She climbed the slope of the cobblestoned bridge. Anasera followed her down the other side and onto the winding path.

From behind flowering trees, two women appeared, immersed in conversation, their words only partially translated by the device behind Syteria's ear. One of the women wore a sharp, black uniform; the other, smart, tailored civilian clothing. They offered murmurs of acknowledgment and nods. Anasera responded in kind as Syteria studied the passing faces.

Moments later, a similar trio came down a path—two men and a woman. Then a larger group jogged by in precision formation, their clothes clinging to them like second skins.

They were all, right down to the last person, perfect in appearance. Not a single scar, nor missing limbs, nor teeth. Their eyes held no fear and their faces were bright with smiles. There was no evidence of deception or strain, of subterfuge or posturing. No one trailed behind another, head bent, back bowed, eyes downcast. No one scurried or flinched. As they passed, they didn't glance backward with suspicion or fear.

There are no slaves here. The thought froze Syteria in her tracks. Her left hand rose, fingers splayed to rest on her collarbones. The *eniseri* collar wasn't there, despite its phantom weight. It wasn't there and it would never be.

Concern played over Anasera's kind face. It was replaced by the questioning one that always made Syteria feel like she was a specimen.

"I take it there are no Rhoan ships like this," Anasera said as a slow smile came to her lips.

Syteria shook her head and asked, "How long have your people been traveling like this?"

"Ten or so human lifetimes," Anasera said.

Syteria swallowed. "And how long is a human lifetime here?"

"A century, give or take."

A century. Like Galen's "two weeks" it was a meaningless number. She needed better, more precise answers, and therefore, better questions.

"How many years until you can bear children?" Syteria asked.

"Our bodies can bear children as early as thirteen, but most of us do not have them until much later."

Syteria lowered her gaze to the path under her feet. The cobblestones had given way to flat, paving stones threaded by moss. The green wove through tans sprinkled with gold and copper flecks.

Thirteen was far closer to the Kappan equivalent of fifteen than Syteria had hoped. It meant their time-keeping was similar to her own. But no Kappan lived to a century.

These people had been traveling between the stars for a millennium. Kappan oral history didn't even go back that far. A chill swept over Syteria's skin.

"Are you alright?" Anasera asked.

"Yes," Syteria lied.

"I'm here to help you, you know."

"I know."

They continued along the path, each step adding to Syteria's sense of clarity. As marvelous as Galen's infirmary was, its shelter had limited the extent of her understanding. Rho's technology paled in comparison to the wonders around her.

Her Rhoan understanding of the universe began to crack, hammered first by the idea of a ship of such size moving through space and second by the thought that a culture more Kappan than Rhoan thrived in unapologetic abundance.

"What will happen to me now?" Syteria asked.

"I don't think that's been decided."

"Will I be allowed to return to Kappa?"

Anasera took her hand gently, rubbing at the dirt and grass stains that still lingered.

"We're still trying to find out how you got here," Anasera said. "We're still trying to figure out where Kappa might be."

Syteria squared her shoulders, pulling her hand free. She hadn't flinched at Anasera's touch. It was both strange comfort and a source of distress.

"I must get back," Syteria said.

A part of her feared recapture. Another recoiled at the idea of giving up the protection of people as powerful as these *donai*. But there was more at stake here than her fears, her unfulfilled needs.

There was duty.

The Rhoans had made her forget her Kappan self with all its outdated notions of duty to..."family." The bittersweet word should've brought a sharp, piercing pain to her temples. She thought it again, not the Rhoan equivalent, for there was none, but the Kappan word itself. Again, no pain. Her fingers danced over her throat.

How long had it been since she'd thought in Kappan? All of her adult life, at least. Speaking in Rhoan instead of Kappan was one of the first things the *eniseri* learned to do. The collar would take away their voices and the longer one wore it, the better it became at punishing thoughts in Kappan.

Syteria probed the area at the back of her neck, just below the base of her skull. The implant that worked in concert with the collar must be gone too for there was no pain.

"We don't know where to send you Syteria," Anasera's voice intruded. "We don't know how you got here. Do you understand?"

"Yes."

Syteria pressed her lips in a tight line. She didn't trust her voice lest she confess her desire to return to Kappa. She wanted to rescue her brother and free her people.

Whoever Galen's people were, whatever they could do, they were not gods. They might live a century. Their cities might travel in ships. They may sail between the stars, but if they didn't know where she was from or how to get her back, it didn't matter.

"Are you tired? Do you want to go back?" Anasera asked.

Syteria shook her head. "I'd like to watch the sunset. I know it's not real, but…"

Anasera led her up to an overlook. They waited on the holographic sunset while insects chirped and birds twittered. Syteria closed her eyes so she could focus on the caress of fading light on her face.

So real.

She didn't ever want to leave. Guilt settled in her heart. Guilt for failing to evade the *eniseri* that had captured her as a child. Guilt for failing her brother and his family.

"Is there a moon?" Syteria asked.

"Of course." Anasera pointed at the sky. "There."

Two pale orbs, as delicate as soap bubbles crested the sky. The lake's placid surface reflected their ascent.

"The sky changes from night to night," Anasera said. "We have people from many different worlds aboard. They come here to be under their own stars. This is our home's—Serigala's—night sky."

Another world's sky. How many wonders could she lose herself in?

"And the lake?" Syteria asked.

They returned to the trail.

129

A male and a female strolled by. The male wrapped his arm along the curve of the female's hip. Unable to look away, Syteria stared at the blatant display. Her jaw clenched. A lump rose in her throat. Her fingers flew to her neck.

"This way," an untroubled Anasera prompted.

Syteria followed, stumbling, still frowning at the female's willingness to allow the male's touch. She glanced back at the couple but the winding path obscured them from view.

Anasera led her through a wooded tract. The trees on either side thickened, and long, languid branches reached down, sweeping into their path.

"This is my favorite spot," Anasera said, parting a curtain of swaying foliage to emerge into a glade.

"It's beautiful," Syteria whispered, yielding to the distraction, admiring the tranquil bay that cut into the open space.

Several couples strolled footpaths leading to secluded places.

A female bolted past, laughter trailing in her wake.

A male ran after her, mumbling a half-hearted apology as he barreled between them. Stunned by his unbowed height, the span of his bare shoulders, Syteria froze.

A Rhoan male wouldn't have dared give chase.

Clenching her fists to hold them immobile, she resisted the compulsion to take him down and kill him.

"Syteria, what's wrong?"

Every fiber of her being insisted she act. Adrenaline made her limbs shake.

"He's going to hurt her," Syteria said.

Even as the words rushed out, she *knew* it was a lie. It was expectation, not observation, but she was already moving, closing the distance. As *eniseri*, she yielded to her training.

Anasera grabbed her by the wrist and yanked her back with surprising strength. "She wants him to follow her."

"What?"

"Wait," Anasera insisted, digging her fingers into Syteria's arm. "Watch."

The fleeing female reached the edge of a pond, shed her clothing, and waded into the water. The male pursued his victim into the pond without stopping to shed his clothes. The female laughed, loudly protesting his tactics as she splashed water at him.

He lunged, his motion half-hearted, as she dove from sight. He disappeared under the water and they emerged together. Their laughter receded as they swam to a secluded alcove.

"See, they're just"—an error tone beeped—"It's only innocent"—another beep.

Anasera's words faded as Syteria blundered towards the lake. She made it to the water's edge and fell to her knees, not knowing how she'd shaken Anasera's iron grip.

"I don't understand," Syteria said, glancing over her shoulder.

Anasera had caught up to her. She repeated the previous phrases, and then followed them with variants that yielded the same results—a bevy of error tones.

Syteria was a strong swimmer. Still, the possibility that her unusual clothing with all its excess fabric might tangle her and drag her to the bottom made her hesitate.

"Why are you letting him hurt her?" Syteria's voice was accusatory and demanding. Her limbs shook hard enough for Anasera to see. Her judging gaze flew to all the details that Syteria could no longer mask—the way her chest heaved, the way her body shivered, her fingers trembled.

Syteria probed the boots for a way to remove them, but there were no clasps, no laces, nothing she could work. They weren't nearly as heavy as the boots of an *eniseri*, but then again, neither was the cloth, so maybe—

"I promise you, he will not hurt her." Anasera's tone said the idea was too absurd to entertain. "They're just playing."

"Playing?" Syteria asked.

Anasera's face lit up with a smile.

Syteria pushed herself up. Was this a ruse then. A test? Or just how these people entertained themselves?

"I'd like to go back now," Syteria said and took off running, the exertion burning through some of the accumulated adrenaline. At a fork, uncertain of which path to take, she slowed.

Anasera grasped her elbow and pulled her to a halt.

"What's wrong?" Anasera asked.

"What you said. It's impossible. Impossible, absurd, wrong!"

"What's impossible?"

"Him. Her," Syteria said.

Anasera's breath hitched.

"Syteria, are you saying that your people don't"—she cleared her throat—"play?"

THE MOLECULAR MACHINE had been seeded into space many months ago, one of millions, all sharing the same mission: float inert inside a hardened shell until swept up in the gravitic wake of a ship. Then, ride along, skimming along the ship's shields, until an opening formed, or some part of it weakened, whether from impact or defective harmonics.

Along with a handful of others, it had been in the right spot, at the right time, when the ship known as the *Edlyn* had irised its shield to allow the imperial courier inside the field. Many more of the machine's clones had perished than had made it inside.

Once within the ship, those that had survived had gone dormant in order to avoid detection, moving slowly enough not to set off the sensors, or hitching a ride along something convenient, like a piece of equipment, or one of the organisms that inhabited the ship.

Their primary mission was to multiply, but not too quickly, not enough for anyone to notice.

Their secondary mission was to tap into the *Edlyn's* communications and stand by for further orders. Those orders had come from an unknown source. The machines had dutifully made their transmissions, masking their signals within the active emissions the *Edlyn* poured out into space for navigation and sensors.

But something had gone wrong, some harmonic had misbehaved, spiking, giving them away.

The *Edlyn* had responded by shutting off its secondary communications array. As it cooled, the machines had ceased all attempts at reproduction, lest it give them away. But it hadn't been enough. They'd been discovered. Protocols engaged, randomly designating a survivor to sneak away while the rest of the batch stayed behind as a decoy.

Tertiary protocols activated when radiation destroyed the decoys.

Those protocols involved new programming, new orders, new mission parameters. As long as the access codes matched, the orders would be obeyed.

The machine authenticated the latest codes as it received them and attached itself to one of the organisms inhabiting the *Edlyn*.

CHAPTER FOURTEEN

*D*arien's stomach grumbled. His dinner with the *Edlyn's* command staff had ended many hours ago. The current batch of intelligence and status reports taunted him. They flowed as two-dimensional images and icons across the surface of his desk, reminding him that indecision was a decision in itself. He brought up an icon and flicked it upward.

The points of light coalesced above the desk into a holographic image of the survivor. She released a protracted whimper as she struggled through another nightmare.

It fascinated him, this human frailty, this unpleasant activation of the amygdalae.

His kind enjoyed dreams without nightmares, a gift from designers who'd deemed it a liability to have the *donai's* rest-state plagued by fear. Instead, they'd given them a semi-conscious state in which to process the analogous disturbances that led to nightmares in humans.

Anasera swept in without permission, her urgent strides consuming the expanse between them.

"Do you always watch my patient while she sleeps?" she asked as she slammed her hands down atop his desk and looked straight into his eyes.

He leaned back, unimpressed. "Do you always allow your patients to linger in such distress?"

"She's refused my help," Anasera said, deflating. "I can't calibrate a sleep field without her cooperation and she doesn't trust us."

Anasera looked like she could use some sleep herself. Her fatigue was evident in her eyes and shoulders. Even her pores exuded frustration.

The hologram showed the woman, Syteria, at rest once again. *Did you earn your peace through surrender or triumph?* He dismissed the image. With a gesture, he invited Anasera to have a seat.

She dropped into one of the couches beside his desk and rubbed at her brow. "I'm trying to undo her people's draconian behavioral controls. I'm trying to help her forget, but she's fighting me. It's like she *wants* to remember. I don't understand her."

"I do."

She shot him a sideways glance full of skepticism.

"She wants to remember her victories because they define her," he said.

"They can't all be victories, Darien," Anasera said, dropping her hands to her lap. "These people, these Rhoans, they're...they're inhuman."

Amusing choice of words.

"Are they?" he asked.

She blew out a frustrated breath. "She should still be in the infirmary."

"Is that why you've come here? To tell me I shouldn't have moved her?"

"Why? Why move her into your own quarters? We have plenty of empty suites, ones more suited for someone from such a primitive culture. She's already overwhelmed and you..."

"Yes?" he prompted, raising a brow.

"You keep throwing her into the deep end to see if she can swim. First with that stroll you had me take her on, instead of letting me acclimate her slowly. And then by dumping her into another alien environment, again without giving her a chance to adapt."

He accepted the assessment with the barest semblance of a shrug.

"We have a traitor aboard. Maybe several. The stroll was a calculated risk, something that might've drawn him or her out."

"But it didn't," Anasera said.

"No, and since we'll be hosting a contingent of imperials soon, my quarters are the logical choice because they are the most secure."

She shook her head in disbelief. "The most secure facilities are in the brig, not the royal wing."

"Are you suggesting I throw her into the brig, this patient you've just told me is too frail to leave the infirmary?"

It earned him a venomous glare which he met with a smile. He stood and crossed to the refreshments table. He poured the sparkling amber liquid Anasera favored into a glass and presented it to her.

"You know," she said, taking it, "I should have far more influence on you than I actually do."

"And why is that?" Darien poured himself a small measure he had no intention of drinking. He hated its cloying sweetness. But the illusion of sharing their enjoyment often put his humans at ease, so he pretended to drink.

"The emperor would die of apoplectic shock," she said, rolling the stem of the glass between thumb and forefinger, sending the liquid into a swirl. "A *donai* serving a human. It's scandalous."

"Perhaps next time, you'd do me the honor of accompanying me to the Imperial Court. If we can unseat Thán Kabrin with such a simple, bloodless act, the Imperium would be far better off."

"Yes, it would be, but let's not pretend we have such power. We are no longer children, reenacting past battles, and wargaming the defeat of a rival House. It's wishful thinking and a dangerous waste of time."

"As *I* recall, I learned this very valuable skill"—he indicated the table service—"because you and your sister loved tea parties."

It earned him a laugh, although the humor didn't quite reach her eyes.

"You played the tolerant, indulgent big 'brother' very well."

Her words pleased him far more than they should have. Few *donai* had natural siblings. He and Anasera may not have shared parents, but they shared childhood memories and a resilient bond. One deepened even further by her status as the pair-bonded mate of one of his father's *donai*. And mother to someone like him—another half-breed son whose very existence made him a target.

"I did, didn't I," he said.

Brother. Uncle. Terms of endearment few *donai* could claim. He raised the glass to his lips.

The semblance of humor faded completely as her dark eyes went hard. "What will happen to her? I think she deserves to know what to expect."

She did. How did Anasera expect him to explain that from the moment he'd used the appearance of the Rhoan ship as an excuse to land on Thertore, he'd cast this woman into a dangerous role—first as unintended consequence, then as collateral damage, and now as casualty?

His silence gave Anasera the answer. Shaking her head, she sighed her disappointment. Behind those dark eyes, thoughts raced. He could tell by the far away look.

"When Lord Dobromil granted my father asylum, he set a precedent," she finally said. "He can do so again."

"Lord Dobromil has refused."

After their last battle of wills, Darien wouldn't have believed himself capable of beseeching his father for *any* favor. Yet, he'd swallowed his pride only to receive nothing in return.

"What then?" Anasera asked.

"My father's refusal has left me no choice. I must comply with imperial demands."

She stood and touched his cheek. "Brother, please..."

"What are you asking of me...sister?" he asked, hissing that last word.

It was a mistake, allowing her this kind of power now. He knew it even as he granted it.

"Refuse the emperor's demand," she said.

Had she dared strike him it would have been easier to take. He gave her time to retract the demand. She stood before him, not as a supplicant seeking favor, nor as a valued retainer offering guidance, but a vassal to whom he owed a boon.

Why was she so willing to spend this currency, this singular coin? Now. For *her*?

He stepped away and turned his back.

"Every other House in the Imperium recognizes my right to treat you as I see fit. The emperor cannot dictate how I treat you or any other human in my domain. He cannot compel me to turn you over to him. You would have me compromise this? You'd have me set a precedent weakening my dominion over you and every human in my domain for a stranger you've known a few weeks?"

"The stranger has a name."

Silence, and then finally, a shaky breath. It wasn't like her to hesitate so.

"Syteria is not of the Imperium," Anasera said. "She is alien. He has no jurisdict—"

"And you think I've not already made that argument?"

"And?" she asked hopefully.

"It was rejected. The other Houses understand the danger of such a precedent."

"We've sheltered humans from the Imperium before and provided a conduit for escape. Life outside the Imperium is harsh and primitive, but she'd be free."

He shook his head. "My last attempt to deceive the emperor failed. And she wouldn't be safe. I cannot protect her outside my realm any more than I could protect those poor souls I tried helping before. Kabrin would hunt her down. She's too valuable a scapegoat for what happened on Thertore. He's going to cast her as a threat. We both know that threat plays well for the Imperial Court."

"You did the right thing, Darien. You know you did. So does your father. If he truly disagreed with what you did—what *we* did—he would have done far worse than assign us to a meaningless picket."

Darien turned around.

"Only because he didn't realize I could turn the most boring detail into an even bigger political nightmare."

"Always the overachiever," she said with a smirk, reaching for his cheek again.

He rewarded her attempt to lighten the mood with a meager smile.

"House Dobromil cannot survive another incident that ends up threatening the autonomy of the Houses and gives the emperor an excuse to grab more power.

"Anasera, I cannot put my father in a position where he would have to choose between his House and his son."

DREA HAD BEEN PROMISED that the paper-thin shielding under her uniform would be like a second skin, its presence as unobtrusive as breathing. It was designed to neutralize the advantage of the *donai's* heightened senses by shielding most of her physiological reactions from them. Instead it felt both like armor worn too long and a fragile shell about to crack.

Galen doesn't promise what he can't deliver. That had been *her* argument.

So why did she feel like she was about to go into battle for the first time?

Because of how hard Galen had argued against this particular tactic, how much he'd insisted that it was both unnecessary and excessive. Because of how much convincing Darien had needed to allow it.

It wasn't just that delegating this task to her had touched Darien's honor and challenged his pride. It was how often he'd reminded her that it was beyond Galen's ability to remedy a beheading.

Nevertheless, he'd agreed. That's why they were both on the bridge, monitoring the *Edlyn's* hangar bay as it received the imperial corvette. She'd cleared a hangar specifically for it. The corvette drifted into the cavernous harbor and settled into its berth with great reluctance, like a royal bird with ruffled feathers settling into an inadequate nest.

The corvette dropped its shields and submitted its fire-control to the *Edlyn*. An agreement between the Imperium and House Dobromil required both parties to pretend that this gesture neutralized the physical threats as well as the passions of the participants. Decades of experience and a growing tension so palpable Drea feared she might choke on it, said that this fiction was about to be tested.

She lovingly caressed an icon at her station, the one that placed twenty-seven imperial lives at her mercy.

Darien loomed behind her as she considered the extent of her power and reined in desires she'd thought quenched.

He cleared his throat.

"Go ahead," he whispered. "I won't stop you."

The lethal edge in his voice turned her stomach. She hoped to never hear that acid-black, arctic tone again—he'd sounded just like the emperor.

"And here, I thought it was *my* job to rein you in," she replied with a nonchalance she did not feel.

All along, she'd imagined herself the tempering force that would aid him. Instead, she'd allowed her personal animus to suggest a dangerous, alternate course of action.

He remained idle at her shoulder, silent, like Death waiting on its prey. His face was cast in shadow, his hands clasped behind him as he stared out into space. His eyes had changed—the superficial amber layer that behaved like human irises dilating to reveal double layers of not-so-human ones atop gold pupils.

"Commander, please welcome our imperial guests."

"Yes, my lord."

She rushed off the bridge, grateful beyond reason.

By the time she reached the *Edlyn's* most isolated hangar bay she'd buried her doubts. She could ill afford them and indulging them would lead to failure.

Their plan was sound, their contingencies as good as they could make them. Ten *donai*, including Palleton, were waiting on her. She greeted him with a silent nod, which he acknowledged thoughtfully as he escorted her to the head of the assembled honor guard.

The ramp from the imperial ship lowered and extended, touching down within a hairbreadth of her foot.

A shavetail *donai* emerged. He was no mere imperial. The crest on the midnight-green uniform marked him as a member of Kabrin's own line, although he looked nothing like the emperor. The young *donai* had pale hair like her own. It was cut short to the scalp, barely there. His pale skin, however, was very much like the emperor's.

He looked her up and down.

Then he looked beyond her and noted her escort before reluctantly acknowledging her with a nod. He had all the overbred qualities of one to whom contempt was as natural as breathing. With great skill he conveyed a sneer without allowing one to actually form on his face.

"I am Kailin Kabrin. Where is your master?" He punctuated his indignation belatedly with, "Commander."

Whelp, I was freed before you were born, she wanted to say.

"My lord is...indisposed," she said. The word was ash in her mouth, doubly so given the context it conveyed, and the necessity that demanded it. Her heart rattled in its cage. Surely, if she could hear it, he could too. And then he'd suspect that something was in play.

I have ten donai at my back. That comfort only did so much. Her heart continued to thrash against her ribs.

Kailin locked gazes with Palleton, who was towering behind her, both a knight and a rook to her queen.

The look on Kailin's young face clearly asked, *Why are you making me deal with this human?*

"How long is this—what did you call it? Ah, yes, an indisposition, going to last?" Kailin asked, his gaze aimed above her head.

A dark, low rumble rose from the back of Palleton's throat. It drove the blood from Kailin's face.

Drea suppressed a smile, pretended to ignore his tone and the insult conveyed by looking past her. She waited expectantly.

Palleton was less patient. He stepped forward, hand on the sword at his side. Among the *donai*, matters of honor were still settled in anachronistic ways.

At double his present age, the whelp's skill with a sword would still lag Palleton's by decades. Engaging an elder *donai* over such a trivial matter would cost Kailin his life and no one would question Palleton's challenge. While acting as her master's proxy, an insult to Drea was an insult to Dobromil's House.

Kailin's face lost even more of its color as Palleton took his time drawing his sword, letting it cantillate its warning.

"Commander, how long is this indiscretion to last?"

Palleton's killing sword paused, halted, and finally slipped back into its scabbard. He stepped back, not to her side, but just far enough behind her to show the imperial that he, an elder *donai*, deferred to her. Kailin's gaze darted from her to Palleton and back. The contempt in his eyes waned and awe took its place.

So, the young Kabrin had never deferred to a human before. He had the perplexed look of someone who had anticipated the experience to be fatal.

I could make it fatal, she thought, tempted.

"Perhaps in a few days," she said.

"A few days?" Kailin's voice was close to breaking. "Really, Commander. I must insist. I represent the emperor."

It was her turn to look him up and down and bask in the act of finding him wanting.

"My master knows whom you represent."

His nostrils flared. Both hands clenched but remained well away from his sword and his sidearm. He had eyes only for her now. "Tell your master that—"

"What?" she cut in, voice rising as she got into his face.

He wasn't as tall as Darien and she'd practiced this particular tone with him often enough during his youth that it had acquired a certain familiarity. But this wasn't Darien. This wasn't Dobromil's indulgent son, the boy she'd known all his life. This was one of the emperor's own blood. Within his veins, blood that was rightfully hers to spill, flowed. Blood she yearned to spill. Blood she'd earned.

Would she ever be this close to the emperor's own again?

"I shall tell him that the emperor has sent a pup to scratch at our door."

She turned to Palleton and said, "See to it he doesn't soil the deck."

"Yes, Commander!" Palleton snappy acknowledgment was somewhere between a bark and a roar as it echoed in the hangar.

She spun on her heel and strode out.

How long had she wanted to put an imperial in his place? A wonderful floating sensation, a lightness of being flowed through Drea.

I really must not get used to this feeling. It could be the death of me.

The door between hangar and passageway closed behind her. Body shaking, she pressed her hand to her aching chest. She reached inside her tunic, tore the paper-thin material off her skin, crumpling it within her tightening grip.

Galen was waiting in the passageway where he'd been ordered to monitor the exchange from afar.

She dropped the shielding to the floor and resealed her tunic.

Galen clapped. "Masterfully done, Commander."

"I must admit"—her breath came in quick gasps—"that was very cathartic."

"I believe you."

"I really must thank our master…and Palleton."

"No doubt." Galen's lips pursed with amusement.

"Darien said to provoke him. Do you think I managed?"

Galen offered her a steadying hand.

"Oh, yes," he said.

CHAPTER FIFTEEN

our days had passed since Syteria had toured the *Edlyn*
with Anasera. Four days since, numb with the weight of
all she'd learned in that brief tour, she'd been deposited into her new
"quarters." Four days of instruction so intense that she felt like she was
drowning. Each time she fought her way to the surface, only to be
pulled into the depths once again. Four days of judiciously avoiding
probing questions about why her people didn't "play."

She'd not acted like a Kappan. She'd acted the way her Rhoan
mistresses had trained her to act, for on Rho, it was death for a male to
touch a female. For a man to touch a woman.

She bounced between the Rhoan and Kappan terms, between her
desire for answers and her fear of asking the question needed to clarify
the social order aboard the *Edlyn*. Her reluctance was born of fear, for
it was an *eniseri's* job to deliver that death, and the last thing she
wanted was for her new hosts to know of the blood on her hands, of the
terrible things she'd done, the terrible things she was capable of.

Not since the *eniseri* had kidnapped her, shaved her bald, and
extracted her obedience, had she had to adapt so quickly.

But Anasera was nothing like the Matrons. The *Edlyn* was nothing
like the *eniseri* crèches. The methods here were nothing like those of

the Rhoans, but the sense that she would never regain any control over her life had soured the experience of transitioning from the infirmary to her new "quarters."

Such an innocuous word.

Absurd, really, for it was a suite of rooms that belonged in a palace, in service to someone else, not someone who'd never had a room of her own. A completely inadequate word for a space made up of arches and columns that soared into the projection of a sky so flawless she had to remind herself she was "indoors."

On a ship. In space. Traveling between the stars.

She'd explored opulent rooms filled with flowers, marveled at furnishings that reshaped themselves. Despite the advanced technology that had obviously gone into allowing them to change form, they nevertheless seemed anachronistic, like relics or museum pieces. Some of them, like the chaise on the other side of this chamber, with its inexplicable curves, seemed mere decoration with no function at all. Over days, her shock had subsided, but she still felt like an invader in someone else's home.

I am safe here. I cannot stay.

She and Anasera faced each other across a small table dwarfed by the atrium-like proportions of the suite's main chamber. They sat just inside a balcony guarded by sheer, fluttering curtains.

Anasera cleared her throat. By the length and volume of it, Syteria guessed it was not the first time.

Cued by the half-remembered prompt, Syteria imitated the sounds of a language far more complex and nuanced than Rhoan. A plate of food, the subject of today's impromptu lesson, rested at her elbow.

"Here..." Syteria brought up the search function on the interface hovering by her hand. It diverted Anasera's attempts to refine her pronunciation for the name of the red fruit nestled among its yellow, orange, and green variants.

"I think this is the word," Syteria said.

"Veg-e-tar-i-an," Anasera enunciated.

"Are your people vegetarian?"

Anasera laughed. "Why would you think so?"

Syteria gestured to the plate's contents in way of explanation.

Anasera explained without using any words known to Syteria so she reached up to activate the translator. It re-engaged with a confirming beep.

"Your ship's stores," Anasera began again, "indicated that your people did not eat meat. Is that not the case?"

Syteria hesitated.

"Rhoans do not, but I…"

She smoothed the folds of her black and red dress in her lap, straightened and looked back up.

"I remember my grandfather teaching us to hunt."

There. An entirely true and exonerating answer. Perfectly Rhoan as well, since through no fault of her own, she'd been taught to kill.

The Rhoans didn't murder animals for food. Only vicious Kappans like herself did such horrific things.

She shook her head, sighing at how easily she fell into old habits, expecting a jolt of pain as punishment. It had taken years, but eventually she'd stopped thinking of eating meat, for every time she had, somehow, the collar knew.

"Are you all right?" Anasera asked, placing her hand atop Syteria's.

Anasera displayed no recoil of disgust, none of the judgement Syteria had expected.

"Yes, I'm fine," Syteria said.

A smile tempered Anasera's curious expression. It looked very much like admiration. But for what? Surely not for admitting that she'd hunted, that she'd been taught to eat animals.

"I'll make sure the *Edlyn* updates the menu for you," Anasera said and withdrew her hand.

Syteria cleared her throat. "So, the *donai* are *not* veg-e-tar-i-an."

Anasera tried to suppress a laugh, but failed. "Absolutely not."

"Have I said something amusing?"

"Yes, very. The idea of the *donai* being vegetarian, is very, very amusing. My father will find it—"

Alarms shrieked, echoing off the stone flooring. Syteria covered her ears.

Thunder cracked as a force field snapped into place over the balcony threshold. The deck shook.

A shimmer crawled over the chamber walls. It turned viscous and flowed like lava over the force field, turning it into a physical barrier and sealing them inside the chamber.

Vibrations crested. The serving tray spilled its contents and tumbled. Lights dimmed and flickered.

Gravity's grip lightened and Syteria's stomach twisted into itself. Her fingers dug into her chair's armrests as her gaze darted to Anasera's for an explanation.

Anasera spoke into the air, issuing urgent requests that Syteria's translator didn't interpret. Anasera's demeanor changed from curious concern to insistent demand.

Syteria's heart raced as gravity shifted once again, pulling her down urgently for an instant before letting her go again.

The vibrations intensified, charging the air, as if a storm were brewing, roiling fast and hard and full of dangerous promise.

She looked for something that she could use as a weapon. Mortified by her lack of options, she reached down for the small, blunted knife that had tumbled to the deck. She tucked it into her sleeve as the door to her quarters exploded.

The shockwave knocked her back, lifting her into the air.

She was dimly aware of Anasera flying across the room beside her.

An opaque fog pursued, mushrooming to fill the chamber. An enormous invisible hand grabbed her, as though she were a mere doll.

The impact with the barrier that had formed over the balcony knocked the air out of her lungs.

She fell, slow and surreal, caught like a pebble sinking into syrup. Landing sent a jolt out from her ribcage. Her vision blurred.

The translator behind her ear sputtered and died.

Breathing became stabbing.

She shook her vision clear, seeking Anasera.

Her crumpled form lay just beyond reach. Syteria crawled to her side. A gash in Anasera's scalp ran red. Her blood pooled on the deck.

The decorative finials that had rested on the back of her chair separated from the toppled seat and floated towards them, transforming into medical rovers. One rover settled at eye-level and a pale blue beam rastered over her, slicing through the intruding fog. The second rover floated toward Anasera.

Syteria's rover chirped words she didn't understand. She touched her ear. The translator's tiny disk was still securely attached, but pressing it didn't bring it back to life.

She cursed, pressing a hand to her side as pain coursed through her. The rover continued speaking to her and circling. She grabbed at it, ready to throw it at the fog, but it zipped out of reach.

"I'm fine," she insisted, hoping it would understand her. "Help Anasera."

It spoke again. Even without understanding its words she knew it was disagreeing. She ignored it, dragging herself toward Anasera. The other rover had cast out a pulsing beam.

Holding her breath hurt like hell, but Syteria had good reason for it —Anasera was too still, her skin ashen, her lips rimmed in blue.

Rhythmic tremors like giant footfalls traveled through the deck and along every bone in her body. She placed herself between Anasera and the entrance. The roiling fog hung thick in the air, cocooning the space around them. She reached into it.

The fog pulled back.

Startled, she withdrew her hand.

"I don't suppose you can tell me what this is," she said to the rover still circling her.

It gave no indication that it understood. Useless, stubborn, little machine.

The tremors from the deck intensified.

Something big and heavy was approaching. She needed to get Anasera under cover. Whatever this cocoon was, it didn't seem solid enough to rely on for protection.

She slid her arms under Anasera, ignoring the protests of her own damaged rib. The rovers took turns zapping her shoulders until she stopped. They bobbed, scolding her with high pitched tones and angry, mechanized voices.

She swatted at the closest one, catching it just right and sent it into the fog. As she'd thought, the cocoon wasn't solid. Not solid at all.

The threatening rhythm grew louder. The vibrations deepened.

Crushed metal.

Splintering glass.

Syteria grabbed Anasera by her feet and pulled, determined not to let her go.

One of the rovers darted into her face, pulling up and away at the last second. Without meaning to, she let go of Anasera's feet and fell back. Fog swirled around her. It caught her, like a giant hand, slowing, then cushioning her fall.

Once it deposited her on the deck, it retreated.

Her gaze followed the receding fog, right to the armored boot that came down near her hand, narrowly missing her splayed fingers. The fog parted to reveal an armor-clad humanoid.

Syteria craned her neck to get a full measure of its height. The wingless, mechanized gargoyle spoke, voice distorted by a smooth, featureless helmet whose surface revealed nothing of whatever was underneath.

It repeated its demand.

She didn't need her translator to grasp its meaning—it wanted her to stand.

Syteria pulled the knife out of her sleeve and plunged it into the armor's only seam. The knife's meager point found its mark on the boot, but slid along the seam without leaving any trace of its passage.

The gargoyle laughed.

There was no mistaking that very human sound, or the mockery it conveyed.

It grabbed her wrist, plucking her off the floor as if she were a rag doll. As she flew upward, the armored gargoyle's twin emerged from the fog.

"Let me go!" She kicked and twisted as she dangled from its grasp. "Put me down!"

It jerked her higher.

The motion launched a wave of agony through her arm and the knife fell out of her grasp, clattering uselessly to the floor. Forming a fist, she drew her free arm back.

The gargoyle's twin grabbed her wrist and held it high. Fire spread through her ribcage.

Syteria's kicking and screaming loosened the clasps in her hair, releasing it.

A voice emerged from the fog, preceding its owner, a young male in a midnight-green uniform, armed with a sneer and a sword. He spoke to her as he cocked his head to the side, peering through the confounding veil of her hair.

Syteria tossed her head to get a better look at him. Tall, pale of hair and skin. Amber eyes. *Gold* pupils that reflected light.

Closing in, he repeated the question.

Waited for an answer.

Struck her.

Searing pain bolted from her cheek down into her jaw. Tasting blood, she snapped her head back, raising her knees for a kick.

Armored hands squeezed tight, threatening to crush her wrists. Kick forgotten, she cried out with the wretched sound of a trapped animal releasing its fury.

Another voice intruded.

The blond male froze, his gaze glued to the tip of a blade that slid along his neck from just underneath his earlobe to caress the underside of his jaw. From behind, a silhouette in black emerged. The blade slid, tracing the plane of the blond male's jaw as the swordsman arced around.

The blond male's eyes widened, the fear in his eyes confirming that a sword tip at the throat had an authority unlike any other.

The black-clad swordsman spoke again, his voice as much a blade as the weapon he wielded—a blade draped in velvet, shielding a cutting edge barely restrained. It sent shivers skating over her skin.

The armored gargoyles released her.

Pain radiated from her tailbone as it struck ground.

She got her knees under her before the weight of the gargoyle's hand on her shoulder pushed her back down.

The swordsman peered down the length of the blade as he spoke to his victim. He raised the blade's edge enough to force the blond male to tilt his head and bare his throat.

Heated talk passed between them, a volley of venomous-sounding words racing back and forth along the curved blade. They spoke in guttural tones she'd never heard before.

The blond male, who looked so very human despite his strange eyes, revealed sharp cuspids as he bared his teeth.

Pulse pounding, Syteria's fingers sought the translator behind her ear again. The unit chimed its start-up tone.

"I claim this woman," that velvet-draped blade of a voice said.

The gargoyle released her shoulder and stepped back as if those words made her untouchable. They stood as far away from her as the room allowed.

Syteria stood, faltering for an instant when her knees threatened to give way.

More than a dozen males had taken up position around the room, their rifles pointed at the two gargoyles behind her.

Only one had drawn a sword.

The blond whose life teetered on the precipice of that sword swallowed.

"She's not marked," the blond said.

A low growl spiraled from deep inside the swordsman's chest. Something dark and inhuman flared in the depths of *his* golden eyes.

She stepped back.

Full of warning, his gaze flickered to hers, freezing her in place. He held her gaze for an instant, sending her heart fluttering.

Nostrils flaring, he turned his gaze back upon the man whose life he held on a blade's edge. A sharp twist of the wrist, so fast it blurred, drew a quantum of blood before he lowered the blade.

"No," the swordsman said, "but *you* are."

The blond staggered backward, one hand at his throat, the other reaching for his sidearm. The swordsman pressed his advantage, holding the tip of the blade level with the hollow of his prey's throat, denying him the chance to draw as he forced a retreat into an enormous gray-haired wall of muscle.

Blurred motions skirted the edge of Syteria's vision. The riflemen disarmed the gargoyles at her back. With the threat behind her contained, she rushed to Anasera's side and fell to her knees.

Anasera's breathing was even. The gash in her scalp had closed. She stroked Anasera's blood-soaked hair.

A shadow loomed over her and she looked up.

Intense amber eyes held her own. Flames of golden light burned beneath the amber. Short, dark facial hair stubbled the symmetrical jaw and framed a set of full lips.

He extended his hand, bending slightly at the waist, an imperious gesture that was more demand than offer.

Syteria's breath caught in her chest. Pain bloomed again as she stood. A slight flutter took wing in her belly. Her hand had risen to his, obeying the silent demand.

He captured her hand, held it to his lips, and graced the top with a kiss. His lips, firm and so warm they burned, touched her hand for the barest instant. They lifted, leaving behind no brand, no mark. The flutter became a coil that tightened, held, and then released.

Heat crawled up her neck.

A smile of pure, male satisfaction formed on his lips as he straightened. She tilted her head back, so very conscious of his towering height.

I'm not used to feeling small.

He stood with such confident ease, his presence commanding the room and projecting strength as if it cost him nothing. Her body tightened at the arrogance born from that lack of effort. She drew herself up to her full height despite her rib's protests.

Syteria withdrew her hand, and…he let it go.

A brief scuffle reminded her they had an audience. The gargoyles were being marched out. The gray-haired wall had removed the blond one's sword and was hauling him out by the scruff of his neck.

She turned back to drink in the sight of *him*, trying desperately to sort out the odd sensation he'd sent coursing through her.

It wasn't his height, nor his manner, nor the power he wielded, that make him so striking. It wasn't. It couldn't be.

She inched closer, instinct moving against prudence, drawn in by the allure imbued in every angle of his face, every muscle, every strand of hair. He was not just exquisitely formed. He was perfection brought to life.

Not just perfection, but menace. He was the very embodiment of threat.

Still, her body refused to draw away and put more space between them.

"What are you?" she asked.

"I am Darien Dayasagar of House Dobromil." His voice was a low, deep rumble, a perfect complement to the authority he wore like a second skin.

"You're not human."

Somehow, she had gotten closer. Stepping back now would only let him know she'd done it without realizing it. Determined not to retreat, she held herself in place.

He reached for her swollen cheek.

Her back found the wall. She opened her hands and slid them behind her. She had two options: to fight or flee. And there was nowhere to run.

"I'm not going to hurt you," he said. "You have my word of honor."

Even though truth rang in his words, she flinched as his thumb caressed her tender cheek. His hand lingered, his touch a welcome warmth, a soothing balm on her skin. Her breath caught again as his eyes flashed gold.

He looked her up and down with a gaze so intense she could almost feel its touch. Unable to bear the scrutiny, she looked away, knowing it was a sign of surrender, one she'd regret.

Galen's voice intruded, demanding access to the chamber.

The fire of *his* touch abandoned her.

She looked up.

Trailed by a floating pallet and two assistants, Galen rushed past the source of her torment to kneel at Anasera's side. Syteria wanted to join him, to apologize for failing to save his daughter, but she dared not move.

One of Galen's two assistants, a young female, appeared at her side and gently gripped Syteria's elbow, attempting to draw her away. Syteria's half-hearted gesture of rejection did nothing to deter her.

"Nestra, my lady is well enough to walk on her own," *he* said casually.

Nestra yielded her grasp.

"Aren't you, my lady?" *he* said in that same low, inviting voice that made her want to lean closer.

It was unlike anything Syteria had heard in a long time. She was used to the whining, interrupting Rhoan males who raised the pitches of their tones to be heard over dominant Rhoan females.

She nodded, the gesture flushing out the heat that had sustained her. Cold seeped into her body and lingered. Her heartbeats quickened to compensate for their sudden weakness. Her cheek and rib throbbed harder. The place where his fingers had caressed continued to burn. Beneath her, her legs were becoming unsteady.

She did not want to fall at *his* feet.

"My lord, Commander Bomani requests your presence on the bridge," a male subordinate dressed in what they called ship fatigues said.

The room was threatening to spin. It took all her will and whatever presence of mind she still possessed to keep herself from leaning on Nestra for support. *His* gaze was still locked on her as if she were the only person in the room.

"My lord," the subordinate insisted.

He nodded, bowed to her and swept out of the room, subordinate in tow.

"Please, my lady," Nestra said. "We need to get you to the infirmary."

Anasera, Galen, and the other assistant were gone. So were the riflemen who'd poured in. She'd remained oblivious to it all.

154

A second floating pallet arrived, escorted by another female dressed in the soft gray garments of the infirmary staff. Syteria resisted Nestra's attempts to shepherd her onto it.

"I'm fine," Syteria said, but the tremor in her voice betrayed her.

DREA GAVE Darien a sour look as he entered the bridge. She allowed it to remain on her face for only the briefest instant, just in case her displeasure wasn't potent enough otherwise. He gave no indication that he noticed or cared, which was not that unusual.

If the *donai* reacted to every human emotion, every pheromone they detected, no human on the ship would live for long, which was, unfortunately, how some Houses ran things. Only the meekest, most docile, and affectless humans tended to survive under *those* conditions.

"My lord," she said, "we've detected further unauthorized transmissions, this time from our secondary array."

His gaze swept the main display with its markers and icons. They showed that the encrypted bursts of data were being aimed at not one, but two, of the transit points connecting this star system to the Imperium.

A slight tightening of his hands slipped his control. Then his eyes changed.

He was primed to fight. She knew he'd been itching for it, for months during their picket. Despite his efforts to accommodate the imperials, he wanted blood as much as she did.

Had their contingencies failed? She knew the imperials had breached the brig as planned, that several crewmen had been injured, but that no one had been killed. Then the transmissions had diverted her attention for...

How long had it been?

She worked the data stream at her fingertips, reading through the status updates—of the brig and infirmary. She swore under her breath. Anasera. No wonder he was primed for a fight.

"How long before our primary is back online?" he asked.

"Several days, maybe more," Drea said.

The repair process had started, but there were rare elements that the *Edlyn's* nanites could not easily replicate. Elements that would be easier to mine, if they could only find the right piece of rock.

"Irradiate our secondary," he ordered.

She logged the order on her console.

"How far to our next transit point?" he asked.

"Three days at our current speed," Nav answered.

His face clouded just as Palleton entered the bridge.

"My lord," Palleton said, "the prisoner is secure in the brig."

Darien turned to Drea. "Lock our other 'guests' in the hangar."

"Yes, my lord."

Drea issued orders for tighter protocols, isolating the hangar from the rest of her ship. She posted additional security at any points they might be able to breach.

"Colonel, you're with me," Darien said. "Let's get some answers from our 'guest.'"

Palleton gave a grunt of acknowledgment.

"Random course changes until I give further orders," Darien said to Nav who acknowledged.

DARIEN'S BLOOD POUNDED, belying the outward calm as he and Palleton made their way from the bridge to the brig.

He'd shifted his vision to survey the woman's internal injuries and he'd been unable to shift it back. Deep inside him, instinct ruled, rattling its cage with ever increasing strength that kept his adrenaline high. His rushed breathing had dried out his throat. Instinct howled at him to quench that dryness with blood.

"My lord, perhaps you should allow me to deal with our imperial 'guest.' You're in no state of mind to do it properly."

"Why do you say that?" Darien asked. He blinked against the brightness of the passageways, the blinding pulses of light from the power conduits hidden behind the bulkheads.

"I see the Cold rise in you."

Darien gave Palleton a sharp look and stopped in his tracks. The difference between what he wanted to do—tear the Kabrin whelp apart —and what he had done were lightyears apart.

"You think I will lose control," Darien said as his breathing slowed.

"No, I think you will remain in perfect control as you peel him layer by layer until he descends into madness and then return him to his emperor with your compliments."

"Really?"

"It's what I would do, had he touched my lover, much less abused my pregnant concubine."

Darien's breathing slipped his control, coming hard and fast once more. Palleton's eyes mirrored his own, glowing with the telltale signs of anticipation. If Darien *were* to peel Kailin Kabrin layer by layer, Palleton would not stop him. The elder *donai* would see it as his duty to advise and assist. And he'd probably enjoy it, unlike Darien who'd have the unemotional detachment of the Cold guiding his hand.

"I had the chance to behead him," Darien said, "and didn't."

"A mistake, in my opinion. A weakness the Imperium will attribute to your human-tainted heritage. "

Darien shrugged the comment off. This was not the first time his behavior would be attributed to his heritage, nor would it be the last.

"I would keep you from making another mistake," Palleton said.

"And what mistake am I about to make?"

"In order to preempt accusations of weakness, we must frame your choice to spare the imperial whelp as something else."

"Such as?"

"When one counts coup, one must follow the proper forms. A claim has been made and it must be formalized. Notice must be placed in the emperor's hands as quickly as possible."

Palleton was correct. In the scramble to bait the imperials, to allow them to infiltrate the *Edlyn* without thinking they were walking into a trap, he had not involved any of the *donai*. Galen and Bomani's concerns—and therefore, their advice—were more prac- tical in nature. Neither human would have anticipated the *donai* traditions involved. Which excused them, but not himself. *He* had been educated about the proper forms, the required protocols of a claim.

"You want to use the imperials to deliver notice," Darien said.

Palleton smiled. "The emperor sends a ship of war into our territory because he knows we won't fire the first shot. His men violate our sovereignty aboard our own ship because they think we're still fleeing before them."

"This will not further the peace my father desires," Darien said, the words hollow and meaningless, every bit the excuse he knew them to be.

"Your father has maintained peace through shows of strength, not weakness. You must do the same. Prepare the claim and let me deal with the imperial whelp. Do not lower yourself to sparing him another thought."

Darien nodded.

"And one more thing, my lord."

Darien waited.

"Why *this* human?"

This was the question Darien had been avoiding. While the Imperial Court might easily accept the notion that it would please him to take one of the emperor's humans to his bed for no other reason than he could, Palleton knew him too well.

"Not many unarmed humans could've killed a *grierugon*," Darien said.

"No doubt, a desirable quality. But while one of Kabrin's humans would have been trained to obey a *donai's* command, to yield to your desires without question, this woman is not of the Imperium, is she?"

When Darien had claimed her, the woman had not acted like a human raised under the imperial yoke. But Palleton had not been there to witness it, having hauled off the Kabrin welp. Of this, he was sure. Those present must have told him. Darien had taken a chance, keeping her from seeing him or any other *donai*. He'd relied on her being too shocked to act inappropriately. For the most part, it had played out well enough.

"Another desirable quality," Darien said. "Is there a matter of honor that concerns you, Palleton? If so, name it now."

Palleton's posture stiffened, muscles bunching underneath the form-fitting fabric of the ship fatigues.

"Humans are prolific creatures, but we *donai* are not."

It was not the answer Darien had expected. Palleton had served House Dobromil since it had formed, four generations ago. He'd executed some of Dobromil's high-born vassals for matters of honor. Yet his concern wasn't that Darien had forced himself on the woman.

"My human-tainted heritage at work," Darien said.

Palleton's right eyebrow rose.

"House Kabrin would rather preside over our extinction than allow humans to save us," Darien said.

"That sounds very much like Galen talking."

"And if it is? A human child is better than no child at all, is it not?"

"A human cannot rule House Dobromil."

"Then perhaps you should spend your efforts convincing my father to take a *donai* wife, breed at the emperor's command, just as if we were still slaves and had traded our human masters for a despot of our own kind."

Darien took a step past Palleton. As he shifted his weight for the next step, the elder *donai* blurred past him and Darien's chest met Palleton's palm. Their gazes locked.

"Let us not pretend that Galen had no hand in this, my lord," Palleton said. "We all know that Galen's hand moves at Lord Dobromil's command."

"And yours moves at mine," Darien reminded him, gaze lowering to where Palleton's dark hand splayed against his chest. There was no way for the elder *donai* to ignore the calm with which he spoke, the detachment that had descended on him. Palleton's concern that he was on the verge of going cold was not without merit.

"I will do as you advise," Darien said.

Palleton's hand dropped. He stepped out of Darien's way, bent at the waist, eyes lowered, the movement quick and precise, just as it should be.

CHAPTER SIXTEEN

Syteria clutched her side. She was standing in the gallery above the surgical suite that Anasera had been rushed into. Galen and his staff worked with an almost indifferent manner as rovers hovered, working their "magic" via streams of light. Although she had a rudimentary understanding of "nanites," one earned as explanation for her rebirth, the molecular machines still seemed magical.

Galen and his nanites had worked miracles with her, but stab wounds and burns were one thing, head trauma another. All she could think of, despite every effort not to, was how easy it was to crush a human skull or break a human neck. She'd done it and with far less force than Anasera's impact with the wall.

Below, a blue, shimmering veil undulated around Anasera, prominently flaring as the physicians reached through it.

She wanted to rush down there even knowing there was nothing she could do. As much as she'd hated the way Anasera had pushed her into doing all the things she didn't want to do, the woman had been endlessly patient and had never hurt her. Once she'd accepted that Anasera was not part of some elaborate Rhoan deception, she'd come to think of her as a friend.

Please, please, please, be well. I will stop being so stubborn.

"My lady, please. I—" Nestra insisted, nudging.

"What was that fog?" Syteria asked. "Why didn't it grab Anasera the way it grabbed me?"

"Because you are our lady."

Syteria frowned, certain that the translator had made an error. "Why do you keep calling me that?"

"It is proper."

"Proper?"

"Needed," Nestra offered as an alternative. "Required."

Syteria let out a sigh of frustration and shifted her weight. The rib insisted on throbbing as she grappled for words that didn't sound completely idiotic.

"How did the fog decide?"

"Protocol, my lady."

Syteria rubbed at her brow. Perhaps later Galen could explain it to her.

"Will Anasera live?"

"Yes, my lady. Now, pl—"

"When she's out of danger," Syteria said, thwarting all of Nestra's attempts to get her into one of the open coffins Galen's people used for repairing bodies.

The so-called medical reconstruction units' confining design brought back unwelcome memories of Rhoan therapy. Of being tied down to be poked and prodded, without reason, without consent, even when she'd done nothing to warrant punishment.

Her cracked rib would heal well enough on its own. So would her cheek. They had done so before. In a way, she welcomed the pain. It cleared her head, allowed her to get the turmoil of unfamiliar emotions that were battering at her under some semblance of control.

She ran the sequence of events leading to Anasera's injuries through her mind again and again, trying to figure out what she should've done instead. For a time, trapping herself in that loop of circular thinking served as a distraction.

Finally, Galen looked up. His eyes widened. A frown clouded his face as his gaze darted to Nestra who still stood stoically at Syteria's side.

He issued instructions to the people around him and exited the surgical suite.

Eager to meet Galen at the stairs, Syteria turned. A fresh flood of agony clouded her sight and sent the room spinning.

Insistent hands prodded her onto a bio-bed. She blinked her vision clear as she leaned back, suddenly exhausted and unable to fight.

Nestra pulled Syteria's hand away from her ribs, then tackled her clothing. A numbing caress spread out from where only seconds before pain had pulsed.

"You need to let my people do their jobs," Galen said from above her.

"I'm sorry, Galen. I'm sorry Anasera got hurt. I tried—"

Nestra's touch re-woke the pain in her cheek.

"I'm sorry, my lady. I must d—"

"It's fine. I'll heal," Syteria said, grabbing at Galen's arm. "Anasera?"

She needed to hear those words from Galen himself, even though it made her feel small about indulging her own fears when he clearly had more reasons to be concerned about his daughter's life.

"Yes, my lady. Anasera will recover," Galen said and pressed his lips into a line like he was holding something back.

"Now," he added, "please, let Nestra treat you."

On her bared abdomen, a large bruise had formed. A rover hovered at the edge of Syteria's vision and painted a blue shimmer across her eyes.

She blinked. The blurriness intensified, tempting her to close her eyes and drift off.

"I can take it from here, Nestra, thank you. Please check on my daughter."

Galen sounded like he was at the bottom of a well, his voice bouncing and echoing off the stone wall. Her eyelids had closed and she couldn't open them they were so heavy.

Nestra also spoke, but she was deeper, farther down that well, and her already soft voice was swallowed by the distance.

Footsteps receded—one, two…three…more…many, many…more. An odd sensation, a surreal type of not-pain, not-pressure, tugged at her abdomen.

Finally, the heaviness of her eyelids receded. She blinked her eyes open. The blue shimmer was still there, although not as intense. The eerie sensation of time lost came and went. It brought with it the return of perception of numbed pain.

"Either the *donai* was tempering his strength," Galen said, "or you were very fortunate, my lady."

"I was thrown," Syteria mumbled. *Flew, really. Right across the room.*

"I meant your cheek. A *donai* can cave in a human's face without even trying."

She closed her eyes against the memory of glowing gold behind amber irises. They'd both had them. The one who'd struck her had bared teeth she'd never seen on a human. She tried to pull herself forward, swatting clumsily at the rover still blurring her vision and mind. It wobbled, dodging her hand. The blue light remained for a second more, then faded.

The bed raised her torso so she was sitting up.

"You are not *donai*?" she asked as her mind cleared.

A wry smile. "No, I'm not. Most of us on the *Edlyn*, in the Imperium, are human."

The revelation jolted her fully awake.

"Another species? Galen, why didn't you tell me?"

"I wanted to make your transition into our world as easy as possible, allow you a little blissful ignorance before you had to find out exactly what we are."

"Galen, I've never found bliss in ignorance."

Sensation returned to her abdomen, along with the reassuring presence of fabric. She touched her injured cheek. There was no pain or tenderness, nothing to indicate swelling, but when Galen tucked an errant hair behind her ear, she flinched.

A curious, paternal look clouded Galen's gray eyes. "Hmm. Did you find bliss in the knowledge you acquired today?"

"All I've learned today is that you think me unworthy of the truth."

He straightened.

"What—" She took a deep breath, expecting pain, but none came. "Who are these *donai*?"

Galen pulled up a seat and sat down beside her. He started to speak a couple of times and stopped himself.

"You must understand," he finally said, "we did this. We didn't want to fight our own wars, risk our own lives, bloody our own hands. So we created a sub-species of disposable soldiers."

He scratched his temple, swiping away a bead of sweat.

"We got caught up in all we could do. We made the *donai* stronger, faster, physically superior in every way. Our enemies were intelligent, so the *donai* had to be *more* intelligent. We found a way to make them loyal as well. It reduced their humanity, but that, too, was to our advantage. It allowed us to think of them as sub-human. Without intending to, we made the *donai* both less, and more, than human."

"But they are still the same species, still...human."

"Human enough to realize their own potential," Galen said, a bitter smile falling into place.

"Human enough," he continued, "to crave freedom and power, to resent the required sacrifices in which they had no say. The *donai* fulfilled their purpose—they eradicated an enemy that would've wiped us out. They were, in a single word, perfect. With our enemies destroyed, we had peace. We had abundance. We had so much control that we no longer worried about the unpleasantness of natural consequences. It gave us too much of the wrong kind of power."

"What happened?" she asked.

"The peace the *donai* won for us had no place for them or what they represented—war, violence, death. They were living, breathing tools with a single purpose: to die fighting. They had no choice—that loyalty we so cunningly wrote into their genetics, made them fight for us, protect us, at all costs. But they had become obsolete. We tried, but could not re-task such a specialized tool, so we ordered them to self-destruct."

Icy understanding swept through her veins.

"They didn't obey that order," she said.

Unlike the *eniseri*, many of whom had obeyed that very order.

"No, they didn't," Galen said, shaking his head. "Humans are no match for the *donai*. We'd been shaped by non-competitive forces for so long..."

Puzzled, she leaned in but stopped short of touching him. She stared at her errant hand.

His gaze followed it as she pulled it back. He sighed and let the quiet linger a moment before clearing his throat.

"Few humans were able to fight," he said, "and many of us were not willing to fight at all, except by proxy, and the *donai* had been our proxies."

"So the humans chose surrender?" Syteria leaned back, repelled.

Her image of these humans changed. They were not as Kappan as she'd thought. Her grandfather would have died fighting. As a child, new to the *eniseri* crèches, she'd fought but succumbed. Her grandfather had never seen what she'd become. She prayed and hoped he forgave her weakness. After all, she had been only a child...

"We chose not just surrender, my lady. We chose slavery."

She sucked in a breath and pulled away. "Humans are slaves here?"

"Yes."

"All humans?"

"Yes," he said.

"Those people I saw by the lake? The crew? *You?*"

"Yes, my lady, all of us."

She stood.

"Galen, something is wrong with your translator. If your people here are slaves, then your definition of slavery is very different from mine." She'd seen no collars, no vacant faces nodding in unison, no voices echoing required speech.

She'd seen nothing to indicate the mistreatment of one group by another. She hadn't even seen groups. Most of all, she didn't want to see them. She didn't want this to be true.

"My lady—"

"Why do you keep calling me that?"

"Please, sit back down. I need to explain."

Perching on the edge of the bed, she folded her hands in her lap and waited.

"House Dobromil is just one of the many smaller powers in the Imperium. The Imperium is the larger, central authority, but the Imperium derives its power from a very limited mandate given to it by the Houses. Most of the power rests with the Houses, but not individually. Do you understand?"

"Yes, but h—"

"The Imperium blames your ship for the destruction of the imperial squadron assigned to protect Thertore—the planet on which you crashed, a planet that belongs to House Kabrin. We, House Dobromil, answered your ship's distress call because House Kabrin—the emperor's House—could not.

"When they found out that you'd survived, they dispatched a ship to pursue us. They made an unauthorized entry into the *Edlyn's* brig. We tried to stop them and a firefight ensued."

"Who is in the brig?" she asked.

"They were looking for you, my lady."

A small, soundless "Oh" formed on her lips.

"When they discovered where you were, they attempted to take you by force."

"They expected you to be holding me as a prisoner, in your brig?"

"Yes."

She locked gazes with him. "Am I a prisoner?"

He stood and straightened his tunic. "*I* would not call you a prisoner, my lady."

"What *would* you call me?"

"A guest."

"Guests can leave when they please," she said.

Her heart was racing now, preparing her body for flight.

"Galen, I would like to leave."

She waited on the answer, terrified at the prospect of not being denied. She had no place to go. Leaving meant abandoning the safest haven she'd ever known. But, if staying meant she'd be a slave, she would flee.

"I will convey your request to my master," Galen said, giving her a shallow, but precise bow. "Where would my lady like to go?"

I want to go home.

But the home her grandfather had built for her no longer existed. At best, "home" meant a death sentence; at worst, Rhoan therapy. They would tear her apart to learn how she'd been reshaped and reborn. Galen's skill and knowledge, *donai* technology, in Rhoan hands... It was unthinkable.

"Nowhere." She whispered it, deflating, wishing she could recall the demand that had prompted the question.

Nowhere was where Aviel was. Where his family was.

Guilt clawed at her soul. It fought with her acceptance of the fact that the *donai* couldn't send her back. Even if they could, she could not risk bringing their technology to Kappa. Her people had fallen so far back technologically that they wouldn't be able to replicate and use it.

She needed more information. Enough to make a meaningful decision.

"Your master," she said. "Tell me about him. Tell me why he's not just turning me over to the Imperium, why he's risking his ship and his people."

"The emperor intends to execute you for landing on Thertore," Galen said, "and for killing the *grierugon*—the monsters that attacked you. Your very existence is compelling evidence of the emperor's questionable activities. Evidence perhaps compelling enough for the Houses to investigate and meddle in his affairs."

Had Syteria not been sitting, her legs would have folded under her. She'd just barely accepted the idea of her own freedom, only to have it torn out of her tentative grasp.

"What does your master gain by preventing my execution?"

"I don't believe he gains anything, my lady."

"Galen, does he gain another slave?" Nausea coiled around her throat at the thought.

"He gains...dominion over you."

She breathed into her hands. Dominion and ownership were not the same, assuming the translation was correct. Frustrated tears pricked her eyes.

"What if I refuse?"

Galen would not meet her gaze. He stared at the pattern his thumb was slowly tracing on his palm.

"If you refuse," Galen said slowly, "he cannot protect you. He is invoking a tradition that ensures your safety and that the emperor is honor-bound to respect. You must understand—you either belong to the emperor, or to him. Being *his* means being safe."

"My freedom means more to me than my safety. Galen, surely you know that."

He nodded.

"You saved me," she continued, voice trembling, "let me have a taste of freedom, only to place me at the mercy of this...this..." She couldn't bring the word to life. Her stomach knotted.

He was so much more than a Rhoan male, or even a Kappan one. That dark, predatory smile, as he baited her. That sonorous echo of a voice as it drew her in. Galen's master embodied everything the Matriarchy had eradicated as it rose to power and everything she'd been taught to hate. Everything she'd been trained to destroy.

"My lady, I only thought to save your life. I didn't realize you'd see this as subjugation."

"What did you think I'd see it as? An honor?" She gave him a scathing look that made his shoulders slump a bit.

"I'm sorry. The ravages of my master's honor were not meant to be borne by a human."

She stood, pushed away from the bio-bed, and paced. Galen waited patiently.

"What is the price for this protection your master bestows on me?" she asked.

She steeled herself for the worst her imagination could conjure. It evoked no specifics, just a turmoil of emotions, like a habit gone awry.

"My master has conveyed only one requi—one request—my lady," Galen said, extending his hand, palm up. "He would have you learn our language."

It brought her to a halt. Staring at the offered hand, she brushed the translator at her ear, making sure it was still there. She made no move to detach it.

"How can I learn if I have no one to talk to?"

"Anasera will continue your lessons and..." he trailed off, fidgeting, tugging at his uniform again.

"What else, Galen? All of it. I want the truth."

"My master does not need a translator."

She crossed her arms. "Why doesn't *he* need a translator?"

"He speaks Rhoan as well as the language files from your ship allow."

The whole of her being froze, denying such absurdity. "That's not possible."

Galen gave her a bland expression that was anything but agreement. Her resentful look did nothing to change his demeanor.

"Can you show me how," she said, "show me the trick he used?"

"Trick?" Galen chuckled. "No trick. Motivation, perhaps. I believe he wants to impress you."

Syteria's fingers carved furrows through her hair until they found the nape of her neck. Galen's motivations appeared simple enough—he was a physician who enjoyed his work, a scientist who enjoyed a challenge. His master, however...

"Why would your master want to impress a slave?" she asked.

Galen studied his hands, as if they held some answer. "Perhaps he considers you worthy."

"Worthy of what, exactly?"

She could not, would not, accept that *he* had a disinterested, selfless concern for her well-being. *He* wasn't like Galen.

"Life," Galen said. "I believe he sees it as his duty to protect one so lost."

It brought her pacing to a halt again. "Galen, I absolve him of his duty. Tell him. I don't want his protection."

"Whether you want it or not, you need it. You are a human with no resources, no allies, and no options. It is dependency that makes you a slave, not my master's desire to protect you."

She sought a rebuttal, but failed to find one.

"Why are you so afraid?" Galen asked.

"I'm not afraid."

His smile was polite, but full of skepticism. "Darien Dayasagar is many things, my lady, but a threat to you he is not. You may take him at his word."

"His word, Galen? What are the words of any male worth?"

His voice intruded. "I don't know what it is worth on Rho, my lady…"

Syteria turned to that blade of a voice.

"…but here, this man's word is the sum of his power, his possessions, his life."

He had entered the room, moving without sound.

The pressure building in her chest threatened to burst.

Galen rose with a curt nod. "My lord."

Fluid motions carried *him* closer.

"Galen, I'm sorry that Anasera was hurt," *he* said. "I didn't think they'd enter the royal wing."

"You expected them to violate House Dobromil's sovereignty," Galen said, "but respect the sanctity of your quarters?"

His quarters?

No. The translator was in error again. It had been damaged. That's why things were no longer making sense.

The *donai's* hands went behind his back as he straightened. "I miscalculated. I'm sorry. It's my fault that Anasera was hurt."

Syteria held her breath at the way Galen spoke to one he called his master and at the way that master admitted to a mistake. It added to the tide of confusion threatening to drown her and cast further doubt on the accuracy of the translation. What master tolerated such tone from a slave?

"She'll be awake in a few hours," Galen said. "I'm sure your apology will mean something to her."

The *donai* made a tight nod of acknowledgment, permitting the familiarity without striking Galen.

"I must apologize to you as well," the *donai* said, turning his attention to her. "Are you fully recovered, my lady?"

Those eyes. So alien with the amber and gold, yet somehow, human as well. Ignoring her tightening throat, she anchored her hands at her sides, tangling them in the folds of her dress.

His gaze flickered to Galen, who'd donned the blandest expression she'd ever seen on anyone. She could expect no help from him. She would have to deal with Galen's master herself.

"I'm not your lady. My name is Syteria."

"I know your name," he replied in an arctic tone. "You are Syteria Kainda, a drudge of the Rhoan Matriarchy, sentenced to terminal therapy for disobeying orders, for—"

"For saving the lives of my brother and his family."

Had such clarity, such conviction come from her own mouth? Where had her fear fled? She waited for an uncontrolled male rage that did not come.

"For an act of honor," he said and the way he said that last word, the power he gave it, made shivers run up her spine.

He closed in, his eyes changing in that strange way that made her wonder if he was somehow appraising her soul once again. A crisp, satisfied nod ended his inspection.

"Did you love your brother?" he asked. "Were you close to him?"

She released the breath burning in her chest. "I have not seen or spoken to him since we were children. I didn't even know he was alive until I was ordered to kill him."

"Does he know of your sacrifice?" he asked, face softening.

"He can't know. It's safer for all of them."

"Does he still live? Did you succeed?" His tone had softened too.

"I don't know. They never told me."

A frown, soft with concern, not harsh with judgement appeared.

171

"You did not ask?" There was no longer an edge behind that velvet smoothness.

"Their answer would be meaningless," she said, "and it would only give them power over me."

A smile tugged at the corners of his mouth.

"I understand this need to deny others power over you," he said. "My lady."

"Don't call me that."

"You cannot shed the title I've bestowed on you any more than you can refuse my protection."

Rho "protected" Kappa as well. For someone who had supposedly learned her language, he couldn't have made a poorer choice of words. She unclenched her fists and took a deep breath.

"I reject your protection. The title. *You,*" she said, aiming the word at him like a weapon.

His breathing quickened. The muscle in his jaw pulsed, but no aborted motion betrayed a desire to strike her.

"A refusal without understanding is meaningless," was all he said.

"Then explain it to me. You're the one who's supposedly mastered Rhoan."

If he'd been made of stone, he couldn't have remained as still.

"I cannot," he said. "This Rhoan language of yours is primitive, incomplete, and inadequate." His voice was strained, the corded muscles of his neck rising against the confines of the tunic's high collar.

"Your language has no concept for"—an error tone sounded, and the groan he made was almost a growl.

Syteria barely stifled an inexplicable laugh. Her language might have been "primitive" by his standards, but it was enough to elicit frustration from the stony façade he presented.

Stoicism fell into place around him, piecemeal, like armor, starting with a stillness in his chest and working its way up to his eyes.

"It is in your interest"—his voice was as devoid of emotion as a machine's—"for your safety, to master Kanthlos as quickly as possible. The translation matrix is incomplete and lacks an adequate depth of meaning. It is also dangerous. Technology fails. The rovers were telling you that help was on the way, that moving Anasera would complicate her injuries."

She flinched backwards as if he had struck her.

"The translator is a crutch," he continued. "One you *will* set aside."

"You must allow m—"

"*You* are in no position to make demands."

She raised her chin and held an amber gaze. This tyrant actually expected her to follow where he led, to respect his word as law, to simply obey. Clearly, he thought of her as just another one of his slaves.

He held out his hand.

She held her ground, not as still as she'd have liked, but a good effort, despite the trembling.

He closed in.

She retreated into a wall as a voice inside her—a Rhoan Matron's voice—shrieked at her to take him down no matter the cost. But no Rhoan Matron had ever set eyes on someone like him. Someone who could cave in a human's skull without realizing it. Someone who stood so still despite the power he could wield.

Her hands slipped behind her, her weight pinning them against the pearlescent surface. Blood drained from her face, but she held his gaze.

With a steadiness she did not feel, she said, "Without a translator, I can't—"

His hand slipped behind her ear, halting briefly at her earlobe. Blood roared, pulsing the pain in her jaw. The translator detached. Fire rushed back into her face.

He leaned in.

"Learn," he whispered in Rhoan.

As he lingered, her heart drummed out a rising rhythm.

The translator's fractured remains slipped from his fingers, dusting her dress. He pulled away, gaze still on her, and spoke in Kanthlos. Galen's response was too brief to be anything but acknowlededgment.

"Galen will destroy the remaining devices," the tyrant said in

Rhoan as perfect as if he'd been born to it. "To remove any temptation."

Her fingers curled, finding unyielding resistance in the wall at her back.

"This is not about temptation," she said. "It is about power."

The corners of his lips curled, making her regret her boldness as he leaned in again.

She didn't wilt, or shrink from him—didn't run. But she was shaking. Galen was right. She *was* afraid.

His breath was an elemental force swirling in her ear. "You're wrong you know. You tempt me."

Shivers raced up her spine.

Her gaze trailed the tyrant's shadow, the query, *What do you mean?* lingering unvoiced on her lips.

~

DARIEN RETURNED TO HIS DESK.

His weapons—parchment, pen, dagger—glimmered under the light. He removed the ceremonial blade from its scabbard. The simple sheath, with its watermarked design, housed an exquisite blade with a nanometer edge.

Tradition had once placed it into his grasp moments after birth, seconds after his father had used it to cut his umbilical.

Tradition made claiming this human woman his first official act. He laughed out loud and set the dagger aside.

Strength. Courage. Mastery. Honor.

Those simple words framed the wolf's head sigil embossed into the parchment.

You need never touch her, Galen had said.

He'd had to allow the emperor's *donai* to touch her first, to hurt her. Despite the injuries she'd suffered at their hands, despite her pain, she'd responded as if she'd been made for him.

Even now the memory of that all too brief touch stoked his desire. The danger had passed, but his protective nature refused to retreat to its dormant state. Galen was right. A claim was the only way to protect her.

He coded and activated the parchment for writing by breathing on its surface. Pen touched paper.

Tradition. *That's* the word that should've preceded the others in House Dobromil's motto.

At one time, the peculiarities of *donai* traditions had seemed frivolous. They had been no more than an amusing collection of anachronisms and affectations.

But not anymore.

Pressing one's thumb to a form on a screen was *the* truly frivolous gesture.

It was the act of inking the claim with his own hand that gave it true meaning. Each breath, each stroke made by his pen, each skin cell he shed as he wrote, authenticated his authorship.

He gave form to the required words, the ones that expressed the proper gratitude for the emperor's generosity, as if Kabrin had granted him a precious gift. In spite of the manuscript's perfect form, it still felt like a confession written by a thief and would be read like a declaration of war, but protocol had been observed. Tradition had been honored.

It was with such fragile things that he bound the emperor's hands… and his own.

Darien added his name and title, set the pen aside, and considered his creation. There was so much power in this arcane act. These were not mere symbols on a form, not words written for him by someone else, not ambiguities subject to interpretation.

They were oath and pledge and promise, and they were…unrealized.

She was an alluring combination of courage and vulnerability.

His first impulse had been to sweep her off her feet and carry her to the infirmary himself. She would have fought him. Of this, he had no doubt. His impulse would have resulted in a dangerous precedent.

Galen was correct. The emperor would have seen—might still see —his claim as a move away from his father and towards the Imperium.

Darien unsheathed the dagger. Once his blood touched the sensors embedded in the parchment, the markers in his blood would code and lock its surface.

He held the blade's edge to his thumb, used its unforgiving sharpness to keep the cut open long enough for a single drop to land on the parchment. Sparks raced across its surface, flashing along the edges as nanites encoded the data for final authentication.

He rolled the parchment and slipped it into a narrow canister. An intricately etched helical pattern decorated its red, enameled surface.

He ran his thumb along the seams, sealing it...and their fate.

CHAPTER SEVENTEEN

*P*alleton adjusted his ship fatigues as he exited the tunnel leading into the *Edlyn's* brig. It was dark, thanks to the trigger-happy imperials, but he didn't need light to make his way to the one remaining operational cell.

The cells ringed an open space set at normal gravity and pressure. A turret protruded from the ceiling. Its muzzle was askew and its casing battered. A strong-smelling industrial lubricant, its scent intense and metallic, dripped into a puddle on the deck. Faint heat images strobed across the bulkheads and decking, indicating that automated repairs were underway.

The scent of scorched metal competed with that of scorched flesh, a remnant from the firefight that had injured eight members of the crew. Bomani had locked the imperial craft in the hangar, containing its *donai*, except for Kailin Kabrin. The whelp whose lineage somehow crossed that of the emperor's was the guest of honor in the *Edlyn's* brig.

Kailin was sprawled on the deck of the sunken cell, crushed and held in place by gravity ten times the norm. The temperature was at the extreme of *donai* tolerance as well. His rasping breaths condensed above a face covered in a mask of frost. Likewise, every exposed part of him was bluing, then pinking, as his body caught up with repairs, only to be overwhelmed again. It was more than an unpleasant sensation and according to the monitors, he was at the very edge of what was considered safe.

The whites of his eyes bloomed with blood as he shifted his gaze to meet Palleton's. His throat worked, but made no sound—the pressure was too low.

Palleton pressed his hand to the control panel and entered a code. Atmosphere rushed into the cell. Gravity loosened its hold. The prisoner gulped down greedy breaths. His chest heaved up, the uniform crackling with frost. He wrapped his hand around his throat and speared Palleton with a baleful glare.

"Now, now," Palleton said, "you should be thanking me. I had to talk my master out of the far worse things he had in mind for you."

Kailin pushed up from the deck, the evidence of his suffering fading as he healed.

Ah, the benefits of youth. There was little that Palleton envied in his fellow *donai* but their youth.

Despite the physical healing, Kailin's pride was, no doubt, an open wound prone to festering. Thoughts of slinking back to the emperor with nothing but failure might cloud the youth's judgment and lead him into further recklessness.

Palleton would never have allowed House Dobromil to send someone so inexperienced on a delicate task requiring finesse rather than ego and a pedigree.

"Out," Palleton ordered as the force field dropped.

Kailin straightened his tunic and climbed the stair with dignity. "Where are you taking me?"

"My master's cut has improved your voice," Palleton said, moving out of the way. "You no longer sound like a pup."

"Your master still kneels before mine. Don't forget that," Kailin said as he strolled out with a swagger more fitting of a man who'd been invited to dinner than one who'd just been released from torturous restraints.

"I'm not the one who forgot my place," Palleton said as his palm landed between the whelp's shoulder blades, breaking Kailin's arrogant stride.

Kailin spun, regaining his balance. Walking backwards, he spat insolently onto the deck.

"Does House Dobromil intend to go to war over a human?" Kailin asked, wiping that last word from his mouth with a swipe of his sleeve.

Palleton closed the gap between them, grabbed Kailin's lapels and hoisted him up for an instant before sending him sprawling to the deck.

"This isn't about the human, whelp! The *Edlyn* is sovereign territory. Our laws apply, not House Kabrin's."

Kailin bared his teeth, but stayed down.

Palleton pulled a message baton from his tunic and tossed it at the young *donai*.

Kailin caught it as he got up. "What's this?"

"Diplomatic communique for your master, errand boy."

"House Kabrin will not accept a written apology. Your master must offer a formal apology, in person."

Palleton's mirthless laughter echoed in the dark, narrow tunnel. "It's not an apology. It's the data from the alien ship; everything to which your master is legally entitled, compliments of Lord Dobromil."

Kailin cast the baton aside. It clattered along the deck as he ignored it in favor of making a great show of wiping residue off his tunic.

"I take no direction from your half-breed master, or his sire."

Palleton donned his most menacing leer. "I was so hoping you'd say that."

"Wait! What?" Kailin squeaked as he backed away, face reddening.

"It takes twenty-five days for a bod-pod to reach the nearest life-sustaining world between here and Kanavar. Imagine it," Palleton said, advancing.

Kailin backed away.

"Twenty-five days of helplessness," Palleton continued, "floating in the darkness with nothing to do, without communication of any kind, hoping your pod wasn't sabotaged, hoping you don't run out of air, hoping nothing knocks you off-course, hoping your beacon doesn't fail, hoping the pod hits atmo just right so you don't burn up."

The instinctive retreat made Kailin hit the bulkhead hard.

"Or worse," Palleton said, pressing his advantage, "you could get shot down. You'll be flashing House Dobromil's sign so you'll never know if it was friend or foe that ended you. And if you make it to the surface, you'll be armed with just your 'wits.' "

"You can't do this to us," Kailin said. "The nearest world is Thertore."

He slid along the bulkhead, edging out of Palleton's threatening reach.

"Oh no, there is no *us*. Just you. Alone." Palleton's finger pinned Kailin to the bulkhead. "You're the one who chose to violate our sovereignty, the one responsible for insult to our House. Don't you understand the burdens of command?"

"What about my men?" Kailin asked, somehow managing an even pitch.

"Your men will wait for the diplomats to work matters out through the appropriate channels. Slow workers, those diplomats."

Kailin sniffed and puffed out his chest. "House Kabrin may not go to war over a human, but they will go to war over me."

"Over someone who doesn't understand the most basic protocols, who thinks his name is the only protection he needs?" Palleton asked, eyebrows rising. "I'm willing to bet that House Kabrin will thank us for culling you before your arrogance got someone valuable killed. I hear House Kabrin is overrun with your kind. You won't be missed."

The muscles in Kailin's jaw twitched.

Palleton grinned at the confirmation that he'd hit a nerve. This member of House Kabrin wasn't as important as he'd made himself out to be. He'd overstepped his authority.

"And if I agree to deliver the data?"

"It serves my master's interests to place that data"—Palleton said, pointing at the discarded communique on the deck—"and his claim, in the emperor's possession as soon as possible."

He allowed Kailin a moment to pretend he had a choice.

"Very well," Kailin said.

He ducked defensively, retrieved the message cylinder, and tucked it away.

"That's what I thought."

Palleton grunted as he reached into his tunic again.

"Inform all pursuing imperial craft that House Kabrin no longer has dominion over the survivor. Make it very clear. We will regard any attempt to board us as a hostile act."

Palleton presented the second message baton with proper formality, raised on the flat of his palm and accompanied by a precisely angled bow.

Kailin snatched it, held it up so it caught some of the low light. He studied the helical pattern etched into the enameled surface with undeserved intensity.

"I've never seen one," Kailin said.

"A claim?"

"No, a coup de grâce."

Kailin's fist tightened on the cylinder as he lowered it and pointed it at Palleton's broad chest.

"House Dobromil is weak and wounded," Kailin said. "It will be my pleasure and my honor to deliver this, the finishing blow that ends your House."

DARIEN WAITED IN SILENCE, lingering in the entry to Galen's domain. Despite the late hour, Galen was tending to his two patients by himself. He moved with the lagging motions of the weary, rubbing at his eyes and dragging his hand through his hair.

The woman Darien had claimed was asleep on a bed not far from the reconstruction unit where Anasera lay. She still looked deathly still, despite the color in her face.

Galen dimmed the lights and dispatched a rover. It rose and hovered above the woman in the half-dark. Its weak glow framed her face in soft, red light, as she slept on her side, hand pillowing her cheek.

Darien took a step inside and cleared his throat.

Galen looked up and joined him a moment later.

"Is it done?" Darien asked, his voice flat and quiet.

"Can't you tell?"

"Not from here."

"Perhaps you should get closer then," Galen said.

"No."

"Then I'll ask Palleton, or one of the other *donai*, to verify it for me," Galen said, moving away.

Darien grabbed Galen's arm and pulled him back.

"I'll do it," Darien said as he allowed Galen to shake himself free.

Vision shifting, he approached the woman. Tendrils of flowing light coursed through her body, wrapping themselves in patterns that swirled around the twin beacons of heart and brain.

"She sleeps," Darien whispered, speaking with lips gone dry.

"I thought she deserved a night of rest and peace," Galen said, his voice so hushed Darien could barely hear him.

"Anasera said she refused a sleep field."

"She did."

"But you're using one anyway," Darien said.

"*I* didn't give her a choice."

Darien cast him a sideways glance.

"My patient, my infirmary, my rules."

"She chose to stay?"

"Let's just say she refused to return to *your* quarters," Galen said.

"We can't allow *that* to stand."

"Allowing her to stay here for a few days would let me work on alleviating some of her nightmares, perhaps even some of her people's draconian conditioning. I'd appreciate it if you didn't push the issue. Let me do some good, for her sake."

"Her being in your care, in the infirmary… " Darien took a deep breath. "That too could work to our advantage."

"Not yet," Galen said. "We have to establish that she's pregnant first so your *donai* can swear to it, if need be."

Darien gave him a tight nod. "I can hear Anasera's heartbeat. Yours. Hers."

"Nothing else?"

Darien shook his head, frowning.

"Good," Galen said. "It hasn't been six weeks."

"Six weeks?"

"That's how long it takes for a human child's heart to start beating."

A sharp sensation pierced Darien's chest and faded to a dull ache. "How close will the *donai* have to get?"

"Closer than this, at least once the implant starts mimicking a heartbeat. As the beats strengthen, the *donai* will be able to hear it from greater distances."

"How long do I have?"

"I can push the heartbeat out five, six, weeks at most. Maybe a little longer given the hybrid nature of your hypothetical offspring. Once it starts, it will mimic one as long as necessary, but I suggest no more than twelve weeks."

"Why twelve?"

"After that you'll need Syteria's cooperation to continue the ruse," Galen said.

Darien shook his head at Galen's word choice. Why not call it what it was? The lie. The fraud. The treason.

"We'll be on Serigala by then," Darien said. "I will have had a chance to explain things to my father."

"Have you considered telling Lord Dobromil the truth?"

"Our communications are compromised. I trust no courier to deliver such condemning words and I dare not implicate my father in this. He must have deniability should he need to separate House Dobromil's reputation from mine."

Whether it was to separate himself from a son thought to have violated a woman or one who'd defied the emperor, he owed it to his father.

Galen sighed. "What do you intend to do?"

"Keep my distance. Bide my time. As you said, I need never touch her," Darien said as his hands tightened into fists, "Once she's out of the Imperium's reach…"

"I see how you look at her," Galen said.

"Good. It lends credibility to my claim."

Galen cleared his throat. "Have you considered perfecting your claim?"

He had. Humans were such prolific creatures. They were the key to *donai* survival. They were the only way to bring fertility back into the *donai* genome.

He'd been fortunate. He'd not only survived, but inherited enough *donai* traits to thrive and to lead. For it to mean anything, he would have to pair-bond with one of his own kind, not a human. The few *donai* traits he might pass onto any human's child might be enough for it to survive, but not to thrive.

"See to it she learns our language, our ways."

Galen nodded and made a polite sound of acknowledgement.

The original plan was sound—a pretend pregnancy followed by a pretend miscarriage. Even if, in the eyes of some, it cast him into the role of rapist, it was worth it to save her life. It was enough to allow his father to use her mysterious origin as a weapon against the emperor.

"And keep her out of my way," Darien said.

CHAPTER EIGHTEEN

*G*alen waited for Anasera's jaw to snap shut. She was still wearing a patient gown, mostly because he'd insisted that she spend another day under observation. Reluctantly, she'd agreed. He'd been relieved, not just at her physical recovery, but that her personality had remained intact.

That is, until now.

He'd just finished briefing her on what had happened while she recovered. She had taken up pacing, eyes focused intently on the deck below her slippered feet, her teeth gnawing gently on her lower lip. Her long hair trailed loose behind her, swirling at each pivot along with the length of the gown.

Galen sat back down into the comfort of the chair he'd dozed in the night before, giving in to the fatigue that had been wearing him down. There had been a few moments during Anasera's surgery when he'd thought they might lose her. Guilt had snuck past his clinical defenses, allowing emotion to take hold.

When he and Darien had laid out the plan to provoke the imperials, Galen had known there would be risks. But they had both thought those risks would be borne by those tasked to stop the imperials.

As he'd watched Anasera's life ebb and flow under his hands he'd wished he would've told her the plan and prepared her. He'd thought it would be safer for her not to know, not to be involved in the treason that came with a false claim.

"This is my fault," Anasera said.

He perked up, blinking heavy lids. "How in the world is this *your* fault?"

"I'm the one that begged Darien not to turn Syteria over to the Imperium. I didn't think he was going to put his honor on the line to save her."

"I think Bomani and I share at least some of the blame," he said.

"But I'm the one that pushed him." She shook her head and placed her hands on her hips. "Pushed him right over the brink."

"Darien has always been his own man. Ultimately, it was always his decision."

"He should have told me."

"He couldn't have. It would've—"

"Yes, yes," she said, waving her hand dismissively. "For my own safety. Didn't you think I'd have to know eventually? That you'd need me to keep your little secret?"

He took a deep breath. "I wasn't sure he was going to do it. Not until he did, and by then…" He turned up his palms with the barest shrug.

She rolled her eyes and her hands traveled up to her neck where they laced together for a handful of steps. At the pivot she swept her hair forward, wrestling it into the beginnings of a braid.

"What about Syteria?" she asked. "How are you going to make her understand?"

"I'm not."

She came to a halt, casting a punishing glare.

Galen steepled his fingers together and cocked his head.

"Father, have you looked at this from Syteria's perspective, even for a moment?"

"What should I have done? Asked her if she'd rather be turned over to the Imperium to be tortured and killed? Perhaps shown her some of our recorded history so that she would have nightmares whenever she looked at or thought of the *donai*. How would that serve Darien's purpose?"

"Darien's purpose? I thought this was about Syteria's survival."

"They are not separate issues, Anasera. Either she belongs to him or she belongs to the emperor. Where would *you*, or any woman, rather be?"

"All right," she said. "I see your point, but there is still that issue with the couple in the park. I don't think the Rhoans share our mating practices."

"It does not change the stakes. The emperor will tear her apart, mind, body, and soul, to learn where she is from. The truth that she does not know will not matter. It will only make tearing her apart more enticing."

Her lingering silence conceded his point.

"I don't think she'll understand what it means to be claimed by Darien," she finally said, finishing off the ends of the braid and looping it around itself at the base of her neck until it made a fist-sized knot.

"I told her it was for her protection. So did he."

"This ship"—she aimed a finger at the deck before returning her hand to her hip—"is all she has seen of our society. It is but a very small window into a more dangerous world. One she will not be able to truly comprehend for years.

"She does not have the capacity to understand the difference between being a slave and belonging to him. And the lack of an actual child in her womb means that the pair-bond that protects a *donai's* concubine won't be there. Do you not see how much this could go awry?"

"Oh, I'm quite aware. Darien's last words to me were to keep her out of his way."

She raised her eyebrows. "Keeping her out of the way is not an option. That is not how pair-bonded mates behave. The *donai* will become suspicious. And if they find out he lied about a claim, a component of that precarious balance that allows them to remain in control of their own destinies..."

He smiled. It stopped her in her tracks. Her dark gaze demanded an answer.

"The implant will do more than mimic a child's heartbeat. She will smell pregnant to the *donai*, including Darien. And in turn, her scent will make him act just like they were pair-bonded."

The profanity spilling from her mouth was lengthy and impressive. He waited for her to finish, a self-satisfied grin on his face.

"You think you've thought of everything, don't you?" she added.

He made an unapologetic shrug.

"What happens when his instinct kicks in? When he's drawn to his pregnant concubine? When he's driven to mate with her as often as he can to strengthen the pair-bond?"

"I seem to recall how much you enjoyed Miquelon's attentions while you were pregnant. How much you both rejoiced at the birth of your son. How much you despaired when, despite enthusiastic attempts, you were unable to conceive again."

"But I chose Miquelon. What did you tell Syteria? Did you ask her if she wanted a *donai* for a mate? Did you explain to her what it would mean to be *his* concubine?"

He shifted uncomfortably. "Darien ordered the translators destroyed before I had a chance to explain."

"Which means we can't even tell her that everyone around her will think she's pregnant?" She bit her lip. "Perhaps I can show her some images. Pantomime the—"

"I wouldn't advise that," he said darkly. "In fact, I forbid it."

"Why? She deserves—"

"We don't know how she'd react. If she betrays him, she betrays us, and herself."

Anasera drew in and let out a pained breath. He stood and drew her into an embrace.

"I know this is going to be hard for her. But there is so much more at stake here than her bruised feelings. We need to let it play out. A pretend pregnancy. A pretend miscarriage. House Dobromil's honor is at stake here, not just Darien's."

"Yes, I know." She pushed him away, looking up into his eyes as she did so. "You've tied all our fates to this."

He narrowed his eyes in question.

"Let's say that by some phenomenal piece of luck," she said, voice trembling, "Syteria enjoys Darien's attentions, gives in to them, conceives and bears a child to term. A human child. Will we suffer the same fate as House Hevonen? What will happen to us when Kabrin kills Lord Dobromil, and Darien? When he demands that all of Dobromil's vassals put their human children and the women who bore them to death as proof of their loyalty? What happens when Miquelon and the other *donai* refuse? I'll tell you, what happens, Father. The emperor will kill everyone—*donai* and human, adults and children."

Her eyes had filled with tears. They sparkled in the light. He used his thumb to sweep them off her face as they trailed down the sides of her cheeks.

"You must be missing your husband and son terribly. We've been gone for far too long and it doesn't look like Darien is in any hurry to return while his actions could compromise his father. Would you like to go home?"

She sniffed and pulled away. "No."

"Why not?"

"I can't abandon Darien now."

"You would not be abandoning him," Galen said.

"I will go if you let me take Syteria with me."

"I doubt that Darien will agree to that."

"Why not?" she asked. "She'd be safer on Serigala."

"If she were pregnant, yes. Lord Dobromil would protect her for the sake of his grandchild."

"But not for her own sake?"

He shook his head, a hard line coming unbidden to his lips.

"He is not like Darien, and I don't think you see Darien as clearly as you should either. There is more to being human than having a human parent. You still see him as the little boy you grew up with. Before his *donai* traits and augmentations manifested, he was merely an amber-eyed

189

adolescent obsessed with being *donai*. Now he is *donai*. And with each passing year he becomes more like them and less like us. We have very little time left to cement what's left of his humanity. Do you not see it?"

"All I see is a good man."

"Then make sure Syteria sees the same."

DARIEN WALKED through the drying field too quickly for it to do its job. Dampness lingered on his skin and in his hair as he emerged from the utilitarian facility attached to his flag cabin. His refreshed uniform waited, as crisp as the first time he'd ever worn it. He was still working the clasps at his throat when he entered his flag cabin.

Bomani stood.

He gestured for her to retake her seat as he gathered his hair.

"Roughing it?" she asked.

He ignored the teasing lilt of her tone as he stepped into his boots. They molded around his feet, anchoring themselves neatly around his trousers.

"The imperials are gone," she said.

"Your point, Commander?"

"Darien, your domestic arrangements are—"

"Not your concern," he said, crossing to his desk. He loomed over its glossy surface, frowning at the contents of the latest reports. "Have you identified the source of the unauthorized transmissions?"

"No," she said.

"Then, the likelihood of a spy aboard the *Edlyn* remains."

She gave him a fractional nod and cleared her throat. "The imperial ship is no longer within sensor range, and I've increased our internal sensor sweeps and tightened our containment procedures."

He nodded absently.

"My lord, I'd like your permission to question everyone who hasn't taken their fealty oaths."

His gaze snapped to hers. "Not everyone."

"I've read Anasera's reports as well. The survivor is hiding something."

"Perhaps you should be reading Galen's reports instead, specifically the ones that show the warm corpse we brought back from Thertore. Do you really believe anyone would allow themselves to be butchered like that on the off-chance that she'd be rescued by us?"

"She wouldn't have to be a willing spy," Bomani said, bracing herself. "Have you already lost sight of your reasons for saving her?"

Had he? Answering her ship's distress call had been duty and honor. And tactic. Her presence had revealed a spy among them. He would put her to use as a catalyst if necessary. His decision to stay away from her had dulled the infatuation that had taken hold of him. It still lingered, present in unguarded moments, in stray thoughts...

"I have not," he said.

CHAPTER NINETEEN

*S*yteria woke with a start.

The pain wasn't real.

Her hands were immaculate, in both form and appearance. The consequences of her disobedient nature no longer embellished their surface.

When the Rhoans had deadened her flesh and she could no longer feel pain, they'd moved elsewhere, allowing the nerves to heal so they'd be receptive again. Had they not needed her hands they would've crippled them as punishment. But a drudge needed her hands.

Here, she was anything but a drudge...

Here, she slept alone on a bed larger than the rooms in which Kappan families huddled together for warmth.

Here, luxurious tangling sheets snared her body.

She shook off their silken embrace with sudden violence, as if they were the talons of the Rhoan dragon that haunted her nightmares. Standing beside the bed, she leaned on one of the posts that curved up towards its center. The soaring ceiling looked like a starry sky obscured by drifting, whisper-thin clouds.

There was no malevolent Rhoan eye. Still, she couldn't shake the sensation that something was wrong. She was in the wrong place, in the wrong time, living someone else's life.

The nightmare had caught her by surprise. A few nights of restful sleep in Galen's infirmary had lulled her into that deep slumber that made dream a prey to nightmare.

The nightmares had returned and with them the reality that she was as much a prisoner as she was a guest.

Guests can leave when they please.

The echo of those words carried her across the room as she pulled on the sleeping gown, a flowing, gossamer thing of pinks and lavenders that left her arms bare. It swirled around her ankles as she stopped just inside the threshold. The doors yawned open and she stuck her head into the corridor.

No guards.

She'd never seen any. But they wouldn't need to be visible. The *donai* could watch and track her in secret, just like—if not better—than the Rhoans.

She stepped through.

No snare field embraced and held her in its blue light.

Her hands clenched against her collarbones, expecting the warning from her *eniseri* collar. She swallowed, feeling the weight of a device her hands insisted was not there. Although wrapping hands around the collar to lessen the shocks never worked, everyone did it. A meager, ineffective defiance was better than nothing at all.

She strode through empty corridors.

Broke into a run.

Continued even when it drew the gazes and interest of people she passed.

It was the wrong thing to do.

She ran faster.

Ran until everything streaked by her in an incoherent, unknowable blur.

Someone hailed her, his voice fading. She knew it was only a matter of time before they brought her to ground.

She kept running. Just like before…

Aviel had run too. Her twin brother had been shorter then, his stride just a bit narrower. She'd slowed to grab his hand. He'd stumbled and drawn her down with him. They'd rolled down the hill and come to a stop at the bottom of a gully overgrown with moss and bracken.

When she'd come to, Aviel was no longer beside her. Frantic, she'd searched for him, digging through the thorny bushes until her arms and hands bled.

Eyes had appeared within the foliage. Cruel eyes in a face streaked with mottled greens and browns. She'd backed away, but the rest of the *eniseri* monster emerged from the trees. The *eniseri* reached out and snatched her.

Impact knocked the air out of lungs.

She had bounced off a broad chest.

A man wearing the *Edlyn's* uniform spoke to her in a soothing voice, like she was an animal in need of gentling. She backed away. He approached her slowly, a frown creeping onto his face. His voice had that lilt that one used with a child...or an idiot.

She surged, aiming for his chin, intending to snap his head back.

Her palm made contact with his raised forearm, the impact of his block reverberating back along her arm. Shifting her balance, she jerked her knee to his middle.

He swept her feet out from under her, rolled her, and drove her face-first into the deck.

Syteria snarled, struggling under a reluctant hold. He spoke again, urgent this time. The moment his weight shifted off her back, she scrambled up and ran, rounding one corner, then another.

A stumble forced her to slow and take stock. This part of the ship was unfamiliar to her. Utilitarian. Functional. No opulence. More like a spaceship, less like a palace. There were no courtyards, flowers, or waterfalls.

She stole a glance around the corner, expecting her pursuer to appear. Alone or with reinforcements, it didn't matter how they dealt with her.

But no one pursued.

She took off again, down a massive tunnel with glass-slick walls and a mirrored floor that should've been as slippery as ice. In she went, running towards the gleaming light that burned brighter as she approached. The tunnel opened right into a cavernous chamber.

There was a chill to the hangar. It cradled ships to its soaring walls. They nestled together in branched clusters, their brown and gray metals gleaming.

Glancing behind her, she climbed spiraling steps leading to a cluster of ships. She expected a small army at any moment, but none of the armored *donai*, nor their human counterparts emerged from the tunnel.

Her hand strayed up to her neck again, feeling for the collar and finding nothing. It halted her, that absence, that lack of weight and the pain that usually came with it.

With another glance over her shoulder, she took a chance and touched her palm to the woodgrain-metal skin of the ship. This simple gesture had brought many things to life in the infirmary.

The hatch flicked aside, leaving her hand hanging in mid-air. She ducked inside. Instrument panels and a seat formed out of the pearly interior. She lowered herself into the seat. It squirmed around her, embracing her as holograms activated in the space where a cockpit console should've been. The hatch flicked closed again.

A disembodied voice posed a question she didn't know how to answer.

Her heart raced, thundering again, aware now of her mistake.

All but one of the holograms blinked out of existence.

The words and tone of the repeating question did not change.

Insistent and threatening, the remaining hologram pulsed with each repetition.

Words caught in her throat. She couldn't bring herself to name Rho as her destination. As futile as it was, she said, "Kappa."

The hologram collapsed into a crimson dot. It blinked against the background of the hangar and its ships, all dormant in their berths, like seedpods waiting to be hurled upon the wind and on to some chance destination.

The crimson dot changed from one cryptic symbol to the next, swirling angrily from one iteration to another.

She reached out to touch it, but pulled back at the last second. Such folly. Such utter foolishness. She knew nothing about their ships or their navigational systems. She couldn't even read their symbols.

The crimson dot faded.

A thousand pearly beads come at her from all directions. They hit her at the same time, combining into a wet sheet around her.

She fought the irrational sensation that she was falling and refused to yield to panic even as she clutched the armrests and darkness surrounded her.

The hatch zipped open and the ship spit her out onto the deck, drenched and dripping something thick and so viscous its sinewy strands tugged at her limbs. It limited her mobility, stuck to her face, and invaded her mouth and nose.

Every breath was like inhaling sand. She coughed a lungful of the substance right onto the deck. As soon as it hit, it sublimated, leaving only a thin layer of powder behind.

Hands gripped her arms, hauling her upward.

She caught a brief glimpse of the man that had tackled her before. His face was hard now, no longer set on gentling her. She wanted to strike out, but her body refused to obey. She couldn't even keep her eyes open much less stand or struggle.

As the disorientation of falling eased, she realized that they were taking her back.

Along the way, the viscous membrane crisped and bits of it fell away. Eventually, the thickness on her eyelids lifted and she could blink again.

The utilitarian decking of the ship gave way to marble.

The pattern of the stone was wrong though. She tried to lift her legs so she could walk on her own. Her mumbled demands resulted only in choking as she inhaled the powder. She wanted to swipe it off her face.

The henchmen deposited her in front of a large, curved desk. She landed with more of a squelch than a thud.

Syteria pushed up, snapping the drying tendrils of the incapacitating substance. She rose from the one-kneed crouch she'd maneuvered into. Her venomous looks bounced off the henchmen.

Their attention was on *him*, their lord and master, the tyrant that ruled them all. The henchmen's faces were blank, wearing the masks of guards merely doing their duty. She'd donned that ill-fitting mask herself in the past.

The tyrant spoke, low and soft, over hands folded in front of him, as he leaned forward on the desk.

His gaze never left her as the man who'd tried to stop her spoke at length, no doubt recounting the incident. The man's stiff demeanor held no pride, but his tone wasn't just deferential; it was cautious. He finished with a curt bow.

The tyrant rose. His unnatural calm would've made the hair on the back of her neck rise if it'd been dry enough. Her skin crawled as the residue cracked and slid off her body.

What must she look like? Something partially chewed and spit out with distaste. Why did her appearance even matter all of a sudden?

She braced herself with a deep lungful of air. The insidious powder had sloughed off, its passage itching as it dropped to the floor.

He rounded the desk to stand in front of her. A terse order and the men who'd brought her here withdrew.

Syteria pushed wet strands off her face. Weighed down and still dripping, they flopped right back with a wet sound and stuck to her cheeks.

With his arms across his chest, his biceps bulged, stretching the fabric of his uniform. The tyrant was the very image of menace practicing self-restraint.

He spoke again, but not to her. Another one of his henchmen—the wall-sized aristocrat—emerged from the shadows and responded with a grumble.

In oppressive silence, *he* studied her.

The tyrant was a resounding contrast to all she'd become. Every hair on his head was obediently tucked away into a clasp at the back of his neck. He wore a crisp, white shirt with precise lines and seams that looked like they had been placed to accentuate his physique. His uniform jacket was no doubt neatly standing at attention somewhere, waiting on him. If she moved in closer she'd probably see her reflection in his boots.

"Exactly where did you think you were going?" the tyrant asked in Rhoan.

Would an admission that she hadn't been thinking, but reacting, that she'd been foolish and naïve, earn her anything worth the humiliation of admitting she'd acted stupidly?

"I thought that guests could leave whenever they pleased."

Her bitter tone earned a frown and a brief flash of golden light that flickered in his eyes.

"Whatever made you think you were a guest?"

Her breath caught. They *had* treated her as such but the admission remained unspoken. *He* smiled, as if it had been his intent to bring her to this very realization.

"So I am your prisoner."

"We should like to treat you as an honored guest," he said, "but you seem intent on demanding a cage instead. Shall I have one set up for you? Escape is impossible because you have nowhere to go and I cannot allow you to leave, but the choice is yours."

"Cage or not, both choices reveal what you are."

"And what is that?" he asked.

His voice was as measured as ever, but its hard edge made it sound like anger sat at its core.

"A slaver," she said.

She must've hit a nerve. He went still. The henchman made a comment that drew the tyrant's gaze. It sent a creeping chill down her spine and it wasn't even directed at her. The tone of *his* reply pulsed with unmasked anger. So did the henchman's.

Syteria balled her hands into fists. She'd never cared for being a subject openly discussed as if her presence didn't matter.

"Have you not been treated well?" the tyrant asked.

She had been. Perhaps too well. Despite how she'd been treated, she still didn't understand their motives.

You mustn't trust them, the Rhoan drudge inside her insisted, bringing to the surface all the fear and hatred the Matrons had taught her. A halting breath silenced the inner voice.

Since she had nothing to offer the *donai*, or their humans, there was no reason for this false courtesy, this façade.

"Even so," she said, "the unpalatable truth remains."

The tyrant's demeanor, that core of controlled anger, did not change. He spoke to someone over the intercom as he held her gaze.

She dared not look away as she waited. Soon enough she would know how they punished escape attempts. The source of the henchman's anger would be revealed. They couldn't question her in their own language. They'd have to return her translator. An interrogation without it would be mere torture.

A terrible thought intruded: unlike the Rhoans, they could take her to the brink of death...and then heal her. And they could do it over and over again.

The doors whispered open behind her. She swallowed the lump that had formed in her throat.

Anasera's gentle voice startled her and Syteria almost folded at the sound of it.

Anasera's eyes blazed, her dark gaze darting between the two *donai*. The henchman crossed his arms at the tone of Anasera's "my lord" while the tyrant remained a looming statue in front of Syteria.

And then Anasera was standing between them, blocking *his* gaze, freeing her from *his* power. She looked disheveled, with a face framed by hair thrown over one shoulder and bound loosely with a ribbon. A dark sleeping robe wrapped around her and her feet were bare.

Syteria shrank back from Anasera's touch. She relented when she realized that the motion was only an attempt to guide her out.

Syteria stopped at the junction leading to the infirmary.

"Are you hurt?" Anasera asked.

At least that's what she thought Anasera said. Syteria shook her head. Maybe they didn't use their medical facilities in the same ways as the Rhoans. The muscles along her shoulders and neck tightened anew. Perhaps the brig was farther down, but why call for Anasera?

Because they'd made a calculated guess that she'd go quietly with her friend.

Anasera put her arm around Syteria's shoulders, speaking in gentle tones full of concern. The space between her eyes furrowed with frustration as she herded Syteria towards—

Her breath caught. Anasera was leading her back to her—no, *his*—quarters. The ones he never used. The ones that were exclusively hers.

She would have preferred a cage. At least a cage didn't pretend to be anything it wasn't.

And an animal confined too long paced its length even when that cage was gone.

IN HIS FLAG CABIN, Darien stood, wrapped in multiple layers of holographic reports. Hand motions dispatched them to their next stop or queued them to be dealt with later. The latest intelligence reports being dispersed through Dobromil's territory were already out of date by the time they got to him. Speculations on Court politics meant just as little.

And still, nothing from his father. He was being left to deal with his own mess, a measure of trust for which he was grateful.

A chime sounded.

"Enter," Darien said, and the doors parted.

Anasera walked in, wearing ship fatigues and a cloak of clinical detachment.

Intent on the data stream, he didn't acknowledge her.

"I cleaned her up," Anasera said. "She's resting."

He nodded, making a polite sound of acknowledgment.

"Syteria was not expecting to be returned to her quarters. What did you say to her?"

"I asked her if she'd prefer a cage," he said, matter-of-factly.

Anasera gasped.

He cast a sideways glance. "I don't intend to confine her."

"Perhaps you should," she said as the shock wore off. "It would be safer to restrict her movements. With a spy aboard, she is a target, now more than ever..."

Confining her was exactly what Palleton had suggested. Not for her safety, but as punishment for challenging Darien's authority. And he had been tempted.

Right up until she had called him a slaver.

He'd translated the epithet for the elder *donai's* benefit and Palleton had offered to show her what she would have experienced had she fallen into the Imperium's hands.

His *donai* saw her as his, but only as long as she behaved as a concubine would. One action, one misspoken word, and the ruse would unravel. This one incident had already made Palleton suspicious, but Darien had slipped in a casual remark about how susceptible humans were to nightmares. It had seemed enough.

"What do you intend to tell the *donai*?" Anasera asked, as if she'd read his thoughts.

"About what?" he asked, stalling.

She crossed her arms and gave him a scolding look. "That which must remain unspoken."

Anasera heaved a frustrated sigh and crossed the room to the refreshments wall. They protruded at her command. She poured two cups of strong tea and shoved one at him.

He took it and collapsed the reports to his desk, thoughtfully lowering himself into the chair behind it. Anasera sat down across from him.

"What does Palleton think about her escape attempt?" she asked.

"I did not ask for his opinion."

"Of course you didn't. That doesn't mean he and the other *donai* won't have one."

She leaned forward, cradling the steaming cup in her hands.

"You ordered us to teach her our ways," Anasera said. "Let me do that. It would be immensely helpful if I could explain things to her. A translator w—"

"No."

"Why not?"

He leaned back.

"Because I cannot afford to be seen indulging her defiance and rejecting our language is a part of her rebellion. Because she must demonstrate intelligence and resilience to survive among us." He looked down at the reports he'd collapsed to the desk surface and set the cup aside. "Pick one. Whichever makes you feel better."

"Do my feelings factor into this?"

"Should they?"

She straightened. "No, my lord."

"Was she hurt?"

"Not physically."

He looked up. "That implies she's wounded in other ways."

"She is, Darien. You know she is, or do you not see her?"

"I see her." He did. Truly, he did. But not as the wounded, fragile victim that Anasera saw.

"The way she reacted to the couple in the park is something I need to resolve. I need to find its root so I can help her overcome it. Do you not understand that, or the need for it? Now that you've taken away my only means of communicating with her, you can't expect her to—"

"I most certainly can. And do. She *will* rise to my expectations."

By the length of her pause, Anasera must've been counting backwards from ten.

"My lord, when you rescued her, she was wearing a control device. One designed to elicit physical pain when the psychological controls failed. Removing that collar removed the source of the external pain, but those other, psychological sources remain."

"So you said in your reports."

He could recite them verbatim. But their content didn't matter. He couldn't afford to indulge Anasera's recommendations. It would take years. Time he simply did not have.

"I monitor her vitals carefully," she said. "I can tell you that her physical reactions are intense, but that she does not act on them—most of the time. Last night was an exception. But I cannot assess what drives them, not without the means to communicate—really communicate—with her. And not without trust. You and your actions are interfering with that process."

Her shoulders were tight, her lips set in a well-schooled line, as her cup cooled alongside his on the desk.

"When you had the means to communicate with her," he said, "to earn her trust, you produced no results."

"That's because I couldn't replicate the cause."

"But now you can?"

"Yes," she said, hesitantly.

"Then I suggest you proceed."

Anasera cleared her throat.

"My lord, that cause is you."

CHAPTER TWENTY

*T*he hemispherical chamber where Bomani held her staff meetings rivaled the bridge itself. Palleton at his side, Darien observed from the shadows.

They had positioned themselves as far away as they could from Bomani's acid tone and the cloud of fear and determination floating around Lieutenant Savas. The young, junior grade lieutenant's brown hair was neatly trimmed, his ship fatigues meticulous, his blue eyes facing straight ahead. Several questions ago, he'd snapped to attention and retained the posture as if he were still a cadet lined up for inspection.

A thread of sympathy for the young human tugged at Darien even as he admired Bomani's ability to intimidate.

He'd never forget that utter dread that went with not knowing what to do or say. That first time under her command, her tone and the look on her face was all it had taken to shatter his confidence in his own abilities.

Even as *donai*, even as Dobromil's heir-apparent, she'd dressed him down as if he'd been the most utter waste of skin she'd ever come across. His ears had burned red-hot and his blood had boiled. She had none of the qualities of a *donai* tester. There were only prey-scent clues

204

and no sheer mass and size for his baser instincts to yield to. He'd lost count of the number of times he'd thought how easy it would've been to snap her neck.

Darien rather preferred his current role as observer, even if the prey-scent clues still got to him.

She circled the hologram and the lieutenant who'd created it. If there were errors, Darien couldn't find them, and he doubted that Bomani had either. Nevertheless, she fired off a bevy of very direct questions, all aimed at Savas' competence and conclusions.

She walked between the image of Thertore and the point where the "theoretical" space-time rift had opened. Her presence distorted a three-dimensional spiral that showed fluctuating gravitational energy levels. The spiral bloomed from a point inside Thertore. It spread out across space to collapse back into a singularity co-located with the rift. She resized the image and called up additional data.

"This is your best guess?" she demanded, the last word spoken with enough contempt to make a young lieutenant slink away, burrow into some hole, and stay there.

"As I said, Commander, this is our best understanding of the data we have," Savas said.

If the lieutenant's back straightened any further Darien thought it might snap. Savas' blood pressure was skyrocketing to a dangerous level now. It would've been much easier to tell Bomani what she wanted to hear: that the hologram showed them something that was impossible rather than probable. Instead, Savas held his ground as if it was the hill on which he'd rather die.

Bomani may not have been able to read Savas like Darien could, but she knew what she was doing. Tempering, she called it. And she was very good at eliminating those inclined to tell her what she wanted to hear and bringing her people to a suitable toughness.

Subtle muscle twitches under Savas' skin betrayed how hard it was for him to stand so firmly on conclusions drawn from theoretical models rather than hard data.

"Well done," Bomani said. "Thank you. You're dismissed."

Savas saluted, spun on his heel, and raced for the door. He had to backtrack a step to bow to Darien and stumbled. Then he reddened and almost tripped. He made it out the door without sprawling.

"We really must bloody them soon," Darien said as the doors shut.

Bloodying, that rite of passage practiced only by House Dobromil and a few of their allies, was more than tradition. It was a means to demolish the psychological barriers between humans and *donai*, to let them earn their place in the hierarchy of the pack. Some humans could never shed the prey mind-set. Those that could, however—

"They *are* overdue," she said.

Her lips widened into a cold smile that reminded Darien of a cat, one that liked to play with her food. Bomani definitely enjoyed the chase and the power of the kill.

"There's nothing suitable on this meandering path you've had us on," she continued as she waved away the hologram. A few quick taps on a control panel in the center of the chamber brought up an image of their position. She manipulated it.

"How about Tir'Hala-Revir?" she asked bringing forth the hologram of a planet. "Suitable biota, unsettled, *and* on the way home."

Darien approached the archived image from a previous survey. He wrapped his hands around it, expanding it until continents, then plains, then herds of animals appeared.

He selected a temperate zone abundant in prey large enough to pose a challenge.

"Yes," he said, nodding. "Tir'Hala-Revir will do nicely."

"Also," she said, "it'll give us a chance to shut off life support on the decks where we have not been able to do so. We can finish up the bug hunt and do a final, proper sweep."

Darien nodded, noncommittally.

Bomani wasn't going to be satisfied until she checked every part of the *Edlyn* and there was no sense in dissuading her from doing her job. It also provided her with something to do beside reminding him that they should return home.

"I have one more item on the agenda," she added as she collapsed the hologram of Tir'Hala-Revir.

Palleton grunted in not-quite silent agreement.

Darien turned towards him. "Do you have something to add as well?"

"Shall I fetch the lady for you, my lord?" The gleam in Palleton's eyes hid nothing.

"As long as she comes under her own power," Darien said.

Another grunt as Palleton crossed his arms and said, "My herding skills are a bit rusty."

Bomani grinned.

He should just send Palleton for "the lady." Out of spite if nothing else. But Darien didn't want to question an already harried human. The elder *donai's* sheer size and demeanor had an unfortunate effect even on humans who'd lived their whole lives in the Imperium.

"I'll take care of it," Darien said.

"When?" Bomani asked.

"In my own time, as always, Commander."

"Time is not on your side in this, my lord," she said in a toneless voice that did not match the warning on her face.

Palleton limited his commentary to a disappointed huff.

"Colonel," Darien said, "her language has no words for 'wormhole' or 'phase jumps' or any of the concepts Lieutenant Savas just finished speculating about. Exactly how would you have me ask her about them?"

"We have far more efficient ways of teaching her Kanthlos," Palleton reminded him.

"Yes we do," he said. "But not ones without risk. Would you endanger my concubine's mental and emotional stability by forcing it on her? Are we adopting all of the Imperium's methods now?"

"No, my lord." There was a hardness to Palleton's eyes, one that said that his patience had limits.

"Commander," Darien said, "set course for Tir'Hala-Revir. Best speed."

THE *EDLYN'S* parkland sprawled below the balcony. Afternoon light fell through the thin veil of the force field around it. Syteria could even feel the breeze against her cheeks and bare arms. Stronger gusts stirred the floor length nightgown she still wore. The scents of freshly turned soil wafted upward, along with the voices of the people working five stories below. They were planting flowers and chatting happily. Yet when she put her hand up against the force field, it would not allow her through.

You seem intent on demanding a cage instead. Shall I have one set up for you? the tyrant had asked.

She formed a fist and put all her weight behind it. It bounced off the field without sound. She struck it again and again until bruises bloomed around her knuckles and the bones in her wrist and forearm resonated with pain.

The doors to her quarters parted without warning. She whirled, intent on unleashing all her pent-up frustration on whomever entered. The human she'd attacked during her escape attempt had taken her down with appalling ease. Her *eniseri* training—effective against Rhoans—had failed her against one of her own kind. That man had been nowhere as muscled as the *donai* tyrant crossing the distance between them.

"A cage is not enough, I see. Would you prefer restraints as well?" His tone was ice, his eyes blazing as he stopped just a few paces from where she stood.

Cradling her arm to her chest Syteria took a step back. Once again instinct betrayed her, marked her as weak. And nothing enticed a predator like weakness.

The tyrant's nostrils flared in confirmation, but he didn't come any closer.

"Anasera sedated me," Syteria said.

"A sleep field is not sedation," he said.

"I don't care what you call it. I refused it."

"You prefer nightmares?"

She could't quite place the tone of his question? It wasn't surprise, nor curiosity.

"Yes," she said.

He inclined his head as a smile tugged at a corner of his mouth.

It made her hesitate as she pondered its fleeting meaning.

"I will forbid the sleep field's use if you give me your word of honor that you will make no further escape attempts."

There was that word again. And not just the word, but the way he said it. It burned her even as it sent a chill down her spine.

"Trading Rhoan mistresses for *donai* masters holds no appeal for me."

"I did not expect it to," he said.

She spread her fingers out against her collarbones. It drew his gaze and strain betrayed the effort of looking away.

"Then why are you here?" she asked.

"To warn you. Refuse to learn our language, our customs at your own peril."

"You cannot force me to—"

"I can, and I will."

There was a finality to the threat so imbued with truth that it struck at her heart as surely as if he'd driven his sword through her chest. Their technology had not only freed her from the Rhoans but it had woken the long-dormant Kappan within. It had been why she had survived. The Rhoans had let her retain just enough of her true self so she could be useful in her role as a drudge, so she could run towards danger. They had corrupted her essence, her true self for their own needs. And now that she was Kappan again, in mind and in body, her spirit was reawakening.

He could take it all away.

"Very well," she said. "My word of honor. I will not try to escape."

"And you will learn."

She counted five breaths. "I will try."

"You will learn."

"You don't want me just to learn," she said. "You want me to surrender."

"I want you to survive."

Sudden cold hit her at the core of her being. "Will you kill me if I fail?"

"No, but you will not survive and I won't be able to save you."

"I don't understand."

"And I cannot explain it any further. *Not* in Rhoan."

"I don't want to be yours. Do you understand that?"

"Until you understand what it means to reject my House's protection, what you want is irrelevant. Which is why you must learn."

Heat spread through her body, all the way to her fingertips and a bead of sweat slid down her spine.

"How did you get here, my lady?"

She held his gaze, biting back the objection to her so-called title. It was nothing but a brand marking her as his property.

"I don't know," she answered. "I was in a cell. We were on our way from Kappa to Rho. It was supposed to be a short flight—less than a day."

"And..."

He clasped his hands behind him, drawing her gaze once again to muscles thinly veiled by what the crew called ship-fatigues. On him, they looked anything but informal.

"I was drugged, restrained."

"Why?"

"There were no Matrons aboard, no other *eniseri*."

"The *eniseri* are drudges, like yourself. The Matrons are..." he prompted.

She wrung her hands, then schooled them to stillness and looked away. There were other chambers connected to this one, places she could flee to but could not hide. On this ship, there were no places for her to hide. And no way off.

Inevitably her gaze met his again, the amber of his irises half dilated to reveal the gold ones underneath. He was watching her again as though stripping her down to her very essence.

She had her own questions. What was he, truly? And what did he want from and of her.

"First tell me, what—"

"No." The word echoed in the chamber. "We are asking the questions here."

"We? I see no 'we,' " she said, looking to distract him.

An amused eyebrow quirked for an instant. "What are the Matrons?"

Her pulse raced, heartbeat pounding. His gaze found the pulse point at her neck and homed in on it as though it were a beacon. She covered it with her hand, drawing farther back from him. He looked away for an instant and when he turned back, the amber of his human irises covered the others.

That possessive look, that intensity remained.

"The Matrons are older *eniseri*," she said. "They have earned the trust of the Matriarchy. They keep us—*eniseri* like me—under control."

He nodded. Nostrils flaring, his irises dilated and contracted once again. More scrutiny. But why?

"There were no Matrons on the ship because I was to remain sedated until we reached Rho."

"Prisoner DRD4," he said.

She turned away. Had he run her through with his sword, it would have hurt less. Her eyes filled and she swept the gathering moisture away with the back of her hand. She'd been called DRD4 more often than she'd been called Syteria, so what did it matter? What if they came from his lips and in his voice?

"I'm sorry."

He'd moved closer. How much she couldn't be sure. As before, he'd moved without sound.

She took a deep breath and faced him. "The rest, you know."

He paced, a thoughtful yet aristocratic frown drawn high over pursed lips.

"It is no small feat for a human to kill a *grierugon*, my lady. As it is no small feat to destroy a shielded imperial craft. Yet your ship had no weapons, not even small arms."

"Is that why I am here? Because I killed that creature? Because I would not succumb to it like the Rhoans?"

"In part, yes," he said. "The emperor believes you and your people are a threat to the Imperium."

A humorless laugh escaped her chest. Perhaps if the Kappans had Rhoan technology. But no, not even then. Not after what she'd seen aboard the *Edlyn*.

"What do *you* believe?" she asked.

An appraising gaze swept her once more. Light blued the brighter strands that wove through the dark ink of his hair. Soundless ventilation drove his plum-tinged scent towards her.

Syteria swallowed the moisture that had pooled in her mouth. Bitterly, she waited, aware of the power he held over her very existence. If he agreed with his emperor, if he perceived her as a threat, she could do nothing to sway him. But if he expected her to beg or bargain for her life, he would be disappointed.

"I believe you both fortunate and brave," he finally said as he stopped to face her.

His statement didn't absolve her of being a threat. Was it a reprieve, or was he giving her a chance to prove his emperor wrong?

"I wasn't brave," she said, offering him the only truth she could. "I was desperate."

"The Rhoans must have been desperate as well. Yet they took their own lives. Why?"

"They were Rhoan."

The dark, brooding, almost-frown returned. "Fighting for their lives is not in Rhoan nature?"

"Physical violence is not in their nature," she said. "The Rhoans prefer other methods. 'Kinder, gentler' methods."

Her fingers drifted to her throat. They were ice against the desperate fluttering of her pulse. The motion drew his gaze.

"But physical violence is in *your* nature," he said.

She nodded, dropping her hand to her side. "I am Kappan."

His eyes widened, smile flashing for an instant like a boy who'd just made some wonderful discovery.

Desperate to hide the rising heat in her cheeks, she turned away. She shouldn't find his admiration pleasing. When the heat in her face faded, she drew in a deep breath and looked him straight in the eyes.

"What do you intend to do with me?"

He donned an inscrutable mask, clearly hiding something as the silence around them grew. He bowed deeper than she'd ever seen him bow before and turned to leave.

"Wait," she said.

DARIEN TURNED TO FACE HER. Her pulse fluttered at the base of her elegant neck. He tore his gaze away only to have it return to the drape of her garments. Her curved body was flawlessly female.

You need never touch her, Galen had said. Galen could never understand just how wrong he was, nor the difficult position in which he'd put Darien.

How could he? Galen was human. It was different for them.

Without a pair-bond, most human relationships were matters of short-lived infatuation or convenience. In this, they were freer than someone in his position could ever be.

She'd taken a solid stance, one with tight fists forced along the seams of her dress. It betrayed her expectation of conflict. His imagination cast her in armor, a goddess riding into battle. He had to restrain the grin that was about to spread on his face.

"I would like different quarters," she said. Her battle stance softened, as though the major obstacle had simply been the asking.

"Are your quarters inadequate?" he asked.

"They are *your* quarters."

"As I am not using them—"

"Please... By placing me in your quarters, you're making a statement, are you not?"

If he'd been human, he'd have flinched.

"You do not understand our customs," he said. "Changing quarters will not change your status."

"What will?"

"You would have to become something...someone else."

"I don't understand."

He needed to make her understand. The necessity of cruel truth waited on his lips.

"Rhoan," he said softly. "You would have to become Rhoan."

He saw the pressure gradient in her tear ducts rise. She trembled with the force of will needed to staunch those tears.

The oddest fusion of need, want, and desire gripped him. He wanted her to need him, to want comfort only he could provide, to surrender to the cradle of protection only he could offer.

Her face lost all its softness. It fled from her eyes, her lips, her voice as she announced, "I would rather face the *grierugon* again, or your emperor, than continue like this."

His blood surged, hot and angry, as Kabrin's title rolled off her lips. He straightened his tunic as a delaying gesture.

"I will see if I can arrange the former and treat the latter as hyperbole," he said. "Will that be all?"

"No, that will not be all. I will not be dismissed."

The defiant tone coursed between them, settled and wrapped around him, raising the fine hairs on his neck. Darien bared his teeth.

He would not be challenged, not about the emperor, not by someone who had no understanding and no right. He straightened his shoulders and clasped his hands behind his back.

"You are addressing the master and commander of this vessel, my lady."

"Putting me in this gilded cage does not make you my master. Everyone aboard this vessel may call you 'master,' but I do not."

His tongue probed the sudden ache around his cuspids. He waited for anger and desire to subside. Challenged by her defiance, they remained paired despite his best efforts to separate them. Unaware, she stoked a dangerous fire, a potent mixture fueled by his need to thwart the emperor.

"Why do you hold me in such contempt?" he asked. "Have I not provided you with every comfort? Have I not met your needs?"

"Every comfort, yes; every need, no."

"What remains unfulfilled?" Somehow hope had made its way into his tone even as he knew she wouldn't give him the answers he sought.

"A purpose," she said. "Everyone and everything on this ship has a purpose, except for me."

"You have a purpose, my lady."

"What? To be at your mercy? To be a pet you indulge when it suits you?"

"A pet?" His breath caught as he smiled. "Pets are tame, compliant, eager to please. You are none of these things."

"I have complied—" A pained expression played across her face. A deep breath betrayed the struggle to choose her words wisely.

"I am learning your language," she continued.

She looked like she was about to bare *her* teeth. He understood the anger for what it was—a balm for the wound he'd inflicted by making her admit to bending to his will.

"Yet here we are," he said. "Speaking yours."

"It was easy for you to learn this—what did you call it? Ah yes, 'incomplete, inadequate, primitive speech'—to make sure you were my only gateway to your world."

"The ease of it does not change that I indulge you by using it."

"I'm honored that my glorious 'master' indulges his pet," she said and gave him a mocking bow, almost a curtsy, something he hadn't seen in years.

"Are you honored, Syteria? Do you find me glorious? Is that why you omit my title? Every. Time."

Her laughter had an edge to it. One he did not care for.

"Do you enjoy being *the* predator that everyone fears?"

His jaw tightened and he forced his lips together, reining in the inhuman growl that would show her just how much of a predator he truly was.

She stood her ground, the jeweled green of her irises a steady, unrelenting weapon he could not resist engaging.

"You shouldn't look at me that way," he said, stalking closer. She remained still, even as he leaned in closer to whisper in her ear. "Your strength intrigues me, tempts me."

Her body tightened, obviously poised for flight, paying the price

215

for standing her ground with the most enticing tremors. Those flutters ebbed and flowed, a sensual dance under her silken skin.

"How should I look at you then…*my lord*?" Contempt dripped off his title.

"You could look at me like someone who *is* at my mercy…and *knows* it."

Her gaze wavered, a fleeting instant so brief, it dispatched his disappointment before it could take form.

"I know my life is in your hands…my lord," she whispered, voice shaking. This time his title wasn't soaked in contempt, merely disdain.

"Yes, it is," he admitted. "I should say that I regret the situation, but I do not. I like having your life in my hands."

A surge of pheromones flooded his senses, drawing him in.

"Why does this knowledge infuriate you so?" he asked.

"You control everything, even the very air I breathe."

"That can be said of everyone aboard this ship. You are not unique."

"But you don't look at them the way you look at me," she said, taking the slightest distancing step.

He blinked. So much for being reserved, controlled, safe from human perceptions. He stalked closer, re-claiming proximity.

"And how is that?" he asked.

"Like I am prey," she said.

A smile tugged at his lips. To his baser side, they were all prey, although not in the same way.

"You need not worry, " he said, pulling a strand of her hair loose.

She didn't flinch, didn't retreat, didn't flee.

"I don't eat my pets…"

Another strand. More. Until they all cascaded down her back. The flutter of her heartbeat launched a new surge of pheromones. He tilted his head and closed his eyes, letting her scent wrap him in its arms.

"…but I do play with them."

He could lose himself in that silken mass of hair. Schooling his hands back into place, he denied himself further exploration. The temptation to explore her curves, ignite her passion and stoke her fire grew with each breath, each beat of her heart.

"That is what you're asking me to do," he whispered. "Is it not?"

"No."

"There it is again," he said. "That look."

She backed away. "What look?"

"You judge, but do not understand."

"I understand."

He rushed forward, his hand landing to curl on her nape in a warning grip. His lips brushed her ear.

"No, you do not. You cannot."

"I—"

"Careful, Syteria," he said, a roughness edging the quiet of his voice. "I can hear your heart beating. I can read your body with great precision, by a dozen different means. Your temperature rises whenever I am near you. Did you know that?"

Her whole body flushed in confirmation.

A satisfied groan rumbled in his chest. Heat pumped through her veins. His grip loosened.

She paled and turned away, hiding her face behind a cascade of chestnut silk.

"Know this then, and understand it," he said. "When the emperor deals with humans, he prefers certain methods not because they are effective, but because they allow him to indulge a darker side, one all *donai* have."

Did he want to feed her fear? It could be useful to him, or it could defeat his purpose.

"But what I do," he added, "what I demand of you, is for honor."

She whirled to face him, sending the chestnut silk flowing to settle behind her.

"Honor? You saved me because you needed a pawn you could use against your emperor."

The truth of it, her dizzying aroma woke that darker side of him, the shadows he'd inherited from his father, the ones that had allowed him to survive and thrive, to claim the title of heir, to stand as more

217

than human. Yet he would not lose her to those shadows. They railed at him, demanding that he break her, that he put her in her place, whether that place was under him or at his feet.

One thing stopped him: he needed her spirit intact. Without it, he would tire of her. Galen's ruse and the need for it aside, he would have her as more than a means to gain leverage over the emperor, more than a temporary companion or paramour. The ache around his cuspids rose with a yearning to bite her, draw blood, and mark her as his.

He shook his head. He really had meant to keep his distance and the stopover on Tir'Hala-Revir would provide him with plenty of opportunity to do so.

"I saved you because no one deserves to be butchered, not even a human, and particularly not one who fought as you did."

She pursed her lips. "You didn't know. Not until after. Not until you'd salvaged the Rhoan logs."

"True. At first, it was about a distress call, about avoiding a blemish to the honor of my House."

Her arched brows knitted in consideration.

"So, it is honor that prevents you from turning me over to the emperor? Honor that compels you to disobey him? Nothing but honor."

"I wouldn't turn anyone over to the emperor, knowing what awaited them."

"I don't believe you," she said.

"Shall I prove it to you?"

A sudden deluge of fear-scent unleashed his darker side. He wrapped one hand behind her neck so he could cradle her head, and forced her chin up.

Despite the rising fear, she held his gaze.

"Were I to deliver you to the emperor, I would gain his favor. My House would advance in status. Everything in my dominion would benefit should I no longer court the emperor's displeasure. He might even give you back to me after he was done—or at least what was left of you. Galen could repair your body again.

"Would you prefer that, my lady? Shall I let him break you for me? You wouldn't be conflicted about being under my dominion anymore.

You'd never be conflicted again. You'd be a blank slate, a hollow vessel to be filled and shaped as *I* saw fit. Is that what you'd prefer?"

He peered into the jade pools of her eyes and saw incredible control, her will overriding her fear, a rare and precious quality.

Beautiful.

His grip loosened, then gave way, and he took a step back, allowing her to twist out of his grasp. She turned to flee but only took a few steps before coming to a stop.

He held his breath.

He'd never considered gaining the emperor's favor in that way. It had been inconceivable to him until the moment she'd provoked him. It made him realize just how important it was to rein in the nature he shared with his imperial brethren.

It would unravel him to gaze into empty jade eyes betraying a will stolen. Even his darker side and all the shadows that lived within it retreated, the image holding no interest for them.

He waited. He would not allow her to flee through those doors, nor to emerge from his chambers and take flight again. It would make his *donai* ask too many questions.

She remained three steps from the door, her body tight with the effort it had taken for her to stop.

"No, that is not what I would prefer." Her voice shook despite the strength behind it.

She turned, facing him as if he were a firing squad.

"What am I to you, my—"

"Say my name," he said.

The seam of her lips tightened like a line drawn in sand. She stood on one side of that line. He, on the other. In that moment, he knew she would not cross it. It would stand as a symbol of her defiance, of her rejection of him.

For now, he would tolerate it, knowing he'd revel in his triumph when he drew it out of her, when it would fall from her lips with reverence.

CHAPTER TWENTY-ONE

Galen gathered his supplies, packing instruments designed for use in a primitive environment. He preferred doing such simple tasks himself, finding calm in the process of placing old, familiar things in their proper place.

Darien's announcement that they were going to make planetfall at Tir'Hala-Revir, had replaced the dull routines of ship life with excitement. After so long on the border and the uncertainty of wandering aimlessly without a mission, the promise of the initiation rites had bolstered the crew's morale.

Anasera entered the lab wearing the remains of a scowl. She rushed to the nearest console and made hurried log entries, handling the holographic images like she wanted to hurl them as weapons.

"I take it the lessons are not going well," Galen said, turning his attention back to his instruments and vials. Pristine, they gleamed in the bright light, lined up like soldiers on parade across the top of a workbench that stretched to fill the lab.

"Syteria is making progress. She's stopped fighting me at least."

Galen joined her as she dueled with the hologram that was part of the Rhoan language matrix. She was filling in blanks for useless words like types of plants and refining terms for bodies of water.

Crucial blanks remained: marriage, courtship, consort, wife, pregnancy.

He shook his head. The pattern of missing concepts no longer seemed incidental to the damage the Rhoan ship had sustained. They needed the services of a linguist, not a cryptologist. Or maybe an anthropologist. One specializing in exotic, long-dead cultures, if there was even such a person still alive in the Imperium.

"Darien threatened her," Anasera said.

He shrugged. "Perhaps he had no choice. You've often complained about her stubbornness."

She closed her eyes for a moment, shaking her head with suppressed frustration.

"The *donai* will notice that he's not spending time with her." She glared at him accusingly. "I told you this was going to go awry."

"Most of the *donai* have never seen pair-bond, much less experienced it themselves."

"Palleton has," Anasera said as she dismissed the language matrix with an angry sweep and crossed her arms. Her teeth tugged on her lower lip as was her habit when in deep thought.

"Then we shall take Syteria to Tir'Hala-Revir," Galen said.

"It's not safe."

"She's not going hunting, not being bloodied or tested. Syteria will be fine."

"Father—"

"She's not a newborn fawn about to take its first steps into the meadow," he said returning to the work table and its ordered splendor.

"A newborn fawn has instincts wrought by its nature and the ability to run. Syteria is not—"

"She's not defenseless. That *grierugon* did not lay down and die."

He used a handheld scanner to check the level of nanite-infused liquids in a dozen vials. It beeped in confirmation, flashing satisfying numbers.

"The immersion will do her good," he said. "She'll have the opportunity to interact with other members of the crew. It'll give her more context, speed up her language acquisition. Meanwhile, Palleton will be too busy bloodying the crew to worry about pair-bonding, and there might just be a few opportunities for Darien and Syteria to interact."

Admittedly, interaction also meant that she'd misbehave or make an error. Perhaps even one that would reveal their ruse, but it was a calculated risk.

"She's just getting used to life on this ship," Anasera said. "Now you want to throw her into the middle of the *donai* bloodying the crew?"

"Her life has to be lived in a bigger world than this ship. That includes everything about our world including human-*donai* interactions."

"I understand that." She stayed his hand as he sealed a container. "But why is she expected to do it over just a few weeks?"

"Because that's all the time we have," he said, giving her a meaningful look.

"Perhaps I should come along," she said, rubbing her forehead. "I know you. You'll lose yourself in your work and forget all about her."

"You and your sister both survived," he reminded her.

Anasera's lips twisted into something that wasn't quite a smile.

His NAME. Syteria measured her victory in denying his name.

How many more days could she feast on such spoils? She let out a bitter laugh as her hands closed around the rail of the balcony. The shield would give way there, humming lightly, sending strange vibrations of warning into her fingers.

Would she trust anyone that had run? The answer was a resounding no.

She had tried to explain the incident to Anasera, but the shocked disbelief on her face was a universal language that needed no words.

Anasera was loyal to *him*. Loyal to a fault.

One of Anasera's questions had been very clear: *Do you want to live?*

It should've been an easy question to answer, because the worst Syteria could say about her new life was that she wanted to live it. She'd realized just how much when he'd described what his emperor planned to do to her.

She'd seen such broken people, devoid of a will of their own. Seen them by the thousands. The Rhoans made use of them, for show, for sport, to prove their power over the physically stronger Kappans. They used them as beasts of burden, ordered them to mutilate themselves and to torture and break their own people. She'd watched the light fade from their eyes even as their hearts continued to beat, their limbs continued to move.

It's why she kept refusing Anasera's offers to use a sleep field to end the nightmares that haunted her. The sleep field sounded too much like a tool of Rhoan therapy.

Syteria would rather hold on to her mind and self than surrender them to anyone again, even if the price for doing so was painful.

The doors opened to allow Anasera and Galen entry. They stepped through, bearing boxes. Anasera set the largest box down on the only empty table and flipped it open.

Syteria groaned.

No, no more gifts.

Her quarters were cluttered enough. Fresh floral arrangements arrived daily. Not one or even a few, but dozens. The crewmen that brought them paired the floral gifts with offers of assistance as well as a constant stream of food and drink. There seemed to be some sort of competition to get her to eat more, to get her to accept and delight in one gift or another.

She'd made it as clear as she could that she did not need help dressing, or undressing, or bathing. She could not only feed herself, she could decide when and if she was hungry. She didn't need to be walked, or entertained, or have her hair brushed or braided.

What she needed was someone to show her how to lock her own door.

"No more, Galen," Syteria insisted, turning away. Perhaps if she retreated to one of the smaller rooms, they'd understand. Failing that, she could always hurl things at them. She'd start with the flower vases. That would clear them out.

"Please, my lady." It was Anasera who answered as she rested her hand on Syteria's shoulder. She kept talking.

Syteria turned at the unfamiliar words.

Anasera held up a square piece of fabric. It had none of the ornamental qualities of the clothing they had so far provided. Syteria took it from her. The fabric was made of tiny cells, a rough honeycomb structure. She flipped it over, running her hands over the underside. It was soft and supple, like skin. Traces of luminescence raced and swirled around her hand and the material warmed under her touch.

Syteria looked up, giving them a puzzled frown.

Galen spoke.

Box in hand, Anasera grabbed Syteria's and pulled her behind a screen.

"What now?" Syteria mumbled in Rhoan as Anasera tugged off her gown.

Anasera's motions were both efficient and patient as she moved Syteria's limbs. The fabric segments fused together when brought into contact.

Curiosity piqued, Syteria assisted with the smaller segments, wrapping them around her calves and forearms. They emerged from behind the screen to Galen's approval.

"A uniform? You're giving me a uniform," she said, suddenly happy.

CHAPTER TWENTY-TWO

*S*yteria waited until everyone had disembarked before approaching the edge of the ramp leading off the transport. The textured metal below her boots rested atop a thick carpet of blue-green grass edged in brown and gold.

One more step, and she'd be the first Kappan to set foot on a world other than the Rho-Kappa binary. A chill slithered up her spine despite the heat.

She tilted her head back and shielded her eyes against a white sun piercing a cloudless blue. Traces of light persisted on her retinas as she closed her eyes.

The bulk of her hair remained tightly braided despite the wind, but a few strands had escaped to tickle her face. She swept them aside, tucking them behind her ears. She'd thought about cutting her hair, but could never bring herself to do it. Shortening it would feel like a betrayal, a rejection of moments like this, moments when she paused to appreciate the enormity of her new universe.

"This way, my lady," Galen called as he led a small army of infirmary staff and equipment away from the shuttle.

On the plain below, sweat-drenched humans and *donai* strained and labored to cut down trees. With saws. By hand.

She passed a group where a *donai* was ordering humans about. Then another where a human was in charge. As the tasks changed, leadership passed from *donai* to human and back.

Beside them, their technology gleamed in the sunlight, idling like a useless ornament.

Like me.

She approached a small group. Work stopped as they gave her their attention and bowed. She caught herself in time, returning a nod instead of mimicking the depth of theirs.

Last time she'd responded with a full bow, she'd set off an extended exchange of increasingly deeper bows that would have been comical had it not been so disconcerting. An amused Anasera had rescued her and untangled the mess, but her usual guide had remained aboard the *Edlyn*.

"May I help you, my lady?" the man—a human?—in charge of the group asked. This man was shorter than some of the others, but well-constructed, with a muscled torso and thick limbs wrapped in the same type of uniform she was wearing. From underneath the brim of his hat, brown eyes met hers.

"What are you doing?" she asked.

What Syteria *wanted* to ask was why they were wasting time with saws and muscle but understanding Kanthlos was easier than speaking it. It wasn't just the sounds or the vocabulary—it was the complexity of the syntax.

"We are making a tower," he answered.

She bent to pick up one of the saws laying on the ground and mimicked its use. Then she crossed the distance to the unused machinery nearby.

"Why?" she asked as she placed her hand on top of the machine.

They formed a semi-circle around her. Swift discussion reminiscent of a debate flowed around her. The leader broke into a satisfied smile. His chest swelled.

"To see if it could be done," the leader said.

Behind him, his compatriots echoed agreement, some with rapid-fire speech that sounded like detailed explanations, others by demonstrating the steps involved—cutting and sizing the wood, placing notches so they could overlap, demonstrating knots and ties to hold the wood together.

As confusion contorted her brow, their speech slowed.

She smiled, said, "Thank you," and hurried away.

Her cheeks burned under her hands. She appreciated their attempts to speak slowly for her benefit. She really did. But the softness of their expectations struck her as harshly as the imperial *donai* had. They'd meant no insult, she was certain. Still, it smarted, reminding her that she'd not come as far as she'd needed to go.

Syteria launched into a litany of sotto voce remarks about the ancestry of the tyrant.

She passed a group where humans directed the stronger *donai* to perform the more physically difficult tasks. It stopped her in her tracks.

Instead of drudgery and servitude there was a hierarchy, or at least the appearance of one. The upper tiers of that hierarchy were inhabited by humans and *donai*, both of whom exhibited a kind of good cheer and tenacity she'd never witnessed on Rho.

One group was making spears, pulling the blades from a box and setting them onto freshly harvested poles. A lone crewman assembled a rack and loaded it with bows and arrows brought down from the ship. Her hands itched to examine these tools.

She found Galen's group farther down the plain, where the trees were scarce and wind rippled the grass.

They too were busy building—no, growing—a new structure.

An enormous transparent egg took shape before her eyes. She stepped back as it rose above her, bulging as if it were about to burst. A sound like a sheet being snapped startled her as the bubble rippled and turned opaque. Its surface hardened to a shell.

"What's this?" she asked Galen.

The equipment around her looked a lot like what was in the infirmary on the *Edlyn*. They were probably setting up a field hospital, but she wanted the actual term so that she could commit it to memory.

"What for?" she asked.

"For wounded," he said.

She put her hands on her hips and cocked her head. "Is this war?"

He nodded, intent on the task of dispatching things in a specific order. He spoke to his staff in short, clipped phrases. They pushed the indicated crates towards different sections of the new structure.

"With what...who...whom?" she asked.

Without looking up, he said, "Darien will bloody the crew. He'll need my help."

She frowned, certain she couldn't have heard him right.

"Why hurt the crew?" she asked. "And why are you helping?"

"Not wound. Bloody."

She tasted the words. The distinction was subtle, but only the former had clear meaning.

A large vehicle with all the grace and aesthetics of a barge floated down and settled into a low hover nearby. It bristled with what could only be weapons. Their large, unfamiliar barrels circled the lower half of the barge.

"Come with," Galen said, extending a hand.

She took it, allowing him to lead her and help her up into the barge.

The pilot greeted them as Galen climbed aboard. A force field snapped into place, creating a transparent canopy. Galen took a seat up front next to the pilot and Syteria settled into the space behind him.

The interior was the same type of pearly white as the *Edlyn's* infirmary. A flock of rovers nestled atop a diagnostic bed. An ambulance, an armed one. Of course it would be armed. Everyone around her was armed. The thing on Galen's hip was clearly some sort of firearm.

The barge rose, whisper quiet, like a leaf on the wind. As they climbed, understanding took form—a wall; towers; a star fort, complete with indentations to prevent dead zones.

How very strange.

"Is this a"—she fumbled for the word that meant simulation, but settled for—"game?"

A distracted Galen nodded without turning to face her.

Apparently, her education would have to wait. She doubted that the *donai* fought battles with such primitive weapons, despite Anasera's explanation that they were prone to affectations like the sword.

Galen pointed towards specks on the plain.

The pilot verified Galen's sighting and closed in, banking as they descended. He maintained an altitude that didn't disturb the herd of large animals below. The creatures ambled across the grass. Beautifully mottled in browns and blacks, they grazed at their leisure. Majestic antlers crowned a vigilant few.

The pilot flew them over a ridge and circled a canyon. They spiraled down. A group—a hunting party by the look of them—waited below, just off a clearing. The ambulance landed just a stone's throw from the group and parted its canopy.

Syteria followed Galen's lead as he disembarked and headed for the group. She lagged behind his determined stride.

A few members of the hunting party were bare-skinned except for black pleated fabric wrapped around their hips and secured with a wide belt. They also sported gloves or gauntlets on one arm. Their amber eyes tracked her like she was prey.

The rest wore skin suits like her own.

Oh, the skin suits are for the humans.

Her hesitation drew the *donai's* attention. She ran for the safety of Galen's shadow.

Two injured humans, a man and a woman, sheltered under a tree with a flat, sprawling, green canopy. The man was leaning against the ashen trunk, cradling an arm bared by a damaged skin suit.

The injured woman sat, propped up against the tree. Sweat and grime covered her face.

Syteria fell behind as Galen knelt at the injured woman's side. The woman smiled up at him, but her set jaw betrayed pain as she tucked bright reddish strands behind her ear. Tears hung on the points of her lashes. She swiped them away with the back of her blood-stained hand and winced.

A *donai* knelt at her side, supporting her injured leg. The small bone in her lower leg protruded between his blood-soaked fingers. He spoke to her in a soothing voice, lowering his shaved head to gaze into her blue eyes.

Movement caught the edge of Syteria's vision as more *donai* joined them. They dragged the carcass of a large-maned feline forward to lay at the injured woman's feet. Its throat had been torn open, raked by four parallel furrows reminiscent of claw marks.

The bald *donai* gently let go of the woman's leg. He dipped a finger in the cat's blood. He smeared some on her forehead, murmuring something that made a smile soften the woman's features. Finger lingering, he smeared her cheek. Their gazes met, and Syteria held her breath along with them.

Galen's scolding tone intruded. The bald *donai* rose, a restrained scowl on his scarred face. He shouted orders and his *donai* compatriots dragged the carcass out of Galen's way.

Syteria knelt beside the cat and ran her hand over the rough pelt of its broad snout. Flint eyes rimmed in pebbled skin stared back. It was quite beautiful. Even in death, its powerful muscles projected a lethal majesty.

She heard a crack and a muffled scream as Galen set the broken leg. The whimpering woman tucked herself into the bald *donai's* arms.

"Aeda refused," a proud male voice said.

It took a heartbeat for Syteria to realize it was in Rhoan. She closed her eyes.

He was behind her.

She turned and opened her eyes to *his* face. Suddenly the beast at her feet seemed less majestic and more trip hazard.

"Refused what?" she whispered as she backed away, then halted. A stumble would place her at *his* feet.

"Anesthetic. That's the reason for that gasp, that look, is it not?" *he* said, frowning down at her.

A lump rose in her throat. She blew out a breath to clear it. "What look?"

"The look that judges what it does not understand."

"I understand," she said, bristling.

"And still you judge."

Syteria bit back further argument. "What happened?" she asked.

"Aeda saved Laleo's life. That's why he's walking away with a scratch to his arm while she has a broken leg."

"And the cat?"

"Kell had the cat brought back for Aeda. It would've been her kill had she not saved her teammate."

"This creature," she argued, gesturing towards the cat, "was killed by another animal, not by a weapon."

He raised an eyebrow, along with his arm. Pearl black fingernails crowned a hand gloved in blood.

Syteria swallowed the tension rebuilding in her throat. None of the *donai* carried weapons of any kind. She'd seen this from her vantage in the ambulance. Seen it as they'd disembarked. Seen it without realizing.

"Humans think of us as weapons…" he said, stepping closer.

Her breath caught.

"…I think it best you do the same," he continued.

Strong male musk mixed with the scent of blood as he closed in. Adrenaline surged. Not the kind that she'd expected. Not the fight-or-flight kind. More like…anticipation. She shook her head to clear it.

"You mean warriors…not weapons."

The curve of his full lips remained skewed. She tore her gaze upward to amber-wrapped gold, lest she linger too long on the broad chest, the chiseled muscle beneath bronzed skin, the sparse trail of short, curly hair leading downward.

"I mean exactly what I say, my lady. Weapons. Although some call us animals as well."

He was so close now, he filled the entirety of her vision. His scent —musk, salt, plums—wrapped around her. She clamped her mouth shut to stifle the desire to lick her lips.

The grin on his face grew, and for an instant she dreaded the shrinking gap between them. Her gaze wanted to wander, to admire all of his…attributes. Her nails curled again to dig into her palms, remaining at her side only by some miracle.

Behind her, blessed commotion gave her cause to glance over her shoulder. A floating pallet trailed, unused, behind the *donai* called Kell as he carried Aeda to the ambulance. Galen called for Syteria to join him.

She turned to face the tyrant again, with further request for explanation on her lips, but he'd disappeared.

Infuriating man.

CHAPTER TWENTY-THREE

*G*alen's frown deepened as he tugged at the strange object under his work station. One of the rovers had failed in its attempts to "clean" it off the floor and flagged it.

The pendant's lanyard, some weak organic material, had been torn. The astroid-shaped pendant had become embedded in the temporary flooring.

Maybe he should return to the *Edlyn*. He'd been reduced to cleaning up after patients who couldn't be bothered to keep track of their belongings. He plucked it off the floor and made a knot in the lanyard to keep the pendant from sliding off.

"Is this yours, Lieutenant?" Galen asked, holding up the lanyard.

Laleo was lounging in the center bed along the far wall of Galen's recovery ward, indulging in holographic entertainment. He was alone, evidently the only patient who needed extra time to recover. One of Galen's assistants had treated his arm and let him stay the night. While everyone else was eager to get out as soon as possible, Laleo had happily settled in.

Laleo waved the hologram off and rose. He clapped his hands together as he rushed towards Galen.

"Thank you," he said, snatching the pendant out of Galen's grasp. "I thought I'd lost it out there and I would never see it again."

His thumb caressed the shiny surface like it was a fetish. The image of a woman with short, amber hair sprouted from the pendant's surface.

"My sister," Laleo announced proudly.

"Very good." Galen turned to leave, certain he could find something interesting to do.

"Sir, can I ask you a question?"

Galen faced Laleo and gave him a polite look of interest. Not too interested though. Laleo had a reputation for being loquacious—even for a communications officer.

Laleo's eyes had that faraway look, as though he weren't seeing the image of his sister spinning and casting blown kisses over her shoulder.

"She's in love with one of *them*," Laleo finally said.

Galen cleared his throat. "Them?"

Laleo cast a meaningful look towards the adjoining room.

One of the *donai* had been gored by one of this planet's more dangerous predators. He would have lived, but the beast had taken him with it as it went over a waterfall. They had smashed onto not one, but two, outcroppings on their way down. Chance had also placed the *donai* under the beast both times. His skull had been crushed on the second landing, brains destroyed beyond even *donai* capacity to heal. His remains awaited funeral rites and a pyre.

"Your question, Mister Laleo."

"I'm afraid for her."

Still not a question. Galen counted to five. Twice.

"Mister Laleo, my daughter is the one you should speak with. She is a *donai's* pair-bonded mate. She'll tell you that there's nothing to fear—"

"Oh no. I mean, you misunderstand, sir. My sister wants to bind him to her, and I promised her I would ask for your help."

The hairs on the nape of Galen's neck rose as fear replaced irritation.

"What kind of help?" Galen asked, frowning.

"What you did with Lord Dobromil's concubine. And with Lady Syteria."

Galen's posture tightened. A deafening roar pounded in his ears, keeping time with his heart. "Exactly what do you think I did for Lord Dobromil or his son?"

Laleo looked at the image of his sister again.

"Made them fertile," Laleo answered. "Fertile enough to breed with humans. Your work has yielded the strongest human-*donai* crosses in the Imperium. That is why the Imperium's bounty for you grows each year. The emperor wants you for your methods, your secrets."

Galen's temper rose with each word. He stretched his lips into a tight, grim line.

"Sir, why won't Lord Dobromil allow you to make the other *donai* of his House fertile?" Laleo asked. "It would serve him, would it not? To have more *donai*, even if they are also the children of humans. It would bring other *donai* under House Dobromil's banner and rally them to his cause. They would come from all over the Imperium. And then we wouldn't have to fight the emperor alone. We woul—"

"Enough," Galen said, his voice louder than he'd intended.

"I'm sor—" Laleo shut his mouth with a snap. He waited, eyes downcast, the image of his sister still dancing in his palm. Hiding his face, he closed his trembling hand around the pendant.

Galen's temper continued to simmer. The bounty had indeed grown every year, but not for the reasons Laleo believed. Everything Laleo had said was true, but also wrong.

The *donai* would come from all over the Imperium but invoking Galen's knowledge would void the very nobility of that cause by reducing humans even further and making them disposable. Nothing would remain to separate House Dobromil and its few allies from the Imperium under House Kabrin.

The knowledge, the "methods," would die with him. In the decades since he'd escaped he'd never used those methods. Before he'd escaped, he'd made every effort to ensure that no one could follow in his steps.

"Lieutenant," he said, making his voice gentle.

Laleo looked up.

"I had nothing to do with Lord Dobromil's—or his son's—success," Galen added, matter-of-factly. "None at all. You must believe me."

"But—"

"None. At. All."

Laleo gulped. "Your daughter. She has a son as well. A *donai* son."

"*One* son. Also not my doing. Any of it."

People only remembered the things that confirmed their biases and conveniently forgot the things that didn't. Like the lack of a *donai*-human population explosion under Lord Dobromil's rule. Like the number of failed *donai*-human pregnancies. Like the overwhelming number of human children with *donai* fathers—children who inherited no *donai* traits at all.

"Do you really think that"—Galen looked Laleo right in the eyes—"if I had a way of increasing House Dobromil's power and strength, I wouldn't use it? That Lord Dobromil would not make me use it? Why stop at one son? Why not make a dozen daughters instead?"

Understanding spread over Laleo's features.

Galen rested his hand atop Laleo's shoulder and said, "A dozen fertile *donai* females to ally with a dozen powerful houses. *They* would be the key to power, would they not?"

SYTERIA UNDERSTOOD the reasons why Galen was having her follow him around: he was keeping her busy while keeping her close and providing her with opportunities to interact with the *Edlyn's* crew. Although the *Edlyn's* infirmary had seemed hers alone, the field hospital was far busier, keeping the staff occupied with a constant influx of injured humans.

It was late afternoon, the sun lingering low in the sky on their third day on Tir'Hala-Revir. They were returning to the field hospital after sharing a late afternoon meal. Sweat trickled down her hairline as dust tainted the air and made it taste of ash.

They passed a row of egg-shaped pods queued up in a line. The life-pods hadn't been there earlier.

She stopped in her tracks, dread flowing in her veins like ice. Galen backed up, a questioning look on his face.

"Ah," he said and launched into an explanation as he placed his hand at the center of her back.

Her feet refused to move, as if they'd grown roots. He spoke again. "Life" was the only word she understood.

He extended his other arm in invitation, encouraging her forward. Her stomach clenched and churned despite his steadying hand. Scorch marks on the compacted soil, the telltale pattern of landing gear, and the distance—well away from the hospital itself—told her that this was a landing pad for the *Edlyn's* shuttles.

"Go on," he said with an encouraging smile.

She'd seen the pods before, when she'd first woken on the *Edlyn*. They had been nestled into the triage area's ceiling, no doubt stowed safely out of the way until needed.

"For *donai* and beasts," he said, placing his hand on one of the larger ones, then moved to a smaller version. "For humans."

"Thertore," Syteria whispered, hugging herself, rubbing her arms to banish a spurious chill.

"Yes," he said as he waved his hand over a symbol etched into the smooth surface. Not even dust seemed able to cling to the pods. Seams appeared on the surface as if carved by an invisible hand. They raced along the long axis and then the seam parted, revealing a pristine interior.

Cold rose in tendrils like fog. It reminded her of the cloud that had grabbed her when the imperials had attacked. Galen placed his hand into the fog. It coalesced around his fingers, coating them in a wet sheen.

He gestured encouragingly for her to do the same. Hesitantly, she stretched her right hand into the fog. Like mist turning to dew, it had a slight chill.

"Nanites," she said and leaned in closer. The pod was slowly filling with a wet shimmer, a liquid that moved as if it were alive.

Memories rushed at her: the agony of razor-sharp edges plunging into her body, acid dissolving her eyelids and burning through her eyes, the strain of breathing liquid. It had been thick and cold, just like the one clinging to her hand.

She raised her hand to her cheek. "New face. New eyes."

Galen nodded, smiling.

Her skin pebbled. She blew out a breath. "Thank you."

He gave her a shallow bow and waved the pod closed. She followed him back into the field hospital, playing with the wetness still clinging to her hand. It evaporated slowly, shimmering as it did.

"Life," she whispered in Kappan. More than life: miracle.

Galen had led her to Aeda's bedside. The red-haired woman was in a deep sleep, a rover floating above her head, casting a pulsing light. Her injured leg was locked in place, surrounded by a sparkling shroud.

"Here," Galen said gesturing towards a chair by Aeda's bed.

Syteria sat down, giving in to a fatigue that had been creeping in since they'd eaten. Tir'Hala-Revir's day was longer than the standard she'd become used to on the *Edlyn*.

Galen worked a nearby console.

"Wait here," he said.

"What do you need me to do?" Syteria asked in Rhoan. She tried again in Kanthlos, haltingly, not quite certain she had the proper verb.

"Guard."

Syteria frowned. "Guard?"

"Watch," he amended. "Watch Aeda. Rest."

He left before she could answer, walking through the adjoining partition to check on his other patients.

Syteria leaned back and pressed the palm of her hand to her breast-bone, rubbing at the phantom pain there. She squeezed her eyes shut at the memory of the *grierugon* pulling its claw out of her chest. Blood had fountained as she'd fallen back in that sickening distortion of slowed time.

A throat cleared and she bolted upright. The scarred *donai*, the one called Kell, was standing beside Aeda's bed. He wore the pleated garment and reeked of blood and sweat. His right arm bore a metal gauntlet fashioned out of the same woodgrain metal that was so prevalent aboard the *Edlyn*, and in his left hand, white and red wildflowers.

He leaned over Aeda, eyes aglow, sweeping his gaze over the red-haired woman just like the tyrant had swept his gaze over Syteria. A slow smile crept across Kell's lips revealing the brilliant white of sharp cuspids.

Syteria sniffed, placing her hand to her nose. His scent was acrid. Not unpleasant, but...wrong.

He blushed and she lowered her hand. "I'm sorry," she said in Rhoan. She had meant no insult.

He spoke, his voice hushed and hurried, ending with her title.

"I don't understand." Those were three words she knew perfectly.

He bowed his head and thrust the wildflowers at Syteria as he said, "Aeda."

He let go of them a bit too quickly—as if he didn't want to risk touching her—and some of them slipped and fell from his grasp . Syteria bent to gather the ones that had fallen.

Galen reentered and fired off what sounded like a half dozen questions, never giving Kell a chance to answer. Kell's demeanor changed, his posture stiffening, his face hardening. He cast one last longing look at Aeda, pivoted on his heel, and strode out.

Syteria turned to Galen. "What's wrong? Why are you so angry? Why did you send him away?" They all came out in Rhoan.

Galen aimed a scowl at the wildflowers and stalked off in the opposite direction.

Syteria took a step to follow, intent on demanding an explanation, but stopped. Not only was an explanation unlikely given her limited understanding of Kanthlos, but perhaps, given the way Kell had looked at Aeda, Galen had good reason for posting a guard at her bedside.

She tried not to think of herself as *eniseri* again, but her hands were shaking. No matter what she did, they continued to tremble as she scrounged around for a container, filled it with water, and arranged the wildflowers as neatly as she could.

There was a perfect place for them at Aeda's bedside. Perhaps in the morning Aeda could be convinced to explain if the conveyance of flowers had a cultural meaning she had missed.

CHAPTER TWENTY-FOUR

*D*arkness and pain. Ice. They flowed around Syteria with a
rough, dry touch like the scales of a snake scorching skin in
their wake. Her skin blistered at their touch. As the snake coiled
around her for purchase it grew limbs and razor-sharp claws.

She startled awake, a scream catching in her throat. Aeda had both
of her hands on Syteria's shoulders, shaking her awake while keeping
her from toppling out of the bedside chair.

Aeda had donned her skin suit and boots. She'd even tamed her red
hair and pulled it back. It was tucked underneath her cap. Concerned
blue eyes were aimed at Syteria, along with gentle words that sounded
like a question.

Syteria took a deep breath. "It was a dream," she said in Rhoan.
"I'm fine," she added in Kanthlos.

Aeda let go of her shoulders, eyes narrowing as if she was
pondering the truth of Syteria's words.

"*Grie-ru-gon,*" Syteria said, forming the word with care as she
stood up and shook herself.

Aeda nodded and said something.

"I don't understand," Syteria said.

Aeda reached across the bio-bed, stretching her tall frame with ease, and plucked the wildflowers from their container. They dripped water down her skin suit as she lifted them to her face, taking in their scent.

"Kell," Syteria said, pantomiming the long scar on the *donai's* face.

A triumphant smile spread across Aeda's lips. She let out a squeak as she wrapped her arms around Syteria and gave her a hard squeeze. She spoke far too fast for Syteria to catch a single word. Aeda let go of her just as abruptly, stepped back, and then gave her a half-bow, along with a "my lady" before she took off.

"Wait!" Syteria shouted. "Galen hasn't—"

Aeda burst through the field hospital's doors, shedding a few blossoms as she ran. Syteria followed, running into the sunlight and down a path towards the center of the star fort.

Other humans were gathering before a platform on which Palleton stood. They clamored, their voices rising for attention. Aeda shouldered her way into the assembled throng and disappeared.

Syteria came to a stop. She could no more force Aeda to come back with her than she could explain her reason for it. Obviously Aeda's leg had healed well enough for her to outrun Syteria. Strong, fierce Aeda who'd refused anesthetic, who'd allowed Kell to carry her like a child, wanted to be here more than she wanted to continue under Galen's care. She could understand that, having had that feeling more than once herself. Attentive, meticulous, paternal, Galen could be overbearing.

She ducked into the shadows to observe. Several other *donai*, including Kell, mounted the platform. Over the shouting and clamoring the *donai* pointed and called out names. Whoops of excitement rose from those named. Small groups formed around each *donai* to be led away, leaving behind a few dozen disappointed humans.

Some went off alone. Others walked in pairs or small groups, consoling each other with pats on the back. They cast longing glances at those leaving the star fort. The few that noticed Syteria greeted her with nods. She trailed a small group to a practice field. As the sun rose she watched them work spears and bows and arrows.

Thirst and hunger called her back to the field hospital's commissary.

For two more perplexing days Galen pretended he needed Syteria's help to set human bones and re-break *donai* ones that had healed improperly in the field. He thundered at exhausted, triumphant humans who refused to remain in the field hospital as ordered. He dispatched his useful aides to track them down and haul them back.

The tyrant breezed in long enough to enjoy the spectacle of Galen threatening his rebellious patients with restraints.

Galen stopped short of asking the tyrant to issue orders reinforcing medical prudence. His frustrated look, that false deference that dared not ask for something that would be denied...Syteria had worn that look often enough to be intimate with its source.

The tyrant departed, leaving the ultimate decision to Galen's patients. Almost to the last, they had fled the hospital as soon as an opening presented itself.

Syteria cornered Galen after things settled down.

"Why?" she asked. "Why are we here?"

It was the best approximation of the real question: Given that your technology doesn't eliminate pain or death, why take all these risks?

Galen led her out of the field hospital. They climbed to a parapet overlooking the interior of the star fort. Dozens of tents ringed the open space in the fort's center.

He spoke, gesturing at the tents, the central area, the bastions that made up the points of the star fort. She didn't understand most of what he'd said, but he rambled on.

"We may be slaves, but this"—he nodded towards the central arena below—"*this* forms us pieces of the pack." He clasped his hands together, intertwining his fingers as he added, "Ties us to *donai* and *donai* to us."

The words weren't quite right to her, but Syteria nodded.

So, Aeda's reluctance to remain in Galen's care had to do with this rite of passage. The *donai* were testing the humans. But for what? Why? They were already crew. They had rank and position.

Why in this dangerous, primitive environment where pain and death remained everyday possibilities despite their technology?

And why were only some humans part of it? Why not all of them?

Some of the *Edlyn's* crew had remained on the ship. And not all the humans on the planet were being tested. Some, like Galen and his staff, as well as others she'd seen teaching, preparing meals, and running things obviously weren't here to prove themselves.

I'm not learning fast enough.

She had seen humans coming together and earning esteem, just like on Kappa. Longing filled her for home, her people, their way of life.

How could these *donai* who were so far ahead of Kappa be so much like her people?

The Rhoans had taught her that societies like their own had achieved advancement, enlightenment, and superiority by rejecting physical violence. They had also taught her that the Kappans were little more than animals because of their physicality and competitiveness. Because of their Kappan nature, her people would never advance. That "truth" had been pounded into her for more than a decade until she'd accepted it.

But these people—both *donai* and humans—were far more advanced than the Rhoans. They embraced not only competition and violence but used it to develop trust. The *donai* relied on their humans as much as the humans relied on the *donai*. And they cared for one another—she had seen it when Anasera and Aeda had been injured.

That's why there were no chains, no overseers. These people, these humans, were slaves in name only. They were part of a hierarchy where people were unequal but valued nevertheless. They were respected only for what they could accomplish.

The *donai* allowed them to succeed, or fail, and placed them accordingly. Just like her tribe on Kappa had, each person valued for what they could do. She yearned for that kind of worth again.

And in order to get it, she'd have to give up her past. It wasn't enough to reject being *eniseri*. She would have to rediscover and nurture her Kappan self, stoke it from the tiny spark that had somehow survived and let it become a roaring flame.

She would have to allow it to consume her.

"I want to belong," she said in Kanthlos, uncertain about the last word. She did not mean being property, being a slave, or a captive. Would Galen understand that?

"You belong, Syteria." There was a kind smile and a pat on the shoulder to go with that reassurance as Galen walked away.

She sighed her frustration.

I've earned nothing. I'm owned, like a prize or a trophy. A useless...pet.

Syteria wanted more. Her teeth worried her lower lip, drawing blood. She'd learned one thing, down here: if she wanted more, she was going to have to take it.

GALEN'S THREAT TO sedate all his disobedient patients still echoed in Darien's ears as he climbed to the top of the north-most tower. He saw Galen's words for the empty threat they were. Sabotaging human efforts to rise to the status of oath-sworn vassal was not in Galen's interests. Many had volunteered to serve on the *Edlyn* just for this opportunity.

All humans needed to demonstrate a certain temperament and intelligence, as well as the ability to survive. A primitive setting remained their best testing ground. Galen understood this as well as the *donai*.

Darien shifted his visual augmentations so he could scan the perimeter far outside the fort. He memorized the locations of the caches of weapons and supplies his father had ordered hidden here. There were thousands such caches throughout his domain. With a potential spy among them, it was a risk but Darien had ordered that a cache be set up on every one of Tir'Hala-Revir's continents.

Below, *donai* and humans were returning from the hunt.

He admired these ordinary humans and their willingness to risk death just so he would take their oaths. It was different for the *donai*. Their instincts dictated required behaviors far more than in humans. Their augmentations reduced the fear and risk of death.

The bloodied, exhausted humans for whom the test had been a joy...*they* were the ones he planned to keep.

His survey halted at the sight of Galen and Syteria standing on a parapet. He couldn't hear them over the din of all the activity.

Galen pointed and gestured to the area reserved for humans.

Darien strained the limits of his visual augmentations to zoom in on Syteria. Her unfocused gaze drifted over the activities around her. Her face—that beautiful face—was expressionless. It filled him with a need to do something, anything, to bring emotion, to it.

As ordered, Galen had kept her out of Darien's way. Coming to Tir'Hala-Revir had kept Palleton and the *donai* focused on all the humans except Syteria. Keeping his distance remained the best course of action. He knew this with deep, painful intensity. Still, the question, *Best for whom?* intruded and refused to be ignored.

He shook his head.

One did not negotiate with desire.

He wanted her. Distance had not changed that. His humanity was intruding in the form of desire despite the lack of proximity. Humans were not driven by pheromones the way the *donai* were. They didn't bind themselves to the only woman who'd proven herself compatible by conceiving.

A shadow streaked along the ground. He looked up just as Bomani's shuttle passed over.

Down the side of the tower he went. He sprinted past the pavilions and tents, rounding the half-finished arena where they would hold the oath-taking ceremony.

He entered the *donai's* courtyard, a small area tucked into the fort's eastern bailey. Triangular canopies perched on spires. They shaded the platform on which Bomani waited. The blandness in her face appeared forced enough to give him pause.

"Will you be joining us after all, Commander?" he asked as he reached for a pitcher of water. He drank some, then poured the rest over his head, shedding some of the day's accumulated grime. He swiped at his wet hair and face.

She shook her head. "No, my lord."

Bomani reached into her tunic and withdrew a thin cylinder enameled in green. The color alone told him it was from the emperor.

"The courier did not wait for a response," she said, presenting him with the message cylinder.

Palleton led several kilted *donai* into the courtyard.

Darien dragged his thumb across the cylinder's edge, shedding skin cells for it to analyze and confirm his identity. Like the slit of a cat-eye, the cylinder opened along the long axis, revealing a rolled up piece of parchment. He pulled it out and smoothed it open. The embedded coding confirming its origin glowed in his enhanced vision as he read it in the fading light.

"Drea, relax. It's just a summons."

She didn't relax. He handed her the message so she could read for herself. Her expression hardened.

"There's no reason given," she said.

"The emperor does not need a reason; he can summon me at any time."

"For aid and counsel, yes. This states neither."

"Don't read too much into this, Commander," he said, shrugging. But his shrug did nothing to dispel the bitter taste of the half-truth.

Palleton had joined them on the platform. He peered over Bomani's shoulder, reading the short, terse message with a quick glance.

"Do you think it's about your claim?" Palleton asked.

"Absolutely. Of that, I have no doubt."

"What if he refuses to recognize it?" Bomani asked.

"A claim has never been rejected," Palleton said. "In this, the emperor truly has no choice."

"Only if the emperor chooses to follow the rules," Bomani said. "Only if the Houses choose to enforce them. Only if there are consequences."

What Bomani was not saying was that the emperor wasn't beyond using dishonorable—and personal—means to strike at Darien. As much rested on the emperor's honor as on Darien's. And if Darien was willing to compromise it—as he had—why wouldn't his imperial cousin?

"Do you think he has ulterior motives, Commander?" Palleton asked.

"Of course he does. He always does..." A heavy sigh joined her pinched, tension-filled posture.

"How many ships did he send?" Darien asked.

"Just the courier ship," Bomani said. "At least, that's all we can detect. It's possible there are imperial ships outside the range of our sensors."

"Did you send out our parasites?" Darien asked.

"Yes, my lord. They haven't reported any imperial contacts."

"Commander, the emperor won't send a fleet, or any significant presence. Not here. To Serigala, maybe. To my father. He'd have my father bring me to heel, because as a half-breed I am not worthy of the emperor's notice. Not his public notice, anyway."

She gave him a reluctant, fractional nod.

"How did the Imperium know where we were?" Darien asked.

Bomani's face reddened. "We suspect additional transmissions, ones beamed to phase-jumping drones we failed to detect until it was too late. We're not certain, but they might have come from here rather than from the *Edlyn*."

Darien paced the depth of the platform. He'd hoped to ferret out the traitor with the testing. If someone who'd already sworn fealty to him was responsible, the problem became...more. No wonder Bomani looked ready to spit nails.

"Kabrin sends only a courier," Darien said. "He still courts me to his side, half-breed that I am, delicately seeking for my defection to his cause. He still hopes that I'll stand against my father and bring House Dobromil in line with the Imperium."

Since the emperor had reluctantly recognized his status, he had been testing Darien's loyalties to his father and his House. The emperor had even offered unreserved recognition of his status as heir, all for the slightest rebuke of Dobromil's unsanctioned practices. Darien's claim had been designed to cater to imperial prejudices, but perhaps it hadn't. There was only one way to find out: speak with the emperor himself.

Bomani cleared her throat and pulled a second cylinder—one bearing Dobromil's sigil—from inside her tunic.

"Perhaps you're right, my lord, " she said as she handed it over.

Between their problems with the communications arrays and his desire to avoid the Imperium, they'd been running silent, but his father would have known he'd stop to bloody the crew. He would have narrowed down candidate planets to a convenient handful. He would have sent courier drones to all possible sites. It still unnerved him to see the cylinder in Bomani's hand.

It didn't serve his father's deniability to know where he was and what he was doing. It didn't serve Darien's plan to be ordered back to Serigala just yet.

He opened the cylinder. It was a very short note, written in a hurried scrawl. *Deploy to Gamma Iramana. End the practice called the Rite of Ascension. Lord Dobromil.*

The brevity of such orders meant that how Darien chose to accomplish his mission was up to him—a cryptic, if welcome—gesture of trust.

There was no second, personal message.

"Something about your claim?" Bomani asked.

He handed her the note. She read it. Her somber nod conveyed a hint of apology.

"We have a new mission," he said for Palleton's benefit.

"The *Edlyn's* crew is due for a reprieve, not another assignment," Bomani said, passing their orders to Palleton. "Was no one else available?"

No one he needed to keep out of the way. Still, his father's orders bought him much-needed time.

"Elva Tavernier was a friend of yours, was she not?" Palleton asked.

The elder *donai* had not misspoken. It was probably the precise nature of Elva's "friendship" that had earned him this assignment. It could be another test. It could simply be political prudence, or mere proximity. Any or all would make compelling reason for his father to send him.

"She *was*," Darien said, retaking possession of his father's note and reading it again.

Even before their exile to the border, it had come to his father's attention that the governor of Gamma Iramana, his so-called friend, the Honorable Elva Tavernier, had been unaware that the barbaric rite continued. Dispatching him and the *Edlyn* could only mean that Elva had somehow failed to end the Rite.

"I'll have a courier sent to request another ship for the Gamma Iramana mission," Bomani said.

Darien's pacing came to a halt. "Whatever for?"

"The imperial summons," Bomani said as if the answer was patently obvious. "You don't intend to go to Kanavar alone." Her tone was crystal clear: it was a command, not a request.

He raised a mocking brow, but she held his gaze, unyielding, practically daring him to defy her. What secret orders had his father given her? A part of him yearned to see just how far he could push Bomani, how much he could get her to reveal.

"No," Darien said. "Not alone. It's been a while since Palleton has enjoyed the emperor's hospitality. We will take the *Glaive* and comply with the summons, then meet up with the *Edlyn* before she reaches Gamma Iramana."

"What if the emperor doesn't allow you to return? My lord," she said.

"Then Gamma Iramana will be the least of my father's concerns." *Or yours.*

He waited, expecting further argument. He didn't envy Bomani's untenable position—protect Dobromil's interests; protect and obey Dobromil's heir. And Dobromil's heir never made it easy.

"Will you be taking Syteria with you?" she asked.

It was a stab at his honor, right into his soul. He waited for the roused monster within, the one Bomani herself had denied existed, to settle.

"She remains under my protection, and the claim denies him dominion over her. That's why the summons doesn't mention her at all. The emperor knows the first rule of command as well as we do."

Never give an order that can't be obeyed.

"Yes, my lord," she said reluctantly.

Bomani bowed and departed.

When she passed out of sight, Darien grabbed his dagger from its sheath, and with a shouted curse, pinned the summons to the table. He stepped back and glared at the parchment. The vibrating dagger came to rest, no longer harmonizing into the silence. He wanted to set it afire, watch it smolder and turn to ash. He wanted its destruction, along with everything it represented.

Palleton stood opposite him. He leaned forward, bracing his massive hands on the table.

"What do you need, my lord?"

"The traitor's head to lay at my liege's feet."

And an overwhelming force at my back.

OWYN TOLEK AIMED his courier ship for one of Tir'Hala-Revir's phase-points. Mere light-seconds behind, two of the Serigalan ship's parasites provided escort, just as they had when he'd first entered the system. According to his sensors, the Serigalan ship called the *Edlyn* had sent out additional parasites, no doubt expecting an imperial fleet.

Disguised as a courier, he was a diplomatic envoy with certain protections that other imperial craft would not enjoy. After the political fallout from Kailin Kabrin's attempt to enforce imperial demands, the emperor had dispatched Tolek. His mission was two-fold. The secondary part of it required the delivery of a message, so he'd acted like a mere courier.

Tolek's ship had been confined to a hangar and he'd been allowed to disembark only after a very thorough, but unnecessary, scan.

He'd been greeted by Bomani. Once she'd identified herself as the ranking officer and a sworn vassal of the message's recipient, he'd placed the cylinder in her hands, turned on his heel, and returned to his ship. The *Edlyn* had cleared him for departure and irised an opening in its shield before he'd re-seated himself in the cockpit.

On his left, one of the smaller displays translated the encrypted signals from the seeds he'd launched on the solar wind, toward

Tir'Hala-Revir. He had released them, fulfilling his primary mission, upon entry into the star system, before his vector had taken him anywhere near the *Edlyn*. Most of the seeds would burn up in the atmosphere, despite their shielding, but some would get through and make it to the surface and into Dayasagar's encampment.

There hadn't been time to tailor the microscopic weapons to a specific individual. Instead, they would invoke a much easier parameter, one already built in—human women. And not just any women, but those favored by *donai*.

He punched through the phase-point, leaving his Serigalan escorts behind.

CHAPTER TWENTY-FIVE

*S*yteria headed to the *donai* courtyard, walking the serpentine path through the pavilions where humans slept. She had not noticed it aboard the *Edlyn*, but in the encampment there was a distinct physical separation between the quartering of humans and *donai*, as well as males and females.

No. Here it was men and women. The distinction between man and male, woman and female, was a nuance reinforced by their vocabulary, another aspect of their culture that reminded her of Kappa.

Homesickness stabbed her heart and gut. She shook her head. Kappa was out of reach, not just now, but maybe forever. It was wasted energy, wasted emotion, to pine for something so impossible.

As the sky darkened and stars appeared, the hunting parties trickled in. She passed bustling activity: meals being prepared and served; filthy people waiting for showers; groups engaged in conversation and friendly competition; tutoring sessions focusing on spear-throwing and archery.

She lingered. Would they allow her to join them?

No. She needed to speak to *him*.

She paused in front of a pair of towering supports. They were topped by two horizontal crosspieces that cast curved shadows. It was a gate of some kind, but one designed to allow entry, not deny it.

A small group of *donai* ringed a large, open fire pit. Some *donai* were sharpening spears; others, knives. She looked for the telltale swords and found none.

Their gazes followed her, reflecting the firelight, but no one moved to bar her entry.

On the other side of the fire pit, staggered canopies shaded a platform. Chairs hedged a long table. Everything looked like it had been constructed "to see if it could be done."

In the time it had taken her to enter their domain, twilight had chased away the setting sun. Soon all the light would be gone, along with her courage.

The tyrant was there, leaning over the wooden table, engaged in a debate with the one called Palleton.

He hesitated mid-sentence as she entered.

Pelts, spears and other primitive weapons she did not recognize framed them. It was as though she had stepped through time, back thousands of years, to what they might have looked like had humans not created them.

There was something primal—so very right—about the way they looked. They were in their element.

The *donai* clustered around her, maintaining a distance they observed only with her. Did they still see her as alien? Or was it the taint of being a pet? Had they seen her escape attempt as a rejection of the new life they'd given her or as ungratefulness for the risks they had taken to rescue her? Did they see it as a rejection of them? She had wanted to be judged for herself, her own worth, not because she was *his*.

"My lady," Palleton acknowledged, his voice a tumbling rumble, but without the strange effect *his* voice had on her.

She gave Palleton one of those curt nods that Galen favored. It brought a hint of a smile to the dark face.

The tyrant continued to ignore her, giving his attention to a thick paper pinned to the table with a dagger. She waited a moment. And another.

Retreat gains me nothing.

"I want to understand," she said in Rhoan.

Nothing. Not a twitch, not a flicker of *his* gaze, not a hesitant breath. She wasn't worthy of his notice. She did not exist.

"I want to understand and not judge."

He leveled those amber eyes at her with such intensity that she took a half step back.

Oh, I have his attention now.

Mouth dry, she swallowed her apprehension.

He straightened and spoke—too low to make out—to Palleton.

She stepped closer, but not too close.

Palleton nodded and a silent signal of some kind must've passed between them. The *donai* to clear the courtyard. She stopped mid-turn as she considered following them out.

Curiosity itched between her shoulder blades, reminding her of why she was here. She squared her shoulders as she faced the platform.

He had pulled a chair forward and gazed down at her from a barbarian throne. Her heart skipped a beat as reality intruded—they were alone. He'd dismissed *all* his men.

He gripped the armrests as he leaned back to consider her through hooded eyes. The rise and fall of his chest drew her gaze to carved muscle underneath skin caked with dust and blood. His feet were streaked with mud. Dirt clung to the coarse hair on his legs.

Her gaze traveled to the belt hugging his hips and then vaulted to his face. A mask of torchlight danced over his features, revealing the brutal line of his jaw, the jumping muscle in his bearded cheek, the thick knitted brow.

She clenched her hands.

"Why are you dressed like that?" she asked.

"It's warm."

The swiftness of the answer and the depth of his impatient tone gave her pause. She kept her gaze on his face. "Too warm for skin suits? The humans—"

"*We* are not human."

255

"I'm trying to understand." *Help me understand.* The plea would not pass her tightening throat and lingered unspoken as a painful thought, a simmering ache.

"Our bodies can withstand the extremes of harsher environments than this," he said. "Aboard ship, to appear human, we wear clothing and boots, but require neither."

She eyed the grime covering his body.

"And the decoration?" she asked, the taunt clearing her lips before she realized she'd spoken aloud.

His frown deepened. "Do blood and dirt offend you?"

Oh, no, that's not what—

She hadn't meant to darken his mood. How had this primal creature come to inhabit the civilized star-farer who'd rescued her, insisted she accept his protection, and whispered to her of temptation?

"Why did you really come here?" he asked.

"You're the only person who underst—the only one I can converse with." She took a deep breath. "I came here to understand. Your language is very difficult. It's not fair."

He leaned on a propped elbow.

"Fair?" he scolded. "Only a child whines about fairness. You're an adult."

"And you're a tyrant." Her breath hitched at the careless choice of words. It made her sound like a child.

"I don't deny it," he said, a steel edge to his voice. His knuckles paled as he tightened his hold on the armrest.

Stubborn, arrogant creature. How had he managed to crawl—and take residence—under her skin so quickly?

"Galen said you're binding the *donai* to the humans and the humans to the *donai*."

"Is there a question in there?"

"Is there a nobleman in *there*?" she demanded, pointing an accusing finger at him. Before her arm could tremble, she lowered it. "I'd like to speak to him."

He stood, muscles flexing in the firelight. "I will have a shuttle take you up to the *Edlyn*. We can continue this discussion when I've finished with the crew."

"I want to stay here. I want to learn. I want to belong."

He took a hesitant step forward, then back. A heartbeat later he lowered himself into the embrace of his throne, golden gaze fixed like a predator studying his prey from shadowed repose.

Shoulders back, Syteria braced for the inevitable silence. She wouldn't break it and allow him to unbalance her further. She too could wait.

"You," he said, softer and calmer than she'd expected, "are not part of the *Edlyn's* crew."

She was about to object, but he held up a staying hand.

"There is a specific intent to what we're doing here," he explained. "The crew is in my chain of command. I have to be prepared to sacrifice every single one of them for the good of the mission, the good of the ship, the good of my House. You are under my protection, and I cannot compromise my vow by treating you as crew."

"I release you from your vow."

He was as still and silent as stone.

She dared not breathe. Could it be that easy? Was that all it would've taken all along?

"Were we to accept," he finally said, "which we do not, our release still wouldn't place you in our chain of command."

She closed her eyes to shield herself from the possessiveness of his gaze.

Time seemed to stop, to gather and loom around her, sweeping her away like a great tide. Something primal, without physical form, caught her in its grasp, wrapped powerful arms around her, and held her close.

It whispered to her without words, *I will never let you go.*

With a startled gasp, she opened her eyes. He was still there on his throne, and she, before him. That tide, that elemental force, hadn't swept her away after all. She licked dry lips. The motion drew his smoldering gaze, bringing breath to his still form.

"I don't want to be part of your crew," she said.

"What then? What do you want to be a part of?"

"The *pack*."

She'd used their word. The Rhoans had two equivalents—mob or herd. The closest Kappan word she'd inferred from context was tribe...or perhaps, family. For a terrible, fleeting instant, she wished he could speak and understand Kappan as well.

His chin rose and a satisfied smile—a knowing grin—took his face as he leaned forward, out into the light.

"*Pack?* Not crew?" he verified.

"Yes. *Pack*."

Her belly tightened, twisting.

"Not crew," she added. "Not in your chain of command."

*P*ACK.

Darien probed his cuspids with his tongue. It had taken her scent only seconds to remind him why he needed to keep his distance.

Everything about her tempted him: the way she controlled her own impulses; the way her lips glistened; the way she filled an earnest tone with challenge.

As if calling him a tyrant would somehow wound him. Or shame him. He knew what he was. And what he was not. The urge to show her the extent of his tyranny dissipated as her scent faded.

He groaned, easing the painful tension in his chest.

He should've never allowed Galen to bring her down here. She belonged on the *Edlyn*, safe from the dangers of this place.

Safe from him.

But he hadn't. Some part of him had found merit in the argument that his crew, and the *donai* in particular, needed to see them interact. Her escape attempt had cast a shadow on his claim, one that couldn't be lifted as long as they believed her caged in his quarters.

"She *is* a good match for you, my lord," Palleton said as he returned to the platform. The elder *donai's* gaze lingered on Syteria's retreating form.

Darien bared his teeth, nostrils flaring. A pulling sensation in his gut joined in, spearing him. It happened every time another *donai's* gaze had lingered on her. If he marked her, the lingering looks would cease, and he need never deal with *that* emotion.

He took a deep, calming breath. It sent a tremor down the length of his body. Let them admire her. The sight of her was his gift to them— his only gift.

"Understood her, did you?" Darien asked.

"Not a word, my lord. Didn't need to." Palleton grinned. "All I need to know, I see in you face."

"See what?"

"Hunger."

Darien's jaw worked, but he couldn't voice a denial. Hunger was one way to describe it—a mundane description, but not inaccurate.

"Pair-bond," Palleton amended with a widening grin. "A strong one."

So, Galen's ruse was working. It was bound to be a double-edged sword. He would have to wield it with great care.

"A pair-bond you do not take advantage of, my lord," Palleton said as if he'd somehow divined Darien's fears. Perhaps he had, in his own subtle way. The elder *donai* had seen generations come and go, been witness to pair-bonds that yielded human children and inhuman ones. He'd been a part of Darien's life since before he'd been born. In some ways, Palleton had been as much a father to him as Lord Dobromil. Over the years, he'd certainly spent more time with him.

"I would take my pleasures in private," Darien said.

Palleton scoffed. "You have the whole planet at your disposal." The elder *donai* scrutinized him with such intensity it was like a knife scraping across Darien's skin.

"You understood one word, didn't you?"

"Pack," Palleton answered.

An ironic laugh pressed past Darien's lips, masking his relief. "She wants to be pack."

"As I said, a good match." Palleton grinned.

Darien scratched his forehead. He was starting to itch. He was of a mind to forego bathing until they returned to the *Edlyn*, just to see her reaction. He could make a point of gathering further "decorations" for her delight.

Palleton cleared his throat. "You're not thinking of allowing it."

"Allowing what?"

"My lord, your thinking seems quite affected," Palleton said, raising an eyebrow.

Darien sighed in agreement. "Advise me, unaffected one."

Palleton grunted in mock derision, then turned serious once again. "The humans will resent it. They worked hard for the opportunity to be here. She's not one of them. She's not crew. This is their rite of passage, not hers."

"And the *donai*?"

"We *donai* recognize your claim, my lord. We are, to the last, happy to finally see you falter before a woman. The hunger of pair-bond looks good on you."

Darien shook off the sarcasm along with the dust on his forearms. He swiped at his face and decided a bath was in order before the night's hunt.

"I have not faltered."

"Of course not, my lord."

"Glad you agree. Set up a weapons test. Let's see what she knows. Then we can decide how to test her mettle."

"*If* we should test her mettle," Palleton corrected.

CHAPTER TWENTY-SIX

*I*nside the field hospital, in one of the chambers set aside for research, Galen perched on the edge of a high stool, working on cataloguing samples of the local microbes.

His patient load was practically nil as the naturally accident-prone took themselves out of the competition early on and were sent back up to the *Edlyn*. Gone too were those too injured for the limited facilities here. It was peaceful and quiet. Just like he liked it. Pure bliss.

"What are you doing here?" Nestra's strained voice drifted in from the adjoining chamber.

Multiple pairs of thudding footsteps approached as Galen looked up from the samples.

"Sorry for the interruption," Palleton said as he ducked into the lab, twisting to enter shoulder first.

Three more *donai* followed, spreading out through the lab, gingerly stepping around workstations cluttered with unprocessed samples.

"What *is* going on?" Galen asked, echoing Nestra's indignation.

Eyes wide, she slid into the lab, stepping around the *donai*.

Palleton was bare-chested and kilted, but the others were in their biomechanical suits—which meant they'd come down from the *Edlyn* and weren't part of the ritual taking place here. The suited *donai* worked specialized scanners as they swept the lab, their faces inscrutable behind their helmets.

One of the *donai* closed in on a specimen inside a spherical containment fields. His scans drove a feedback loop that hummed in angry resonance. Galen winced as the resonant pulse caused the specimen to sizzle and spark. It turned to ash. A tendril of smoke swirled, clouding the containment field.

"Colonel," Galen said, rising, "would you care to explain why you're invading my domain?"

Palleton was busy consulting the scanner held out to him by his subordinate. A scowl animated his usually stoic face. His men continued sweeping the lab, overturning equipment in their haste.

Nestra ducked out of their way only to bump into a console. She tried to steady a tray full of vials before it fell over.

Palleton's hand snaked out just in time, their arms colliding, sending the vials crashing to the floor. Some broke. Others rolled away. He handed her the empty tray. His enormous hands dug into her shoulders, pushed her aside.

She'd have bruises there tomorrow. Galen bit down on a warning. It wasn't like Palleton to man-handle women. Something had him, and his men, too agitated for the niceties they usually practiced.

Palleton's bare feet crushed the vials that had fallen off the tray. Nestra hastily reached for the surviving samples. She cast a fearful look toward Galen. The *donai* may be immune, the humans curable, but—

"That's enough," Galen bellowed.

The *donai* ignored him, intent gazes glued to their scanners. They swept the area again, faces grim. Palleton looked up and pinned Galen with a glare.

"We detected an anomaly in your lab," Palleton said.

"My lab is full of anomalies," Galen said. "We specialize in studying them."

The corners of Palleton's mouth contorted into not-quite-a-sneer. "Transmission anomalies."

Curiosity piqued, Galen shuffled closer to the *donai* to catch a glimpse of the scanner's display, only to be disappointed by what looked like normal readings.

"Gone now, I take it," Galen said.

Another scowl, paired this time with a ruder noise, as Palleton waved the other *donai* away. They were a little more careful on their way out, avoiding instruments and what was left of the samples. A crunch, followed by a muttered curse, told Galen they didn't quite succeed.

Nestra followed the *donai* out, clutching the few vials she'd rescued to her torso.

The prospect of bulls cleaning up his china shop made Galen forego the demand that the *donai* clean up the mess they made.

"Commander Bomani believes the spy is down here now," Palleton said.

Galen glanced around, the hairs on the back of his neck rising. Palleton huffed.

Things he'd dismissed before tugged at the edge of Galen's consciousness as he surveyed the lab. He'd found several things out of order, but assumed that his staff had simply been careless. The field hospital didn't sport the sophisticated countermeasures hard-wired into the *Edlyn* and her infirmary. It was easy to forget that field protocols were in place. He'd caught himself being careless a couple of times.

A weight settled on his shoulders. Someone could've painted a target on his back, and he'd just become aware of it. He tugged at his collar. Not just *his* back. There was another target of interest to the Imperium.

"I better get Syteria back to the *Edlyn*, then," Galen said.

"No," Palleton said.

"Why not? She'd be safer there."

"My lord intends to test her."

Galen blinked away the initial shock. "When?"

"Tomorrow. She needs to earn her marks," Palleton said as he ducked out.

Galen swallowed and unbuttoned his collar, the disarray of his lab forgotten. He'd promised Anasera that he'd keep Syteria safe, that she was in no danger of being bloodied. But he'd never thought that Darien would mark her. Syteria couldn't understand what a marking ceremony truly entailed. And there was no need for it. None at all.

Out of all the archaic, barbaric *donai* practices…

Stick to the plan, boy, he wanted to shout, knowing there was no private place down here where he could approach Darien with a demand for explanation, much less a direct challenge. He couldn't take the chance that the *donai* could overhear anything that might lead them to think their lord's claim was a ruse.

But he could take Syteria out of their reach, keep her safe.

HOT WATER PELTED Syteria's sore back muscles. Her hands were splayed against the blued shower wall, head tucked under the flowing water. She lingered under the soothing caress, profoundly grateful for small pleasures like the well-earned ache of taxed muscles.

Perhaps it was such pleasures that brought the *donai* here, to remind themselves of how far they'd come, how far they'd risen, how far they could fall. Or perhaps it was a return to a past where humans and *donai* had been one.

The tyrant hadn't denied her request to join in the rituals binding the humans to the *donai*. He hadn't had her hauled up to the ship either. She'd taken that as implied agreement.

When *he* hadn't sent for her, she'd made her way to the practice range. Her poorly worded request had resulted in an impromptu spear-throwing lesson from the range master. His indulgence and enthusiasm at having such a willing student had been a welcome alternative to spending the day idly waiting for a summons that hadn't come.

"My lady."

The urgent but muffled voice cut through the water, jolting her from her musings.

She opened her eyes and turned the lever until the flow of water stopped. Swiping at her wet face, she pivoted. The back of Galen's head protruded above the stall door as he turned away.

Blood raced to her face, leaving her cold. Shivering, she reached for a large, beige towel as Galen cleared his throat.

Back still to her, he stammered something about needing or wanting or expecting her help. His tone implied that whatever it was, it couldn't wait.

"Have the *donai* sent for me?" she asked.

He stalked away, rubbing the back of his neck, ignoring her question.

Moments later, barely dry, coiled hair still damp, she emerged wearing her skin suit and boots. Galen paced the staging area outside the women's shower stalls. It was still early enough that the rising sun was barely a promise and the stalls still empty.

He beckoned, gaze bouncing from place to place.

As he headed out, she followed, stopping only to grab a spear someone had abandoned outside the stalls. It was a short walk to an ambulance. At Galen's gestured invitation, she climbed aboard and moved to the back. She wedged herself between stacked boxes, to be whisked off as if staging an escape. Clutching her spear, she looked down at the fort as it slipped below the horizon. She wanted to train with the *donai*, prove that she belonged, not participate in the make-work Galen had been throwing at her.

"Galen, where are you taking me?" she asked.

"Yes," he said without turning to face her.

"I want to go back."

"Thank you."

Folding her arms, she dropped back onto her makeshift seat. Her words had been correct enough. She was certain of it. They should have elicited more than token acknowledgements. It wasn't like Galen to use a single word when dozens would do.

She sulked for the remainder of the flight.

The sun was nearly a quarter of the way to its zenith when the ambulance left them and most of the crates at the base of a waterfall near a forest clearing. Galen's casual attitude and his relaxed manner, suggested that their surroundings were safe from predators and other dangers. She asked why he'd brought no guards, but he

265

waved her question away with a smile and a reassuring pat on the shoulder.

"I make a poor guard," she said.

Galen nodded, avoiding her gaze, and opened a crate. He rearranged several others, staging them, and issued instructions, demonstrating when necessary to clarify what he wanted. She played along, helping him set up a shelter and a field lab.

He kept her busy and distracted all morning, sending her out to collect specimens—anything and everything that crawled, flew, burrowed, or swam.

Hours later, still silent, he picked at the food she'd prepared. He'd shown no previous aversion to speaking to her as if she understood. He could go on for hours.

She played with a fresh cut on her finger, earned while digging out a particularly stubborn, worm-like thing that had hissed and spat at her.

This wasn't the kind of hunting she'd hoped for. The tyrant was the real hunter. Hard body. Broad shoulders. Powerful limbs. No longer hidden by the uniform, no longer wearing the thin veneer of civilization, he'd revealed himself for what he truly was, and in that terrible presence, an illness had taken her, tightening her belly, quickening her heart and breath.

"Galen, what's wrong with me?"

He looked up and frowned.

"Why do I feel sick around *him*?"

Galen answered with silence.

"What did he mean when he said I tempted him?" she asked. "How am I tempting him?" Surely she'd done nothing anyone could mistake for temptation.

Galen picked at his food, separating the chunks of glistening meat from the striped vegetables and setting them up on opposite sides of his plate, like forces about to engage in combat on the field between. He traced circles in the thick sauce and then redeployed his edible army.

"Galen, what did you do to me?"

She placed her hand on his wrist. His gaze rose to hers. She repeated her question.

"I saved your life," he said.

She sat back, breath stalling, uncertain if he'd understood her question at all.

Galen rose to refill a glass not empty and returned to the table. He activated a holographic interface and gave the list that appeared his full attention. Absently, he picked at his fruit salad.

She eyed some of the plant and insect specimens she'd collected. Dropping a few choice bugs on his plate would be a good test of his concentration. She weighed the risk against the satisfaction of grabbing his attention.

By mid-afternoon he was completely immersed in his work.

She strayed from the camp, spear in hand, ready to inflict damage on the thick, reddish-brown trunks that ringed the clearing. Passing breezes stirred the amber-bronze canopies of nearby trees.

Placing the shaft of the spear atop a finger, she determined its balance point. With her grip centered so it lay flat in her hand, she brought her right arm straight back as she pointed her left towards the target.

She whipped the spear out.

It landed a few steps short of the target.

Glancing toward camp to check on Galen, she retrieved it to try again.

Adding a body twist gave her more power; her spear landed just short of the nearest tree. Aligning her left foot toward the target gave her accuracy, making the spear land in line with the tree trunk's center.

Moving closer, she rolled her aching shoulders, letting them recover a bit.

The spear's short range meant it had been designed for hunting. If she ever intended to use it against a live target, she'd have to stalk in close. She had no illusions about the differences between stalking live prey and using trees for target practice, but it was a start—one that made her inexplicably content.

She launched the spear again. It made a satisfying sound as it hit its mark.

She looked behind her towards the camp again, half-expecting to see Galen coming after her with another request for rocks or roots or perhaps some slime or scat.

Bracing one foot against the trunk, she grasped the spear shaft with both hands. She struggled to pull it out of the reddish-brown bark. It finally gave way, and she set up to repeat her throw.

She halted mid-motion as the echoes of a thundering roar blended with the crush of sound from the waterfall. Distorting metal added a screech.

"Galen—"

Fear images propelled her legs as she sprinted towards the camp, spear in hand.

A shredded canopy.

Smashed equipment.

Galen, missing.

She sought a target. At the back of the camp, drag marks marred the bloody soil.

"No, no, no," she chanted in a broken voice.

She followed the trail of drag marks and blood towards the waterfall. Drops blurred to streaks, coating the grass.

Legs pumped. Lungs burned. Vision blurred.

Galen lay prone before her, unmoving.

She sucked in a hesitant breath. Flint eyes blinked back at her as the cat let go of his leg and raised its head with a warning growl.

Releasing the breath to steady her nerves, she lowered to a crouch, intent on the threat in front of her.

"That's right. I'm just a furless little primate," she said, searching the ground, feeling for something small and sharp without breaking eye contact.

The cat's flint eyes barely moved. Head lowering, its body coiled, ready to unleash the full force of its power.

Syteria closed her fingers around what felt like one of the sharp-edged pebbles that littered the area.

"See? No fangs, no claws."

Hopefully, the cat had never faced an adversary armed with a spear, and it wouldn't see it as a threat.

Galen still hadn't moved.

"Please don't be dead."

She had to buy him some time, just long enough for the ambulance to return for them.

"Soft. Softer than him."

She opened the skin suit's neck seal, and raked the sharp-edged pebble across her collar bone. On Kappa similar predators were enticed by blood. Perhaps this one would be too.

Warmth welled. Good. She'd broken skin. She let the pebble fall.

"Tastier too."

The mouthful of pearl scimitars roared another warning. She backed off as she locked fear into the cold, dark corner where it belonged.

And rushed forward.

The flurry of belligerent yowls leapt at her, its razor-sharp claws sparkling in the sunlight. She ducked under the leaping cat's body and aimed the tip of the spear at the center of its soft underside.

Obedient to gravity, the cat fell.

Torque wrenched the spear out of Syteria's grip as a hot, sticky torrent rained down on her, obscuring her vision.

She stumbled towards Galen and fell, placing herself between him and the cat. Swiping tears and gore off her face, she waited for the cat to rise.

It didn't. A gash split its belly from sternum to groin. Fluids oozed and viscera slithered across the grass.

Sounds returned: the whisper of wind; chirps and hums; the flow of water splashing over rock. No growls, no purrs, no keening wails.

Syteria scrambled to her knees. Bending over Galen, she rolled him to his back and tried not to look at the raw open wound of his face. No pulse. A semblance of his chest rising gave her false hope, baiting her imagination.

She tucked her head to his chest and listened. Desperately, she searched the sky. Clouds. A blinding white sun. Moisture on the breeze. She closed her eyes and pressed her ear into his chest.

A muted squelch prickled her eyes open as a spurt of blood painted

Galen's leg. Her hand flew to the seam on his thigh. She searched for the femoral pulse.

Nothing.

She bit down on her bottom lip, opened the skin suit's seam and shoved her hand inside. His pulse was faint. Almost too faint to sense through the roar of her own heartbeat.

She had to keep him warm. Get back to camp. See if any of the surviving equipment included a way to call for help.

Galen's threadbare pulse fluttered under her hand. She drew it back out and the suit re-sealed itself.

It would take too long to build any kind of litter. She could drag him. It wasn't that far.

She stood and hooked her hands under his arms. A dozen steps later she stumbled on the uneven ground and dropped him.

"Sorry."

She slid her arms under his, pulling him higher. Every few steps, she checked over her shoulder. It was easier to keep going than to start again. Galen was heavier than he looked.

Catching her breath, she searched the skies. The ambulance carried a life pod that could sustain humans on the verge of death. She only had to get him so far.

"Galen, what were you thinking?" she mumbled, hooking him under the arms again.

His leg no longer bled. Segments of the skin suit had tightened around the injury. She took a deep breath to brace herself for the starting lift.

A shadow flew down and struck her, setting her right shoulder blade afire. Galen's head hit her boot as she twisted and backed away.

Shrieks echoed around her.

A medley of color streaked across the edge of her vision.

Something reptilian knocked her back and perched atop her chest. Saurian eyes separated by a square muzzle blinked at her. A flailed tail tipped with colorful barbs swayed as the creature studied her, contorting its neck to get a better view.

Syteria punched, aiming for its torso, but it leapt away. It joined two of its companions on Galen's chest, then scurried toward his head. Razor-sharp talons clawed at his face, bringing fresh blood to the surface for them to lick.

"No!"

She rushed forward, swatting one scavenger aside to get to Galen's sidearm. Her palm closed around it. Gun in hand, she raised her arm to sight the larger of the creatures as it leapt away. The gun gripped back as it shifted in her hand.

She dropped it.

The creatures launched themselves at her.

Crossing her arms, she shielded her face.

One creature landed on her back and snaked its tail around her neck. She wrapped one hand around the cord of its tail before it could pull tight.

The second creature landed and balanced on her head, its barbed whip of a tail flailing, its talons digging into her scalp.

The third tangled her feet with its tail and yanked.

She lost her balance and fell on her back. The creature underneath her stopped moving, dead or stunned, its tail loosening around her neck. She pulled her hand free and grabbed at the reptile balancing on her head, but it got its tail around her throat and squeezed.

Syteria raised her legs and the reptile clinging to them, and beat the creature into the ground. It let go, hissed at her, and skittered toward Galen as she rolled for the gun.

The tail around her neck tightened. Her vision tunneled.

Her body went limp, defying her will.

The world went quiet and dark.

DAYS AGO, when it had been launched from the imperial courier ship, the seed was one of thousands.

By the time it reached orbit around Tir'Hala-Revir, it didn't know if it was still one of thousands or one of hundreds. It had no means by which to communicate with the others. This was a precaution, just like the hardwired internal countdown mechanism.

Generations before, designers had learned the hard way not to deploy molecular machines that could replicate or operate as long as resources were available.

The seed plunged through the atmosphere, shedding its skin to friction, keeping its interior components dormant. The plunge into ice-cold water woke the rudimentary intelligence at its core.

Sections of the seed's skin were almost gone, so it set out in search of raw materials with which to reinforce the weak spots. As it tumbled along the bottom of a fast-moving river, it found stone and silt. The seed had many candidate materials to choose from and it opted to supplement its repairs with camouflage.

It woke and deployed the molecular machines resting inside it. Within a day, it looked more or less like an insect that had adapted to survive in its rocky surroundings.

The seed moved a set of its optical sensors to where the eyes on the insect would be and created a realistic approximation of the organ. Its remaining sensors remained on its body so it could maintain its full field of vision.

Its "brain" sought out the pulsing beacon designated in its mission parameters. It deployed membranes filled with hydrogen split from water molecules and floated along the river for as long as it took it in the right direction.

It walked the rest of the way, drawing power from the sun during the day, and from other sources of natural radiation when it found them.

Two days into the mission, the source of the beacon was within its sight. The telltale signature of a shield and the time remaining on its clock triggered a decision pathway: stay far away enough from the shield as to remain undetected.

The seed climbed atop a rock with full exposure to the sun, extruded and spread wing-like solar collectors, and started assembling the weapons inside it.

CHAPTER TWENTY-SEVEN

A vibrant, healthy herd glowed in Darien's enhanced vision. The complacent animals grazed on thick, verdant grasses. Their short tails flicked over striped haunches. Those crowned with antlers stood almost twice as tall as any *donai*.

Darien and Palleton stood on a ridge overlooking the lush grasslands. Sparse trees intruded along the boundary between plain and hill, clustered mostly along overflowing streams. The water, fed by a glacial source farther to the north, ran cold.

"You said you needed to work on your herding skills," Darien joked.

"Darting back and forth," Palleton said as he crossed his arms, "causing confusion, preventing escape. Such undignified wastes of energy hold no interest for me. They're completely unsuitable for someone like me."

"Is that so?" Darien asked.

Palleton grunted assent.

"For whom *are* they suitable?" Darien asked, knowing the answer.

"Smaller, less powerful men." Palleton shot Darien a sideways look. "Or puppies."

Darien hid a smile. The banter was part of their ritual, a light-hearted acknowledgment of their hierarchy. Darien didn't have the size to take this particular type of animal down on his own, but as leader, the decision to do so was still his.

"You'd better pick one," Palleton said. "They're about to—"

The wind shifted.

One of the grazing animals sniffed, caught a whiff of something unsettling—perhaps another predator or spilt blood. The beast dashed for open territory, the first to spook, to display the required sign of weakness and vulnerability.

Neither injured, sick, nor old, the animal's strength promised a challenge. Darien and Palleton exchanged satisfied grins in the split second before taking off along the ridge.

As the herd scattered, they pursued the spooked animal. Darien overtook Palleton as they raced over the grassland. Together, they blurred past lone gray-green trees and patches of thorny red scrub, trailing the panicked beast.

Fear billowed behind their prey on thick tendrils of invisible fog. The beast's heart pumped loudly, robust and full of promise. Gloss-black hooves dug into the hard soil, kicking up a trail of brown dust. The beast's heartbeat turned erratic and panic rose like a cloud around it.

Another burst of speed.

One Darien and Palleton couldn't quite keep up with.

Relentless, they followed.

It was only a matter of time. The sun was high, as much an enemy to the overheating beast as the *donai* pursuing it.

The animal slowed.

Darien raced alongside so the beast would see how close he was.

Its fear was palpable as it leapt over the ground.

Darien swiftly circled around the animal, driving it.

Its body heat soared again. It veered north, towards cover. Darien's feigns and darts forced it the other way.

The source of the river, a waterfall, was close. He could hear its susurrations. He crisscrossed the beast's path, avoiding the serrated antlers.

Panting, the animal slowed to a gallop. Darien persisted, closing the distance, taking advantage of a human-sourced *donai* trait—the ability to sweat and reduce body heat. The same breeze that carried his prey's scent soothed and cooled.

The potent tang of fear, the satisfaction of the chase, tugged at Darien's non-human instincts. Only yesterday, a similar beast's flailing hooves and slashing antlers had broken a *donai's* jaw. Darien had reprimanded the man for not harassing the animal to exhaustion before moving in. It had been an important lesson.

A predator without a *donai's* healing abilities would've died a slow, excruciating death from either trauma or the resulting starvation. Such lessons were a powerful reminder to both human and *donai*, that the seeming cruelty of a drawn-out chase served a purpose: self-preservation.

But the *donai* were not just passive participants in the endless cycle of predator pursuing prey. They didn't have to wait for their prey to die of shock or blood loss. They didn't have to wait for muscle damage to take its toll. They were armed, holding their knives in reserve so as to give the beast a quick, merciful death, an indulgence no unarmed predator could afford.

The beast slowed, eyes wide, head low, sharp antlers ready, but Darien remained out of reach. He roared, feeding the beast's fear. He didn't have to kill it, just keep it from running off.

As it thrust its antlers at Darien's chest, Palleton came upon the beast, leapt, and seized its muscular neck.

Bones snapped.

The beast's front legs folded. Before it could hit the ground, Palleton slashed through its jugular, freeing a torrent of life in a quick, merciful knife-stroke.

The light faded from the beast's eyes.

Chests heaving, Darien and Palleton stood facing each other, teeth bared, breathing in the intoxicating scent of blood-salted air.

Darien stepped forward and knelt. He plunged his hand into the pooling blood and raised it to his lips. Iron and copper. Liquid heat. Life become death for a blink in time before death fed life.

He stood, his shifting vision painfully intense now. Life flowed around him, as the blood spilling onto the ground called to everything around it, begging to be taken in and consumed.

Waste not.

One death meant life for many.

Wings flapped. Scales slithered and slid. Insects shuffled, closing in. They all came to feast.

Palleton knelt in homage. Darien's elder, his mentor and friend, waited for permission. Even when it was just the two of them, even when it had been Palleton's kill, it was the alpha's job to decide who shared and in what order.

Darien nodded and Palleton cupped his hands to catch the ebbing flow of life. He drank deep.

A satisfied growl emerged from Palleton's throat.

Darien smiled.

As adrenaline faded, his senses dulled, but movement caught his gaze. Other predators. The kind that weren't above scavenging.

A small canid with bristly grey fur and tufted ears emerged from the tall grass. It sniffed the air. Darien and Palleton remained still as it prowled closer.

Darien extended his hand. The canid sniffed at it, vigilant eyes cast balefully on Palleton. A hesitant tongue snaked out from between sharp, needle-like teeth. Rough, like sandpaper, but smoother than Darien had expected.

Body slung low, the canid turned to the carcass. A too-smooth, too-soft abdomen, recently swollen, sagged with emptiness.

She glanced around and flicked her black tail, then let out a long hooting call. The sweet melody of it lingered in the air and was answered from multiple directions.

"We're being courted," Palleton said.

Two furrows appeared in the tall grass, flowing in smooth darts. The paired furrows split into four. Smaller versions of the canid emerged and waited. She called to them again, and they fell on the kill as if it were their own.

Darien laughed. "Seems our friends have taken ownership."

The canid hunched lower, her teeth bared at Palleton as he ambled closer.

"Where's your pack, little mother?" Darien asked as he crouched low to extend his hand once again. He made soothing sounds. She blinked at him over a blood-soaked muzzle. With a low growl, she jumped away to tear into *her* kill.

"Seems she's gotten what she needs from you," Palleton said, smiling as he came to stand by Darien's side.

The pups had torn an opening in the beast's abdomen. They buried their heads into the rich viscera. Satisfied yipping sounds and grunts competed with their mother's rumbling. She couldn't seem to make up her mind, alternately growling and purring.

"Seems so," Darien said as he stood. "We n—"

The gauntlet on his right arm vibrated.

"My lord." Kell's voice had an edge to it as it rose from the gauntlet. "Galen and Lady Syteria are missing."

"Since when?"

"Galen commandeered an ambulance before first light and invoked your name to order the pilot to take them outside the safe zone. He is not answering his comm."

"Where did he go?" Darien asked.

"Sending co-ordinates."

A map flowed across the gauntlet, the destination blinking crimson.

"Meet us there," Darien said.

He ran. Palleton followed.

An ache swelled, then tightened Darien's chest. It was unlike anything caused by exertion. It was deeper, agonizing.

He'd seen Syteria after the *grierugon* had reduced her to a mound of flesh. He'd seen her draw breath through a face melted away right down to the bone. And he'd been unaffected. Unlike now.

The fact that Galen was always armed, that he would protect her, was little consolation. Tight muscles fueled Darien's stride as he confirmed his heading. Palleton's steps pounded the dirt behind him. They leaped over a stream. Then another.

As Darien landed, uneven ground gave way. He rolled and came upright, barely avoiding Palleton's falling bulk. The terrain changed, rockier now. They darted through a forest following a signal that might or might not lead them where they needed to go.

They only had Galen's last known position.

The unthinkable occurred to Darien and persisted as he closed on the signal. When Syteria had declared her desire to belong, he'd judged her sincere; he'd allowed his delight to cloud his thinking, to...trust.

A second escape attempt could not go unpunished.

As they passed the remnants of the field lab, the scent of human blood lingered in the air. Two figures in biomechanical suits—Kell and Aeson— had reached the clearing before them.

Darien's gauntlet spoke, reporting that an ambulance had been dispatched and was moments away.

His throat suddenly dry, Darien joined his *donai*.

Chief Aeson knelt, tending a bloodied figure. Galen's torn face was barely recognizable. His damaged skin suit looked like a rind that had worked its way back onto the battered, bloodied fruit from which it had been torn.

"He's going to need a life-pod," Aeson said as he worked. "The skin suit wasn't designed to repair this much damage."

Darien nodded.

Vision shifting, he surveyed the area. Streaks of blood, human and otherwise, were paired with drag marks angled toward the waterfall.

Galen would've carried Syteria, but she could not have carried him. Darien ran to the cooling carcass of a large cat still impaled by a training spear. It was covered with small hand-marks dried in blood. Aeson was right behind him.

"My lady?" Darien asked, sniffing the wind for her scent.

"She was attacked by reptilian scavengers, over there," Aeson said, pointing downwind. "They'd just knocked her down when we arrived. Looks like she killed one. Beat another into the ground, stunning it. The third one we took out before it finished strangling her."

The ambulance circled overhead, racing its shadow.

The wind shifted, reversing direction, allowing Darien to catch Syteria's scent at last. As he closed the distance between them, all of his *donai* senses intensified, driven by the scent of her blood. The copper, iron, and salt of it triggered baser instincts than those of a predator. His nails dug painfully into his palms as he dueled with protective instincts that insisted he run to her. It felt like forever before he reached her.

"She is unconscious, but her injuries are minor," Kell said as he stood above her. "The skin suits are working very well."

Darien shouldn't have sighed in relief. It's what a human would've done.

A *donai* would've ripped the skin suit off his pair-bonded mate. He would have dripped his own blood into her wounds. He would have used a kiss to flood her with his nanites. He could do none of these things, no matter how much his instincts drove him. There was only the illusion of a pair-bond. His nanites could kill her.

"It looks like she saved Galen's life, from the cat at least..." Kell's voice drifted on the wind, distant and fading despite its proximity.

Darien's shadow fell over Syteria's sprawled form.

The woman at his feet would never know that she'd saved Galen's life three times today. First from the cat. Then from the scavengers. And again, from Darien's wrath.

Galen had violated protocol by ordering the pilot to land in an unsafe area. He'd falsely invoked Darien's name to dismiss his armed escort. Whatever his reasons, such acts weren't mere disobedience. They were public challenges to his authority.

There had to be more to this than a sudden desire to collect samples. Galen had an infirmary full of staff, specially trained for just that purpose, and plenty of crew to draft as guards if all he wanted was a jaunt in an uncleared area.

There was no reason to endanger *her*.

Palleton joined him, bloodied spear in hand. "At least now we know that she can use one of these."

For a split second Darien couldn't breathe. It was a slow buildup to a deliberate inhale as realization hit him. Galen had endangered her because he hadn't wanted her tested. This ill-advised, ill-conceived scenario was Galen's clumsy attempt to take the decision out of Darien's hands.

As if she belonged to Galen. As if her life were his. As if he were her father.

He placed Galen in the life pod himself.

He ordered a shuttle prepared to lift him to the *Edlyn*.

He considered the reinstitution of public floggings.

As Aeson shepherded Galen's life pod into the ambulance Darien returned to kneel at Syteria's side.

There was a tremor in his hands, one felt but not manifested, as he tore her skin suit so he could read her. She had no internal injuries, so he cradled her body against his to keep her warm, tarnishing her porcelain skin with sweat and grime.

"Collect her trophies," Darien told Kell.

Three reptilian tails and a cat's mane made a fine start for any collection. They weren't the trophies he'd planned for her, but she'd earned them, and he wasn't going to deny her—not the trophies, not her victories, perhaps nothing. Not today.

Welcome to the pack.

As though she might have heard him, she responded with a mumble, without coming to full consciousness. Her lashes fluttered as he carried her to the ambulance. Covered in her prey's blood, a well-*"decorated"* Syteria made a fit, worthy predator.

"Persistent creature," Darien said with affection. His cuspids ached as his mouth filled with saliva. The heat of multiplying nanites burned as he swallowed, as he thwarted the instinct to mark her.

He climbed into the back of the ambulance and refused to yield her. Her breath on his neck, the weight of her body in his arms, the steady rhythm of her heartbeat—these were *his* trophies.

She stirred and he held his breath, expecting rejection, but she settled deeper into his embrace. He swiped at angry streaks weeping ichor into the chestnut hair that had loosened and settled over her shoulder blade.

"My lord," Aeson said, indicating a nearby pallet, "perhaps if she were prone,"

Darien bared his teeth. No one could make him give her up until he was ready.

A dark corner of his mind whispered to him that his reactions were not his own, that they were driven by the implant Galen had placed inside her. Its whispers faded as he held her, as her blood mixed with his sweat. The telltale signs of nanite blooms glowed wherever her blood touched his skin. He didn't need to see them to know what they were doing: taking the mixture of blood and sweat, deciding if the blood was a threat, and finding that it was not, looking for pair-bond markers. How far had Galen gone with the implant? There was no ersatz child's heartbeat—not yet.

The way Aeson held his breath as he worked around Darien's embrace told him what he needed to know. She smelled pregnant to him too. Darien should have rejoiced at the success of the ruse. Instead the shame of dishonor, of deceiving men sworn to him, stabbed at his conscience.

Have you considered perfecting your claim? Galen had asked.

Aeson finished dressing the wound as the ambulance landed. Galen's staff rushed the ambulance.

He stood, holding Syteria in his arms, sweeping an angry gaze driven by shame and guilt. The medical staff stopped in their tracks, then made a path for him, eyes downcast. Their fear-scent clouded the air despite the skin suits.

Once inside, he set her down on a bio-bed. For an instant, her hand caught his. It could have been his imagination or the viscosity of drying blood. Whatever had caused it, didn't matter to the intense ache in his chest.

He backed away from the bio-bed and nodded. The medical staff rushed forward, stripped her of the skin suit, their fearful gazes darting his way for instants of time that felt like minutes. He should leave, let them do their work without fear. So few had ever seen him like this.

But he could not move. His skin still burned where her blood lingered. Saliva continued to pool and burn in his mouth.

The staff immersed Syteria in a tank of nanite-enriched fluid. Nanites swarmed to the damaged sites—shoulder blade, neck, scalp, forearms, and hands—darkening the color of the fluid. As they repaired her injuries, they erased the evidence of her valor. It would have to live on in his memory.

Palleton approached the tank, Galen's sidearm in his hand. He too passed an assessing gaze and for a moment, Darien's heart froze in his chest: a careful enough look and the presence of the implant would betray them.

Instead Palleton grunted in satisfaction and came to stand beside Darien.

"She tried to use this," Palleton said. "Probably dropped it when its center of mass shifted to balance her grip."

Darien made a sound of agreement.

"My lord, it would be my honor to bring the lady up to regulation."

Everyone aboard the *Edlyn*, right down to the lowliest human was up to regulation. Dobromil's domain was one of the few where humans were armed. Darien had vowed to protect her, but instead, he'd left her defenseless. He'd never doubted her spirit, yet he'd denied her the means to protect herself, as if she were truly a slave.

Hands stained with her blood mocked the honorable intention of saving her life with his ulterior motives—his intent to use her against the emperor.

"Guilt is a useless emotion," Darien reminded himself.

"Yes, my lord. It is still my duty to remedy the situation," Palleton responded.

Just as Galen is mine.

Darien had never taken Galen's oath. That technically made Galen his father's problem. Lord Dobromil would be the one who got to decide if this foolish and public act merited forgiveness.

But the pawn called Syteria was no longer in play, and it was Darien's turn to teach. Galen was still part of the game, but bishops didn't decide when, or how, to sacrifice his—

"The *Edlyn* did confirm," Palleton said, "Galen is alive and should make a full recovery."

Some of the tension that knotted Darien's shoulders released.

Palleton cleared his throat.

It was a reminder: Galen had dishonored Darien's name; he'd endangered the woman they believed bore his heir.

Palleton was right. He had faltered. The *donai* understood human nature and didn't hold it against him. But a failure to lead was another matter: an unforgivable sin. *Their* expectations, he was forced to meet.

"When he's well enough," Darien said, "throw him in the brig."

Palleton nodded. "For how long?"

Forever.

CHAPTER TWENTY-EIGHT

*S*yteria had woken in the field-hospital to a hyper-vigilant staff in constant attendance, fussing over her every move-ment. Other than a twinge when she lifted her arm above her head, Syteria would've never known that her back had been sliced open. She kept running her fingers over her shoulder blade, feeling for the scar that should've been there.

"Sore-pain dims above days," Nestra said.

"The soreness will fade over a few days?" Syteria asked tentatively.

It was worth the effort of rephrasing to see if she understood the subtler differences of their language, even though it still made her ears burn with embarrassment. It was getting easier, however, and they never noticed, or at least they went to great lengths to pretend they didn't. Either way, she was grateful.

"Yes, my lady."

"Where's Galen?"

Nestra examined Syteria's throat. "Inhale please."

Syteria took a deep breath.

"No, like this." Nestra swallowed dramatically.

Swallow, not inhale. Syteria complied.

"Again, please."

"Where's Galen?"

She must've asked for Galen a dozen times since she'd woken. Other than confirmation that he was alive, her question had been ignored or evaded. His injuries had been severe, but nowhere near as severe as some of the patients she'd helped him treat.

"Hurts?" Nestra asked, sweeping her finger across Syteria's neck, right along where the scars and bruising from the reptile's tails should have been.

Syteria shook her head.

Someone called for Nestra and she excused herself, leaving Syteria sitting atop the exam table.

Syteria rotated the shoulder as she stood, the soreness fading as motion loosened the muscles there.

Perhaps Galen had been healed and returned to duty. As the man in charge, perhaps he was busy. Still, it was odd, how all morning, patients had trickled in and were treated and released by the staff, all without so much as a mention of Galen. Even when a human had been brought in and required a life-pod, Galen had not made an appearance.

Done with idling, done with "recovery" as they called it, she returned to the communal tent she shared with the female staff.

The bloody spear she'd used to save Galen was propped against the tent wall by her bed. It was framed by three tails and the cat's mane, a makeshift trophy wall.

Syteria grabbed the mane. She didn't deserve trophies. If she hadn't run off to play with the spear because she was bored and annoyed about being whisked away from what she wanted to do, the cat would not have snuck up on Galen and dragged him away.

Her belly churned and twisted, digesting guilt and excuses. The mane was heavy in her hands, a prickly, rather than soft, bundle. They had cured and treated it—and the tails—so quickly. It shouldn't have surprised her, yet...

She dropped the mane atop her bed, and left to go looking for Galen.

After checking every other place within the star fort's walls, Syteria made her way to the *donai's* courtyard. The tyrant would know where Galen was. She was ready to swallow her pride and ask him to translate, so she could ask for Galen's forgiveness. And, perhaps, the tyrant might just tell her why *he* had not sent for her.

Had her failure to protect Galen proved that she wasn't worthy of being pack?

With the growing knot of tension in her shoulders as her only companion, she walked up to Kell. He was standing outside the gate. Gone was the surreptitious smile he'd worn when he'd come to watch Aeda sleep. Gone was the light in his eyes when he'd brought flowers. His gaze was hard under furrowed brows. He put his arm out, blocking her from walking through.

Syteria took a small step back, eyeing the gauntleted arm, set out at eye level. She ran a finger under her nose to block out his scent and took another step back. Breathing through her mouth only made his scent linger on her tongue, an aftertaste not at all to her liking. Ducking under his arm would be easy. Getting out of his reach in time would not.

She'd rather not suffer the indignity of being hoisted over his shoulder and dumped back in her tent, or worse, at the tyrant's feet. She peered under Kell's bicep.

The court was empty; the tyrant, absent.

"Where's Galen?"

"In the *Edlyn*," Kell said.

She made to move around him. He stepped in front of her and crossed his arms, rumbling something. A challenge or admonition by the tone, the obligatory "my lady" tagged on the end.

The lump in her throat kept the question about *him* unvoiced.

Kell seemed intent on standing there, aspiring to the stoicism of a wall.

"Where is your lord?" she asked, not quite certain if her usage of the pronoun was correct. Kell was smart. Surely he could extrapolate.

The silence between them stretched, casting doubt on her expectations.

"Not here," he finally said, disgust coloring both face and tone.

Then why was he so intent on keeping her out? She turned away. Maybe Aeda could help. Kell would be more amenable to a request from her.

Fruitless hours later, unable to find Aeda within the fort, Syteria returned to the tent.

Inside, Nestra sat, peering into a mirror. Her arms contorted, she struggled to wind a thick plait of glossy, ebony hair around her head. Her fingers worked, flowing through the strands as if she were playing a musical instrument. From what she'd braided so far, it looked like she was attempting an artistic arrangement instead of the practical one she usually sported. Her hair's unwieldy length wouldn't succumb to her efforts.

Syteria came up behind her and smiled. "May I?"

Nestra's face lit up. She shook her hair loose, sat up straight and expectantly held out the brush.

Syteria took it and ran it through the ebony veil of Nestra's hair.

"Beautiful," Syteria whispered.

Nestra's hair reached almost to her waist and reflected thick dark indigo as light played in it.

"Thank you, my lady."

Syteria divided Nestra's hair into sections like Anasera had done countless times for her.

"Can you reveal answer for me?" Syteria asked, threading a plait through its fellows, weaving it back and forth.

"If I can, my lady."

"Where are the *donai* women?" she asked as she crowned Nestra with a tiny braid.

"There are none," Nestra said, turning her head from side to side, admiring her reflection. She handed Syteria a set of pins. "Not on *Edlyn*."

"Why?" Syteria asked as she pinned the braid.

"None serve."

Syteria frowned at the simple, if cryptic answer, as she ran the brush through the rest of Nestra's hair.

Is this why the Rhoans had shaved the *eniseri* bald? She'd always thought it was to make them look the same and keep them focused on their duties.

"Your round," Nestra said, rising.

She pulled the brush out of Syteria's grasp and pushed her onto the stool. Before Syteria could think of the words for a polite objection, Nestra had loosened the clasp that held Syteria's hair together behind her neck.

My turn? For what?

"Like my lord," Nestra said.

"Like what?" Syteria asked. It ended on a high pitch. A flush swept over her neck and rose to her face.

"Your hair like *donai*."

Schooling her features to hide her frustration, Syteria blew out a breath. All of the *donai* wore their hair short, cut almost to the scalp, more like the *eniseri*. All but one. Even amongst the humans, the men favored shorter hair like the *donai*, while the women had long hair like her own.

"Like emperor," Nestra added.

Syteria's heart raced. "I don't understand."

Nestra tilted her head and repeated the same line, then added several variants, none familiar to Syteria.

Shrugging, Nestra gave up and returned her attention to Syteria's hair. Smooth, even motions trailed downward along its entire length as Nestra worked out some tangles.

Syteria's gaze darted to the tent flap, expecting a Matron to burst through at any moment. More than one *eniseri* sported deep scars, drawn into her face by the sharp edges of a shattered contraband mirror. Scars drawn in by the other *eniseri* under a Matron's watchful eye. Make the cut too shallow and risk one yourself. A joint punishment, clear in its message.

The Rhoan penalty for allowing one's hair to grow too long too often was to peel the skin off until nothing but a bloody cap of tissue remained. This, along with other similar punishments kept the *eniseri* from focusing on their appearance.

Syteria shook herself.

"You well, my lady?"

Nodding, Syteria smiled, but she couldn't make words flow past her tightening throat.

This is not Rho. These are not Rhoans. I am no longer eniseri.

What had started with just her and Nestra soon drew forth the entirety of Galen's female staff. They seemed to discuss strategy, braiding and unbraiding various configurations, arguing and running off excitedly. Some returned with combs. Others with pins and clips. They spun Syteria around, chattering far too quickly for her to catch any words she understood.

Mostly she nodded and kept a smile on her face, surrendering any semblance of control. It felt like another rite of passage, another step towards being accepted into their world. And they were *giving* her a place in it. The thought warmed her, dispelling the heavy gnawing sensation in her belly.

Flowers joined pins and ribbons and beads. Where had it all come from?

One of Galen's older physicians, a severe man of middle age ducked into the tent.

"It's time," he said with a smile and added a few more words that sounded like a warning.

The women ignored him.

He aimed an apologetic shrug at Syteria and ducked back out.

Coward.

Their aesthetic ambitions exhausted, the women launched into what sounded like another debate. In the mirror, jade eyes widened at a face crowned with a dozen layers of tiny rosettes.

Nestra had run off and now returned to pose a sober question.

"Sorry, other than *donai*..." Syteria said in halting Kanthlos and finished with, "I don't understand."

Nestra pushed forward, through the assembled women. She lifted and held out her hands. The reptilian scavengers' barbed tails were cradled in her palms.

Syteria searched the women's faces. Their neutral façades provided no clue to the right answer. Nestra repeated the question, raising the supple leathery bundles with their lustrous, pointed ends.

The leathery scales of the scavengers' whipcord tails gleamed like a jeweled rainbow in the light. How had something so delicate come so close to taking her life? A beautiful weapon now reduced to nothing more than frivolous ornamentation.

A trophy for a prize.

She took a deep breath, refusal poised on her lips. It caught there, in the waiting silence. These customs must have meaning. This was their world, not hers.

She nodded and delight swept over the women like a wave. No one posed a question in regard to the cat's mane. Having consented to one, she had accepted the other.

Syteria emerged from the tent with the tails braided into her hair. The cured tails dangled down her back in a trio of woven layers. Their barbed tips bounced and swayed between her hips as the women surrounding her provided escort. She pulled her hair over one shoulder, through the spiked mantle of feline mane, and ran her fingers over the intricacy of the binding.

"Where are we going?" Syteria asked.

A CHEER WENT UP JUST as Syteria and her escorts reached the vast arena that Galen had shown her days ago. They'd missed some important announcement, she was sure.

The women herded her up an embankment and pulled her down to sit amongst them, settling her in the middle of a circle of rugs and pillows.

Below, torches ringed the arena, giving off a sharp, clean smell. In the center, a bonfire had been lit. Embers took to the sky, the larger ones meeting their end with a hiss and a puff of smoke thanks to the force field above.

On the other side of the arena, a platform hosted *donai* and humans.

The *Edlyn's* crew, the ones that had remained aboard ship, wandered about, offering food and drink from the ship's stores. Syteria smiled as she took the offered delicacies. She'd missed the carved, candied fruits and mysterious layered finger foods that were more art than sustenance.

She sipped a chilled drink from a chalice. It gave her hiccups, so she had some more.

The women around her conversed in excited, satisfied tones. They took turns pointing out people, explaining things, and encouraging her to sample one delicacy or another.

They named things, teaching her the correct words. She repeated them, some more easily than others. Her efforts were rewarded with encouraging smiles that she returned. What had she done to merit such sudden inclusion and indulgence?

Aeda approached with a broad grin on her face. A cat's mane adorned her shoulders as well. She bowed to Syteria.

"My lady, profoundness and gratitude redeeming Galen's continuance."

Syteria frowned.

"My lady, Aeda thanks you for saving Galen's life," Nestra said.

Syteria blinked, speechless, her mouth hanging open for a moment. Why had Nestra's words made sense but Aeda's had not?

"High Kanthlos for *donai*," Nestra said, apparently answering Syteria's confused look. "Umm, ruler. Kanthlos for us." Nestra pointed an index finger at herself and then turned it towards Syteria. "You, my lady, High Kanthlos."

Two languages. She'd been trying to learn *two* languages.

"Bastard," she said in Rhoan, and then embellished it with a few choicer Kappan words. While they may not have understood the words themselves, her tone was clear. The women's expressions ranged from puzzled to stoic to worried.

"My lady, I—" Aeda stumbled over words as her cheeks colored.

Syteria shook her head and put on a sincere smile. "No, Aeda. Not you. I regret."

Aeda relaxed, as did the women around her.

"I failed Galen," Syteria said. "Them," she pointed to the *donai* gathered in the arena, "they saved Galen, me."

Aeda's nod had a slight tilt to it, as though she was not readily accepting the explanation, but was being too polite to disagree.

Nestra leaned in and whispered in Syteria's ear, then made an encouraging gesture towards Aeda.

Syteria repeated the unfamiliar words, an equivalent of "my pleasure" she hoped.

Aeda's face lit up. She bowed again, deeper this time, before turning to leave.

Syteria sipped from the chalice again, hoping the chill of the drink would cool the burn in her neck and face. She felt like a thief, accepting praise for something she didn't do.

Further offerings of food and drink were made. Her chalice was refreshed. She ate and drank in self-defense.

Below them, on the arena's raised platform, the tyrant—clean, but still dressed as sparsely as before—held court. A similarly attired Palleton stood at his side.

Aeda climbed the steps leading up to the platform and dropped to one knee before the tyrant. She placed her hands between his and spoke. He nodded, responding with what sounded to Syteria's straining, untrained ear, as agreeable words.

Aeda stood and bowed again. When she stepped off the platform, another human, a man, took her place.

Nestra leaned in and explained, but "Human oath...loyalty...duty..." were the only words Syteria recognized.

She nodded.

"...bind...lord...honor..." Nestra continued

Surrounded by his people, the tyrant stood like a king with a giant as his knight. As with Aeda, he spoke, the words now ringing with the familiarity of a script. One by one, the humans knelt before him. *He* always responded, sometimes at length, sometimes with brevity. When the last of the humans stepped off the platform, Palleton made an announcement.

Cheers erupted from the crowd.

Drums thrummed out a rhythmic beat. Other instruments joined in. As the music rose, it enticed couples to dance.

Several of Syteria's companions abandoned her to join the festivities. She remained nestled in the safety of her pillows and arranged them around herself like battlements.

With each chilled sip, with each pulsing drum beat, tension slipped down her body and slithered out her toes. Warmth rose from within.

While she'd been entranced by the oath-taking below, Nestra had shed her skin suit altogether to reveal sheer undergarments. On her belly, with elbows propped, she lounged at the edge of the rugs, a satisfied smile on her face. She stretched, languid and glassy eyed, the very image of satisfaction.

Someone—not all of her escorts had abandoned her after all— refilled Syteria's chalice.

"Thank you," she mumbled and sipped.

Her blood burned as it coursed through her body. Syteria tugged at the collar of the skin suit, struggling with the seams. Nestra rose and moved towards her as if through syrup. She pulled the mane off Syteria's shoulders and pulled her free of the skin suit that had somehow become too complicated for Syteria to work on her own.

A question from Nestra, more lyrical than usual, had Syteria cocking her head in puzzlement. Nestra grabbed her wrists and tugged her upward.

Syteria's legs felt wobbly underneath her, like she couldn't trust them. In fact, all her limbs seemed unusually heavy, while her head felt light. She sank back down, a happy puddle contained by the safety of the pillows. Nestra shrugged and abandoned her with a cheerful departing wave.

Syteria propped her elbow on a pillow. That light, fuzzy feeling in her head continued, but now her eyelids were heavy. Blinking became an effort. A haze alloyed her thoughts, and they quieted.

Drumbeats muffled. Flames leapt. Wind stirred the canopies, fluttered the flags, and caressed her limbs.

She surrendered to the sweet lull delivered by too much food and drink. The stars above winked at her through the force field. Had her arm not been too heavy she'd have reached out to try to touch them.

Her gaze followed a speck floating on the wind as it drifted back down to the arena. There, Aeda sauntered up to Kell. Aeda wrapped her arms around his neck. Aeda rose on her toes and kissed him.

Kell morphed into the tyrant. Aeda morphed into someone that looked like herself. Syteria blinked the surreal image away with a swipe of her hand.

A fierce, proud Kell held Aeda in his arms, his body glued to hers, his lips at her throat, then her ear. His kiss wasn't the chaste, tender, touching of lips that Aeda's had been. It was primal, possessive, branding. Aeda arched against him, offering herself up, that look of satisfaction from before, heightened and mixed in with utter joy.

Syteria fought heavy-lidded eyes. When they opened, Aeda and her *donai* were gone. Syteria's eyes closed again.

CHAPTER TWENTY-NINE

*M*otion woke Syteria—despite *his* grace, the fluid glide of his gait woke her. Her breath caught, right there in her rib cage, like an ache. She kept her head tucked into his chest, slitting her eyes only a fraction.

The drumbeats and jubilation trailed behind them. Away from the bonfire, the night air was crisp.

He stopped. Underneath her ear, his heart thundered. His breathing was ragged, as if he were straining under her weight.

I'm not that heavy. Not to him.

In the back of her mind, something whispered for her to be still, to wait, to see what he would do.

He paused at a fork in the road. One path led towards the eastern bailey, towards the gate that guarded his barbarian throne. The other, towards the field hospital.

Bare skin pressed against hers as he moved again. She wanted to nestle closer, but dared not; she barely dared to breathe.

Warmth rose in waves from his chest, floating around her, imbued with his scent. Salt, spice, plums and musk. She could lick the column of his neck and get a taste.

On Rho, this is treason.

Somewhere along the way she'd lost her skin suit and she was barely covered in thin undergarments that left nothing to the imagination.

Treason for me.

She'd lost the cat's mane.

Death for him.

The motion that tugged at the weight of her braids told her that the tails were still twined in her hair. They made the barest sound as they slapped against his hip, like tiny coins chiming. Their resonance became an anchor for her awareness.

Clink...

This is not Rho.

On Rho someone like him could not exist. Someone like her couldn't either. She'd been irrevocably changed, transformed into someone else's image of her.

His? Clink...

Galen's? Clink...

Hers? Clink...

I am a traitor. A proper Rhoan would never allow this violation, this reforging of her soul. A proper Rhoan wouldn't crave superior strength or see confidence where others saw arrogance. A proper Rhoan wouldn't find beauty in his cruelly chiseled face or the depth of his rumbling voice. A Rhoan would find threat and menace and she'd succumb to fear and call it violence.

Clink...

I've always been a traitor.

Moisture flowed into the seam between her eyelids, clouding the little bit of vision she'd allowed herself. Moisture flowed into the seam between her thighs.

I was never Rhoan.

He had brought her to the tent she shared with the other women. He stood outside its entrance, his breathing going ragged again.

She strained to hear. The human commotion so prevalent in these communal tents, even at night, wasn't there.

The tent flaps were pinned back, and he ducked to enter, bringing her closer in, smothering her in silk-covered muscle. His scent threat-ened to overwhelm her, drown her, pull her into depths from which she'd never escape.

She gasped for breath and opened her eyes.

Within the giant tent, every bed was meticulously empty, just as it had been when she'd been shepherded out. He took her to her bed, hesitated, then lowered her into it.

His gaze met hers. The molten gold there swirled and spiraled. His arms flexed as his hands tightened and then relaxed. Light gleamed off the hard muscles of his chest, betraying the hitch of breath.

His rough hands skimmed her defenseless, semi-nude body as he set her down. He closed in, his bearded face hovering over hers, his eyes burning with desire. There was a second of hesitation, one that would've allowed her to move, to push him away, to voice a protest. One second became two, then three.

His lips touched hers with the barest pressure. They didn't linger long enough for her to press back, to respond in any way. Instead his nose trailed a path to her ear, then down her throat. He inhaled, filling his chest and a tremor passed over him.

When his nostrils flared and his face darkened, she knew that the pooling moisture between her thighs had betrayed her. She waited for him to tear off her garments, to pin her under him, to silence her and part her and enter her, to do all the things that Rhoans considered a crime, all the things that an *eniseri* would take his life for.

And for a moment, she thought that he might. But the moment passed, unfulfilled.

She blinked. And when she opened her eyes, he was gone.

You tempt me, he'd whispered once, long ago.

THE SEED WAS CRAWLING with nanite pods. Like the insect it was emulating, the seed was near-sighted, but its heat vision had no trouble distinguishing between humans and *donai*, even as the sun rose. As long as it deployed the pods before the ambient temperature made distinguishing between its targets too hard, its "brain" would consider its mission a success.

It lumbered through the grass, emitting a discordant hum at any rival insect or predator that might mistake it for prey. When a human passed, one of the nanite pods would sprout wings and fly off.

Since the humans were covered in artificial membranes, the pods flew toward human mouths and noses.

Once inside, the nanites would be released into those with female chromosomes. Otherwise, the pod held onto the nanite packet until it could deliver it to a suitable candidate.

Now empty, the seed crawled off, as far from human activity as its energy reserves allowed. When its internal clock hit zero, the seed used the last of its energy to self-destruct.

SYTERIA KNEW that she was dreaming. It was as clear and certain as the fact that she could not wake. She had to let the nightmare run its course. The beginning was always the same.

The lightning-split sky above her glowed crimson. She was high above the ground, on a barren peak, her body broken on the jagged rocks. Swirling clouds of pitch and ash chased each other.

A dragon with green and black scales perched atop the peak, its triple rows of razor-sharp teeth dripping with Kappan blood. The beast wasn't feasting on her corpse. It had, instead, torn her soul from her body.

With lifeless eyes, she watched, devoid of emotion, of pain. As a hollow vessel, an empty shell, she was nothing and no one.

A howl carried on the wind, swept up by the air currents swirling around the peak. The dragon roared, clutching her soul tightly in its talons.

Again, the howling stirred and swelled, cutting through the gusting winds.

Her re-animated corpse rose to stand between the ledge and the dragon. From the boiling mists below, a wolf emerged, scrambling upward, its dark claws digging into the rock.

Her corpse stood its ground, ready to protect the dragon.

The wolf advanced, amber eyes glowing.

Syteria bolted upright, torn from the nightmare, sweat-soaked sheets clinging to her skin as a hand gripped her shoulder.

Nestra wore a mix of fear and clinical concern as she stood at her side.

Sunshine stabbed through the tent opening. Syteria turned away, as much from the glare as for the opportunity to wipe away the moisture from her face.

"My lady," Nestra said and followed with quick, rushed words that made no sense.

Syteria's head pounded like one of the drums from the night before. She groaned and rubbed at her temples.

"See me on duty," Nestra said, her tone definitely a clinician's order.

Nodding, Syteria pulled the sheets around her.

Nestra stood over her for a second more, as though assessing her intent to comply. From outside the tent, someone called her name. She rushed off.

Syteria pushed up and away from the bed on unsteady legs. Hand shading her eyes, she pulled the tent-flap closed. The beds were all empty. Some looked as if they hadn't been slept in at all.

Someone had set her skin suit at the foot of her bed. She fumbled her way into it, mixing up left and right gauntlets, then right and left boots.

Her hair had come loose sometime during the night, shedding the rosettes. After two attempts, she gave up on working the bindings that held the tails, and ventured forth, squinting against the punishing sun that was already at its zenith.

There were fewer tents and the bustling activity centered around crates suggested they were de-camping. She ducked into the large, hospital tent, seeking refuge from the sun and a remedy for the pounding in her head.

Nestra was attending to Aeda who reclined on a bio-bed. Kell stood at her side, his face grim, his mouth set in a hard line. Aeda smiled up at him, her face glowing, and patted his hand as if she was reassuring him of something.

He nodded, clearly unconvinced.

Nestra issued instructions, speaking first to Aeda, then in a more admonishing tone to Kell. He made that slight tilted nod the *donai* used as a sign of deference to humans.

Aeda stood, Kell hovering as if he meant to catch her lest she fall. She waved him away. Undeterred, he placed his hand at the small of her back.

They walked past Syteria, exchanging greetings. Aeda's gait was off.

"Does Aeda hurt?" Syteria asked, touching her own leg at the spot where Aeda's had broken hers just days before.

Nestra gave her the strangest look—a mixture of surprise and humor—then donned her clinician's mask.

Syteria must've mis-spoken again. She turned the phrase over in her mind, grasping for better, clearer wording. "Does—"

Nestra handed Syteria a glass of glowing water and waited expectantly. Knowing better than to argue, Syteria drained the glass only to have another thrust at her.

"Does Aeda's leg still hurt?" Syteria asked as her head cleared.

"No, my lady," Nestra said with a grin.

CHAPTER THIRTY

*D*arien had changed into ship fatigues and ordered internal surveillance cut before he descended into Galen's cell. Under the intense light, Galen lay flat on his back atop the lone platform. His arm was draped over his eyes. His breath puffed small clouds into the chill air.

It had been days since Galen had been thrown into this oubliette and deprived of the sense of time. The relentless white light never dimmed.

Unopened rations lay about, rejected.

He'd been isolated from everything and everyone, left only with his own thoughts for distraction or torment. Galen's discomfort and boredom served Darien's purpose without taking the physician too far into the horrors of his past.

Back ramrod straight, hands clasped tightly behind him, Darien spoke. "*My* lady lives."

Galen's chest rose steadily, its rhythm—and his pulse—suggesting relief. He pressed the heels of his palms to his eyes. "I didn't intend—"

"Do *not* speak to me of intent," Darien said. "You of all people should understand that a public challenge cannot go unanswered, that it leaves me no choice. *You* taught me that."

"And you learned it so well," Galen grumbled as he rolled over, turning to face the wall.

Darien held his breath and let the insult go. They were alone after all, and the insult was to his ego, not to his position.

"Do you find me difficult?" Darien asked.

Galen's back answered with utter stillness.

"Consider the difficulty of carrying out Lord Dobromil's orders from Serigala," Darien said.

Galen answered with an indifferent grunt.

Very well. There were other ways to prey on the tendencies Galen had so ineptly displayed.

"Then consider the difficulty of satisfying your duty to my lady if you're no longer aboard my ship."

Galen turned and sat up, blinking swollen eyes rimmed in red.

"What duty is that, my lord?"

"My lady has become quite attached to you. For her own reasons, she's cast you in some sort of paternal role. Did you know?" Darien asked, tilting his head, mocking Galen's attempt at indifference.

Galen's small, well-schooled smile answered for him. His hunched posture uncurled. He straightened the coarse prisoner's garb, an attempt at dignity thwarted by the loose fit.

"I mention this not to please you, Galen, but to warn you. Do not interfere."

Galen's gaze lifted to his and did not stray as Darien added, "I intend to perfect my claim."

"For your honor," Galen added, his tone clearly a mockery.

Darien's jaw muscles beat in rhythm as if his heart had moved into his throat. The edges of his vision darkened. He had done everything in his power to stay away, to carry out Galen's plan. He had tread the fine line between duty and honor, between what was expected of him as heir and vassal. But he could no longer do so. Not after last night. Not after he'd tasted her lips, smelled the desire pooling between her thighs, lost himself in the scent of her. Everything he was, the very fiber of his being called out for him to pair-bond with Syteria.

"My reasons need not concern you," Darien said when he trusted his voice again.

"They concern me if you cultivate my paternal tendencies," Galen said as he ran his hands through unkempt hair. "Make up your mind. Do you want me to feel protective towards her as a father, or not?"

"I am not catering to *your* sensibilities."

"Hmm. I should provoke you further, then. Make you thrash me. See which is more important to you? Your honor or her image of you."

"My honor and that image are inseparable."

A derisive laugh burst from Galen's chest. "That's a beautiful delusion, my lord. Do you indulge it often?"

"More and more, with you out of my way. It's liberating," Darien said as he swept the confining space with his gaze and the arc of his open palm.

Galen sneered and crossed his arms.

"My lady requires your…company. I, require your parole."

SYTERIA SAT atop a hill as one of the *Edlyn's* shuttles took off. Like clockwork, another arrived to take its place. *He* had never sent for her. She'd never had the opportunity to ask him about becoming "pack," about proving her worth. Her thoughts incessantly circled around the question of why he'd only kissed her.

From what she'd seen, humans and *donai* were not forbidden contact. Humans were allowed to give their affections freely.

Learn, he'd commanded and then taken away the easiest means to do so. Perhaps *that* had been her test, her trial.

You belong, Galen had insisted.

Other than when she'd demanded other quarters, the tyrant had treated her with a kind of benign neglect. Yet, he'd carried her to the tent and despite that kiss, despite the hunger burning in his eyes, he'd fled. And not just her tent, but the planet. He'd retreated all the way to the *Edlyn* and never returned.

She scoffed. There were, no doubt, other matters of concern for someone like him. As the lowliest of drudges, she'd never commanded. The Matrons had not trusted her. She had never been willing to do what was necessary to gain their trust. She'd had opportunities to report on one drudge or another, but she'd never taken advantage of those, never even been tempted.

Despite the illusion that the Matrons monitored the *eniseri* constantly, it must not have been true. She'd seen enough *eniseri* snatch moments of forbidden pleasure at their own hands. Yet, they had gone unpunished. Either the collars were not always active or those around them were being tested.

But when the *eniseri* betrayed each other, the Matrons had punished those who'd found their own pleasure. That tiny scrap of flesh and the folds around it were torn off, the offender chained to a post and allowed to bleed out. If she didn't die from that punishment, cutting off her hands finished her.

Syteria shuddered, wrapped her arms around her knees, and rested her forehead atop them. She'd buried such memories so deep and now they were coming back, sometimes as a trickle, sometimes as flood. This was the price of regaining her true self. She would break the Matron's hold on her, no matter the cost. This was part of it. Bit by bit, she would again become Syteria Kainda, a hunter's daughter, a war-chief's granddaughter, a Kappan.

She looked up. Somewhere up there, the *Edlyn* and all its wonders orbited.

Below, the fort remained, left behind as if they intended to return. The field hospital and its attendant structures had been collapsed and packed away. Everyone else was busy, moving with intent and purpose.

She savored the flower-scented air, the tang promising a storm. Distant hills beckoned. With a few weapons she could survive here. There was a lifetime supply of primitive weapons being left behind in the fort.

How far could she get before they caught her? She'd given her word of honor that she would not attempt another escape.

You will not survive and I won't be able to save you. There had been a certainty behind the tyrant's words, a heavy meaning that still weighed her down with the question of why her survival was so important to him.

A shift in the wind betrayed Palleton's approach as he strode up the hill. He was wearing ship fatigues, a sidearm, and a sword. Although he looked freshly scrubbed and clean his scent made her catch and hold her breath. Like Kell's scent, its acrid undertones made her want to keep her distance.

"My lady," he said, deep voice rumbling as he swept her with a critical eye.

"Syteria," she insisted, surging to her feet.

"*My lady*, it's time."

Standing her ground, she titled her head back to look into his amber eyes. If she could've grown roots, she would have.

"My lord says, it's time," he said a little slower.

If she pretended that she didn't understand, how many slower and louder attempts could she get him to make? Maybe they could make a game of it.

She laughed.

His eyes narrowed.

In Rhoan, she said, "Well, if your master says it is, then of course, it must be."

Her tone must've conveyed as much as her words. Before she could blink, he had her up over his shoulder and was carrying her down the hill.

She thrashed about, kicking. Her fists and feet connected with no effect. He was as solid as any armor, as indifferent as a mountain to a breeze.

"Put me down."

There was nothing to cushion the hard, unceremonious landing as her tailbone hit the ground. Momentum propelled her spine and shoulders into the grass.

Palleton's hand snaked out, keeping her head from hitting the ground. He pulled his hand away just as quickly.

She gasped for breath in his kneeling shadow. Her skin still crawled where his hands had touched her. The breeze pelted her with his scent. She needed to clear the acrid taste in her mouth. She rolled on her side, spat on the grass and wiped her lips with the back of her hand, turning to give him a scathing look.

He had a vicious grin on his face as he pushed up and placed his hands on his hips.

"Act a child and I will treat you as one," he said. "Insult *our* master and I will cage you."

She made a rude, dismissive noise.

He lowered himself and grabbed her chin, his grip firm. "Do you understand?"

"Yes."

He released her and extended his hand as though he'd had nothing to do with her undignified position.

Syteria stood on her own, refusing to take the offered hand and suffer his touch again. She made a show of dusting off her skin suit and rearranging her hair. He grunted amusement and made an inviting gesture towards the shuttle.

"It's time to retreat," she said. "To the *Edlyn*."

A sneer replaced the amusement. "We are *returning*, not retreating, to the *Edlyn*. My lady."

"Returning," she acknowledged.

Despite having the shuttle to themselves, he sat right across from her the entire flight. She squirmed in her seat, favoring the sudden tenderness of her bottom. At least the span between them—or the shuttle's filtration system—was enough to mute his scent. Despite the closed eyes, the head propped back like he was sleeping, a smug grin occasionally tugged the corners of his mouth.

Once aboard the *Edlyn*, he grabbed her by the elbow and hurried her along. She fumed in silence, grateful for the skin suit between him and his touch and the fact that everyone they passed seemed too busy to take notice.

"Where do you guide me?" she asked.

"I'm *taking* you to Galen."

Oh. She lengthened her stride.

Palleton's grip loosened.

She rushed through the passageways, through the arch that opened before her. The main infirmary compartment, with its bio-beds and staff passed with a blur.

The doors to Galen's lab parted. She skidded to a stop.

Galen had his back to her as he worked a console. He turned, eyes widening. His gaze darted to Palleton, whom he acknowledged with a hard look and a minuscule nod.

"Galen," she said, as she pulled him into a possessive embrace.

Words rushed out in Rhoan. "I was so worried. They wouldn't tell me anything. I tried, I really tried, but—"

He pushed her out at arm's length, hands tight on her shoulders, hard look softening.

"My lady," he said as he let her go and bowed.

She froze at the formality of his words.

"Are you wounded?" he asked, straightening.

"Me? No," she said. *Are you?*

There was a haunted look about him. He'd been severely injured, but he looked, at least physically, no worse for the experience.

His gaze darted yet again to Palleton. An unspoken question, and answer, seemed to pass between them.

"How may I serve you?" Galen asked.

"Serve? No. I'm sorry I couldn't'"—she fell into Rhoan with the rest—"protect you from that cat. I should've never left you alone. I was mad and selfish and I just wanted to…"

He cleared his throat and went to one knee before her.

She stepped back, but not before he captured her right hand between his.

"No, my lady. I'm sorry for"—something that sounded like their word for endangering or maybe even harming—"you."

She pulled her hand out of his grasp, revolted by his deference, his lowered eyes. She was no Matriarch to have a lesser kneel before her and no tyrant either.

She backed away.

Galen stood, continuing in soft, placating tones.

Caught up in her disgust, she shook her head and fled. She raced past Palleton and out of the infirmary, eager to get to her quarters and wash off the revulsion clinging to her like a second skin.

CHAPTER THIRTY-ONE

*S*yteria tossed and turned in her bed.

The days on Tir'Hala-Revir hadn't quite matched the *Edlyn's* timekeeping system. It was past midnight here, instead of late afternoon, as her body insisted.

The bedposts curved into a soaring ceiling that simulated a night sky she'd never seen before. Rho was not a disk of malevolence to be feared. There was no giant dragon's eye, forever staring down at her.

The Rhoan dragon in her dreams only bore a slight resemblance to the mark that the *eniseri* had branded onto her shoulder. During one of her first escape attempts, she'd peeled the mark from her skin with a blade and thrown it into a fire. She rubbed at the spot, gagging at the memory of scorched flesh.

Her stomach turned again. She rushed for the sink in the adjoining chamber and dry-heaved until the remembered stench faded.

Braced over the sink, she rinsed her mouth out, again and again. The water sparkled as it flowed over her new hands. She turned to look at the flawless spot on her shoulder and ran trembling fingers over it. The self-inflicted wound had not healed well, despite her attempt to cauterize it. The Matrons had recaptured her because she'd been too weak from the infection.

Rather than let her die, they had healed her so she could survive her punishment. Syteria splashed cold water onto her face and looked into the mirror. A shade of the *eniseri* known as DRD4 stared back.

Branded. Burned. Beaten.

Jagged scars criss-crossed her brow, her cheeks, her lips. Her scalp showed through the short hair. Her eyes were sunken, lifeless, the whites bruised and bloody. Only the "jade" of them betrayed that once she had been a Kappan child called Syteria. The collar around DRD4's neck defined her.

Syteria's throat tightened. She swallowed and reached for the collar. As the fingers in the reflection touched her bare collarbones, the illusion of the collar faded, and so did DRD4.

Instead the Kappan woman the Rhoans had sought to destroy stood tall.

You tempt me, the tyrant's whisper echoed again.

Amid strangers, separated from everything she'd ever known, of her place in this world, she obsessed about why a man who'd already named her slave had only kissed her. She needed an answer. And she knew exactly where to get it.

She dried her face and shrugged into a robe. Anasera had once told her that the *donai* didn't sleep. A quick query to the chamber presence provided her with *his* location.

The emptiness of the passageways spoke of the late hour as she made her way to the royal swordhall.

She entered a vast, wood-paneled room. Silken banners fluttered from a high ceiling. A lone sword rack stood off to the side. A viewscreen dominated the far wall. Distant stars shone or pulsed. The wisp of a nebula that looked like a lightning-lit cloud filled a corner.

A silhouette moved in the dimness.

He was alone, performing what looked like weapon drills, but in fluid, precise motions that were more dance than combat. His right hand held a curved sword slightly longer than the one in his left.

She approached slowly, whisper-quiet, giving her eyes time to adjust to the threadbare light.

A sheen of sweat glistened on his bare chest. Staccato exhalations accompanied his movements. The seven-pleated design of his long, black trousers flowed, allowing him to move without foreshadowing his intent. She ventured farther within, fascinated by the deadliness of his dance, the song sung by swords cutting through the air, the accompanying chorus of his voice.

His back to her, he froze mid-motion. He whirled, the fabric flowing around him as he lowered the swords. His smile almost stole her faltering courage.

She looked down.

His feet were bare, just visible under the fabric. She forced her gaze upward as he approached with a grace that verbalized power, strength...and death.

Galen had said that humans had created the *donai* to fight for them. They'd created predators that healed like magic, moved in utter silence, and ran too fast for the human eye to see, and that had not been enough—they had also given them swords.

With care born of reverence, he placed the long blade horizontally on the sword rack's curved pegs. The short blade followed, coming to rest above the long one. He grabbed a towel hanging off the rack, wiped his face and scrubbed at dark hair streaked with sweat.

A hint of musk drifted towards her. It settled in her nose, on her tongue as if were an invading mist. More. She would have more and that was exactly why she should leave.

Her body cast a veto and remained in place. It insisted she stay even as the predator's amber irises swirled open.

"You never sent for me," she said. "Why?"

"You went with Galen," he said darkly.

I did not, lingered on her lips but she dared not speak it. She'd never forget that haunted look on Galen's face, nor his cowed demeanor. Had Galen defied his master, risked his wrath for her? Why would he? He had nothing to gain, and perhaps, everything to lose.

"You misunderstand," she said.

"Do I?" It was flat, emotionless and framed by a predator's gaze.

"I—"

311

"Choose your words carefully, my lady. It is very easy for my kind to know when a human lies."

"I did not know his intentions," she said. "You took away my only means of communicating with him, remember?"

"You know how to say 'no' in Kanthlos."

"No to what? He didn't tell me his plan. And even had I said, 'no,' it's not as if he would have obeyed me."

He considered her for an overlong moment. "He will obey you now."

She gasped air tinted with his distracting scent. It cleared faster than before thanks to the anger flowing through her veins.

"You punished him?"

"Yes."

"Why?" She dared not ask what he had done to the man who'd given her new life, who'd given her Kappan self the means to rise again.

"It was a matter of honor," he said.

"I don't understand."

"And I don't have the means to explain it to you. You keep defying me, refusing to learn."

"I am learning." She waited for her temper to fade. "For example, I learned that your people speak two languages. I learned that your slaves compete to swear their fealty to you, and that you are willing to punish even someone like Galen if it suits your mood."

"They are two dialects," he said. "Not two languages."

Syteria bit her lip before she said something she might regret.

"And I punished him not because it suited my mood, but because he defied me." He looked down at the towel in his hand. "I had no choice."

"Another matter of honor," she said. It came out a whisper, without derision.

He looked up, and for a fleeting moment, what looked like pain and regret on a human raced across. From his barbarian throne he had told her that he and his kind were not human, despite appearances.

As with so many things, she'd not grasped the true meaning of it.

And she never would, not without his help. Despite all the obstacles that stood between her and understanding, here they were, discussing honor once again.

Honor and swords. Perhaps that was enough, a small patch of common ground whose boundaries she could expand.

"Swords?" she asked, with a hint of amusement in her voice.

An untainted smile crossed his face. "Ceremonial, of course."

"Those blades don't look ceremonial. They look… deadly."

"Even our ceremonies prepare us for combat. Otherwise they would be mere affectation."

"You drew your own kind's blood for me. Why?"

"Honor."

Again, he said that word without derision, without contempt, almost like a prayer.

"I was their target, not you. Not your honor."

"You are wrong," he said.

She expected more but silence lingered. When she could no longer bear the scrutiny of his gaze, she moved towards the sword rack and its viciously sharp blades.

She wrapped her hand around the hilt of the short sword he'd returned to its place. His hand covered hers and an inviting, masculine scent swirled around her. Her breath hitched, then resumed a slower rhythm.

"Humans are forbidden the sword." His voice was a caress floating through her hair. Heat radiated off his bare chest, blazing, a fire at her back.

His hand engulfed hers, the pressure light, effortless. Skin burned against skin, her hand greedily absorbing the warmth as if it were life itself. A different kind of heat pooled inside her.

Hand tightened around the hilt, she turned to meet those golden pupils.

"Who says?" she asked.

"The Imperium," he said.

The Imperium. Not him. An inexplicable sense of gratitude unfurled within her. She gripped the hilt even tighter.

313

"What's the punishment for a human handling a sword?" she asked.

"Death."

Of course it was death. She had expected no less. And now she wanted the sword even more. Not because she wanted to die. Because she wanted to live. She wanted the power to determine her own fate, make her own choices.

"They can't execute me twice," she said.

An ironic smile tugged at those full lips and he whispered words that sounded like disagreement.

With fingers that were curiously gentle for an enemy—no, not an enemy...an adversary—he pulled her hand free of the sword.

She let him lead her towards a paneled wall.

"This way," he said. "We start with wood so you can see it for what it is, without the sword's shroud of secrets, without...enigma."

He let go of her hand and opened a compartment filled with wooden variants of the sword.

His gaze skated up and down her body. He selected a curved, wooden sword without a hilt-guard and moved to stand beside her.

"Hold the bokken like this," he said as he held it loosely at his side. "It should not touch the ground."

He lifted the bokken with both hands, holding it parallel to the ground, presenting it with the thinner, "cutting" edge towards him.

She took the bokken and held it at her side as he had.

"Good," he said as he picked up a longer one. He grasped it with both hands, placing one above the other.

She followed suit.

"Relax. Let it come down a bit."

She mimicked his stance.

Tucking his bokken through the twisted fabric at his waist, he moved to stand behind her. Muscular arms engulfed her. He pushed her right hand up towards the top of the grip and repositioned her fingers. Then he slid her left hand towards the bottom and covered both hands with his. His shoulders loomed above her, casting a shadow both felt and seen.

The overpowering instinct to move into his embrace pulled and tugged at her self-control.

"Exert pressure while rolling inward as if you're wringing water out of it." His hand stroked over hers. "Tighten your grip."

She complied despite the ache rising within her.

"Good." His voice whispered in her ear.

"Adjust your stance like this," he said, nudging her feet apart.

The oddest sensation, one of being caged, but not trapped, took her in its hold. Deep, visceral sensations slipped their bindings, making her body clench. If he continued holding her like this, breathing fire on her neck, igniting her blood, she would be consumed.

The sound of a throat clearing shattered the moment. They turned as one. The cage of his arms withdrew. Cold replaced heat. Doubt replaced protection. Dread replaced anticipation.

Palleton had entered the swordhall. Like a child caught at mischief, she dropped the bokken. It made a resounding noise that echoed, mocking her attempt to distance herself.

"Forgive me, my lord," Palleton said, sparing her a brief smile. He continued speaking, his words a rushing river. She caught bits and pieces, some words suggesting a reminder; others, a reunion.

"Not today, Palleton. Thank you," *he* said, his voice flat.

Palleton quirked a smile. "Of course."

The next sentence might have been an apology, but for what? And why offered to her? He bowed. The doors closed behind him.

"Chamber, privacy," *he* said and bent closer.

She followed the line of his throat, the exquisite lines of his face. The curve of his lips beckoned invitingly. She closed the gap, intrigued by the golden flames licking at his irises.

"In the tent. I would know why you stopped," she said.

He blinked, surprise flickering in his eyes.

"You were not yourself," he said.

"Not myself?"

"The celebration."

She frowned.

"The drink," he said. "It dulls judgement. Did you not feel its effects?"

Oh. She had. It had dulled her thoughts, lulled her into a dreamlike state.

"My judgement is not dulled now," she said carefully watching for his reaction.

"There are...differences between *donai* and humans."

She smiled up at him. "Ones overcome by Aeda and Kell."

"You believe yourself ready?" His tone was tinged with warning.

"Show me what you are," she whispered.

He smiled, showing his slightly elongated cuspids. A low growl emanated from his throat when she traced her finger along them, testing their sharpness.

"Careful," he whispered.

"Why?"

"Never mind."

He guided her hand up towards his ear and she rose on her toes so she could trace its outline. She pushed his hair away, drawing closer still until the entire length of her body touched his. Unlike the other *donai*, the tips barely merited distinction from human ones.

"These are enhancements?" she asked.

"No. The enhancements are engineered from human analogues. These are...unintended consequences."

She cocked her head. "Consequences of what?"

"Our creators also wanted certain non-human behaviors."

"Like what?"

"Like my desire for you."

His hand was at the small of her back, holding her tight against his body.

She wanted *him*. For the first time in her life she wanted a man.

Like the sword, he was forbidden. The Matrons must've known she'd be drawn to her own kind, someone so Kappan, and had built these barriers. She would tear them down, set them ablaze and turn them to ash.

The spark for that cleansing fire held her in his grasp. It was the way he looked at her, as though she was worthy of interest, of conquest. Desire flooded her veins, drowning out, then silencing the *eniseri* voices.

Desire is the key. She drew in *his* scent, wanting nothing more than to drown in it. He reciprocated, burying his face in her neck and reaching for the clasp in her hair. It cascaded down as a shudder flowed over him.

Her ragged breathing deepened.

He continued to play with her hair, twisting small strands of it around his fingers until his tangled grasp angled her head and bared her throat. He feathered kisses along her neck.

When—how—had her hands wrapped around him? She wanted to play with his hair, experience the same pleasure he seemed to enjoy by toying with hers. The vitriol of *eniseri* voices stayed her hand.

She waited for the voices to fade, drawing in his scent until she floated on a cloud of musk, until the melody of his breathing drowned the *eniseri* out.

His feather-light lips continued across her chin, her face.

"Kiss me," he said.

She blinked at the masculine demand, at the lust, unbidden but sharp, that made her comply. Carefully, Syteria's tongue explored his cuspids. She'd expected the taste of her own blood, but instead...

This is what ambrosia must taste like—a blend of exotic spices and forbidden fruits demanding to be savored. He kissed her back, as gently and tentatively as her own hesitant explorations.

Fearing gluttony, she pulled away.

His eyes opened, irises retreating, revealing golden light fixated on the pulse in her throat. Her heart pounded.

A sound, more animal than human, resonated low in his throat. He widened the gap between them, but barely.

"Don't stop," she whispered and discovered that her nails were digging into his back.

"It's Galen." He carefully untwisted his hand from her hair. "He's on his way here. I can hear his footsteps racing across the deck."

She tilted her head to listen. "I don't hear anything."

He made a low sound of amusement. "Galen must still be monitoring your vitals. He is rushing to stop me lest I hurt you."

The chime requesting entry sounded.

"Why would Galen think that?"

Face darkening, he compressed his lips into a thin line.

"Is it your intent to hurt me?" she asked.

The chime sounded again.

"I gave you my word that I would not," he said. "But humans are fragile."

Another chime. It drew his gaze to the entry.

"Are you going to let him in?"

"No. I don't want or need an audience."

The possessiveness in that phrase sent her heart pounding again. She caressed his bearded cheek.

His gaze returned to hers, and he was about to kiss her when the door slid open.

No.

Not when her body had been quickening, ripening under his touch. She turned around in his grasp, but he held her against him like a captive shield.

Her arms curled around her middle only to find *his* arms already firmly entrenched.

Had it been anyone but Galen, she would have borne it and fought off the shame that was twisting pleasure into confusion. But she could not bear the thought of having Galen witness her surrender.

Galen paused, jaw agape, his gaze quickly moving from her to him. Urgent steps had brought Galen just outside *his* reach. Galen dropped to one knee and bowed his head.

"Apologies, my lord."

"You have my leave," *he* said. "And Galen, the next time you override the lock on my door, someone better be dying." He said it first in Rhoan and then again in what must have been High Kanthlos because Galen's name was the only word she understood.

Galen gave him a curt nod. It was the same quick motion that *he* had used when Galen had reprimanded *him*.

318

"My lady," Galen said. "May I escort you to quarters?"

The sound of her heartbeat crashed in her ears. She wanted to disappear, to fade from this world and its intense, confusing emotions. *His* grasp around her middle tightened, no longer merely protective.

It sent a jolt through her body. She licked her lips, preparing to remind him that she was only human—she could only bear so much. But she dared no move, no gesture, no sound.

Tighter and tighter, his arms curled around her abdomen, drawing Galen's gaze. Heat caressed the bare slope of her shoulder—when had her robe slipped off? A brush of *his* lips followed at that tender spot where shoulder met neck. A spasm at her very core sent caressing aftershocks through her.

Galen raised his eyes, and his gaze was harsh and fixed to the spot above her bared shoulder where his master reigned.

"Syteria."

The word caressed her ear. Her abdomen grew tight at the potency of her name on *his* lips. His teeth grazed at the tender point, his lips tracing a line of fire on her skin. An ugly parody of pleasure manifested itself as a shiver born of all the wrong emotions.

She surged forward, suddenly free, stumbling from the shock of being released with sudden ease. She turned to look back, but Galen caught her and placed his body between them, blocking her view. He herded her out, and she barely caught a glimpse of some dark monument that looked like *him.*

Anger and other dark, dangerous things she didn't want to see or know shone from *his* eyes.

THE NANITE POD did not know it was a weapon.

It *did* know that its host had the right chromosomes and that it had not encountered any *donai* nanites. It also knew, that once it did, it would be destroyed in microseconds.

The pod had no countermeasures. In fact, countermeasures would have prevented it from fulfilling its mission. So it hid inside the host, camouflaging itself by surrounding its shell with epithelial cells.

Replication, at least in its current, dormant form, was not an option. It might draw attention from the host's own immune system or from active scanners designed to seek out and hunt its kind.

A flood of hormones and pheromones permeated the host. Then another.

A small army—just a few thousand—of *donai* nanites accompanied the next surge, and microseconds later, they consumed the pod's shell. With the shell gone, the contents escaped.

The *donai* nanites surrounding it recognized the contents as harmless human epithelial cells and ignored them.

DREA SETTLED into her day-cabin's favorite chair to sip her morning tea. She inhaled the delicate scent. Heated sweetness slid down her tongue as she scrolled through the reports.

A rise in visits to the infirmary, mostly due to the celebratory misadventures that inevitably occurred after the initiation rites.

Verification scans of the decks they'd cleared of imperial bugs while most of the crew were on Tir'Hala-Revir.

Reports from their parasites indicating a lack of imperial contacts.

She frowned. Darien's personal ship, the *Glaive*, was not being prepped for its trip to Kanavar. Setting the steaming cup aside, she verified Darien's current whereabouts and made her way to the swordhall.

The doors parted to reveal a battlefield. No phantom had been spared. Only the swords remained intact.

Darien stood before the sprawling viewscreen, his sweat-drenched back to her, the killing sword held out at his side.

"Commander Bomani," he said.

The arctic tone sent chills down her spine. She had to lock her knees to keep from running. It took a few seconds to regain her voice.

"My lord. The summons."

"Yes."

A puddle of cream silk caught her eye. She approached and picked it up. Cast aside and abandoned? Or torn off? She swallowed the lump in her throat.

"Have your intentions toward Syteria changed, my lord?"

"I am *not* returning her to the emperor," he said, his voice colder still. And harsh.

Harsher than she'd ever thought possible. Had he even considered it? Or was he just anticipating her argument? She drew herself up, as though projecting height would help her.

"That's not what I meant," she said.

"I am in no mood for guessing games, Commander. What do you mean?"

Are you in love with your prisoner?

Did Galen create the right woman for you?

Are you insane?

They went unspoken because she didn't want answers to any of those questions. The dire consequences of a "yes" to any of them could tear Dobromil's House apart. She let the silk slip back down onto the floor.

"What happened on Tir'Hala-Revir?" she asked.

"Nothing."

"And here?"

"Nothing that concerns you," he said.

"It will concern your *donai*."

"My *donai*. My concern. Not yours."

His intentions towards Syteria *were* changing. She clamped her mouth shut. If he was developing emotional attachments, abandoning Galen's ruse, then—

"Palleton and I are going to Kanavar. Prepare my ship."

"Yes, my lord."

CHAPTER THIRTY-TWO

*L*ast night, when Galen had escorted Syteria to her quarters, she'd been grateful that he'd not insisted on having yet another poorly understood conversation. She needed time to sort out what had happened.

Her body still awash with desire, she'd lingered under the falling water of a shower so cold it had made her teeth chatter. Even after she'd thought she'd washed him off her, she'd wanted to go back. It was only by sheer force of will that she'd remained in her quarters.

She wanted more. More of *him*, his touch, his scent. And alongside desire, there was a fear of returning to him while she remained so ready to yield.

She'd eventually fallen into a fitful sleep plagued by nightmares. Despite them, she dressed and steeled herself for another encounter. She should've never left with Galen, never allowed his presence to twist her desires into shame.

The way *he* had held her, had been so possessive, so primal. If only he hadn't let her go.

Syteria moved through the *Edlyn's* passageways. Crewmen greeted her. She nodded her response.

She entered the swordhall expecting *him* to still be there. Instead, she found a battlefield. Things that looked like people—identically featureless in face and form—had been hacked to pieces. She squatted to get a better look at a torso that had a sword sticking out of its chest. The head had been smashed. It felt as real as any corpse, its skin and the tissue beneath it all-too-human to her probing touch. No blood though. Practice dummies of some kind.

The sword rack was in splinters. The banners that had fluttered above had been pulled down and torn to shreds. There was even a section of the viewscreen where a glowing crack pulsed with the light of nanites at work.

She looked about for her discarded robe, shoving limbs aside with her foot. Lifting her skirt, she stepped over debris, but the pile of fabric turned out to be part of a banner. It fell from her grasp, floating down to settle upon a bare patch of flooring.

Looking about, she noticed four portraits against the far wall. Her footsteps echoed across the wood floor as she approached them.

The *donai* within those frames looked at her with archaic, unseeing eyes. These weren't the life-like holograms she'd become used to. They were, like so much of this chamber, anachronisms.

Symbols had been carved into the frames. They glowed at her approach and sped along the frame itself, trailing additional writings that flowed by too quickly to read. She touched the right edge of the frame and the words stopped.

One of the *donai* in the images had harsher lines permanently set into his face as he cast a brooding look at everything before him.

The whisper-quiet of parting doors and the echo of footsteps made Syteria look over her shoulder.

"I'm glad to see you out and about," Anasera said as she came to a stop beside her. She seemed unaffected by the chamber's disarray, or what it implied.

"Who is this?" Syteria asked.

"Lord Dobromil. Darien's father."

"And this?" she asked, gesturing to the next portrait.

There was a twinge at her back. Syteria winced and put her hand on the troublesome spot.

"Are you in pain?"

"It's nothing."

Anasera pushed Syteria's hand away and placed her own over the bloom of pain.

"How long?" Anasera asked.

"Just now—" It was like a knife had been plunged into her lower back, just below her waist. A tearing pain followed it, ripping inward from her spine to her hip.

She took a deep breath and let it out as Anasera watched her with concern.

"There," Syteria said, straightening. "It's gone."

Anasera's brows drew together.

"Really, I'm fine."

Anasera heaved a deep, weighed sigh.

"Please, let me check," Anasera said, taking a step back and bowing her head. "My lady."

Syteria's hands tightened at her sides.

Anasera had never bowed her head like this. Not to her. Had she done it to hide how ashen her face had become?

As intense as the pain had been, it hadn't made her heart beat like it was now at Anasera's obvious fear.

THE WEAPONIZED EPITHELIAL "CELLS" had replicated.

They formed a sheet of slime one cell thick and made their way through the host's body. They did so, slowly, making sure to repair the damage they caused as they crossed through barriers they couldn't go around.

They drew resources from their host, stealing needed molecules she used to nourish herself. Her body's defenses responded, attaching themselves to the sheet. They would be tolerated as long as they didn't become a direct threat.

In fact, letting them ride along provided a sort of camouflage as the sheet of slime made its way to its target—the largest cell in the host's body.

"EVERYONE OUT!" Galen's voice boomed so loud it echoed.

It was the ashen look on Anasera's face, paired with Syteria's bristling annoyance that made his tone harsher than what he'd intended, but his staff was used to his moods. They also knew better than not to clear out.

Nestra's eyes went wide. She pivoted left, then right, like she was uncertain which route to take, and followed two other assistants who obeyed without hesitation.

She cast a backward glance that clearly asked, *Are you sure?*

He gave her a tight nod as the chime of the lock sounded behind her.

"Galen, I'm fine," Syteria insisted, shaking off Anasera's grip.

"I will be the judge of that."

She mumbled something in Rhoan.

"The pain is gone," she said in clear, precise Kanthlos.

"Pain is a symptom. It is there for a reason," he said, gesturing to the bio-bed.

She stood her ground, arms rigid at her sides, shoulders set with defiance.

A few commands sent two rovers to hover around her. They wrapped her in sweeping veils of light. He routed the resulting images to a console so she couldn't see the results.

It had been less than a month since he'd inserted the implant. It was designed to be harmless, painless, and undetectable to the host. The scans confirmed its presence, and that it hadn't inadvertently started simulating a child's heartbeat.

Pregnancy hormones designed to give the *donai* the right scent clues, but spare her the physiological changes of pregnancy, were being slowly released, right on schedule. The implant was sparing her a little too well, apparently. He adjusted its programing to mask the scent of ovulation.

No wonder she had sought Darien out. No wonder her emotions had overwhelmed her.

His sigh of relief was quickly followed by regret. If Darien intended to perfect his claim—to get her pregnant and trigger a pair-bond—the window of opportunity was getting narrower every day.

Syteria, however, wasn't ready. Not yet. In time, perhaps. Time. Always time. No matter how much humans advanced, they remained slaves to time.

He recalled the rovers as Anasera joined him at the console. She took a confirming look and purged the records.

"Our apologies, my lady," she said.

Syteria shifted her weight and crossed her arms.

"It was, as you said, nothing," Galen said and gave her his most charming smile. "How did you sleep?"

Her brows drew together with suspicion. "Fine. Why?"

"You slept for almost two days."

"Oh?" She was clearly taken aback. "Did you use a...how do you say?"

"Sleep field? No, my lady."

She crossed her arms, considering him, then Anasera.

Uncomfortable silence hung in the room. He couldn't say that he blamed her. If Darien had explained to her why he'd taken her away from the fort on Tir'Hala-Revir, she'd have just cause not to trust him.

She cleared her throat. "I have a request."

Galen nodded.

She approached and hesitantly tugged at his sleeve. "I want this."

"A uniform?" Galen asked.

"You are not crew," Anasera said.

"I know. He, the *donai*"—she licked dry lips—"the..."

"Darien," Galen said helpfully.

She threw him a glare.

"Why won't you say Darien's name?" he asked.

The glare grew in intensity. She answered in Rhoan, her tone one of pure frustration. He waited for her to rephrase. She remained silent instead.

"Perhaps some ship fatigues," Galen said. "She is not crew, but she is pack."

Anasera gave him a puzzled frown. "Since when? Father, you promised she'd not be bloodied on Tir'Ha—"

"Since she saved my life. My lord decreed it so, before he left."

Syteria's eyes widened and a slow smile crept across her lips. She gave him a look of noblesse oblige so perfect he'd have thought her *donai*.

"This way," Anasera said. "I will show you how to have the *Edlyn* make them for you."

"Thank you," Syteria said.

It was only after they had both exited the lab that Galen realized that it had been in High Kanthlos. He rushed to the console to see if he could still retrieve the scans they'd just made, but the data was gone. They had set it up just for this purpose—to keep Syteria's condition a secret—and hardwired the protocols ensuring that once data was erased, it could not be retrieved.

He scrubbed a hand over his face. It had to be coincidence. She had been studying diligently, that's all. That she was intelligent had never been in doubt and Darien had been pushing her. That had to be it.

They couldn't have exchanged more than a kiss or two. They could not have exchanged blood. There hadn't been time. She showed none of the damaging signs of a human whose blood had been contaminated with *donai* nanites. And Darien had not bitten her. Galen had stopped them in time. He was sure of it.

He reactivated the monitors that tracked Syteria's vitals, defying Darien's orders once again.

CHAPTER THIRTY-THREE

*T*he *Glaive* circled the emperor's palace for the hundred-and-thirty-fifth time.

The imperial residence stabbed high into the clouds, crowning the cliffs into which it was built. Over a precipice, waterfalls spilled like veils, becoming fog and mist. Battlements postured their functionality, crowding flying buttresses and towers designed to glorify and intimidate.

It had been hours since Darien had surrendered control of his craft to the Imperium only to be assigned a holding pattern.

He groaned as he tugged at the sleeves of his formal uniform. Crimson braid circled the black fabric as his House's embroidered sigil stared back at him.

"We get the message," he said under his breath and dug his nails into the arms of the command chair.

"What message is that, my lord?" Palleton asked, his tone holding far too much amusement for Darien's tastes. Decades of service had given Palleton the ability to wait patiently on a master's whims. Darien had no intention of developing that trait.

He shot Palleton a frustrated look.

"If you allow the emperor to unnerve you before you even step off this ship," Palleton said, "we might as well skip the audience and head home."

Darien took a deep breath and closed his eyes.

Memories haunted him: Syteria in his arms, the curious gleam in her eyes, the cheery curiosity at his more obvious *donai* traits. She had kissed him, pressed her body against his, all of her own free will. Every gesture, every look, even her scent had signaled her interest, her arousal, her acceptance. Since she was human, she was not ruled by pair-bond. Her reactions were entirely her own.

She hadn't recoiled. She hadn't been afraid.

Not until Galen had intruded.

It had been in those painful moments when her scent had changed that he'd almost bitten her. To bite one's pregnant mate was instinct, a way of infusing additional *donai* nanites into her blood, nanites that would reduce her pain and increase the chances for a healthy child.

His conscience had finally reminded him, that there was no child. Sending nanites into her bloodstream was likely to kill her. He'd stopped, just in time. Just barely.

Her choice to go with Galen, to accept his offer of safety had been...prudent, no matter how much it felt like a betrayal and throbbed like a wound in his chest.

Darien had made his intentions clear to Galen in the brig. He'd ordered him not to interfere. And Galen had disobeyed. Again. He'd disobeyed because he'd known that she'd smell pregnant, that Darien's *donai* instincts would take over, that he'd act as if they were already a bonded pair.

There is no child.

Perhaps if he repeated it often enough, he'd remember himself around her and take a step back. Perfecting his claim meant seducing her, getting her pregnant. Not marking her. Once she was pregnant, once he was pair-bonded, only then was it proper to consider—and very carefully—marking her. Even then, it would not be without risk.

"Stop thinking about her," Palleton said.

Darien bolted out of his seat to pace the deck and regain control of all the outward signs that would unmask him. He needed to cast aside his humanity and all its attendant faults. He needed the calm, cold detachment of being just *donai*. He needed to concentrate on the matter at hand, not on lost opportunities.

The *Glaive* banked, altering its course towards the setting sun, slowly surrendering altitude.

Palleton checked the controls and said, "They're taking us out of the main imperial quarter."

"More theatre," Darien complained as he peeked over Palleton's shoulder.

"The Imperial Gardens," Palleton said.

From above, the Imperial Gardens looked like the work of a giant child who'd broken the ground to mix the upturned soil with his hoard of smashed toys. Into the haphazard layout, pathways had been carved and paved.

The *Glaive* landed in a clearing just outside the Gardens' perimeter.

An armed escort greeted Darien and Palleton as the ramp lowered. Imperial *donai*, ceremonially garbed in formal attire similar to Darien's but in Kabrin's colors waited. They lined both sides of the path leading from the landing pad to the Gardens' arched entryway.

The arch had once been part of a ship. Its dark, twisted metal absorbed more light than it reflected, making it seem darker in the light of the setting sun. Serrated edges pointed inward like a clawed hand curling shut.

A makeshift wall constructed of stone slabs circled the enormity of the Gardens.

"Your master awaits, my lord," the detail commander said.

Darien nodded and followed him, striding through the imperial gauntlet with ease. As he and Palleton approached, it became clear that the Garden's encircling slabs were actually grave markers.

The paving stones under his feet also bore the names of the fallen. The scripts on both markers and stones were a dull rainbow of grays and blacks. They were written in scripts as varied as the material into which they were carved. Flashes of light sparked across the pathway and up the encircling wall as the sun sank into the horizon.

"A private audience, my lord," the detail commander clarified as they were about to pass under the arch.

"Wait here," Darien said, casting a glance over his shoulder.

Palleton's lip twitched into the barest sneer, but he obeyed.

Darien passed under the arch. He followed the winding path to the first exhibit, a crumbling structure of aged stone columns arrayed around a marble throne. The silent trophy had been plucked from the ruins of a conquered capital. The remnants of a bloodied banner fluttered in the backdrop. House Hevonen's sigil—a screeching raptor—was barely recognizable.

True to his word, Emperor Thán Kabrin stood alone, his back angled toward Darien. His waist-length black hair was pulled away from his face, held back by a simple clasp stamped with House Kabrin's sigil, the silhouette of a dragon. Black trousers and a dark green tunic—undecorated, devoid of braid and accoutrement—stretched over a tall, broad frame.

In the fading light, a sideways glance revealed the glowing gold behind his amber irises. Cut from the same genetic cloth, they could've been brothers, but everything muted in Darien by his human mother was strengthened in Thán Kabrin. He was of *donai* stock undiluted over the generations. The points of his ears were prominent, as were his cuspids, his height, the speed with which he healed and moved. His senses were sharper, keener. Older than Darien by two decades, the emperor stood childless despite the dozens of female *donai* who cluttered his Court in the hopes of ascending to the title of empress.

"Sire." Darien bowed and straightened.

"We have received your claim," Kabrin said as he unhurriedly took a fork that veered southward.

Darien followed, remaining a step behind and to the emperor's left.

"A mere human, Darien?" he asked, his tone light, chiding, as though they were friends or brothers-in-arms. "Really? Not even one such as yourself."

"Yes, Sire."

"The invader, nonetheless. One responsible for the loss of many *donai* lives."

Darien remained silent. Denying the charge was as dangerous as acknowledging it.

"What are the chances that you would be so compatible?" Kabrin's tone mocked as he cocked his head.

They paused in front of the next exhibit—a war-torn hill. A set of spears, embedded in the hill, crossed each other at the top. A flame that had represented freedom to its people burned in a raised bowl under the crossed spears of subjugation.

"I do not know, Sire. I can ask my House physician to calculate the changes of comp—"

"That is not what I mean, and you know it. How did you woo and court our enemy in such a short time?"

Darien locked his features into a neutral mask as the emperor's unquestioning gaze searched his face.

"Or did House Dobromil finally fall off that pedestal upon which your father placed it?"

Something in Darien's eyes must have betrayed him. Kabrin's grin widened in triumph. A chill ran through Darien, as Galen's words about how the emperor would perceive a claim rang true.

"Is my claim rejected, Sire?"

The emperor resumed his stroll, past monoliths inscribed with names and separated by curtains of flame. Darien followed, like a man determined to make his way to the gallows without a hint of dread.

"You know as well as we do, that we have no choice but to recognize your claim."

"Thank you, Sire," Darien said, his dread swelling in anticipation of Kabrin's countermove. Kabrin had yielded too easily, mocked too lightly, implied too softly.

"But I do have a choice in recognizing your status as heir."

"Sire?"

"Your father has been a thorn in the Imperium's side from the beginning, weakening the *donai*, empowering humans. Your House has been providing safe harbor for our enemies, providing aid and comfort to imperial traitors—"

"Sire, House Dobr—"

"Do you know how surprised I was when you were born?"

"Sire?" Darien kept pace with the emperor's easy stride. His mind raced, emotions reeling at the sudden change of subject. Adrenaline pumped through his veins. He kept his hand away from his sword.

"I was certain," Kabrin said, "absolutely certain, you would be *donai*, not some abomination, not some half-truth."

Distracted by the revelation, Darien passed the emperor who'd come to a stop.

Kabrin's laugh was low and satisfied.

"Does it not bother you," Kabrin said, "knowing that your father had the means to give you everything and chose instead, to diminish you?"

Darien raised his gaze to the emperor's and held it. Humans and *donai* were not that different. Otherwise he would not exist.

What had his father denied him besides a *donai* mother?

The emperor's lip curled in satisfaction. "Ah...you did not know."

That his father had not sought a *donai* wife was no secret. Was the emperor implying something else or merely playing on Darien's insecurities?

"Unfortunate that Lord Dobromil does not trust his own heir—his own son—with the truth."

"What truth is that, Sire?"

"That he values human lives over *donai*. Even over his own son's."

Darien wiped the incredulous look off his face before it could fully form. He wasn't sure which façade would entice the emperor more.

"I believe Galen's success rate was about ten percent, at its best," Kabrin continued. "Before he—what's the polite word? Ah, yes, defected."

"Success with what, Sire?"

"Using human surrogates to bear *donai* offspring. Brilliant man, that human of yours. A method with limited risk to the *donai*, that required only human sacrifice. I found a sort of cosmic justice in it— repayment for the way the humans used us. Most satisfying, don't you think?"

The emperor resumed walking with a slight spring in his step.

333

Darien followed, steps echoing off the stones, breathing steady only by sheer force of will.

"His first attempt was a complete success," the emperor said. "Even the surrogate survived. A child with all of a *donai's* traits, and no human ones. A female *donai*, no less. Something we thought forever out of our reach."

The emperor looked at Darien sideways, every bit the predator baiting his prey.

Their human creators had skewed the sex ratios of the *donai* on purpose so that even if they managed to breed on their own, they could not sustain any significant numbers. Both the original source material used to create them and the knowledge to recreate it had been lost in the chaos of their rebellion. What the *donai* themselves had not destroyed, their Ryhman creators had.

"But then failure followed," Kabrin said. "Failed attempt after failed attempt. Galen developed something of a conscience about the deaths of the surrogates. Human guilt, I suppose. Sympathy for his own kind. At first I thought him merely defiant, so I broke him. It would never stick for long. I had to do it several times. Resilient for a human, that one. Does he still serve you?"

"No, Sire."

"Really?" The emperor stopped and scrutinized Darien's face.

"Galen serves my father."

A smile formed, the first genuine smile Darien had ever seen on Kabrin's face. The emperor clasped his hands behind his back and headed down the path. They passed statue after statue, each a symbol of conquest. Some ancient, some recent.

The remnants of something that might have been a ship, twisted and melted, or perhaps dipped in acid, loomed ahead. Skeletons with partially melted bones formed a pile next to it.

They stopped in front of it as the setting sun glinted off the remains of the hull, the remains of its crew.

For several seconds there was silence. Realization crashed over Darien, an invisible tidal wave poised to destroy him and everything he'd tried to accomplish. The melted hull, the remains. It was the Rhoan ship.

"When your claim fails to bear the proper fruit," Kabrin said, "I will vacate your status as heir designate. Should Lord Dobromil die without a proper *donai* heir, I will place one of my own choosing on that throne. Someone willing to bring House Dobromil in line with the Imperium. Someone willing to sacrifice as many humans as are required for our survival. Someone willing to rule humans with a heavy hand."

Kabrin resumed walking.

Careful to remain a step behind, Darien's thoughts were a tempest sweeping aside a game board, sending the pieces toppling. His queen. His bishops, knights, and rooks. His pawns. The game was rigged, and the board was awash in blood. If the emperor changed the conditions, then Darien would play a game he could win, a game where he had the advantage, where he made the rules.

"And if my claim *does* bear the proper fruit?"

A tiny corner of his conscience howled at him in his father's voice: *Fool. Arrogant, young fool.*

The emperor raised a skeptical brow. "Impossible."

"Yes, Sire." Darien's tone was so flat, it startled even him.

The emperor faltered, fell behind. Darien slowed, then stopped, waiting with a practiced, polite subservience that was anything but.

"You jest," the emperor insisted, but there was no confidence in it.

Darien lowered his head and shoulders in something like a nod, something non-committal.

THE *GLAIVE* LIFTED off its landing pad and streaked across Kanavar's sky like a meteor. The half-breed lord's stench lingered on the path as Tolek approached the emperor's still form. His liege was facing the Rhoan ship, one hand clenched into a fist behind his back. His other hand was wrapped around what was left of a human femur he'd plucked off the pile before him.

Tolek bent at the waist and held his position until the emperor acknowledged him with a nod.

"Sire, does he lie?" The entire time Tolek had remained out of sight, barely within hearing distance, a secret witness to the entire exchange.

"Perhaps," Kabrin said. "If so, it is with great skill."

"Do you want me to recall the bio-weapon while it is still possible?"

Kabrin threw the bone back atop the pile. It made a hollow sound as it landed and skidded off to the side.

"Why would we wish to recall it?" Kabrin asked as he walked down the path.

Tolek followed. "We still cannot find the woman's system of origin and everything about the ship and its people, suggests a previously unknown human tribe. Perhaps, they are the source material the Ryhmans used to create us."

The emperor's footfalls barely echoed.

"Imagine it, Sire, *donai* fertility restored."

"You suggest I allow this human's child to live. And then what?"

"Order Dobromil to present it, and the woman who bore it, to the Court. Proof of its *donai* traits will be required to allow it to inherit anyway. Genetic proof that must be presented at Court, and vetted by House Kabrin's physicians."

"Years from now," Kabrin said. "Even now, Dobromil moves to outmaneuver us. He consolidates power within the Court, slowly drawing allies. A *donai* grandchild will only aid his cause. Imagine it. Dobromil 'sires' a half-breed that inherits as many *donai* traits as those of true *donai* descent. And then the half-breed begets a stronger strain, whatever the source. No, I will not have even the possibility of such a thing hang over us."

"Your will, Sire," Tolek said with all the required deference. His own thoughts on the matter would remain unvoiced. His loyalty was, no matter what, to the *donai* that allowed him to stand beside the imperial throne itself.

"This is the second time Dobromil has taken something from us. We would have them both—Galen and this woman—dead."

For almost three decades Galen had had a bounty on his head. All of those who'd taken to the task had failed because the emperor had made it known that he wanted Galen alive.

"If there is an heir," the emperor said, "particularly a *donai* heir, Dobromil and every House in the Imperium will try to locate this tribe."

"Sire, this world of hers is not within space known to us. There is only one way to reach it, and that is with the same technology that brought her ship here. Let Dobromil and all the Houses waste time and treasure trying to find it. They will fail."

"You are certain of this?"

"Yes, Sire. There is no indication that any of the Houses are working to develop wormholes."

"And if that changes?"

"They are decades behind us on this, a disadvantage that cannot be overcome."

The emperor let out a sigh. "How does your pet scientist fare?"

"Luuedei Kennen has recovered from her injuries and seems well-satisfied with her vengeance. She works as diligently as ever to reconstruct the generator, properly this time."

"Does she have everything she needs?"

"I have provided her with everything she has asked for and set others to confirm every step of her work, in secret of course."

"How long before she can deliver results?"

"A year, Sire. Perhaps longer."

"That is unacceptable," Kabrin said.

"Sire, I would advise against pushing or threatening her. Not until one of those aiding her has acquired the knowledge required to carry on her work."

Kabrin nodded.

"Should Dayasagar's boast prove true, Sire, this tribe—"

"This tribe will be destroyed," Kabrin said.

"But Sire, if the human stock..." Tolek stopped before he said something that would justify the removal of his head. "Forgive me, Sire."

"The wormhole must be large enough for our flagship to go through. We will bear witness to the destruction of this Rho-Kappa."

"Yes, Sire."

It would delay things further, there was no doubt of that, but again, Tolek kept it to himself. Should it prove fruitful, the wormhole technology would eventually necessitate just that feature. The wormhole would have to accommodate ships of war, allowing them to move directly from origin to destination without suffering delays at the whim of other Houses, without wasting time crossing an entire solar system to get from one transit point to another.

If Luuedei was right it would give them almost instantaneous communication as well, with tight-beamed data transmission through smaller wormholes. Even if transmitting signals through wormholes failed, the use of message drones would still be vastly improved. And as long as the technology remained only in House Kabrin's hands, the emperor would have the means to destroy all those who stood in his way. No more checks and balances. The scales would tilt heavily in his favor and remain that way.

"Tomorrow we will recognize Dayasagar's claim on this woman."

Tolek made a small nod, and said, "The destruction of Thertore must still be explained. Sire."

"All in due time," the emperor said.

It took months for information to propagate through the Imperium. The Imperium's charter required the entirety of the peerage to attend the emperor on Kanavar only once every two to three years. Having just adjourned less than three months ago, time was on their side.

Once Luuedei succeeded, the emperor would never have to explain himself to the peerage again. Should she fail, Tolek would provide the Houses with reasons to fight amongst themselves.

Tolek's mind churned with possibilities, with plots of betrayal and matters of ideological division. He followed the emperor across a bridge made of fossilized human skulls. Each had once belonged to one of the *donai's* creators.

~

SYTERIA FOLLOWED the rat-tat-tap of wooden sticks colliding. They were coming from one of the small amphitheaters tucked into the *Edlyn's* parkland.

Above, the ersatz sky was overcast with the promise of a rainstorm. She made her way down the stone steps without worrying about tripping over the long skirts that had not, despite frequent wear, become easier to deal with.

The plain, unmarked ship fatigues fit her perfectly—mind, body, and soul.

In the center of the amphitheater, Aeda and a statuesque woman with short, black hair were sparring, using long wooden staffs. Two others—a tall, brown-haired woman and a petite blonde—were sitting on the steps, watching.

Aeda called a stop. The women stood and everyone bowed.

She acknowledged them with a nod. "Please. Con-tin-ue." The word had popped into her mind so readily, she blinked in surprise.

Aeda and her sparring partner resumed, moving back and forth over the patch of grass. Words were exchanged. By their tone, probably insults and taunts, but clearly without malice.

Sweat beaded on their brows as the pace intensified.

The statuesque woman's staff made it past Aeda's defenses, right into her abdomen. Aeda folded and fell back, using momentum to roll away a split second before the staff came down on the patch of grass she'd just cleared. Her staff made a wide arc as she swung it at her opponent's legs. The statuesque woman jumped back and held her pole at the ready, grinning.

Clutching at her abdomen, Aeda pushed up and conceded the match. They finished with bows, and the blonde stood to take Aeda's place.

"Are you hurt?" Syteria asked as Aeda limped over and sat down beside her.

Aeda rolled up her shirt to reveal a forming bruise. "No, not really. Lowran was holding back."

Syteria's brows rose. Given their technology, it made sense. They were willing to risk injury, knowing there would be no permanent damage. Pain was, after all, only temporary here.

Remembered pains made themselves known. She braced her hands on the stone ledge beneath her, knuckles turning white, breathing through the memory of *grierugon* claws piercing her again and again.

"My lady," Aeda was saying, in that tone that said she was repeating herself.

"Teach me," Syteria said without meeting Aeda's gaze.

Aeda stood and Syteria rose with her. The sparring couple halted at their approach. Aeda explained the request.

"My lady, this is Cyra," Lowran said, introducing the blonde.

Cyra gave Syteria a half-bow and handed her a staff. She repositioned Syteria's hands several times and taught her some basic strikes.

As they went through motions, warmth flooded Syteria's muscles. The phantom pains faded. Working the staff provided a psychological balm against the pain and fear.

Aeda shouted encouragement and half-understood pointers. Cyra set up opposite Syteria, and held her staff at an angle. Lowran encouraged her to strike.

Syteria lifted the staff and brought it down dead center at the intended target. Then they switched, with her playing defense and Cyra attacking. They switched again, adding more power. It was all rote and artificial, building muscle memory, but it was a start.

As Syteria brought the staff up for a block, Cyra stopped midmotion and took a startled step back.

Syteria spun to find Kell standing a few steps behind her. Muscles and veins strained against the skin on his neck and his face had darkened.

He spoke with threat in his voice.

Placing herself between Kell and Cyra, Aeda spoke softly, soothing him.

He bared his teeth.

"What's going on?" Syteria asked, realizing too late that it had been in Rhoan.

340

"My lady," Kell said in that low, warning tone they all used. He went on to explain, but while she didn't understand the specifics, she did recognize the pattern of High Kanthlos.

"My lady," Aeda said, swallowing hard. "He forbids it."

"Does he?" Syteria asked, leveling her gaze up toward Kell's hard-set eyes. "Speak to me in Kanthlos."

His nostrils flared, gaze darting between Syteria and Aeda as though he was lost.

"My lady," Aeda said, "he cannot. You cannot ask him to."

"I'm not asking." She planted the end of the sparring pole by her foot, holding it defiantly.

Kell's amber gaze met hers. She held it as the layered pupils irised open and shut. He spoke in High Kanthlos again.

Syteria shook her head. "No."

Kell glared at Aeda.

"My lady," Aeda whispered as she leaned closer and threaded her hand through Syteria's arm.

"Please," Aeda said, louder, her voice cracking as she revealed the blooming bruise on her abdomen and gestured towards Syteria's middle. "You get hurt."

"I. Don't. Care."

Kell's visage darkened further. The muscles in his jaw pulsed. He ripped the pole from Syteria's grasp before she'd even realized he'd moved.

Four equally sized pieces with jagged ends—as if the staffs had been mere kindling—landed at her feet as golden pupils flared in the scarred face looming above her.

CHAPTER THIRTY-FOUR

*W*orried sick was not a phrase that Drea liked to apply to herself. But she had been, right up to the moment when the *Glaive* had returned through the phase-point.

It wasn't just for Darien or Palleton, both of whom she'd willingly give her life for. It was the bloody aftermath that was certain to follow. She'd witnessed the demise of more than one House. She did not have it in her to see another.

Not this House. Not my House.

A welcoming chill accompanied the *Glaive* as it settled into the hangar and the ramp lowered. She stood alone, without fanfare or honor guard, ready to deliver a report on the *Edlyn's* status. The entire list of facts and minutiae evaporated from her mind the instant the *Glaive's* hatch opened and Darien appeared.

His face was like stone, cold and hard. Inhuman in a way she'd never seen it before.

Welcome back, my lord, caught in her throat and she swallowed to prevent the words from inadvertently coming out as a squeak.

Darien stalked down the ramp without acknowledging her. On pure instinct, she took a clumsy side-step to avoid being mowed down.

Palleton's steadying hand materialized at the small of her back and disappeared just as soon as she regained her balance. She glared an unspoken question at him. It bounced off Palleton's well-cultivated impression of a wall. An impression which still looked more human than Darien had.

"What happened?" she asked.

Had she been right about the emperor refusing to recognize Darien's claim? Were imperial ships coming to enforce the emperor's will? Was Darien going to risk war over a woman?

Stupid, stupid boy.

House Dobromil didn't have the allies or strength for another engagement with the Imperium. Not now. Not yet. Not soon.

Sweet, young fool.

There was a side of her that wanted to embrace him for that very foolishness. What Dobromil had not done for her kind, Darien just might. A powerful enough House could free its humans without fearing that other *donai* would hunt them down or enslave them. A powerful enough House could declare humans citizens. A powerful enough House could prevent the Imperium from destroying Outer Region worlds to wipe out the humans hiding on them.

She followed them through the passageways without breaking into a run. She was *not* going to trot after them like some junior officer. This was her ship.

Drea followed Darien into the flag cabin. With an angry motion he tore his tunic open and cast it aside. He whirled, sheathed sword in one hand, ready to be drawn, and she knew what it felt like to truly be prey.

Drop to your knees. Show him your throat.

She locked her legs to remain upright. This was why their tunics had such high collars. The collars were decorated with markers of rank and fealty to give humans some level of dignity and remind the *donai* that *this* prey was protected. She was not going to undo those small safeguards by giving in to fear and dread.

"Darien?"

Behind her, doors whispered open, but she dared not turn. It might look too much like she was preparing to run or retreat.

Palleton appeared at her side.

"Not now, Commander," he whispered.

His whisper tore her gaze from Darien.

Several *donai* flanked Palleton. As before, they stood at her back, but this time they were neither honor guard, nor protection detail.

Palleton jerked her out of Darien's way. The throbbing told her that there were going to be some impressive bruises where his fingers dug into her arm. The *donai* parted before their master and trailed in his wake.

Circulation returned to her arm and her legs wobbled as Palleton let her go and made for the door.

"What happened?" she called to his back.

She broke in to a run. By the time she made it to the restored swordhall, they were already inside and a mêlée was in progress.

Palleton appeared in the doorway. She bounced off of him, landing on her rear. She scrambled up, but Palleton grabbed her by the shoulders and propelled her around.

"We'll take good care of him, Commander," he said as he pushed her down the passage.

Drea recovered without grace, but also without sprawling face-forward on the deck. She whirled around, swiping away hair that had come undone. The roar of swords and inhuman *donai* war-calls penetrated the closed doors. Palleton stood guard outside, eyes glowing in warning.

"He's gone cold," she said, bringing her hands to cover her lips. *Cold? A half-human* donai—

"Yes," Palleton said as a frigid, calculating look fell into place.

She swallowed the lump in her throat as her heartbeat soared.

His nostrils flared, the frown deepening.

"It's too bad that my lady is already pregnant. I would prefer a warchild over a human one."

Drea was thankful for the fact that Palleton was an elder *donai*, one tempered by lifetimes among humans. Someone with less experience would be enticed to violence by her dread. If Darien stayed Cold, if his *donai* did not bring him out of it...

"Her life is not yours to risk," she said. "Darien would never forgive you."

His threatening glare was locked on her for far too long, but she stood her ground.

"It would break him," she added.

"Yes. But House Dobromil would have a wort—"

"Darien is a worthy heir," she said, temper and courage rising. "You don't have the authority to cast him aside. You are not his father."

A low growl rumbled in his throat.

"I will not allow it," she said.

He stepped closer and still she stood her ground. "It would be nothing to snap your neck. Commander."

"What are you waiting for then?"

He sneered. "I do not believe her child is merely human. But don't worry, Commander. Even I won't risk the child she carries now for a hypothetical one."

She sighed in relief.

"Go," Palleton said. "We will bring him out of the Cold ourselves. And tell Galen to prepare himself."

"Galen's off duty now," she said matter-of-factly. "Wait. What's he going to do to Galen?"

"I believe my lord will wish to *speak* with him."

The door behind Palleton buckled outward.

"After," he added.

Clashing swords thundered. She took a step forward. Palleton spun her around and had his hand around her throat before her foot came down.

"He doesn't want you to see him like this, Drea. You know this."

Despite the hand around her throat, she said, "I am the captain of the *Edlyn*. Everything aboard this ship concerns me."

"You are not *donai*, Commander. Please don't forget that. Or I will have to remind you."

His hand tightened ever so slightly around her throat, lifting her until she balanced on her toes. He held her there, against his chest, his breath scalding her ear.

Drea's fingertips dug into the forearm holding her up. Her heart raced, the adrenaline in her blood diluting her sense of pain. A lifetime among the *donai* had taught her when to push, and when not to. With tempers already stoked, now was not the time to challenge. Palleton would assert his dominance, one way or the other. And taking her life was not the only way to do it.

"So after all," she said. "It still comes to 'We are *donai* and you are not.'?"

"So it would seem."

AEDA HAD hold of Syteria's wrist. She was leading her out of the royal wing towards a section of the ship that she'd never been to before.

Syteria cast wary backward glances, expecting an alarm to sound or for one of the *donai* to stop them. Aeda seemed to have no such concerns. Instead there was a big grin on her face as she turned to encourage Syteria to follow her.

The compartment was obviously used for training. Not quite as ornate as the swordhall, its walls were still lined with the same feature-less humanoid forms called "sparring phantoms." There were no swords. Instead, about a dozen different kinds of pole arms, shields of all kinds and other weapons Syteria didn't recognize, were stacked or mounted. Unlike the swordhall, there was no viewscreen. It was a fully enclosed space and the floor wasn't made of rich, polished wood, but metal.

"No one will bother us here," Aeda said as the doors closed behind them.

"Are you sure?"

Aeda nodded and handed Syteria a fighting staff.

"But you're wounded," Syteria said.

Aeda rolled up her shirt to reveal a bruise-free abdomen.

"But you have…" she trailed off and, in Rhoan, added, "orders."

As soon as the Rhoan word left her mouth, it came to her in Kanthlos.

"I mean, orders," she corrected. The last thing she wanted, was for Aeda to be punished for disobeying a *donai*.

Aeda pulled the shirt down as she grabbed another staff. She held it loosely in both hands so the staff was at an angle.

"No wounds," Aeda said. "Practice. Like this."

Smoothly, she flowed through lunges and strikes, crossing the length of the chamber. She reversed direction, added some spins to her repertoire and returned to Syteria's side.

Breathing hard from the exertion, Aeda toed off her shoes and encouraged Syteria to do the same.

Syteria laughed. "Practice." Aeda was complying with the letter of her orders, although perhaps, not their spirit.

"Katas," Aeda said.

Syteria gave her a grateful smile.

Aeda nodded. "Let's begin."

DREA RUBBED at her eyes and face. Darien had gone cold. She had not thought it possible. Even among the purest *donai*, it was a rare trait. The way Galen had explained it to her, it was a state of hyper-awareness and detachment, one that even Galen did not fully understand.

It was useful for short periods of time, allowing the *donai* to function without emotional burdens, to make the cold, harsh decisions needed to win. Once danger passed, most came out of the cold on their own. Others, had to be brought out of it.

What had happened on Kanavar to put Darien in such a state? What threats had the emperor made? Did the emperor know that Darien was capable of going cold?

Drea had never seen Galen as nervous as when she'd told him about her encounter with Palleton and delivered the elder *donai's* warning. Galen's hand had drifted to his tunic's collar, tugging, adjusting. It had been his signature move—a Galenism as it were—and over the years, he'd become quite adept at hiding it. Sometimes she caught the slight twitch of his hand betraying just how hard he worked at masking his trademark mannerism.

She had spent the last few hours at her station on the bridge, checking with the infirmary, making sure everyone knew to let her know when it was time. As each hour ticked by, her patience had run thin and her attentiveness to her job had been compromised. She'd left Exton in charge and headed back to the infirmary to wait.

Anasera was watching her father carefully as well, her dark gaze ever-vigilant in the silence.

Ask the right question and Galen became impossible to shut up. Ask him the wrong one and he would not speak.

He busied himself by silently inspecting equipment. Several of the infirmary staff ran through checklists, readied bio-beds, and tweaked nanite packages.

Everyone turned when Palleton entered. A floating pallet trailed him. Its force field canopy only showed a vague human form in its depths, denying curious onlookers a glimpse within. The *donai* followed, wearing haunted looks and sporting rapidly healing injuries.

Two seriously injured *donai* limped in with support and were corralled elsewhere by Galen's subordinates.

If Palleton had been involved in the battle, Drea couldn't tell. She could see him standing by, allowing the others to bloody Darien. It was considered an honor for a lord's vassals to be allowed to bring him out of the cold.

Palleton thanked the uninjured *donai* and asked them to leave. They retreated, casting backward glances. They would obey, but they didn't have to like it.

The elder *donai* pushed the floating pallet over the space reserved for it and locked it into place.

Galen dropped the canopy.

Drea looked away. She braced herself with a deep breath and turned to look again, but Palleton had placed himself in her way, blocking her view.

She shot him a glare.

"Really?" Palleton asked. "You really want to see him like this?"

"The real question is why you don't want me to see him like this? Afraid the human will see just how vulnerable the *donai* can be? Get ideas she shouldn't?"

He harrumphed, but moved out of her way.

Darien was covered in blood, his face, unrecognizable. Nothing was left of his clothing. Skin hung from his body in vast strips. Deep gashes crisscrossed an opened abdomen. She knew that in the time it had taken to bring him here, he must've healed somewhat. This was not the worst of it.

She swallowed bile.

"Gods, what did he look like when you were done with him?"

"Worse," Palleton answered. "Satisfied?"

"Stand here, Commander," Galen said, indicating a spot by Darien's head. "I need you out of the way."

She complied. In a way, it was a relief. She could concentrate on Darien's face, which was healing into recognizable form.

"I didn't think he could go cold," Drea said as she swept the hair out of Darien's eyes.

"All leaders go cold," Palleton said, "or they could not lead."

"But, he's..." Drea licked dry lips. "I mean, his mother..."

"What a mess," Galen muttered as he reattached Darien's ear.

The invisible nanites in Darien's body "stitched" it to his scalp as Drea looked on.

"Did your men have to go this far?" Galen asked over his shoulder.

"Better him than you," Palleton said. "He heals. You don't."

Galen had the good grace to nod sheepishly and remain silent.

"Is this the first time?" Drea asked Palleton.

"No."

What else had they withheld from her? And not just Darien and Palleton. Dobromil as well. Dobromil who'd placed his one and only child into her hands, who'd tasked her with mentoring him, tempering him...

"And you chose not to tell me, because..."

"It was not my place to tell," Palleton said.

"Know your place, human," she said bitterly.

Palleton tilted his head. "If you wish."

Anger flushed through her body. She made no effort to hide it, or to calm herself. She turned towards Galen.

He was preparing Darien's chest, returning salvageable strips of torn skin to their place so they could heal properly. Once they were in place, he worked on Darien's leg. The muscles had come away from the bone and his femur looked like it might come apart at any moment.

When Galen was done, Palleton picked Darien up like a father cradling a child who'd fallen asleep. He lowered Darien into a tank filled with thick, nanite-enriched fluid.

Darien's body sank into it slowly. Palleton pushed him down. Even in his unconscious state, Darien instinctively bucked and thrashed as the fluid entered his lungs. Grimacing, Palleton bore down, pushing Darien deeper with both hands until he stopped struggling.

"Can I help?" Drea asked.

Palleton gave her a sardonic look. "Maybe if you sat on his chest."

She could just see it. Tiny, bird-like human perched atop the bigger *donai*, hoping he didn't wake suddenly and tear her to bits.

Drea demurred with a smirk and circled the tank. The reconstruction of Darien's leg was already visible even to her untrained eye.

Galen was waving his hands in the air like a conductor leading an orchestra, manipulating the haptic interfaces floating around him.

"Where is my lady?" Palleton asked.

"I didn't send for her," Galen said.

"His mate should be here."

"We have no way of explaining to her what happened or that he will heal," Anasera said as she worked at her own station. "We would spare her the distress."

Palleton seemed to accept the answer without further comment.

The color of the liquid in the tank darkened as additional nanites poured into it. While severe, Darien's injuries would have healed on their own, but he'd have emerged weak. Nanites still required energy to work. It was one of the few weaknesses the *donai* had.

Drea shuddered. She'd seen *donai* on the battlefield. Some had incredible self-control, even as their bodies cannibalized themselves.

Others did not. Old ones like Palleton who'd grown to full size were harder to kill not just because their mass and experience gave them an advantage, but because they had more tissue to metabolize for healing.

"What happened?" Drea asked. "With the emperor I mean."

"I don't know. My lord wouldn't tell me. Said five words to me the entire trip back: 'Don't let me kill Galen.' "

Hands frozen mid-gesture, Galen looked up, but ignored the meaningful look.

"He waited three days to go cold?" Galen asked.

"No. I think he was in that state the entire time. Didn't do or say anything. Barely moved. I couldn't engage him. I tried."

"No one can stay cold for that long," Galen said with certainty as he collapsed the interfaces.

Palleton's eyebrows shot up.

"He's your pet project, physician. *You* would know."

CHAPTER THIRTY-FIVE

*T*he pain in Darien's chest was heavy despite the floating sensation. His lungs strained against liquid. He opened his eyes. The pearly luminescence of Galen's lab surrounded him.

A cloudy, distorted Bomani sat across from him, dozing in a chair. She startled awake. Her muffled voice echoed as she stood and rushed to the tank's side.

He braced himself against the sides of the tank, coming up and out of the fluid, pulling himself upright. Each breath brought forth a fresh flood as his lungs expelled their contents. Gulped air drove the liquid out of his throat and nose.

"There has got to be an easier way to do this," Bomani said as she pounded Darien's back.

The edges of his vision caught a blurring motion. He blinked and swiped the thick liquid out of his eyes and off his face, sending it flying with an impatient motion.

"It's a bit like being born, I imagine," Palleton said. He stood at the edge of the tank by Darien's feet. Given his assessing gaze, he was no doubt deciding whether or not to push him back down and drown him again. Darien must've passed muster because Palleton offered him a helping hand.

A warm blanket landed around his shoulders, courtesy of Bomani. Another coughing fit took him.

"You imagine?" she asked as she pounded Darien's back again.

"I don't actually remember being decanted," Palleton clarified. "Do humans remember being born?"

"No, humans do not."

Darien bent over and wheezed. Palleton's strategically placed pounding almost sent him to his knees, but it dislodged the last of the fluid and sent it sluicing across the floor. A flock of rovers floated from their stations to attend to the mess.

"Darien?" Bomani asked.

He blinked and offered her a weak smile. Instead of words, he produced gasps and wheezes. He barely turned away in time to avoid drenching her in sputum.

Darien hated this part. Hated it with a passion. Hated not having control over his own body.

"I'm fine, Commander, thank you," he said in a voice a little weaker than normal. He coughed into his fist. "Status report. Please."

"We are sixteen transit points from Gamma Iramana. There have been no further unauthorized transmissions. No imperial contacts. No courier drones received or dispatched. No anomalous readings of any kind, my lord."

He nodded.

She reached for the soaked tendrils on his forehead. He blocked her hand and shook his head. He was about to ask her why she was tending to him instead of manning her station on the bridge, when Galen entered.

Darien pulled the blanket tighter around himself, and stood, as if he hadn't been breathing liquid just moments ago, as if he wasn't dripping wet.

"Please excuse us," Darien said to Bomani and Palleton.

There was no weakness in his voice this time. Palleton grabbed Bomani's bicep, encouraging, then insisting on her obedience.

"Are you going to let me work while you threaten me, or should I just report to the brig?" Galen asked, voice flat despite the staccato beat of his heart, the betraying aroma of fear. "Or do you intend to kill me? If so, I'd like to say farewell to my daughter."

"Your life doesn't belong to me, remember?"

"You threatened my life readily enough when I suggested we save a stranger from the tender mercies of the Imperium."

The retort should have had an effect on him. Instead, there was only calm, the kind brought on by clarity of purpose, remnants of having gone cold. The inner conflict that had been plaguing him was gone. Darien knew what he had to do, the path he had to take, and what it was going to cost him.

Galen cleared his throat. "The brig then?"

"Not just yet."

"Very well."

Galen crossed to a console and dispatched a second flight of rovers. They floated toward Darien. He dropped the blanket.

The rovers spiraled around him, their beams scraping the remaining fluid off his body.

Galen handed him a robe. Darien shrugged into it, pulling its silken embrace over raw nerves and skin.

"How do you feel?" Galen asked.

"Better."

"How does your leg feel?"

Darien flexed the muscles in his thighs and calves, rocked up and down on his toes. "Fine. It all seems to be working."

"Do you remember what happened?"

Do I remember wanting to kill everyone and destroy everything in my path?

Do I remember not caring if I did?

Do I remember having to be beaten to a bloody pulp by my men until the feeling went away?

"I remember," Darien said.

"All of it?"

"Perfectly."

"I'm sorry," Galen said.

"I'm not."

Galen cleared his throat. "Anasera will be very interested."

"She will not know of it." He didn't want to be the recipient of Anasera's professional or personal curiosities.

"Yes, my lord."

It actually sounded like Galen meant it. Perhaps, this time, he did.

"When were you going to tell me?" Darien asked.

"Tell you what, my lord?"

"That you can create *donai*—fertile, full-blooded *donai*."

"Is that what you really want to know?" Galen asked. "Not why you aren't one?"

HOUSE DOBROMIL'S RECONNAISSANCE DRONE—LABELED C56—looked like a small, grayish asteroid that had been captured by the star known as EDC9.

It was one of several nearly identical drones with mass signatures mimicking the composition of a carbonaceous asteroid. As the most common type of asteroid, C56 would be of no interest to anyone or anything. It would take a very close look to determine that C56 and its cohorts were interstellar wanderers with orbits that allowed the sensors in their bellies to closely monitor EDC9's transit-points.

C56 had been in-system for the better part of a decade, sending regular reports via messengers disguised as chunks of rock. Every year or so, a collision with another asteroid would allow C56 to receive new instructions as the nanites spreading out from the impact crater bore into its shell. It made for secure, if slow, communications.

Besides its cohorts, C56 knew that similarly disguised spies from other Houses kept them company. It wasn't sure how many, just that it was statistically probable based on how many suspiciously small "asteroids" collided with bigger ones at somewhat regular intervals. Per its programming, C56 would compile the data and send it off with its surveillance whenever a ship entered or exited the system. Someone on Serigala probably had a best guess, perhaps even a solid idea.

Most Houses had an interest in transit-point traffic within the

Imperium. It was the only way to know when activity spiked, when to send in people to make direct observations. Few Houses, however, would have an interest in something as inconsequential as the traffic in a system so far from the Imperium.

Energy levels around the phase-point currently under C56's purview, spiked. Active sensors came online. The phase-point "shimmered." Energy continued to leak from it as it grew. Based on the rate of escaping energy, C56 estimated that it would more than triple in size. It kept the phase-point in its sights for another forty hours before its orbit took it too far out.

Seven messengers were dispatched, shot out from the bottom of a deep crater. It gave C56 away to anyone that might have been watching, but its protocols were clear. Anything that massive was valuable enough intelligence to risk C56's discovery. The messengers powered up. Four headed for a transit-point that would allow them to take four separate routes to Serigala. EDC9 itself would shield the remaining messengers as they headed for a transit-point well on the other side of the system. Their packages were intended for Serigalan ships known to be along those transit routes.

In another hundred-twenty-four hours, C56 would be in position again to observe the expanding transit-point.

CHAPTER THIRTY-SIX

*F*eeling nostalgic for home, Darien ordered the chamber presence to create holographic torches. They cast an incandescent glow around the flag cabin. The chamber painted a distant mountain range and its night sky across the viewscreen and merged it with the ceiling above.

He quickly penned a message to his father. It was brief, factual, and offered no apology or excuse.

Sending the message by courier drone prevented him from elaborating on his claim's dubious nature, or his decision to perfect it, or how he'd staked their future on his success. He did not seek his father's advice or permission, nor his forgiveness. But he did owe him a warning and his biggest regret was that he couldn't deliver the message in person.

His father deserved more than the vague brevity of his written words.

The one question he did not hint at was Galen's. All his life he had heard rumors about the things that flowed from Galen's genius; things that some called miracles and others called abominations. The emperor had called him a half-truth, but Darien knew who he was: Darien *Dayasagar* of House Dobromil.

He bore his mother's name for a reason. His birth had earned Ilithyia Dayasagar the title of wife. His inherited *donai* traits had even been enough to earn her the title of queen, one which she had rejected.

At first, the Imperial Court had been abuzz with the meaning behind such a decision. Pair-bonded *donai* did not seek the opportunity to find additional *donai* wives to breed heirs of higher station. It was one of the reasons the Imperium considered mixed-breeding among the peerage to be such a threat. So they had waited, hoping for a change that would show them that a pair-bond had failed, that there was a way to free themselves to take on more than one mate.

Some in the Court, the few that knew Dobromil well, that had met Darien's mother, knew the truth of it: his father had fallen in love before the pair-bond of Darien's conception had bound him to her. He would have never cast an eye towards another before the bond, much less after.

Until the title of Lord Dobromil was thrust upon him, every imperial that spoke Darien's name would speak hers and be reminded that they stood before the son of a human.

Because his father had a purpose for him, Darien would forever straddle the boundary between two worlds. That purpose wasn't just to place him on the throne of Serigala. It was to reunite humans and *donai*, to free them from being locked into the station of their birth, to let them succeed, and fail, on their own deeds. This was why he was not a full-blooded *donai* born of human sacrifice.

Darien had no illusions. He knew the source of his newfound calm and clarity. The Cold still flowed in his veins. It always gave him a new way of seeing things. And it always faded too quickly. The emperor had chosen his words with care, hoping to provoke and enrage him. Had the Cold not seeped into him at the crucial moment his rage might have drawn his sword.

Kabrin had been conveniently unarmed. He'd baited the trap further with the Rhoan ship, then upped the stakes by threatening his status as heir, as if that was his heart's desire. To the emperor it made perfect sense. He could not imagine that anyone would crave something other than what he craved: power.

Now, as the Cold lingered, Darien saw his heart's desire with utmost clarity. And it was not a throne or the unending politics of the Court. It was Syteria at his side, growing old together in peace, surrounded by children safe from imperial threats.

The emperor did not understand Darien's heart at all. Darien's rage hadn't risen because the emperor had threatened his status as heir. It had risen because he'd threatened the people he loved, the people that were bound to him by loyalty and fealty, the masses who were his responsibility.

The dream of hearth and home, of a peaceful life, were not to be his. Not with his parents' blood flowing in his veins. His father had been born to the burden. His mother had chosen it, sacrificing her freedom to save her people.

Perhaps Syteria would be willing to do the same.

SYTERIA COULD BARELY CATCH her breath as she retreated before Aeda's advance. They were both panting, sweat-soaked hair plastered to dripping faces. Their ship fatigues were dry only because the fabric seemed to destroy any sweat that touched it. Pivoting on bare feet, Syteria raised her staff to block Aeda's strike. The vibrations hummed under her slippery hands but she heaved upward, forcing Aeda back.

It was a limited contest. No body shots, nothing that might leave bruises or require a trip to the infirmary, lest their secret be revealed. Aeda had proven not just a patient teacher, but a true friend, showing up just at the right time. She had shown Syteria safe, hidden routes to the sparring gym. She had called in favors of friends to distract the *donai* that might become curious, even hinted at confusing the *Edlyn's* internal sensors.

As soon as Aeda was clear, Syteria switched her stance so she faced her opponent at an angle. She pointed the staff down, allowing part of it to rest behind her back as she carefully watched Aeda's face.

"No," Aeda said, holding her staff at the ready. "Watch my shoulde—"

Aeda's eyes widened. She moved her staff to her right side, planting it by her foot, and lowered herself to one knee, eyes downcast.

"My lord," Aeda said.

Syteria whirled.

He had found them. Despite Syteria asking, Anasera had not warned her that he had returned.

Hands clasped behind his back, he stood in black ship fatigues with red piping, short sword on his left, sidearm on the right. Whether he'd been standing there a while or just entered, was impossible to tell. Unlike Kell, however, there was no rage in his eyes, just an arctic calm.

Syteria raised her chin defiantly. "I am responsible," she said in Kanthlos. It might even have been High Kanthlos, or part of it was. She wasn't sure if she'd used the right form of the pronoun. Nor did she care. She would place herself between Aeda and *him* if need be.

"My lady," he said. "If you'd accompany me."

There was a slight flare to his nostrils, followed by a deep breath, but no other signs of emotion, no hint of what she could expect. Even at his most stoic there had been some subtle hint at his displeasure. Today there was nothing.

She breathed a sigh of relief.

His gaze skimmed the length of the staff, pausing at her grip as though he was judging how well she held it.

"You'd better leave that here, or risk your secret," he said.

She gulped, grip tightening around the staff's balance-point.

"Aeda, take my lady's staff."

Aeda stood and closed the distance between them to stand at Syteria's side, but she did not take the staff. Syteria held onto it for a second more, finally surrendering it.

"Thank you, Aeda."

"Yes, my lady."

Syteria's boots were neatly arranged beside Aeda's by the entryway. She moved towards them. He barred her way with an effortless, fluid motion.

"Do you expect me to accompany you barefoot?"

The corners of his lips twitched. "Not at all." He picked up the boots and gestured for her to take a seat on one of the benches lining the wall.

She complied, lowering herself carefully as he knelt before her. The boots were simple enough to slip into, designed to optimally form themselves around the foot. Instead, he made a ritual of it, carefully placing each one on the deck, lining them up precisely.

He wrapped his hands around her right foot. His thumbs caressed the thin, sensitive skin atop her foot. His head was lowered so she couldn't see his face, just the ink of his hair, every shining strand in its proper place, held together by the simple clasp he favored, the one that had a tiny sword passing through the holes of the half-cylinder of silver metal.

The caress of his thumbs lingered, sending shivers up her leg and into the space between her thighs. The shivers turned into tiny jolts.

Syteria's heart raced. Cheeks ablaze, she sought out Aeda only to find her gone.

"My lord."

"Say my name," he said, as his touch intensified. He stroked the sore muscles on the bottom of her feet. They yielded to his touch. She curled her fingers around the bench rim, lest she bolt upright somehow.

"Please, stop," she whispered.

"Why?" His fingers worked harder now, tracing along her instep.

Her toes curled in response.

"Please…"

"Say my name." It was a command. It plucked at a string deep inside her, one that ran from her core to her chest. The string vibrated, harmonizing like it wanted to be plucked again.

He raised his head and looked in her eyes. The amber irises were threadbare slivers, revealing the burnished gold ones underneath.

He pressed harder, harsh fingers easing belligerent muscles.

She had measured victory in refusing his name. The victory turned hollow as his fingers moved up to her calf and moisture flooded her thighs.

The smile on his face told her that the ship fatigues were no barrier for the scent. He worked her left calf now, finding tender spots she hadn't known were there.

"You don't play fair," she said, squeezing her thighs together just a bit, hoping to find some relief for the ache between them. It was as if her heart had found a new home in that spot and was content to beat happily there.

He used his grip to pull her legs apart once more. Her breath hitched.

"Say my name."

The string vibrated again.

"Darien," she said.

His face lit with triumph. "Again," he demanded.

"What?"

"Say my name again."

It was a soft, gentle, almost-whisper, caressing her just as his fingers were. They moved lower, back to the top of her feet. Her refusal drove them upward again.

"Darien," she repeated.

"Still alive. See, it's not fatal after all."

No, not yet.

"Please. Stop." It came out in a breathy, needy voice that was the exact opposite of what she'd intended.

He titled his head, that triumphant smile still on his face. "Why? I see, and smell, the pleasure my touch gives you."

"I am not some pet, to be stroked, to be calmed, because doing so serves you."

His fingers stopped their work, but his grip remained firm.

"Why do you seem so intent of thinking of yourself as a pet, Syteria? It does not suit you. After all, a pet is a creature kept for the pleasure of her master, and I've taken no pleasure from you—not yet."

She pinned him with a glare. "Haven't you?"

"Taken? No."

She opened her mouth to object, but snapped it shut. She had gone to him. She had asked him to show her what he was. It was her tongue that had opened his lips.

"Someone so obstinate, so capable...You would make too dangerous a pet."

She glared at him and grabbed for her boot. His hand captured her wrist just as her fingertips came into contact with it. Her face was so close to his that his breath sent puffs of heat along her jawline. He drew in a long, savoring breath.

"Allow me, my lady," he murmured. There was no mockery in his eyes. She would have used the memory of it to harden herself against him, but it wasn't there. The tenderness in his eyes, denied her steel, offered her velvet and silk instead.

Meticulously, he slipped her right foot into its boot. He took his time, like someone ritualizing the simple act of pouring a cup of tea. Moments later, he cradled the other boot in his hand, bringing it closer.

"No one else calls you 'Darien.' "

He made a small sound, not quite a scoff, but something softer, gentler, as he repeated the ritual.

"In public, 'my lord' is still appropriate and expected."

"And if I forget?"

"I will remind you." A self-satisfied grin accompanied his answer.

She'd seen the darkness that could rest in the amber and gold of his eyes. Yielding hadn't made that unspoken darkness retreat, hadn't diminished its intensity, but it had changed.

She'd seen it before, when Kell had looked at Aeda. It was more potent and more restrained at the same time. No longer did *he* look like control cost him nothing.

"You didn't come here to help me dress," she said as he lowered her foot to the ground.

He pushed himself up and extended his hand. She stared at the offering and braced herself. When their fingers met that string in her chest thrummed once more, sending a spark coursing from her hand into his.

"I'd like to show you something," he said.

Her mouth went dry.

❀

C56 HAD BEEN on passive sensors for over a hundred-and-twenty hours. In all that time, the system had been quiet. As far as it knew, none of its cohorts had launched messengers. Nothing had impacted the asteroid's surface.

It turned its sensors towards the dilating transit-point. The bursts of energy coming through were erratic as the disk-like "surface" reached its limit. More than one transit-point had been collapsed, some permanently, by too much energy being dumped too quickly into them.

The surface was analogous to what happened when two soap bubbles touched. The size of the smaller soap bubble determined the stable surface-area of the disk. The size of the larger soap bubble determined the maximum. Expanding the disk beyond the maximum destabilized the connection between the bubbles, or rather, the area of space they represented, since such space didn't actually grow in size.

The excess energy would go elsewhere, leak out as it were, creating an unstable pocket of space, temporarily bringing a third "bubble" into contact to distort the resulting surface. Once the energy dump stopped, the third "bubble" popped, using the energy that it still retained to push the other two bubbles apart, sometimes breaking the connection, sometimes distorting it until the energy flows stabilized again.

Ships were very cautious when dilating a transit-point. Getting caught up in the instability meant destruction or a slow, lingering demise in null-space without a point of reference to navigate by, without the means to escape as the space around the ship shrunk.

The prow of a warship pierced the dilated transit-point as it pulsed dangerously. They had stretched it to the limit. In a few hours C56 would know to which House it belonged.

CHAPTER THIRTY-SEVEN

*D*arien led Syteria through unfamiliar passageways. Despite her previous wanderings this was a part of the *Edlyn* she had not seen.

Sweat beaded and ran down her spine, pooling at the small of her back where his hand exerted subtle control. She was so wrapped up in the power of his touch that she was certain, if she'd needed to find her way back she could not.

When he took his hand away, she longed for its return.

Doors parted to reveal a large chamber, the curving walls decorated with hundreds of weapons. Her boots echoed off the etched metal decking. A black and red banner hung from the domed ceiling, its silk filtering the light, casting red-tinged shadows.

Syteria rushed past Darien to the primitive weapons familiar to her eye: matchlocks with wicks; intricately decorated wheel-locks; lavish flint-locks paired for dueling.

The scent of leather and wood tickled her nose. There was a hint of copper and sulfur as well. She inhaled, long and deep, savoring the aromas of home, of her grandfather, of Kappa. As she walked along-side the carefully mounted relics, she ran her finger across them to make sure they were real.

They were. Hundreds of them.

Her steps quickened and came to a stop in front of a percussion revolver. Stepping back, she admired them all, her skin pebbling. The display revealed a parallel history complete with everything from breech-loaded to cartridge guns. She covered her gasp with both hands.

"Are they functional?" she asked, as she moved in close enough to touch the ported barrel of a long gun.

"What use would they be otherwise?"

Two more steps took her to a sidearm surrounded by matched ammunition. She picked up a fat cartridge with a rosette tip. Something like it had been one of her grandfather's most treasured possessions, although the gun used to shoot it had been lost when he'd been a young child. He'd never been able to scrounge up another like it, not even the parts to make one. Their war had been one of attrition. The Kappans hadn't started with bows and arrows. They'd been reduced to them.

"Sub-sonic ammunition?" she asked.

"Yes."

"And this?" she asked moving past several items that skipped decades, if not centuries, of development. "This is Galen's gun, isn't it?"

"One like it, yes. It is a popular choice among the crew."

"It's very familiar," she said. "Almost like a relic, but...it moved."

"It was optimizing itself for your grip by realigning its center of mass, to reduce recoil."

"For accuracy?"

"Yes. Why did you drop it?"

She ran hesitant fingers over the gun, but this time it retained its static form. It had looked so familiar, so unlike the other technology here, she'd thought it another affectation like their swords.

"The Rhoans coded our weapons to prevent misuse. I thought it was going to...to hurt me."

He had moved behind her, so close she could feel the heat radiating off him. She turned without backing away. The scent of plums lingered in a cloud around her as she faced the sigil embroidered on the right side of his chest.

"Syteria," he said, hooking a finger under her chin, driving her gaze upward to meet his. "We have nothing like that here. We trust our people more than our technology."

He held her chin a moment longer, then reluctantly let it go.

The truth dancing in his eyes, his smile, sent shivers over her. It was like he'd unmasked himself and was drawing her further into his world. He was offering her trust and purpose, fulfilling desires both revealed and hidden.

"Show me what you know," he said, clasping his hands behind his back

She turned to the tools around them. She searched for and found a Rhoan analogue—a rifle.

"This is familiar," she said placing her hand on the stock. She picked up the long cartridge next to it and turned it over, running her finger over the casing. It was white, like chalk, but not as brittle.

"Not the caseless ammunition though," she said. "The Rhoans never solved the overheating issue."

"No energy weapons?"

"I never saw any."

Farther along the walls, archaic pieces beckoned, among them, a war fan. She opened it carefully. Light caught the wolf's head embossed into the lacquered canvas. It shimmered with oily iridescence. It was unwieldy in her hands. Built for him, no doubt.

Her chest tightened. She traced her finger around the wolf's head. "What is this?"

"My House's sigil."

She closed her eyes, breathing for calm. It was coincidence. Nothing more. She must've seen the sigil before, somewhere on the ship. Her mind was simply processing information, taking familiar patterns and placing them in her dreams.

"Is *this* an ornament?" she asked, collapsing the fan.

"No more than you are."

She bit her lip, using the pain as an anchor.

"The *Edlyn* is headed to Gamma Iramana," he said. "It is there that

I must mingle with my peers, posture in service to my father's political dictates. And you will posture with me."

She turned to find him towering over her.

"Why?" she asked.

He quirked a smile.

"You said you wanted a purpose, that you wanted to belong, to be a part of the pack. You proved yourself worthy enough to stand among us when you saved Galen's life."

Her heart raced. It thundered in her chest so loudly that he must've heard it. His lips stretched into a smile that reached his eyes and transformed his face. It took her breath away.

"As members of House Dobromil," he continued, "we each have a role to play. Mine is to hide from the consequences of an ill-timed challenge to the emperor. Because of this, I will seek refuge in an isolated place and wait for the political turmoil to die down. I will seek favor as Darien Dayasagar, friend to Gamma Iramana's governor, but not as Dobromil's heir."

His face clouded on the last sentence, as if there was something distasteful with the words themselves.

"And you need me because I'm the ill-timed challenge to your emperor. The reason you seek refuge."

He gave her a fractional nod.

"How do you expect an outsider, who can barely speak your language, who knows so little of your world, your traditions, to be part of such a dangerous game?"

"You will learn." His fingers caressed the spines of the closed fan. They ventured farther, along her hand, to her wrist. It made a sumptuous warmth uncurl low in her body.

"We were created as weapons," he was saying. "I, by my father. You, by the Rhoans. Like the fan, a weapon can serve as ornament, but no mere ornament can serve as a weapon."

"Is that how you intend to use me? As a weapon?" she asked, raising a dubious eyebrow.

"It is one of the ways I intend to use you."

The hairs on the back of her neck and along her arms all stubbornly refused to lay back down. He caressed her arm, his touch not unlike a wind stoking a flame. She wanted him to stop. She couldn't bear the thought of him doing so. Her heart beat faster.

He smiled.

"I'm about to go into a different kind of battle. I offer you purpose —a place by my side—as ornament, as weapon, as companion."

He smiled mischievously at that last word as if doing so gave it special meaning.

"Do you accept?"

DREA'S BODY felt like it had turned to putty. It was the only way to describe it. She'd been enjoying Hemin's ministrations for almost an hour now. The crewman, whose primary job was maintenance of the *Edlyn's* gravitic drive, used skilled hands to coax her tight muscles to loosen. There was something utterly sinful about his skills, about accepting them, even though he insisted it was no different than allowing the hobbyist musicians aboard to perform their art.

As she lay on the table, eyes closed, face cradled by a cushioned ring, it was human touch that she valued—the infirmary might be able to accomplish the same effects for her body, but not for her soul.

Isolated by her rank, her position, she was the only person aboard the *Edlyn* who could not take refuge in the intimacies that even division heads enjoyed. There was always some counterpart who was not in their chain of command, whereas everyone was in Drea's.

Technically, Palleton was her counterpart, but while their banter often bordered on long-familiarity, while rumor-loving tongues wagged, speculating on the long history between them, Drea would never yield to a *donai*. Not the way he would need her to.

Hemin worked out the last kink in her neck and she sighed with repletion. He pulled the sheet covering her back down to her waist. Warm, floral-scented oil dripped onto her skin.

The chime requesting entry made its discordant sound just as Hemin's hands took to the important task of spreading the oil around.

"Lieutenant Exton is requesting entry," the chamber presence announced on the third chime.

"Tell her I'm off duty and I left her in command for a reason," Drea mumbled. Hemin's fingers were at her shoulders soothing them again although this time they resisted.

"Override requested. Privacy screen engaged," the chamber said and a life-size hologram of boots topped by trousers with the bridge crew's silver piping sprouted from the floor below her face.

Drea sighed. At least Lieutenant Exton wouldn't get a hologram of her half-naked body and Hemin's hands kneading her shoulders. She lifted her head just enough to get a glimpse at the rest of Exton's avatar. The young woman had proven herself an excellent XO and was not known to skirt responsibilities or fear making decisions. The pained look on her face said that she'd rather be anywhere else, doing anything else, than interrupting her captain's privacy.

"I'm sorry to interrupt, Commander," Exton's avatar said. "We've received high priority communiques and intelligence."

Drea pushed herself off the table, drawing the sheet around her. The unsecured bun Hemin had made of her hair, unraveled, sweeping down her shoulder blade to cover her back.

"What happened?" Drea asked as she thanked Hemin with a smile.

Hemin returned it in silence and bowed, sending loose pants and an even looser tunic swinging above bare feet. He stepped into his sandals as the chamber presence brought the lights up from half-dark to full-day. Hemin took to packing up his supplies.

"The encoding is for the captain or higher," Exton said. "Shall I take it to—"

"No," Drea said. "Chamber, allow entry."

Drea ducked into her dressing room and hurriedly put on her uniform, wishing she had the time to at least shower. The last thing she wanted was to deliver what was no doubt going to be bad news, while smelling like a rose garden.

She returned to the main chamber as she worked a braid into her hair and secured it off her collar.

Exton snapped to attention. Three communiques, each a thin grey cylinder were held tightly in her right hand. Drones. They were all from drones. And all coded for command staff which meant raw intelligence. Good news never traveled this way.

"Where is my lord?" Drea asked.

"In the armory, Commander."

As she stood in the armory, surrounded by weapons of war, both ancient and recent, Syteria looked every bit the woman Darien needed at his side.

"Companion?" she said, her enunciation of the Rhoan word, uncertain. "Like Kell and Aeda?"

The right corner of his lip turned upward.

"No. Nothing so simple, I'm afraid."

"Simple?" She took a deep breath. "If you know anything about the *eniseri*, about Rho, how could you think that what Kell and Aeda have is at all simple?"

He frowned, and took her hand, drawing her closer. She yielded. He swept the hair off her face. The tips of his fingers tingled as they came into contact with the almost dry sweat there. He brought them to his nose, drawing in a deep breath.

"What does your brother call his woman?" he asked.

She pulled her hand away and brought her fingers down to her throat and fanned her hand out against her breastbone.

"You do not mean her name," she said, her voice shaking.

He tore his gaze from her carotid. Her pheromones were on his skin. The moisture he'd drawn to her thighs still lingered in the air, whispering to him of promises unfulfilled, of duties neglected.

There is no child, he reminded himself. The instinct to pair-bond insisted that he take his mate to his bed, that he worship her for the precious gift she bore, that he bind them one to the other forever.

He cleared his throat. "How can your language not have any words for the pairings required to produce children?"

She stepped back, her hand still splayed at her sternum as she

371

struggled to breathe. Fear-scent cleared the wonderful aroma that had been floating around her.

He frowned. "Are you all ri—"

The doors behind him opened, and he whirled, his lips already set into a snarl, his hand going for his sword.

The blade clicked free from the collar as he faced Bomani and Palleton. Bomani in particular looked like prey while Palleton looked very much a rival.

Darien exhaled, driving Syteria's scent from his nose. He forced the blade back into its sheath but his visual augmentations remained active.

Palleton's gaze darted to Syteria.

A growl rumbled in Darien's throat for a second. Palleton's gaze dropped and he stepped between Darien and Bomani.

"My lord," Palleton said, "the Imperium has destroyed a human world. My lady's 'world.' "

THERE WAS a painful pressure behind Syteria's eyes, one that would result in a river of tears she could not shed. She swallowed them instead.

"My world?" she asked.

Palleton's eyes widened in surprise like he had not expected her to understand. Something that might have been regret flickered over his features. The *Edlyn's* captain, the one called Bomani stepped forward. She clutched three dark grey cylinders in her hand.

"Let us go to your flag cabin, my lord," Bomani said.

"This concerns her as well, does it not?" Darien said as he wrapped his arm around Syteria's shoulder.

She frowned up at him and realized she was trembling. The depths of her new-found soul were slowly turning to ice. If it hadn't been for his arm around her, his soothing scent, she would have been weeping, or worse, an *eniseri* husk who felt nothing.

Ghosts danced in her smearing vision: Aviel; his woman; their children. And with them, millions of faceless Kappans. The thought of being the last Kappan lay heavy on her shoulders. Even with Darien's arm around her, that weight grew, threatening to crush her.

"You said you didn't know where, or when, Rho-Kappa was," she said, her voice barely a whisper. "That you had no means of getting there."

He translated her words.

"With your permission, my lord," Bomani said.

Darien nodded.

Bomani slipped two of the cylinders into a pocket and uncapped the third one. Her hand filled with small metallic spheres. She tossed them into the space between them.

They landed on the etched metal decking, flowing into the hollows that made up House Dobromil's sigil. Syteria took a surprised step back as one bounced off the edge of her boot and settled into a carved hollow.

Staggered holograms sprouted from the spheres, some blazing upward to touch the banner above.

Open space. A planet. A ship materializing from nothing. Streams of data in their still-cryptic alphabet. Numbers without meaning. Star charts threaded with color-coded flight paths and icons flashing two sigils—one was like the wolf's head etched into the floor; the other, a creature resembling a dragon.

Syteria's heart raced. She let go of Darien and moved toward the central hologram, the one showing a star and the small planet orbiting it. The dragon-like icon was on an intercept trajectory.

"Forward to key event," Bomani said.

The holograms obeyed, skipping forward in time to show an enormous ship approaching a world mostly covered in dark, blue oceans. Clouds swirled in its sky. Four small moons circled the planet in close formation.

Syteria breathed a sigh of relief. This was not Rho-Kappa. She cast a questioning gaze at Darien.

"Watch, my lady," Bomani said, eyes hard.

The ship launched asteroids at the world. They cut through the atmosphere and landed with devastating impact, sending up a boiling wave of yellow, orange, and red, that formed a cloud of death and destruction.

"Next event," Bomani said, her voice toneless.

The holograms skipped time again. Another bombardment. Two asteroids this time, on the far side of the same continent.

"Next eve—"

"Enough," Darien said and the holograms collapsed.

The spheres returned to Bomani's outstretched hand. She held them in her open palm, her penetrating blue gaze aimed at Syteria.

"The Imperium just killed a million humans, because of you." Bomani enunciated her words, speaking in common Kanthlos.

A low growl emanated from Darien's chest. He spoke to Bomani in the rapid-fire cadence of the higher dialect, his tone thick with a rage that clung to the air like a fog.

Bomani inclined her head at a slight angle, in that gesture of deference that wasn't. She spoke again, at significant length in a monotone that betrayed that she was simply giving a report.

"Commander Bomani says that the Imperium announced that a human world, an outpost in the Outer Regions was responsible for the loss of its squadron at Thertore and has been dealt with accordingly."

"I don't understand," Syteria said with a calm she did not feel.

"The emperor has changed tactics," Darien said. "You are no longer an alien from an unknown world. You are from the world he just destroyed, a human outpost outside the Imperium that came across a relic from our past—a pre-Ryhman ship. These renegade, Houseless humans used the relic to destroy House Kabrin's ships and make an unauthorized landing on Thertore."

"Why?" Syteria asked in Kanthlos. "Why spin such lies? Why kill a million innocent people?"

"To save face," Palleton said.

Bomani scoffed.

"You have another theory, Commander?" Darien asked.

Bomani's answer was full of warning and framed with a tinge of pity.

Darien took a deep breath, considering. He and Palleton exchanged dark, meaningful glances.

"I agree," Palleton said.

"The commander's theory is that this is a feint," Darien said. "We may not know where Rho-Kappa is or how to get you there, but the Imperium does. Otherwise they would not have been able to bring you here."

"Your world is still a target, my lady," Bomani said. "And so is our House," she added as she met Darien's gaze. "You know him. You know he will not be satisfied until he's truly had his vengeance."

"Unfortunately, the commander is right," Darien said.

"Can you stop him?" Syteria asked.

Darien stood in silence. His face was closed off, as were his eyes. She understood it for what it was—a "no."

Syteria rushed past Bomani sprinting for the safety of her quarters, her thoughts outpacing her strides as she ricocheted down passageways.

She tried to shed the guilt that a million strangers did not matter to her as much as her own people. Apparently, she'd not shed her past as completely as she had thought.

Syteria still believed that Aviel was alive. Even if he wasn't, even if time had indeed separated them forever, there was still a world out there where his descendants might still draw breath. Where they still suffered at the hands of the Rhoans. And now, they were likely to face an imperial threat that would wipe them out.

All because she had survived.

She wished the grierugon had killed her. She wished Darien would have left her for dead. She wished she could trade herself to the emperor, offer herself in payment for whatever slight he perceived so egregious that a million lives were not enough.

Surely she was not worth this.

To anyone.

CHAPTER THIRTY-EIGHT

The helical pattern of Syteria's biological blueprint floated before Galen. It stretched from floor to ceiling, a rendering accurate in every last detail.

He'd tried to match her genetics with those of known human populations, hoping to find—or narrow down—her planet of origin. All to no avail.

Her genetics were peculiar as well. There was a great deal of variation hidden in her alleles, far more than he'd seen in anyone else's. Wherever she was from, her people had been isolated from the rest of humanity for a very long time. Potentially, if evolutionary pressures had been sufficient enough, they might have forged humans who were naturally compatible with the *donai*. And their nanites.

Galen moved to one of the sample vaults and pressed his palm to it. With sure fingers, he tapped in the codes for the required samples. They were presented to him on a tray, each one contained within its own protective field.

The Ryhmans who had designed the *donai* had never intended for them to breed with humans. They had gone to great lengths to prevent it. But they could only base their preventive measures on humans available to them. They would not have been able to take into account the variations of a group of "wild" humans isolated who-knows-where. And not just isolated, but ones who'd diverged as much as Syteria's biology suggested.

Control had been everything to the Ryhmans who had, no doubt, realized the danger of engineering weapons capable of breeding.

All that it would've taken for an enemy to make use of the Ryhman's own weapons against them, was to capture enough *donai* and breed their own super soldiers. So they'd made it almost impossible for the *donai* to procreate on their own. It had been easier and safer to create them in a test tube and gestate them in pods. More convenient too, as no *donai* needed to be taken out of combat for the process.

That technology—the ability to create life—had been lost when the *donai* revolted and destroyed the Ryhmans. Their rebellion had inaugurated a Dark Age, at least from the perspective of those like Galen, who'd been trying to regain that knowledge, that power.

Thousands of attempts to replicate the lost technology had failed, and each failure had come at the price of many lives—both human and *donai*.

Heat flowed off the protective fields as the samples thawed, a contrast to the sudden chill that had settled over Galen.

Once, long ago, he'd sworn he'd never again help the *donai* procreate. And he'd stayed true to his oath.

Ghostly whispers rose around him, turning into whimpers that chilled the air further, making the collar of his uniform uncomfortable again.

DARIEN HAD ISSUED orders to continue on to Gamma Iramana. Nothing about the destruction of the human outpost changed his father's orders.

House Dobromil was not in the habit of challenging the Imperium for its military actions in the Outer Regions—not yet, anyway. The face-saving gesture worried him far less than the possibility that the emperor knew where Rho-Kappa was. Bomani was correct in that the emperor was going to target it, even though she didn't understand the reason why. For Bomani it was simply about revenge.

As Palleton had pointed out, recreating the wormhole technology that had been lost on Thertore was the greater threat.

His bluff—his pride—had cost a million people their lives and was going to end the lives of everyone on Rho-Kappa. It was just a matter of time before the emperor's scientists figured out what had gone wrong. They might have brought Syteria's ship here by mistake, but they were not going to give up just because they had lost Thertore. Abandoning the idea of wormhole travel might never have occurred to the emperor—it was too valuable strategically as a way to consolidate power—but Darien had given him reason to prioritize it.

He entered Syteria's quarters. They were much as he had left them, except for the fresh flowers he'd sent every day. Even the lights remained set low, a *donai* preference, but far too dark for a human's eyes.

The flowers were tradition, like so much of what was expected of someone undergoing pair-bond. Despite the mingling of the floral bouquets, it was Syteria's scent that permeated the chamber and everything in it.

"Surrender me to the emperor," she said, her broken voice ghosting out of the dark.

She was poised on a curved mating chaise. She'd nestled into the lower section of it, knees drawn up to her chin, arms wrapped around her legs. The pain radiating off her assaulted his senses, drove his vision to shift against his will. Traces of bitter light flowed across her body, firing in quick bursts of energy that faded to black.

"I will not," he said.

"Why?" It was almost a whimper.

"Because it wouldn't change anything. He will still seek out Rho, and Kappa, and destroy them."

"You don't know that," she said.

"I do know it." He was as certain of it as he was of his name. And it was his fault. He should've never let the emperor think she bore a *donai* child.

"No, you don't." She surged upward, her arms held tightly at her side. She had been crying. Her eyes were swollen, the jade in them bright with sorrow, even in the low light. "Let me try to make this right."

"I won't allow it," he said, the finality of it as clear as the verdict of a gavel.

She shivered and wrapped her arms around herself. "You once told me that were you to turn me over to your emperor, everyone and everything under your dominion would benefit. Why deny your people, your House, for me?"

"You are still evidence that the emperor lied about Thertore."

"Am I? Still? A million deaths have not made that irrelevant? Surely, whatever political advantage that might still hold, it is nothing compared to giving the emperor what he wants. He might spare my people if I—the enemy he can blame for his loss of face—were to surrender."

"Syteria, if you need someone to surrender to, surrender to me."

She backed away from him until she came into contact with the chaise. Her arms dropped to her sides. She placed her fingers on the back of the mating chaise and traced a line across its crest. There was an implied invitation with the gesture, one she could not have known. It was nerves, he was sure, because the hormones spiking through her body, scented the air with fear. They were mixing with the residue of desire still clinging to her from before.

The part of him that wanted to be the balm for her soul, sparing her from all pain, fled before the darkness rising in him. He no longer wanted to contain it, nor could he afford to. He needed to make her understand.

This was not how he'd imagined perfecting his claim. He'd meant to give her options, for should she bear his child, courage would no longer be a choice. No quarter would be given to her.

He'd always found her to be a woman of courage. Even her maddening demand, imperfect as it was in its motive, in its lack of understanding, was an act of self-sacrifice born of courage. And he would not waste it, or her.

379

He'd wanted their first night together to be filled with kindness, with tenderness, with all the proper rituals designed for her protection solidly in place. Instead, he moved with a speed that gave her no time to react. He closed in on her, wrapped his hand around the back of her neck and pulled her to him.

It knocked the breath out of her, but she looked up at him, eyes wide with the same stricken need that had hold of him. Her heart raced against his chest, beating like a drum in complement to his own.

Her body was taut against his. Lips half-parted, she did not struggle, but she also did not yield. There was some inner battle behind those eyes, an intriguing contest between fear and want.

Making a small sound low in his throat, he lowered his face to hers, scraping the roughness of his cheek against the dried tears on hers. Their residue sizzled into his skin.

Her breath hitched and her fingers tangled in his hair.

He took hold of her wrists and yanked them away. Her breathing had deepened, pulse quickening again, its thud drowning out everything around him. Cuspids ached as his mouth filled, the heat of the nanites searing as he forced them down his throat.

He spun her around, certain that if he did not, the sight of her pulsing carotid would drive him to mark her.

That chestnut mass that she'd twisted into a fist-sized bun had come loose. He swept it over her shoulder and tore through the shirt covering her back. The fabric fell away in ragged strips torn from shoulder to hip. He reached around the front and pulled her arms away from her heaving chest. The remaining cloth fell away.

"Don't move," he whispered, low and frayed. "Don't run."

The muscles in her back did a sinuous dance under her silken skin. Despite the force with which he'd torn her garment, he'd not broken her skin. Three welts were rising, their color darkening the paleness of her. He licked the welt at her shoulder. She didn't even flinch.

The welt did not turn red. He sighed in relief. But it was not enough of a test. Not one to satisfy him. He needed to be sure before he took it further.

Wrapping one arm around her waist, he lowered himself to one knee. He took her boot in one hand, lifting her foot so he could yank it off. It landed behind them with the accompanying thud of a breaking vase.

The sound startled her, but she set her bare foot down and lifted the other without prompting. The sound from his throat was half groan, half laugh as he rested his forehead at the small of her back, drinking in the scent from between her thighs. He tore at the other boot.

He traced a cutting line up the sides of her well-toned legs, feeling her muscles quiver as he rose. The fabric covering her legs fell away. He rested his hands on her bare hips, bringing them back against the hard length of him.

She pushed into his body. Before she could complete the turn, he drove her back onto the chaise. She landed with a thud, her arms crossed to cover herself.

"Don't hide from me," he said in High Kanthlos. He'd made it a command, not a request. The space between her thighs betrayed the moisture there, but she did not obey.

He stripped, freeing himself from his clothing as violently as he'd freed her.

Her ebony pupils were as wide as saucers. The scent of her was filled with invitation. She scooted back against the chaise's raised curve, spine bowing, pushing her shielded chest upward, denying him the view he wanted.

He was a blur, pinning both her wrists above her. As he stretched her out on the chaise's raised hump, he straddled her hips. She looked every bit the delightful feast he'd always imagined. Long, shapely legs with more than a hint of muscle. Flaring hips that begged to be held. A slight swell to her belly. A tapering waist. Her breasts were round and ample with dark nipples that matched her lips.

She was perfect. Beyond perfect. And she was his. She just didn't know it yet.

Writhing under him, she stretched her neck invitingly, arching her back, offering him more, offering him everything.

He let up, testing them both. Himself for control; her with desire.

She arched her back, turning the offering first into a demand, then a plea.

He denied her.

She pressed her thighs together. He placed his knee between them and she ground herself into him, bathing his skin with moisture. It made every nerve in his body throb, narrowing the universe down to the need to slip inside her.

~

SYTERIA CLOSED HER EYES, basking in the strong masculine scent of him. Her whole body thrummed like the string in her chest.

Nothing seemed to hold her down, not even the rough hands around her wrists.

Darien was nuzzling her neck again as she rubbed herself against him, trying to soothe the throbbing ache, the mindless need clenching at the emptiness he refused to fill.

His teeth replaced his tongue, scraping against her neck in warning. It made her chest heave, her breath catch in anticipation. The tips of his teeth as they tested her skin kept promising a bite, but he held back.

She moaned her disappointment when he nuzzled further down her neck, and then lower, to her breasts. Jolts of pleasure coursed maddeningly right through her core, plucking that string once again.

As his tongue moved to her belly he let her wrists go. Through a haze, she tangled her hands in his hair again. His insistent tongue alternately circled her belly button and his teeth scraped her sides, the warring signals turning all the muscles in her abdomen into a quivering mess.

He went lower, circling the little nub between her thighs. He seemed intent on licking her clean, an impossible task. She let go of his hair, drew herself up and grabbed his shoulders. His muscles flexed under her insistent fingers.

Raising himself to tower over her, he looked down with pleased eyes that glowed with a golden light all their own. Her hips moved in invitation, trying to find something hard to ease the persistent ache he'd stoked. A smirk crossed his face as his hands grabbed her hips and held her in place, keeping her from working herself against his thigh.

She stared at the hard, gleaming length of him, and the silver droplet poised on his organ's tip.

"Hands at the small of your back," he said. His voice was no longer velvet, no longer silk, just bare steel.

She fell back against the curve of the chaise, slipping her hands behind her. She did so without remorse, without regret, without shame. It's as if he knew that all her life, desire had been denied her, and that she could not overcome a lifetime of being told this was wrong on her own.

"You are mine," he said, slipping a finger into her opening. He made small circles with just the tip of his finger, again and again, each one wider, making her gush for him.

Her fingers curled, digging into the plushness of the chaise. When her hips moved, trying to take more, he pressed her down with his free hand. The circles slowed, lightened, until he was barely inside her.

"Say it."

"I am yours." It wasn't her speaking. It was someone else. Some creature driven mad with desire, someone who thought she could escape her fate. Someone who had been told countless times that what she felt, what she wanted, were treason.

"Not the emperor's, not the Rhoan's," he said.

The string between her core and her heart hummed in agreement. She closed her eyes. Her hands were fists now, struggling against the need to be taken. To be freed.

"I am yours."

He slid his length along the folds between her thighs.

"Mine alone," he said.

"Yours alone."

The muscles in her arms strained against the curve of the chaise. He pulled back.

"Forever," he demanded.

She would not cry. She would not whimper. She would not beg.

"Forever."

He slid inside her with excruciating slowness, despite the ready wetness. In and out, he worked her until she offered him a whimper. She bit down on her plea as tears slid from beneath closed lids. She thought he would tease her forever, never fill her, never push her over the precipice.

He slammed into her.

She gasped at the sudden pain as he broke through. The splitting apart, the invasion of it was as brutal and absolute as her yearning to be stretched and filled.

He cursed in Kanthlos, damning some deity, before becoming utterly still.

Her hands were on his shoulders, using him to pull herself up, nails anchored firmly into his back lest he dare pull away. She wrapped her legs around his hips, moving with a rhythm that said that she needed all of it—the brutality, the savagery, the excruciating pleasure. She needed them all to re-awaken the deepest, most feminine parts of her, to vanquish the last vestiges of the *eniseri* within, to free her from the Rhoan dragon and its lies.

The copper-iron tang of blood scented the air. The first blow had been struck. And if the Rhoan dragon bled, it could be killed. And if it could be killed, she wanted to bathe in its blood.

"Darien."

It was a tiny, helpless noise as she shuddered beneath him. The hot tears burning beneath her eyelids were nothing compared to the burning, scorching blood between her thighs, or the need for him to continue.

"Syteria," he whispered, his body tensed like a coil.

Every chiseled muscle was like stone. Only the pulse at his throat betrayed the man and the power he restrained.

Shadows flickered in those golden eyes. Flickered, rose and came to life, reined in by that unreadable stillness.

"Make me yours," she demanded as her nails raked down his back.

That predator—the one taking his ease in shadowed repose—finally stirred and gave breath and savage motion to the man inside her.

She bit into his shoulder, riding the tide of pain-become-pleasure, trembling as he filled her again and again, finally pulsing his own plea-sure deep within. A cresting tidal wave caught her, sent her to spiraling new heights from which she never wanted to descend.

Descent came anyway, transforming her into some primal being that melted into a sated, careless puddle and faded into blissful oblivion.

CHAPTER THIRTY-NINE

*F*ive chimes, the whisper of them almost too faint to hear, singed the edges of Syteria's consciousness as she drifted in and out of sleep. He had moved them. The memory of it was like a dream. They'd coupled again and again, each time, with the same demand: *You are mine.*

Even now, the memory of it pulsed inside her like a living being with its own mind, its own intent.

She had needed to be just one thing. And it was not a woman for whom a madman had killed a million people in order to give credibility to his lies; nor a child who'd been torn from her people and turned into their enemy; nor a sister who could not save her brother and his family.

She had needed to be his.

Her head rested on a silken pillow. A matching sheet covered her body. Every muscle throbbed with the same type of ache that followed an intense sparring session.

Feeling well-used, she sat up carefully, drawing the sheet up with her. Her breasts still ached from Darien's attentions. As she slid off the bed, the soreness between her thighs throbbed. The sheets were stained with blood, and by the feel of it, so was she.

She dangled her feet off the bed and slid off carefully. The quivering muscles in her thighs gave a small protest, but held as she flexed her toes into the plush rug. She dragged the sheet behind her as she moved from the bedroom to the main chamber. The area where the balcony usually stood had been transformed: an impressive fire roared within a wall. Slate tiles framed the fire, each one a carved relief of predators hunting prey.

A glowing red split the flame-engulfed logs and heat radiated outward, casting light onto the sprawling animal hides. A tea set waited, nestled among them.

He'd piled the remnants of their clothing atop the chaise.

She hesitated.

It had been the one piece of furniture whose utility she'd not been able to figure out until he'd stretched her atop it and made its intended use obvious. She rummaged through the shredded clothing, looking for the clasp that she'd used to hold her hair up. It wasn't there. She looked around. It had landed well away from the "mating" chaise.

Anasera should've warned her.

She'd seen few displays of affection among the crew. Given that her first exposure to their practices had resulted in trying to stop the man that had been "playing" with his "companion," perhaps her lack of exposure had been by design. It hadn't been until the festivities on Tir'Hala-Revir that she'd seen anything of their "courtship" (she switched to Kappan for the right word) practices.

There was a story that her grandfather used to tell her when she was little. It was one of her most treasured memories, and she had thought it just a story, because it had seemed as implausible as his tales about monsters and flying ships.

He had been a young man, wearing the pair of curved knives he'd earned by proving his prowess in battle. They announced his status as an adult. Kappan custom dictated that he never surrender the knives, never be without them, except for the brief time of courtship where he could give one of them only to the woman he was courting. Unlike his peers, he'd held onto both knives for years deemed far too many.

Until one day he passed through a village market and saw a woman wearing an empty knife-sheath on her thigh. She still wore the crown of flowers that had been placed on her head at the ceremony where her childhood braids had been undone. A woman come of age, she'd donned the empty sheath for the first time.

Once a man placed a blade in the sheath she could reject it outright, or wear it for the rest of the day, denying all others. She could then send it back privately or leave it at home, but if she wore it for more than three days, she signaled her acceptance of the marriage proposal. Whenever she appeared in public with an empty sheath, she invited another suitor to show his interest.

Instead of passing through the village as Syteria's grandfather had intended, he stayed. For four days, he'd watched suitors woo the young woman who'd caught his eye. Four candidates had placed their blades on her thigh, yet she appeared again on the fifth day, with an empty sheath.

It had been a risk for him, a stranger from outside her tribe, to boldly block her path. Cheeks flushed, she had looked up at him.

He'd taken advantage of her surprise, and placed his blade in her sheath without introducing himself, without asking for her permission. Doing so could earn him an outright rejection, one where she took the blade and threw it on the ground, humiliating him. He would never be allowed to approach again. He placed the blade, not knowing if she'd sent the others back or if they decorated her tent waiting on a decision. Or if she invited a contest for her hand, one that ended in first blood.

Syteria's brothers had moaned and groaned as they'd listened to the beginning of the story, demanding that Grandfather get to the good part, the one where he'd defeated another man to win his bride's hand. Syteria had always suspected some embellishment on Grandfather's part, for the sake of Aviel and the other boys, when the fight didn't end in first blood as tradition demanded.

The other suitor had not stopped when Grandfather had drawn first blood. He'd attacked Grandfather from behind, aiming for his back. Only Grandmother's scream had warned him and he'd turned just in time. The fight had become one to the death, one in which her grandfather had prevailed, but at great cost. He'd had to flee, kidnapping his bride on the way out.

In another version of the story—the one he told to her alone—there had been no kidnapping, just the customary festivities and a feast. In that version, no one had died.

How much of what he'd told her had been true, and how much had been story, she could not be sure. Syteria could not remember a time when the Rhoans had not been a threat, where anything like her grandfather's story had played out for her to witness. The curved blades had been real enough though, although by her time, the men rarely wore them in pairs. Necessity had forced them to place the blades into inexperienced hands that hadn't earned them. Most had been lost to defeat and time and wear.

Syteria had been too young to understand the symbolism of the bride's sheath or the groom's blade when the Rhoans had taken her. It hadn't been until she'd seen Matrons castrate Kappan men and boys before they killed them that she'd understood. Or she'd thought she had.

Since intimacies of any kind were forbidden to them, nothing had prepared her for that peak she'd reached with Darien, despite the painful climb to get there. She had not expected to rise to such peaks again and again, at his will, as if her body was some musical instrument designed precisely for him. He'd drawn out sounds she'd never made before. He'd made her pant and claw at his flesh, made her bite him and call out his name.

Syteria had never been considered an ideal *eniseri*. She'd escaped only to be recaptured. She'd been re-indoctrinated more than any other *eniseri* she had known of. There had been others, more defiant ones, but they had died—either at their own hands or by execution.

What would a proper *eniseri*, plunged into the *donai's* world, have done? She would've attacked Galen and ended up in a cage, or dead. The Rhoan whispers that had first haunted her had made no appearance last night. Not once. Not when Darien had torn her clothes off. Not when he'd raised welts down her back. Not when he'd pinned her down or taken her.

She picked up the clasp and finger-combed her hair, finishing it off with a twist and pinning it high atop her head. The fall of water and a jasmine scent drifted on hot, moist air from the bathing chamber beyond.

"In here." Darien's voice drifted from the adjoining chamber.

That invisible string by her heart seemed to tug her towards him. Dragging the sheet with her, she moved under the arch separating the two chambers.

He sat in the middle of a ridiculously oversized tub. Circular and deep, it was centered between four columns that looked like stone but gave off a light of their own. Towels and sponges, delicate bottles of oils and bowls of coarse salt waited. He was sitting on the far side, his arms stretched out and draped over the ledge, waiting.

"Join me," he said, plucking the string once again.

SHE WAS WEARING the same goddess-at-war expression she'd enticed him with before. The delicate skin around her thick, fluttering lashes tightened. The pulse point flared, making Darien's mouth water.

His vision shifted to reveal the air currents streaming around her, chilling her through her silk cocoon and raising pebbles on her skin. The blood coursing through her veins flowed like a sinuous stream of light. Darien blinked away the augmented vision, reining it in along with his other *donai* impulses.

A tightening cascade of tension flowed along every muscle in her body.

"The cleansing and drying fields are—"

"That's not how this works, Syteria. You will join me."

Her eyes widened, lips parting with a gasp. Jewel-bright eyes held his gaze as she dropped the sheet.

As the fabric pooled at her feet the scent of her hymen's blood and the mixed aromas of their coupling made his cuspids ache. His care, his restraint had left no bruises. Relief flowed out of him with a small exhale.

She reached up to undo her hair.

"Leave it up."

Her gaze never left his. The mass of curls atop her head unfurled, spilling down over her shoulders. She shook her head in a calculated gesture, one designed to reposition those tresses over her breasts, and dropped the clip. Its impact echoed off the variegated stone, punctuating her defiance lest he disregard it.

She entered the water, neither hesitating nor rushing.

He eased back. He had already won. If she needed such petty defiances, he would allow them.

Her hands skimmed the water's surface, playing with the swirls of light that gathered around her. By the time she stopped in the middle of the pool, a shimmering army of healing nanites had spread over her skin.

"Come here." Desire roughened his voice.

A neatly groomed brow rose in challenge. She took one step, then another, rationing her compliance, as if she knew his preferences...

"Closer, Syteria."

...knew he preferred being the aggressor.

"Turn around," he said.

She did not move.

He suppressed a groan. Not yet. She needed time to heal. Just a little more time. This was part of having a human concubine. He hadn't thought it would make a difference. He'd been so wrong, underestimating the power of pair-bond. Its tug before—the one driven by Galen's manipulations—had been nothing compared to what it had become in the hours since he'd taken her.

A calming breath allowed him to add, "Please."

She turned, her hair floating outward, wheeling around her.

He rose and gathered the protective veil of hair into his hands. She'd deployed it as a shield, but he had no intention of letting her use it that way.

With his free hand, he released the clasp holding his queue at the base of his neck.

Her breath hitched as he pulled her hair over her shoulder and secured it, leaving only a few shorter strands free.

"Compromise," he whispered in her ear. "Don't get used to it."

She shifted her weight away from him, but he wrapped his arms around her and dipped his head to breathe in her scent. He held her in place, arms resting on her abdomen, gentle but uncompromising as he pulled them both down to the underwater ledge he'd been using as a seat. He pulled her closer, pressing his growing erection into the curve of her back.

She pushed back into him then stopped, as if she hadn't intended to.

"Will it always be like this?" she asked, her voice like that of a child who had made a wonderful discovery whose power she now feared and craved.

"Do you mean the blood?"

He had hesitated in that moment, cursed the mindless perfection of Galen's work, but she had anchored herself to him, and insisted he continue.

The muted cry as he'd torn through her hymen had been pure revelation. Even in pain, she was glorious, sating his shadows without luring them to the surface. As she'd braced against the pain, she'd bitten into his shoulder, marking him.

The gesture and the blood had roused and thrilled the shadows, bringing them to power. It had been a test of his ability to rein himself in even as he chose the path into that dark domain he'd avoided for so long. Even as he'd taken his pleasure, filled her with his seed, he'd maintained control, terrified and tempted.

"Yes," she said. "The blood. And the pain."

He parted her thighs. Her muscles quivered as he held them open.

"No. No more blood. I didn't realize that Galen had restored your hymen. I'm sorry. He and I shall have words."

Her heart skipped a beat, then resumed a steadier rhythm. He ran his fingers along the long muscles of her thighs, pushing out to her knees, holding her open.

"Let the nanites do their work," he whispered into her neck.

She let her head fall back along the slope of his shoulder, easing herself further down into the water. He kept caressing, easing the tension he'd put there. More than once he stopped his hands from drifting upward to that bud of flesh that made her clench and thrust.

"Don't punish him," she whispered. Her hands came to rest atop his. She pushed his hands off her legs and twisted around.

"He didn't restore it," she said, looking up at him.

He frowned down at her, teetering between disbelief and shock.

"What?" she asked. "We were less than animals to them. One does not allow carnal desires to animals not meant to be bred. Did you think the Rhoans would allow us such 'companionship'? "

Had he? Her naïveté had been a puzzle to him but at first he'd had no intention of touching her, and then he'd been too caught up in walking the fine line between acting the pair-bonded mate and fighting urges he couldn't give into.

It had been the lack of Rhoan terminology. Their language had no words for courtship, wife or husband, marriage. His linguists had found no Rhoan references to human sex, not even as an act of procreation. One of his linguist had proposed the theory that such words, and the concepts they represented, had been deliberately eradicated. He'd rejected the theory. It was far more likely that the damage to the ship's data core was to blame. Or perhaps, because the database of a short-range transport was unlikely to contain such information.

Even the Rhoan concept of love had been stripped of any meaning that would serve his intent. It had been used in only one context, and that was as "love" for the Matriarchy. All good flowed from them and their beneficence. All that opposed them was evil.

He took a sponge from the basket on the pool's edge, dipped it in the water, then trailed it above Syteria's shoulder. Light danced as the water fell, leaving a silver trail in its wake. He washed away the welts he'd left on her back.

"I promise," he whispered in her ear, "I will give you nothing but pleasure from now on."

"Stop making promises you cannot keep," she said. It was neither reprimand nor blame and he'd almost rather had either than the detachment with which she'd spoken.

His hand returned to minister to the low notch of her shoulder blade. He dripped a liquid stream of nanites onto the fading welts.

"Were you not the one who dug her fingernails into my back as you begged me to make you mine?"

Her breathing deepened, muscles tensing again.

"I was," she said, her voice no longer detached. There was a hint of pride in it, one that made Darien smile as he traced the swell of hip, then swept up her back. He ran his palms along the curves of her neck, chasing the straining muscles. Her breathing eased and the rush of blood coursing through her veins dulled to a roar.

Her head eased forward with a sigh—a deep, satisfying sound. His thumbs circled in the notches of her shoulder blades. Her moan was a needy, delicious sound, just like she'd made last night. As she gave in to his caresses, she rested her head against his shoulder, eyes closed, her breathing deep and slow.

Time. She needed to heal. He reminded himself, once again, that being *donai* was not about being in control as much as it was about self-control. He trailed kisses, soft and delicate, up her neck, and back down, letting more of his saliva touch her. He needed more confirmation that his nanites weren't hurting her, that they wouldn't burn through her like acid, destroying what they perceived to be a threat.

Last night had been all the proof he should have needed, but there was a part of him that wanted more. He wanted to be in her blood so that no other *donai* could touch her. How had his father borne it, this incessant need, one that would have grown even more powerful with Darien's birth?

Dipping his head again, his lips met her pulse point, and time slowed. There was only she: her heart, beating; her blood, roaring.

She turned her face towards him.

Vulnerable, dazed irises glinted from behind half-open eyes. He licked the seam of her lips. Once, twice, nudging with a feather touch until she opened to allow him entrance. She tasted of warm, silken sunshine and cool, soothing breezes, of every sensation in his life that had ever brought him pleasure. His body responded, impatiently filling with need.

As his kiss deepened, she tensed, driving out all that hard-earned languor he'd stolen.

He captured her wrist, and held it, rising behind her as she stood.

"Don't run," he whispered along the slope of her neck. "You have nowhere to go. And I'm faster."

She glanced over the shoulder of her captive arm. "And stronger too. Don't forget that."

"I won't."

"Let me go," she said, jerking her captive arm.

"I can't."

There was finality in his words, for he was now, thanks to his recklessness before the emperor, truly bereft of choice. For his claim to stand, for the pair-bond he craved with every fiber of his being—for survival, for victory—there had to be a child.

"You accepted my claim, Syteria, did you not?"

Her breathing quickened. "Must you do this?"

"Make you mine? Yes."

Straining against his grip, she jerked forward. "I am not yours."

"Are you sure? You were mine until a moment ago. Blissfully mine."

He wrapped his free hand around her throat, tilting her head back towards him.

"Were you not mine?" he demanded. Her pulse pounded beneath his hand. His own heart responded in dangerous resonance. He eased off.

"Yes." The word was pure venom.

He let go of her and spun her around, his hands on her shoulders. His grip was tight enough to break capillaries. Bruises would form.

She looked away. He let go of one shoulder so he could jerk her chin up, force her to look at him. She grabbed his wrist with both hands.

"Why are you fighting me now, Syteria?"

Her breathing became strained, painful. The scent of her pain could drown him if he allowed it. Drown him and feed the baser side of his nature. It could make a feast of her, gorge itself on the potency of such fear.

"You asked me what my brother calls his woman," she said. "There is no Rhoan word for it, just a Kappan one."

"Teach it to me."

"My brother would call her *feleshee*."

"*Fe-le-shee*." The Kappan term was as different from anything Rhoan as it was from any of the languages spoken in the Imperium.

"Is that what I am, to you. Now. After last night?" There was a panic to her tone, unlike anything he'd heard from her before.

He cupped her cheek.

"You are my concubine," he said switching to Kanthlos.

"Con-cu-bine? This is one of the pairings you spoke of before."

"Yes."

"And the others?" She seemed very intent, like her life depended on his answers.

"The others are consort and wife."

"How are they different?" she asked, the line between her brows creasing.

"Let me mark you and trade the title of concubine for that of consort. Give me a *donai* child and become wife."

The panic returned. It oozed out of her pores like a poison.

"This is why you asked about my brother. Because he had children?"

"Yes."

Her whole body shook. She hid her face behind her hands.

He wanted to reach out, comfort her, to soothe the trusting, vulnerable side of her that was his and only his, but she backed out of his reach.

When she dropped her hands, her face was a mask, one hiding a great deal of pain, far more than the kind he'd taken as a toll last night. The instinct to banish the thing that caused her pain clawed at him again, made his hands turn into fists.

"Tell me," he commanded, his voice like the crystals of ice taking form in his veins. The Cold whispered in his ear like an old friend, calling him into its embrace. It had never beckoned to him so easily before, as if it was a cloak he could shrug into any time he wanted or needed it. The call of the Cold was supposed to be rare, not familiar.

"I cannot give you what you want," she said. Somehow the Cold had crept into her voice as well, like it had flowed from him into her, like their coupling had provided some conduit for a *donai* trait to make its way into a human.

He could not bear to hear it in her voice.

"For some of us," she said with cold detachment, "we never get our woman's blood. It's what they did to us, when they changed us. But for others, the changes didn't take, or at least, not as well. For us, the blood would come. At first, it was easy enough to hide. But somehow, as time passed, the Matrons always knew. If therapy didn't—"

"Torture," he corrected. "What they did to you was not therapy. It was torture."

Pain bloomed in her body. He didn't need his augmented vision to see it. The nanites in the water swarmed around her like a cloud. They flowed over her, burrowing into her pores. She didn't seem to notice. Her gaze was distant, a universe away, back on Rho.

If he ever had the opportunity, he would take Rho and everything it represented and obliterate it from the universe. The *Edlyn's* firepower could render Rho's surface to ash. He would lay the planet at her feet, make an offering of it. He could do it without regret or remorse. The Cold would make sure he felt neither.

"No," she said in that distant voice. "They did that too. Torture came next, when the therapy failed. Although sometimes...sometimes the lines did blur, one flowing into the other and back. I thought I would be one of the ones spared. The therapy didn't allow me to grow useless breasts."

"Useless?" It was more growl than speech, something that only the nuances of High Kanthlos could imbue with the right amount of shock, derision, and anger.

"But I wasn't spared," she said. "The blood came. A spot at first. Easy to hide. Then it became harder. If you could get enough rags, if you could burn them after, if there wasn't enough to overflow them and stain the sheets. We did our own laundry, you see, us drudges. Took turns with the task. The blood came and went for months. I thought I could trust them."

"The other *eniseri?*"

She nodded. Her silence thickened the air around them as though she were trying to erect a barrier. Despite the nanites' efforts she was still in pain. They kept swarming over her. She seemed unaware of them or their effects. He would have it so. She might think their efforts akin to therapy. Like the sleep field, like the nightmares, she might refuse them and he would not have her linger in such pain.

"One of the other *eniseri* must have wanted something—a lighter punishment for whatever she did, or perhaps, to gain the favor of a Matron. The older ones were that way. I don't know at what point, but after so many years, so much therapy, they not only ceased being Kappan, but their loyalties switched to Rho."

"Tell me what they did to you, Syteria." He made his voice gentle.

He moved closer and drew her into his arms. Lowering them into the water, he trapped her legs with his. She settled into him like he was a comfortable chair, turning slightly to the side, her hair flowing behind her and catching on her shoulder.

Despite the comfort that his touch seemed to bring her, he wanted her as submerged as possible. He wanted the healing nanites in every pore, in every cell, doing what they needed to alleviate this unnecessary pain.

"They called me forward at formation. A Matron paced behind me, repeating one of the inane chants they loved so much. There was a part of me that knew. And a part of me that hoped. A shock-stick to the small of my back killed the hope. I dropped to my knees and fell forward. My cheek hit the ground. I tried to push back up but they were on me. They bound me, dragged me to the surgery."

"Surgery?" Darien put a careful kiss atop her head. He caressed her shoulder, drawing her tighter into the shelter of his body.

"They strapped me to a table, gave me a paralytic so I could not move, and cut me open. The Rhoan surgeon..."

"Were you able to feel it all?" He had to know.

398

"Yes."

"How long did it take?" He would use the answer as a measure for justice.

"I'm not sure. It felt like hours, but I don't think it was. The sun was up the entire time, leaking through the windows. They took it out. It was a small thing, smaller than my fist. The surgeon held it up for the Matrons to see. She told them that the therapy had worked, just not well enough. That it was small and shriveled, and that my body could not take larger doses of therapy and still live, so it was fortunate that I had bled, that my body had betrayed me. I would be easier to control now, with fewer doses of...I don't remember what they called it."

She pushed away from him then, sliding away, her face still a mask.

"Don't you see, Darien," she said. "I cannot give you what you want. I cannot be 'concubine' or 'consort' or 'wife' for I cannot have children."

He pulled her onto his lap, drawing her around him, placing her hands on his shoulders. She yielded, like a rag doll, a lifeless thing. It made him shudder. He looked into her eyes and fear gelled in his heart, for if there was no will there, there was only one way to bring it back. She had been right. He needed to stop making promises he could not keep.

Darien swept an errant strand of hair from her face. It had dried and curled, as was its tendency, hanging in a delicate spiral over those thick lashes. A tear traced down her face, a delicate jewel, bright like a diamond. And he was grateful for it. It meant there was still emotion within her, that his nanites had not contaminated her and stripped her of emotion that mimicked the ability to go Cold. It had been just his imagination.

Holding her jade gaze, he laced his fingers at the small of her back. Flickers of will still lingered there. She was back in his arms, on his ship, in his dominion, not on that forsaken planet and its insane Matriarchy. He would do more than raze Rho's surface. He would see each Matriarch crucified, resurrected, and crucified again. He would make them suffer as they had made others suffer. He would be the hand of justice wielding the whip of vengeance. And he would enjoy every moment of it and never regret it for he would have wiped out an Evil from the universe.

"Syteria, do you really believe that Galen could not restore your ability to have children?"

~

SHE DID.

She had.

She shouldn't have.

After all she'd seen, she'd never once dared think...

Darien lifted her out of the water, carried her up the steps and set her down. She swayed on unsteady feet as he wrapped a soft, thick robe around her.

He slipped into ebony silk that flowed off his shoulders like a waterfall. It was decoration, nothing more. He did not need it to keep him warm. He did not need the modesty it imparted. Like he'd said on Tir'Hala-Revir, *Aboard ship, to appear human, we wear clothing.*

"How can we even have a child?" she asked. "I am not *donai*."

"Neither was my mother."

She made a soundless "oh." She'd have expected him to be treated more like the humans, yet every other *donai* on the ship had bowed to him. It was his hand that had brought down the cat for Aeda, his own voice that had so often referred to himself as "us," as *donai*.

"Why me?" she asked.

"Your will to live. You survived the *grierugon*. You survived Rho."

The admiration in his eyes was not new. She had seen it there before. She'd just not understood it.

"You are outside the barrier of class or command," he continued. "Without the complications of fealty, you are the only one for whom I can lower my mask, the companion who will see me for what I truly am. And more than that."

"More how?"

"At first it was not just about saving your life, but about denying

400

you to the emperor. You were, and still are, proof that he was developing a technology that would shift the balance of power in his favor."

"The wormholes. The way to Kappa?"

"Yes."

She closed her eyes. In that dark place she'd buried away, where guilt and hope battled, that place that only made itself known in unguarded moments or nightmares, she saw Aviel. The proud, unkempt savage her brother had become turned old and feeble, his flesh crinkling, his eyes closing for the last time. His body became an empty husk. His bones turned to dust, and with him, everything—

Darien's voice intruded. "Galen can show that you do not share genetics with any humans we've come into contact with. You are proof that the emperor lied, that he killed a million people to hide what he was doing. Some Houses will consider such an act a war crime."

Gentle hands bracketed her shoulders. She opened her eyes to a face full of concern. His beard had dried, but the tips of his shoulder-length hair were still damp. The mark she'd bit into his shoulder had faded to nothing. Her gaze drifted back up to his amber irises.

"In the armory you said you could not stop the emperor, could not save my people."

"In the armory, I could not pledge my father's word in front of Palleton, in front of any *donai,* because my father would only challenge the emperor if there was a reason to save Kappa."

"What kind of reason?"

He played with the coil of hair draped over her shoulder and flowing down her breast, pulling it out of the robe one thick bundle at a time. The inky thickness of his lashes against the pale contrast of his skin cast shadows on his cheek. It changed his face. No longer the careful, attentive lover, he looked up at her with the hardened look of a warrior going into battle.

"Pregnancy is a very rare thing among the *donai*," he said, his voice distant and neutral, like he was not speaking of his people. "The Ryhmans engineered us that way, so they could control our numbers. When we destroyed our creators, we also destroyed the knowledge and the genetic source material used to create us."

Irony played over his stoic features. He headed for the main chamber. She trailed after him.

The chamber radiated with warmth. The flames of the fire sent dancing shadows into the darkened room. He lowered himself onto the animal hides, resting his back against the chaise. He raised a knee so he could rest his elbow on it, casting his gaze into the flames.

She sank to her knees on the other side of the teapot and filled both cups.

"You can tell me the truth, you know," she said, prompting. "If I am the companion to whom you can truly show your face..."

She had watched him before, but never in profile, never so thoughtful. She sipped at her tea. It was very hot, warming her from the inside. The waves of heat came off the fire as if it were real. She almost wanted to test it. Between the fire and the tea the thick weight of the robe turned heavy. She loosened its grip.

"I don't think the *donai* meant to destroy the source material," he finally said. "They didn't know about it. We thought we'd been sourced from humans."

Interesting how he wavered between being one of them and not. Had it always been like this for him? Sometimes *donai*, sometimes human, never quite one or the other.

"Well, mostly from humans," he added. "After our 'victory' we found the remnants of Ryhman Arks, but were never able to replicate our 'creation.' "

"Why are *donai* pregnancies rare?" She had already suspected that *donai* females were rare. For a ship as large as the *Edlyn*, one under a lord's heir to have none "serve" as Nestra had put it, there had to be a reason.

"Unlike human women, *donai* undergo only three to five fertile cycles their entire lives."

"So you mate with humans."

He gave her a sideways glance.

"When the Imperium was still forming, a *donai* warlord hosted his rivals in an attempt to draw allies to his House's cause. He sent women to them for entertainment and for pleasure. Human women."

Syteria sipped at her tea. Her cup made a sound like the chime of a bell as she set it down on its saucer. His tea remained untouched.

She stretched her legs out from underneath her, freeing them from the robe. No longer cold, her skin felt like it was on fire.

"When one of the human women conceived, the warlord insisted that her child—the first child fathered by one of us on a human—belonged to him. She was after all, part of the chattels of his domain."

"Like me because I crashed on Thertore, because Thertore belonged to your emperor."

He nodded, his gaze intent on the flames.

"The *donai* father objected. So did the lord of his House. They would not allow anyone of their genome to be raised, or controlled by another House, even an ally. As far as they were concerned, the child, and by extension, the child's mother, belonged to them, and not just for the duration of the pregnancy. Someone compatible enough to conceive once, might conceive again. It was hope for our kind, hope that we were not destined for extinction."

"What happened?"

"We fought a war over one child, hastening the very extinction we sought to avoid."

"A war?" she asked. "Over *one* child?"

"You don't believe me?" he said turning. He shifted position, reaching for the tea and watched her over the brim of the cup.

Compared to the heat of the flames, his gaze was scorching. The robe still covered most of her breasts, but its touch had turned from warm and comforting to suffocating. She wanted it off of her.

"Why was the life of one child worth so many deaths?" she asked, squirming. The robe slipped off one shoulder, granting her some relief.

"Because we sought to breed fertility back into our genome. One fertile *donai* child's value was—is—priceless."

"Was the child fertile?"

"Yes." The word was so filled with power it was almost a hiss.

"But?"

"Over time, and at great cost, we learned the danger of human-*donai* pregnancies."

403

Syteria was cold again. The sensation started in the pit of her stomach, like a seed crystal. It became a fist. She shrugged into the robe.

"Tell me," she said.

He crawled over to her, his robe falling free, and settled beside her. "Give me your hand."

She slipped her hand into his waiting palm. He turned it over, running his thumb across the delicate skin of her inner wrist.

"Imagine this muscle here," he said tracing the meaty flesh connecting her wrist and thumb. "It is connected to tendons, to bone, covered by skin. Now imagine that the muscle is strong like a *donai's*. But the tendons, the bones, the skin, are not. They are human."

"It would tear the tendon, the bone. Burst the skin."

"Yes."

"But the nanites."

"A child inherits nanites only from the *donai* parent. They will repair only *donai* cells and sometimes even attack and destroy human ones.

"Oh," she said. "All human cells?"

He nodded, his thumb still caressing her palm as her hand rested in his own.

"Our nanites can be dangerous to humans," he said. "Even the ones we pass along to our children. If they don't go dormant, and we don't know why or how to make them go dormant, they will destroy the human cells—child's and mother's."

She frowned down at their hands, hers so pale and unmarred against his darker, rougher one. Hers seemed almost child-sized in comparison and she was not a small woman, not by Kappan standards, and not by Serigalan ones either. Most of the women she'd seen aboard the *Edlyn* were smaller.

"That's why you didn't kiss me. Why you demanded that I kiss you."

"Yes. If my nanites hurt you, you would stop, pull away and never touch me again."

"It's why you licked me last night. To make sure."

She pulled her hand out of his and looked up at his face.

"Pair-bonded *donai* can heal each other with their blood," he said shifting his weight to sit on the rug. "It can help maintain a successful pregnancy, bring a *donai* child to term. It is why we pair-bond. Because once we find a compatible mate, we monopolize her. We can't afford not to."

"But I am human."

"A compatible human. Like my mother." His face darkened like he was remembering something dark and painful.

"Tell me everything," she said gently.

"The emperor had her killed," he said, his voice suddenly small. "He could not afford for a fertile member of the peerage—my father— to remain bound to a human."

"I'm sorry." Her understanding of his loss was both visceral and defining. She'd lost both her parents early. Bits and pieces of their gruesome deaths flickered to life sometimes. They were pain-filled shadows of a life filled with struggle, suffering, and death.

"The emperor is going after Kappa for the same reason," Darien said. "And it is my doing."

She frowned. If the fault lay with anyone, it was with her. As much as it pained her, she said, "I don't understand."

His gaze locked with hers, the gold embers of his pupils swirling like the center of a storm gathering its power.

"I stood before my emperor and placed the honor of my House on the line by claiming a human woman as mine because she carried my child."

Syteria could not speak. She could barely breathe.

"A claim," he continued, "is the only mechanism that allows one *donai* to take a human from another. It is not a perfect solution. Some call it theft. But it protects the woman. It protects each House's genome, bringing it valuable heirs. It stabilizes the Imperium, because when a *donai* sovereign dies without issue, it is the Imperium that decides on an heir of its choosing. That is why the emperor had to honor my claim. Not recognizing it would be seen as a threat to the power held by the Houses.

"So you see, I had the perfect solution. A way to save you and have every House in the Imperium stand with me. But I miscalculated. I didn't realize that the emperor would see Kappa as a threat because it might be a source for a very rare commodity—compatible humans."

"You lied," she said, spitting the words at him. All his talk of honor, of virtue, had been based on a lie, one made worse because she could not fault him for it. He had saved her life. A life she wanted to live.

"Not just lied. Committed fraud and treason. Put my honor on the line, for once my *donai* find out that I falsely invoked the sanctity of a claim, they will no longer follow me, no matter who my father is."

She pushed to her feet. He did the same, towering over her like a golden-eyed titan. The darkness that played over his face was no longer cast by the flames in the hearth. They were from within, that dark side he'd warned her about.

"You are a 'bastard,'" she said, using the Kappan word.

His raised brow asked for clarification.

"A man without honor," she explained.

A sneer formed on his face as he looked down at her. "Everything I have done, I did for the honor of my House, for its survival. I could have sacrificed you, but didn't. I could have left you to die, but didn't. I could have surrendered you to the tender mercies of the Imperium, but didn't."

"You are no less a 'bastard' for it."

She turned to walk away, but he'd grabbed her, brought her to his chest. "And I am the 'bastard' to whom you surrendered, remember."

"Is that why you made me put my hands behind my back?"

"It was what you needed."

It was true. She had.

"When we first met you did it on your own," he said. "Do you remember?"

Her face heated at the memory.

"Why?" he asked.

"Because on Rho it is death for a man to touch a woman. And an *eniseri's* duty to carry out that sentence."

He laughed. It was a soft, restrained amusement.

"It would have been interesting for you to try," he said, his grip loosening. "The emperor's *donai* would have enjoyed it. Rumors would be flying throughout the Imperium that I had violated my father's edict and taken a woman by force. The emperor would be torn between publicly praising me for going against my father and condemning me for not being able to follow my own House's laws."

"Is that what you did last night? Followed your own House's laws?"

"Yes. I prevented you from throwing away your life, saved you from succumbing to your own baseless sentiment."

"It wasn't baseless. I wanted to—still want to—save my people. I thought you would understand. If they are alive out there, somewhere, I have to do the honorable thing. I have to save them."

"Then save them."

"How?"

"Give me a *donai* heir. My father will have reason to protect your people."

Her mind raced her heart, careening into an unknown wilderness, for how could she give him what he sought? She was just beginning to understand, but...

"And if the child is human? Will your father still protect my people then?"

He gave her a fragile smile as his hand cupped her chin. His gaze so piercing she could feel it inside her, not where it was aimed, but in that low, dark place where desire was anchored. He'd plucked it before and she could feel it strain within her in anticipation. It had always been there, she realized. It's why whenever he'd looked at her, she'd felt so conflicted. Her old *eniseri* self had gotten in the way until he'd vanquished everything within her that was Rhoan.

"You drew me in from the beginning," he said. "From when you were in Galen's lab, fighting even when he had rendered you unconscious. It was your scent and I didn't understand it then, but I understand it now. I thought it was what Galen had done to fool my *donai* into thinking you were already pregnant—"

"What do you mean? What did Galen do to me?"

407

His grip tightened. "He made you smell pregnant so they would believe my claim."

It all fell into place: the tearing pain in her abdomen; Anasera's concern; Galen's carefully chosen words. Even Kell's anger and Aeda's cautious choice of training. They had all known. Everyone had known. Everyone, except for her.

"You need not worry," he continued. "Humans don't pair-bond. Your reactions, your will are still your own. That is one thing I would never take from you."

Once more, the universe mocked her understanding of it. She had been living in a world made of the most delicate glass, one that had cracked so often it was held together by the barest threads of trust. As the world spun, it came apart, flinging a thousand delicate shards to the darkest reaches of the universe.

"I don't believe you," she said.

"Have you not been as obstinate and stubborn as ever? Did I not have to bend you to my will? Did you even once fall on your knees for me? Crawl for me?"

There was truth not only in his tone, but in his eyes. But it was too late. One could only take a shattered piece of glass and reassemble it so often before it became dust.

"When you saved Galen's life," he said, "I knew you to be more than mere infatuation. I knew that you would make a fit and worthy queen. I would not dilute that quality. It has far too much value to me."

Would not dilute it did not mean he couldn't. It shook her to her core. With desire. With rage. With guilt.

"And if I refuse? If I don't agree to help you continue fooling your *donai*? If I can't conceive?"

"Galen will say you miscarried. It was his plan all along. A pretend pregnancy, followed by a pretend miscarriage. For mixed pregnancies, miscarriages are far more common than successful ones. No one would think it unusual. You would, however, remain under House Dobromil's protection for the rest of your life. I had hoped, that once you learned the truth, you'd forgive me."

Tears pushed at the barrier of her eyes, threatening to spill and flow, to flood all the paths before her: give truth to his deception and then mourn a child that never was; betray him to his *donai* and see him cast out; give him up and never enjoy the all-encompassing power of his passion again; or bind him to her, risking her life and that of any child she might bear for the chance to perform one last duty for her people.

The sound of shattering glass that only she could hear was drowned out by the thrumming beat of duty, of...honor.

"A Kappan risks her life with every child she bears," she said. "The Rhoans might have torn that from me for a while, but it was always a part of my reality."

CHAPTER FORTY

*G*alen pushed his half-eaten lunch farther away to make room for a cylindrical container and the specimen within. It was one of the thousands they'd picked up on Tir'Hala-Revir. The *Edlyn* had detected unusual activity inside the stasis field, so it had flagged it for his review.

A few dozen red flags were fairly common, often errors in the stasis field's harmonics rather than activity within.

Commotion outside his lab made him look up. Syteria entered, wearing ship fatigues. She was trying to keep her face neutral, but she was failing.

Anasera came in right behind her, aiming an I-told-you-so look at him.

"Chamber, privacy." It was Syteria, speaking High Kanthlos without hesitation. Her cadence conveyed rage so well that, had she been *donai*, Galen would've been wondering who was about to die.

His hand strayed to his collar, giving it a tug. Her wrath was aimed at him. And he knew exactly why.

"Take it out," she said.

He didn't need to be told what "it" was. He thought about asking for specifics, just to be sure, but reconsidered. Darien would not have told her without good cause. It had to have been him, otherwise the *donai* would be involved and she wouldn't have called for privacy.

There was a part of him that was glad that their time together had yielded truth, and a part of him that was afraid. He balled up the fear that Syteria was about to fall into imperial hands and surrounded it with plans of what it would take to get her off the *Edlyn*. He knew how to avoid all the obstacles between here and the Outer Regions. He'd miss his wife and daughters, but maybe with Bomani's help...

"Yes, my lady," he answered, speaking to her in High Kanthlos for the first time.

Her eyes widened. The wrath was replaced with the revulsion he'd seen when he'd knelt to her and she'd fled.

You cannot have it both ways, child.

"This way, my lady," Anasera said. "It cannot be done here."

Syteria looked at her as if she was seeing her for the first time but nodded and followed Anasera into the adjoining compartment.

Galen followed.

Anasera had her climb on the bio-bed. Syteria drew up the shirt and lowered the trousers down to her hips. Task complete, she looked up at the ceiling, her hands clasped together above her waist.

Galen activated the sterile field and bio-monitors came to life, their quiet susurrations filling the uncomfortable silence around them.

"This is treason for both of us," Galen said in the common dialect. "For Anasera and me."

Syteria looked at Anasera first, concern flickering across her face. Then she met Galen's gaze. "Darien will not punish you."

Anasera summoned a rover and set it to hover above Syteria's abdomen. Its blue beam caressed her so she'd feel no pain.

"It's not Darien we're speaking of," Anasera said. "It's the emperor."

"Why would the emperor—"

"It is treason to lie to the emperor as our master did," Galen said. "We not only knew, but aided him."

"But you are slaves," Syteria argued. "You had no choice."

"It is still treason," Anasera whispered. "For any other order, it

411

would be as you say. We are slaves compelled to obey our master. But the Right to Claim, because of its impact on all the Houses, on the balance of power between them and the emperor, it is sacrosanct."

"Do you understand this word, 'sacrosanct'?" Galen asked.

The rover used one of its beams to cut through Syteria's abdomen and pulled out the implant. The size of a fingertip, it looked like a bundle of fat cells, except for the glow. The rover deposited it into a tray and streamed nanites into the cut, reforming the flesh so that when it was all done, no one would ever be able to determine it had ever been there.

"Sacrosanct means too important to be interfered with," Syteria said.

Galen raised an eyebrow in surprise.

"It also means that you are now part of his treason," he said gently.

"If that's your way of asking me if I will betray him, or us, be at ease. I will not."

"Syteria, do you understand what you're doing?" Anasera asked.

She seemed to struggle for an answer. It wasn't so much a struggle for words as it was for something deeper. Galen couldn't put his finger on it.

"How long before I am myself again?" Syteria asked.

"What do you mean, my lady?" Anasera said as she fine-tuned the rover's work.

"These urges, these emotions..."

Galen drifted closer. Tears were leaking from the corners of Syteria's eyes. She blinked and let them roll down her face rather than swipe them away. Perhaps one gesture was more of an acknowledgement of her inner conflicts than the other. He could guess at her inner turmoil. After what the Rhoans had done to her, she did not trust that her body's responses were her own, a reaction he should have considered. He'd had enough of the same types of experience that he should have.

He leaned in and looked down at her. She turned her head, refusing to meet his gaze.

"The implant did not give you—"

"Stop lying to me," she said, squeezing her eyes tighter.

Anasera sent the rover back to its cradle.

"The numbness should be gone in a few moments," she said. "Please lay still until it wears off."

Syteria nodded.

Anasera took hold of her hand. "I'm sorry."

"You should have told me," Syteria said, turning to face them.

"Had we told you, would you have understood?" Galen asked.

She shot him a scathing look. "We'll never know now, will we?"

Galen opened his mouth to speak, but then Syteria's demeanor changed. She drew herself up, and her anger was no longer aimed at them.

Anasera turned first and bowed.

At first glance Galen thought Dobromil stood before him, but it was Darien, looking like he had prepared for an inspection. His hair was pulled back and neat. He was wearing not ship fatigues, but his day uniform, armed with short sword and sidearm. He did not acknowledge either bow, and technically, they should have held them, but habits were hard to break.

"Galen," he said. "Have you ever known *donai* nanites to impart language?"

Galen blinked and took far too long to answer. "No my lord."

"What about lust?"

"No my lord."

"Infatuation?"

"No."

"Do humans undergo pair-bond?"

"No."

Darien's gaze had been on Syteria but he shifted it to Anasera. "Sister, your husband is *donai*. Your son as well. See to it that my lady learns the proper customs and what is expected of her."

"Yes my lord."

Darien turned on his heel and left them.

～

"JUST HOW MUCH HAS YOUR language improved, my lady?" Galen asked as Syteria swung her legs off the bio-bed.

Anasera put a steadying hand on Syteria's shoulder. She shook it off, drawing herself up to her full height.

"I don't know," she said. "Some."

Darien had slipped into Kanthlos, both High and common, and she'd understood him. She'd been too caught up in everything around her, as well as the sudden understanding that she was part of an even bigger game than she'd first imagined. It hardly seemed to matter now.

Galen cleared his throat. "I'd like to do a thorough scan of—"

"No. Unless I'm dying, I don't want any more of your kind of help, Galen. Even then, think twice."

He met her venom with a hard look. "I serve Lord Dobromil, our master—mine and his—but this is my domain."

"Then I shall stay out of it," she said and stepped off, towards the exit.

Anasera blocked her way. "Syteria, please. You're right. We should not have withheld the truth. But now we are trying to serve you with the truth. How will refusing to listen help you?"

Syteria looked into Anasera's dark eyes and saw nothing but concern. She nodded.

"There are," Anasera said, "expectations of address, signs of respect, courtesies that must be observed in public. The omission of any one of these would force his hand, touch his honor, and require him to act, publicly and swiftly. You haven't been amongst us very long, so it will be hard for you to understand, but you must trust me.

"These expectations, some of which you will find unpleasant, and their consequences are there as much for your protection, as for their honor."

"For example?" Syteria asked.

"All of us, myself included," Anasera said, "as well as Bomani, have spoken and acted freely in private. Some of us have gone beyond speaking freely to outright challenge, and survived." She cast an accusatory glance at her father.

Galen's face was a particularly virulent shade of pink. "I would not recommend it."

"He gave me his word that he would not hurt me," Syteria said.

"And has he broken it?" This from Anasera.

Sister, he had called her. A term of endearment, no doubt. But she'd heard the power in the word as he'd spoken it.

"We have an agreement," Syteria said. "I will give him the *donai* heir he wants. In exchange, House Dobromil will protect my people. Tell me, Sister, can I trust him to keep his word?"

"Syteria, why don't y—"

"What?" she asked. "Betray him? Ruin his reputation? What will the *donai* do to him if they found out he lied to them?"

"They would insist that his father cast him out. Some of the *donai* on this ship might join him in exile, but if too many do, it would be a threat to his father's power. Lord Dobromil's remaining *donai* might challenge his sovereignty. It would not end well."

So not just imperial entanglements, as Darien had implied. Dynastic difficulties as well. An endless tapestry of complications where one weak, unraveling thread could collapse everything.

She was not going to be that thread.

"You should have told me," Syteria said.

Galen said, "We couldn't be sure of your loyalty, of your feelings toward him. *He* could never have been sure of your...love."

The word hit her at the center of her being, for it reflected her own fears, and it wasn't all about the noble cause of saving her people, or even her family. Somewhere between shedding the past and embracing the present, some notion of romantic expectation had taken root, only to be thrown in doubt and crushed.

"Galen, he speaks to me of honor and duty, of fitness and worth, not of love."

"My lady, for a *donai*, there is no greater testament of love."

Syteria cast a questioning look in Anasera's direction.

"My father understands the *donai* better than any human."

"And yet you are the one that calls one husband and another son."

"Yes, but my husband is not Dobromil's heir. We have freedoms you and Darien will never have. And you *do* understand, human-*donai* pairings rarely yield viable offspring."

"He told me."

"Yet you're still willing to try? To risk it?"

"His nanites healed me."

Galen's eyes widened. He moved quietly towards a console.

"Galen," Syteria said, her tone full of threat, "if you scan me I will test my new status—now that I know of it—by ordering Palleton to break your hands."

He put his hands in his pockets and gave her a small nod.

"You risk yourself, my lady," Anasera said.

"*You* risked yourself, didn't you?"

"A *donai* child was not our goal, merely a human one."

"And the method? Is it not the same?"

A frustrated look came over Anasera, one she quelled very quickly. "The method is the same, yes. But Darien is very much an unknown. His mother was human yet he inherited almost all of his father's *donai* traits."

"And no human ones?" Syteria asked. There was a drop of hope in there, driven by that romantic sentimentality that had somehow taken root.

Anasera shook her head. It didn't have as much certainty as it should have. Syteria had struck a bargain, whether it was with a *donai* or a human, or something in between. She was certain Darien moved across that line as it suited him.

"Yet his mother survived," Syteria said.

Galen's pallor turned green for a moment. Then he turned very pale. His hand drifted to his collar but he caught himself and lowered it. He would not meet her gaze.

"Yes, she survived," Anasera said. "You need to know, that the more *donai* traits a child inherits, the longer the pregnancy. If they are viable to begin with, if their nanites go dormant at the right time, *donai* take longer to bring to term. Darien's mother was pregnant for a year and a half."

"And you? How long were you with child?"

"Ten months."

"And your son?"

"Most *donai* traits don't manifest until puberty. My son is yet too young. He has amber irises, but he still sees like a human. He is fast and strong and healthy, but we won't know for at least a few more years."

"Did your husband's nanites heal you?" Syteria asked.

Anasera shook her head. "They also did not hurt me."

"Darien's nanites healed me. He said it meant that I was compatible. That such a compatibility was very unique, very rare. Galen, when you had me in your lab, when you remade me, did you also make me compatible?"

"No."

It was spoken so that Syteria had no doubts that he was telling the truth. Relief and disappointment warred within her, for if it wasn't his doing, then the fate of Kappa truly rested on her shoulders. She was both the reason why her people were in danger, and the means to save them.

"My lady, this compatibility is beyond my power, although many believe otherwise. I swear it."

"So, there is a chance then. For me. For us. To have a child."

"Yes."

"A *donai* child?"

"That I do not know," he said.

There was so much pain in those words that she wanted to comfort him, to tell him it wasn't his fault. But she could not do it. If she gave in to this sentiment she might forgive him.

"Thank you," she said instead and headed out the door.

CHAPTER FORTY-ONE

he second time she "surrendered" to him, she lay back on the mating chaise, determined to make it about fulfilling her side of the bargain. The people she'd come to trust the most, Galen and Anasera had betrayed her. Even with the implant removed, she did not trust her emotions.

She'd been told, repeatedly now, that humans did not pair-bond. But what else could explain the cord that deep within her, twisted with such vicious pleasure. She'd thought of it as her femininity restored. She'd seen it as her freedom from the Rhoans. Now she thought of it as Galen's doing.

Until she was sure that she'd not traded Rhoan mistresses for a *donai* master, she would fight and deny these emotions. Darien could have her body, use it, make a child with her, but it would remain a bargain struck for her people, an alliance of necessity, not of...love.

He'd started out by kissing her, careful of the sharp cuspids, an intimacy he'd denied her the first time. She trembled despite her best efforts, failing in her determination as she kissed him back. Her eyes widened with realization and she pulled away. When he went for her neck again, she went still.

He growled, deep in his chest. Straddling her hips, he looked down at her with nothing but molten gold swirling in his eyes.

"Is this the hand you wish to play?" he asked.

She looked away, letting her silence speak her confirmation.

Between one breath and the next, he moved, repositioning her over the hump of the chaise. Face down, he pressed her into the cushion. His erection was at her entrance and her hands were pinned together at the small of her back.

He bent lower, the bristling hair of his legs scraping against the back of her thighs, the weight of him pressing down on her until she struggled to breathe. With his free hand he yanked her head up by her hair.

"Do you have any idea what I could do to you?" he whispered.

It was threat. It was promise. They joined, twisting around each other like two separate strands of metal that eventually melted into each other, creating an alloy that was both and neither.

The tip of his organ found her entrance. She was slick with moisture and it drew another growl from him. It rumbled in his chest as he pushed in to the hilt, stretching and filling her. He let go of her hands and his arm wrapped around her midriff. He pulled her upward, his embrace tight, his hold on her hair fast.

It was easier to breathe now. She knew that it was not without reason.

"Two can play this game, Syteria," he said. "I can hold you here, like this, with me filling you, for hours if need be." His lips brushed down from her ear to her neck. "In fact, I think I will."

His hand caressed one breast, then the other, making the tight little buds harden. He tweaked each nipple, sending little shocks down to her core. She spasmed around him.

A soft laugh of satisfaction vibrated against her back.

He squeezed her left nipple tight. Her arms were still crossed and pinned between them and she anchored her fingers against her fore-arms, refusing to pull them free. With her hands freed, she might dig her fingers into his muscled thighs and draw him to her instead. There were a thousand things she wanted to do with her hands: play with his hair, caress the length of him, pull him into her. It was what lovers did.

They were not lovers.

He continued caressing her breasts as though he'd become obsessed with them, as though he knew what it did to her when he touched them. Whether his touch was tender or rough, they always responded, just like the rest of her body, whether she wanted it to or not.

" 'Useless' you said. Is that what they taught you on Rho? That these treasures were useless?"

He let go of one nipple and clamped on to the other. "Answer me." He squeezed harder.

"Yes," she breathed out, more a gasp than a word. It earned her no respite. The pressure on her nipple made her hips twitch, her thighs squeeze together. He pushed her ankles apart, burying himself even deeper, hitting her cervix.

"Are they useless, Syteria?"

"No."

He eased up on the pressure to make maddening little circles around the tender flesh he'd pinched.

"Why aren't they useless?" he asked.

"They feed a child."

"Yes." There was a smile there. She could hear it. "But that's not why they're useless now, are they?"

She shook her head, squeezing her eyes shut.

"Tell me."

"They give you pleasure," she said.

"Really? Are you sure it is my pleasure you are feeling?"

She shuddered and her hips moved again. She stopped them just in time. He pulled her further up, making her rise all the way up on her toes, bending her so he went in deeper. The arches of her feet were spasming, as were the insides of her thighs. She would have to lower herself on him. She drew it out, milking minutes of defiance out of it.

His hand found the tiny bud between her folds and began circling it. A moan built up in her throat, burning in her chest like a lump of coal.

"I will not move until you do. Do you understand? We will stay locked like this, until you've taken my seed from me, for I will not have you play the passive, dutiful concubine taking no pleasure from her master's use."

"Why do you care?" She was still holding still, but barely. She knew she was going to lose the battle sooner or later. Her will was like cracked glass making that slight, whispering sound that signaled that it was about to shatter. She sought to drown it out with words, with anything that would deny him, even if it was just for a few moments.

He traced a drenched finger upward, giving her swollen bud a moment of relief. She almost sighed in acknowledgement. The finger came back down and she stifled a whimper.

"An orgasm will draw my seed in further. And I will see it done, over and over, until I have perfected my claim, until I have restored our honor."

"You still speak of honor as if you had any." Her hips swayed on their own, imparting such delicious friction she barely stopped them in time.

"You cannot make me angry about this, any more than you can stop me, Syteria, but I will enjoy your efforts, have no doubt."

She twisted her right foot, trying to ease her weight from one leg to another. His fist tightened in her hair, halting her attempt.

"I could've taken you any time," he continued, his voice deepening.

"Why didn't you?"

"Because I could not restore my honor with a dishonorable act."

"No one would've cared how you restored your honor."

"You would have."

She closed her eyes. She was surrounded by scent. His. Hers. Theirs. It floated thick in the air. She swayed, giving in to the need for friction, lowering herself onto him. True to his word, he did not move, even as she drove herself mad along the length of him.

He eased his grip, letting her move further up and down. If she slowed, his grip tightened, pulled her upwards. She quaked around him, her toes curling into the rug.

"Well done," he whispered, teasing her neckline with his teeth. "Again."

He was still hard and ready inside her. There was no gush of fluid. "Bastard."

He laughed. "That just earned you another orgasm, my lady. And I was going to be so giving, so generous. I was going to let you sleep tonight."

Pressure was building up inside her, tightening. She may not be willing to go at it again, but her body was. She bit down on the word "bastard" and rode him.

~

As SHE SHOOK from her third orgasm, Darien lowered her to the chaise, let go of her hair, and thrust into her. He was far kinder than she had been with herself. Gently, he pried her fingers from where she'd anchored them to her forearms.

Her whole body was alight, a concert of pleasure signals playing out in harmonies and melodies unlike anything he'd seen before. They danced under her skin as she brought her arms to her sides and dug her fingers into the cushion.

More than anything, he wanted to look into her eyes, to watch pleasure play over her face. But that would also mean seeing her carotid flare and the desire to mark her had only grown. He shook his head, driving the image from his mind, concentrating on that one spot deep inside her. He slid over it again and again, as she buried her head into the chaise. Its cushions muffled the sounds she was making.

He would rather have her scream his name or curse him. She must've bit her lip because the scent of blood invaded his nostrils. He pulsed his release inside her and placed his hands atop hers. The scent of blood faded as he leaned over her, just breathing and trembling.

Slowly, he caressed her with his cheek and pressed his lips against her shoulder. The taste of her was bittersweet. An aftertaste of salt rode in behind it.

"Don't do that," she said.

"Do what?"

"Don't kiss me." It was soft and broken, every bit as bittersweet as the taste on her skin.

"You would deny me this?" He'd tried to make his voice neutral, but there was a tremor to it.

"Yes."

"Why?"

"We are done, are we not?"

He took a deep breath and pulled out of her. She stepped away, but he grabbed her, turned her to face him and drew her close.

A confounding veil of hair had fallen over her face, but she shook her head defiantly and stared at him with challenge in her eyes. The blood on her lip drew his gaze.

He bent down, cradling her head in his hand, denying her distance. She was utterly still as he licked at her bleeding lip. He would have his kiss. He would heal that cut and bruise her in the taking of it. Her fingers tangled in his hair as her tongue dueled his.

Then her hands were at his chest, palms flat, pushing him away. The jade in her eyes was darker now, as though a cloud had risen to obscure its glow.

"Do you still deny what you feel for me?" he asked, running his finger over her healed lip.

She shrugged out of his grasp, going for the robe she'd shed and slipping into it.

"I don't deny it," she said, combing her hair with her fingers. "But until I'm sure that everything I feel, everything I want is not part of your ruse..."

She moved away, towards the bed, robe trailing behind her. His gaze followed. For a woman who'd just spent the last hour coupling, she moved with a grace he'd not expected.

She stood by the bed, working her hair into a loose braid. It would be untangled by morning, as it always was. She never secured it properly and it would come undone.

"How long before you trust yourself again?" he asked as he approached the bed.

"I don't know. I've never done this before."

He leaned on one of the posts.

"Can you sleep?" she asked.

"I have not slept since I was a child. Once my *donai* traits manifested, I found no need for it."

"Will you sleep tonight?"

"Are you inviting me to your bed?"

"I'm inviting you to share sleep."

He climbed in beside her and propped himself up on an elbow. When she didn't pull away at his touch, he pressed in closer and draped his leg over hers.

She looked up at him through the feathers of her lashes, her gaze settling on his lips. She closed her eyes and slipped into sleep, her muscles relaxing in a wave that seemed to flow down from her shoulders.

His vision had shifted, drifting over her, for he wanted to memorize what she looked like in this state.

It was then that he saw it, an almost invisible flare of energy within her abdomen—the chemical reaction announcing a new life.

THE CHEMICAL REACTION of an ovum being fertilized woke the molecular killing machine. To it, the chemical reaction's relatively small energy discharge was like a flare.

Protocols kicked in.

Wait for the remaining sperm to die.

Build a thicker layer of epithelial cells as camouflage.

Avoid the additional *donai* nanites that would no doubt follow over the coming days, weeks, or months.

Wait for the kill.

CHAPTER FORTY-TWO

*S*yteria woke with a start. She was still wrapped in the silken bedding but the space beside her was cold and bare. How long had Darien remained beside her? Had he slept?

There was commotion on the other side of the door leading to the main chamber. By the sound of it, a small army was making camp outside that door.

She pulled herself out of the bed, using one of the posts as an anchor and wiped sleep from her face. Her hair had come mostly undone. She shook it loose, letting it spill over her shoulders. She slipped into a robe, cinched it tight, and headed for the main chamber.

Hanging curtains that looked like rich, detailed art pieces were everywhere, like a forest that had sprouted and grown to full size while she'd been sleeping.

She pushed a teal curtain aside. It wobbled slightly, rotating as it floated out of her way. Long sleeves flapped with the motion.

Not a curtain, but a robe.

She swept the next one aside as well. It floated out of the way just as gently, trailing its flowing silk across her arm. Then another and another, each a different color vividly drawing the eye. She emerged from the forest to find four crewmen and a dozen ornate trunks sporting Dobromil's sigil.

"What is this?" she asked.

The crewmen bowed out of the way to reveal Darien standing atop a newly formed platform.

He was resplendent in a white, naval uniform covered with martial braid. A tug to the archaic tunic altered the fit, bringing it in at the waist. Separate tugs to each sleeve in turn yielded further adjustments.

A bump to her shoulder propelled her forward, tangling her in the swaying robes.

There was a mumbled apology from the crewman wrestling a floating, see-through locker filled with other elaborate uniforms. She stepped out of his way as more trunks and lockers were brought forward and set down around the platform. Rather than go fumbling and climbing over the trunks, she knelt before an open one.

It was stuffed with rich, textured silks—warm golds, soft silvers, everything from white to ebony. Such impractical finery, so different from the practical uniforms and ship fatigues she'd seen so far.

"Excuse me, my lady, may I?" one of the crewmen asked before pulling out a white, sleeveless under-robe. He gave it a shake and inserted a long, flat rover through the armholes.

The rover sent out a pulse, and the robe's wrinkles smoothed out. It floated away. He rummaged deeper, selecting a robe that looked black but was actually a deep, dark red when the light hit it right.

"More relics?" she asked.

Darien laughed. It was light and amused, a sound that made the cord vibrate happily in resonance.

The crewman pulled the white tunic, and the shirt underneath it, off Darien's shoulders, leaving him bare-chested.

She looked down on impulse, closing her hands around a moss-green sash so she'd have something to do, some reason to look down while blood flowed back out of her cheeks. She'd seen him naked, down to his soul, but they had been alone.

"The trappings of duty," Darien said.

Irony had returned to his voice, causing her to look up at him and find it also in his eyes.

"But yes," he continued, "relics as well. Nothing as mundane as tech-formed facsimiles or replicas are allowed. Not unless one wishes to insult one's host."

"Is this about Gamma Ira... Gamma..."

"Gamma Iramana," he said.

He spoke to the crewman who'd been dressing him. The man bowed and retreated from the room, taking his cohorts with him.

"The under-robe, please. Bring it to me."

She bit down on defiance. It had been an order, even with its semblance of a request. Nothing personal. Nothing to take as offense. Everyone aboard obeyed him.

But, they were alone. She could test him, push the boundary of what was expected. What would it gain her though? Not the knowledge and clarity she craved. Would defying him prove that her emotions were her own? That what she felt for him was real?

She stood and tugged the white robe off its rover. It cascaded into her arms with a caress. As it spilled downward, she almost lost her grip on it.

Without meeting his gaze, she moved through the narrow space between the trunks. She held the robe out to him, along with the sash she'd forgotten to drop, like she was making some sort of offering.

A ghost of a smile formed on his lips. He raised his arms from his sides and held them aloft.

The gossamer fabric in her arms felt suddenly, inexplicably, burdensome. She draped the sash and robe across one shoulder so she'd have both hands free to lift her robe and avoid stumbling. Three steps took her to the top of the platform. She ducked behind him and faced his broad, well-muscled back.

Fumbling with the garment, she finally turned it out properly and slid it up one arm, then the other.

He lowered his arms to his sides.

"Smooth out the fabric across the top," he said.

She obeyed, painfully aware of the heat from his skin seeping through the fabric. His hair kissed her fingertips as they slid beneath the tight silk bundle of his queue. Something like static, but far more subtle, more ghostlike, passed between them. The sensation was gone so quickly she wondered if it had been real.

"Reach around me or stand in front, but the right side must cross under the left."

"Must I do this?"

"You sound offended."

"You've turned me into a body servant."

"We all serve someone, Syteria. That is what it means to have a purpose, to be useful. There is no shame in work, not in our domain." He lifted his chin. "This is a necessary task, as essential as that of an ornament, or a weapon, and a prerequisite to many others. It will take some time to acquire the skills needed to stand at my side."

She tucked her hand underneath his right arm but could not reach the fabric on the opposite side.

"You need to become part of our world," he was saying, "with all its idiosyncrasies. One of them is that dressing me is part of a concubine's duties. Another is that it doesn't matter if my peers can tell if I'm wearing a relic or not. I will know. It is still my duty to wear them at appropriate times."

"Turn," she said.

"No."

The amber eyes in the mirror were rock hard, the jaw set.

Syteria moved to his left side and lowered herself to the middle step. She joined the ties.

A thinly disguised, smug grin beamed down at her.

"Smooth out the collar," he said, the timbre of his voice changing to that deep softness that always drew her in.

She tucked her fingers between the fabric and his skin, running them down the glide of the collar, smoothing out nonexistent wrinkles. That ghost of a sensation returned and faded, but this time, she didn't doubt that it was real.

Keeping her eyes downcast, she concentrated on her task, intent on the feel of his chest slipping under her fingers. She rested her hand on the juncture of the collar and waited.

"Secure the opposing side over the first," he said.

A strange form of satisfaction joined the completion of the task. A part of her reveled in it. Another rose to reject it. She did not understand why. They had done far more intimate things than this.

"Who usually does this for you?" she asked. "Perhaps he or she would be better suited for the task."

"You," he said. "And you are perfectly suited to the task."

"Should I consider this an honor then?" A bit of venom had slipped into her tone.

His lip quirked in amusement.

She continued smoothing the other side, this time without tucking her hand between chest and fabric. There was no tie to secure it, but he placed his open palm over the corner, holding it in place.

"The sash," he said. "Get behind me and bring it around the front, then cross it at the back. Bring the tips forward so you can tie it at the front."

She fumbled at first, in spite of his help, or because of it. Her hands were trembling, thwarting her effort to complete this simple task. It was his scent and the tug of that visceral thread between them.

And before she was done, she'd have to get closer. Setting herself to the task, she wrapped her arms around his waist. She pressed into him and held onto the finished knot, her defiance swept away by the rising gust of some storm. He placed his hands atop hers. It was a tentative touch, but it still sent invisible sparks across her skin.

"The red robe next."

That low, dark place pulsed. Inside her, it twisted and contorted. It sent her breath out in little gasps and then was gone as suddenly as it had come.

"Syteria," he whispered.

The red robe was within reach, floating beside her like a veil of blood. Light sparkled off a wetness that wasn't there. She pulled it closer and slipped it off the rover.

"I could make myself unsuitable to the task," she said.

"But you do not."

"And if I did, would it get me a reprieve?"

She yanked one edge of the robe underneath the other. She'd meant it to be forceful, to unbalance him, but he didn't acknowledge her intent. Not even a smirk, or the barest raise of an eyebrow.

"No," he said, his pulse thrumming at eye level. "It would simply take longer as I had you do it again and again, until you gave in."

"So, it's my obedience that pleases you."

She grabbed the collar of the outer robe tight and leaned in forcefully, capturing his gaze so he couldn't mistake her displeasure.

"Yes," he said. There was not a trace of guilt; not in his tone, not in his eyes.

"Does my obstinance please you as well?" she asked.

This time he did raise an eyebrow, his gaze searching, questioning. "As long as you present that obstinate side only to me, yes. You must not challenge me in public and never in front of the *donai*."

Done. She'd dressed him.

Her hands remained splayed on his chest, deriving pleasure from that salty muskiness mixed with plums that surrounded him. It made her mouth water.

She took a deeper breath. It was a mistake. His scent, as always, reminded her of what he felt like inside her. Determined to keep the seeping moisture confined, she squeezed her thighs together.

"If my humans won't obey me," he was saying, "or show me the proper respect, why should my peers? Do you understand?"

She pushed away, backing down the steps. Distance. How much distance did she need between them so her body wouldn't crave his, so it wouldn't send out flares demanding attention.

"You don't mean humans," she said. "You mean slaves."

"I cannot change what they are," he said, following her down and veering off towards a control panel. He entered commands and the sartorial army floating around them lined up and maneuvered into the closet like well-regulated soldiers.

The platform morphed into a semi-circular couch with deep, brown cushions.

"But you indulge in it," she said. "You benefit from it."

His face darkened, but he did not deny it. She was going to need something to do if her obstinance was going to outlast his stubbornness. The nest of rovers the crewmen had left behind waited, so she set herself to the task of emptying the rest of the trunks.

"Why not free your humans?" she asked.

He sank into the center of the couch, resting an ankle atop the opposing knee as he draped an arm along the back. His hand made an idle gesture along the back of the couch. Had he been human she would have said he was uncertain and the gesture betrayed an inner conflict.

She continued working under his considering gaze, hiding within the simple repetition: shake out the garment; hang it up; watch it float away; repeat.

"I understand your distaste," he said. "I really do. So perverse is man that he prefers to be misgoverned by his own kind than to be well-ruled by another."

"Are you a good ruler?" she asked as she stood and gathered her robe about her legs. She negotiated a path to another trunk without getting it caught in the tight spacing. "As good as you are arrogant?"

Soft laughter rolled toward her.

"We value our humans. They are free to choose mates, occupations, free in practice if not in law."

Again, there was no mockery in his tone. His eyes flashed a brighter gold.

"What does that mean?" she asked as she opened the trunk and knelt beside it. Inside, small boxes of polished woods were arranged in neat rows. They wouldn't open at her touch.

"It means that we require service in arms to defend and protect our domain. We require loyalty. We require personal responsibility for one's own actions. In exchange, the humans in our dominion lead unaffected lives, encumbered by few limitations."

"It is still not freedom," she insisted, picking up another box that wouldn't open. She struggled with it, turning it over, attempting to pry it loose from several directions.

"Syteria, there is more to freedom than the lack of a master."

She set the mysterious box aside and stood, considering his words.

"They still fear you," she said.

"Do they?" His gaze was level.

"If they did not, you would not call yourselves rulers," she said.

That unnerving *donai* stillness descended on him once again. It lingered for several breaths he did not take.

"My father does not rule with the heavy hand of the Imperium," he said.

"Why not? A heavy hand would make it easier to rule, wouldn't it?"

"In some ways, yes. We do not seek those who need a heavy hand and the dependence that comes with it. We do not seek or desire a nation of victims, of...pets. For if we did, everything that was not forbidden would have to be mandated. Can you imagine the tyranny of such an existence?"

"I don't have to imagine," she whispered.

She lowered herself to the floor and rummaged through the mysterious treasures inside.

"You're saying the Imperium is like Rho," she said, bringing some of her pain to the surface. Maybe if she allowed her pain to bubble up a bit at a time—

"In what way?"

He propped his chin on his fist and studied her, the layered irises dilating. Clearly, he did not believe her, and perhaps with just cause. From what she had told him, she could understand why. But tyranny was tyranny, whether it was the tyranny of one like the emperor, or the tyranny of many like the Matriarchy.

"It is a place where all are equals," she said. "You could not rule there."

He narrowed his gaze. "Equal in liberty or equal in restraint?"

She stopped fiddling with the lacquered box and set it aside. That word, "equality," had a very different meaning on Rho than on Kappa. On Rho, he would not exist, for he would stand above everyone there. He was faster, stronger, smarter. He exuded power. The Rhoans could not elevate themselves to his level. The only way to remedy that inequality was to bring him down to theirs.

"I was never given a choice in anything on Rho, my lord, but I was always equal."

"Darien," he insisted.

She nodded in a just-so gesture, as she needlessly reordered the small boxes inside the trunk. Despite their simple design, the wood, the inlay, the ornate script were works of art. She picked one up and brought it to her ear, shaking it. Something rattled within.

He'd moved in that soundless way of his, to stand above her. His hand was out, that same imperious gesture that was both order and request. A smile played across his lips.

"Allow me," he said.

She pushed up and placed the box in his hand. It opened like a blooming flower, the top splitting and pulling away as if the threads of dawn had woken it.

He held it out for her. She leaned in, curious. A pair of rings rested inside.

"Go on," he prompted.

The ring was far too small, even for her smallest finger. It was made of the same woodgrain metal as their spaceships.

She cast him a skeptical look. He merely smiled. She slipped the ring onto the tip of her finger, expecting it to reshape itself, but it didn't. She set it back in the box and took the other one out, repeating the process.

"You're amused," she said as she set the ring back in its place. Heat had risen in her cheeks. "Why?"

He watched her with the intensity of his *donai* vision. "Perhaps I will show you tonight."

She frowned. Her skin tingled as she set the second ring back by its mate and handed him the box.

He waved the box closed and leaned down to place it back in the trunk. He retrieved another, a longer, rectangular box. Dark red swirls that looked like an inscription, but not of a kind she'd seen before, were etched into the lid.

"I would like for you to have this," he said, placing the box in her hands.

It was heavier than the others and still warm from his touch.

"Open it," he prompted.

She ran her hand over the top. It opened to reveal a sheath of red and black silk, betraying the outline of a dagger.

"Go on," he said, taking a step back.

She set the box down and slipped the sheath off the dagger. The straight blade was exquisite, catching the light and reflecting it like diamonds. The watermarked sigil played with light and shadow as she wrapped her hand around the hilt. The dagger was perfectly balanced as if it had been forged specifically for her hand.

"I don't understand."

"This was my mother's dagger," he said. "Tradition places it in your hands until it's time for me to cut our child's umbilical. Once I have done so, it returns to your hand, and yours alone."

She tightened her grip around the hilt as her gaze rose to meet his. He had to be speaking metaphorically again. Pregnancies were rare, they'd said. Surely, it hadn't been so...easy.

"Our child?"

"The one we conceived last night."

Her left hand went to her belly. His hand came to rest atop hers. She was wrapped in his scent again, drowning in it. She swayed into him, holding the dagger out at her side. He pulled her head to his chest with a touch so gentle that it made her heart ache.

The light seeping through her eyelids was brighter, his scent sweeter, her body lighter. He put his arms around her and the universe and all its threats, all its sorrows, all its ugliness disappeared.

Her people believed that bringing new life into the world was an act of defiance, a defeat of death. They believed that new life was a bright spark, kindling that could start a roaring fire, not something that would merely consume and then fade away.

The cord in her chest resonated not just with him, but with the child, creating a singular, perfect moment in time.

~

SHE PULLED out of Darien's embrace, taking two steps back, the dagger still held out at her side.

"What happens now?" she asked.

"We ensure the survival of our child."

"How?" Her pulse quickened, making her carotid flare like a beacon.

Darien tore his gaze away from it and said, "We couple so that additional nanites can enter your body and protect the child."

Her grip on the dagger tightened. Her free hand dangled at her side, but as a fist. She was shaking.

She raised her left fist towards her chest and pressed it there.

"There is this thing," she said, voice full of unshed tears, "inside my chest. It vibrates when you are near. You pluck it when you speak, when you hold me tight, when you're inside me. What is it?"

He blew out a slow breath. "It's what pair-bond feels like."

"Galen said that humans can't pair-bond."

"It is something only we *donai* feel," he said, choosing his words with caution. "The nanites in our bodies vibrate at certain frequencies. They set up resonances with each other. The feeling of a string, a cord, it's just a manifestation, a phantom, if you will. And we feel it not just with pair-bond, but with..."

"With what?"

"When my father commands, I feel the compulsion to obey my master. But it is different with one's mate, with you. The compulsion is to protect you, to please you."

She paled. "It would make *you* slaves, to each other, to your human concubines."

"We were slaves, Syteria. Bred for one specific purpose—to fight and die. They wanted to make us obedient to those in charge. It's much easier to control us as if we were a pack. Control the leader and the rest will follow. To some extent we can resist it, but the stronger the resonance, the more we don't want to. Most humans think that we are merely animals, acting on instinct. And maybe we are. Better they think of us as such than as slaves so easily made to obey."

Her breathing became strained. "And the concubines?"

"We assert our dominance over them in order to maintain the illusion that they do not have this power over us."

"And they accept it. Even with this," she pounded her chest once again.

"They don't feel the pair-bond for they are human," he said. "Now, give me the dagger, Syteria."

Her nostrils flared. "Tradition places it in my hand. Your words. For my hand alone. Again, your words."

Darien's vision had shifted, seeing her as heat and light, and that nascent spark inside her where his child was nestled. "You are not *donai*, Syteria."

She lifted her hand, bringing the dagger's point towards herself. He could move fast enough to tear it from her hands. He could disarm her before she brought the dagger down, but then he'd never be able to trust her again. They both knew that as long as she was on this ship, almost any harm that came to her could be remedied. Except for the harm to her reputation, to his claim, to their future together.

"Compel me," she said.

Ice crystallized in Darien's blood. The Cold whispered to him once again, gently nudging him, tempting him. *I am here*, it whispered. *Use me.*

He shook his head, not trusting the Cold with his voice.

"I need this," she said, her voice a strange combination of pleading and demand. "I need to know what it feels like to be compelled. To know if what I feel, is me, and only me."

"There is no longer only you, Syteria."

"Compel me," she said.

There were a thousand reasons he didn't want to do it. And only one that mattered. He let the Cold seep into him, sweep through his veins, holding it at bay enough that it would not consume him like it had in the emperor's presence.

"Drop the dagger, Syteria," the Cold said.

She pulled her hand away from her chest. Her hand was still wrapped around the hilt, knuckles white, trembling as she held it as far out from her body as she could.

She was strong, his woman. Stronger than he'd ever imagined. He would know how strong.

"Drop the dagger," the Cold said once again, this time no longer restrained.

He saw the pain lancing through her as surely as if he'd taken his sword and driven it through her heart. The dagger dropped, embedding itself into the marble between them.

She stared at her open hand, unbelieving eyes wide.

"It hurts," she whispered.

It always hurt the first time. And with each use, a bit of will was stolen and the pain reduced. The *donai* obeyed as the compulsion became easier to bear. Over time, obedience became rewarding. It was why his father used it sparingly, if at all.

"Yes," Darien said. "And we are not done."

Her eyes widened further.

He picked up the dagger. She backed away from him, almost stumbling over one of the trunks, her robe slipping off her shoulder as the hem caught under her retreating feet.

"I should mark you," he said. "That way all that see you will know you are mine. So that no one will touch you without pain of death, just as if you were my pair-bonded *donai* mate."

Her gaze darted to the dagger in his hand, but it wasn't fear he saw in her eyes. It was wonder. And expectation.

"On Kappa—"

He cut her off with, "Get on the mating chaise."

No longer stumbling, she drew herself to her full height. "Not like before. I will look at your face this time."

He shook his head, advancing. The Cold was still with him. Once the Cold came, once it had hold of them, it could not simply be cast off, unused. It reminded him of its presence with a fresh surge of chilled blood.

"On the chaise," Darien said.

437

She didn't move.

"Would you have me compel you again?"

"No," she said. "I see the difference now."

"Chaise."

She remained in place as if she'd grown roots, as if this was the hill she was willing to die on.

"First you deny me the intimacy of a kiss," he said. "Now you would keep me from my duty to pair-bond, to ensure our child's survival?"

"I deny you nothing," she said, dropping the robe to pool at her feet.

And she was true to her word. She did not deny him. But when she tried to face him as he neared his completion, he forced her back down, and denied her hers.

A growl came from her chest as she whipped her head around to look behind her. He lowered his head to rub his cheek against hers.

"All defiance comes with a price, my lady." The Cold was still with him, threading itself into his voice.

She strained against him, not to free herself, but to tempt him.

"Be still," he said, compelling her. It drove the breath out of her as her inner muscles tightened around him.

He looked down on the perfect swell of her hips, the taper of her waist, the curve of shoulders quivering with the power of his compulsion.

Darien didn't want her facing him. The urge to mark her was stronger than ever. Putting his nanites directly into her blood would give him a *donai* child, but at great cost.

And he would not risk her, not even for a warchild.

As soon as he pulled out and away from her, Syteria whirled about to face him. He looked down at her without remorse, or regret. The dagger was tucked into the moss-colored sash. He had not bothered to undress and the folds of his robe had settled to hide him.

"You have something of mine," she said and stuck her hand out.

"If you raise it against yourself again, you will not like the consequences."

"You have my word of honor. I will not raise it against myself, or against you or our child. But you must give it back to me."

"Must I?" The amber irises swirled back into place.

"You expect me to honor your traditions, but deny me mine?" She closed the distance between them and placed her hand on the dagger's hilt.

His hand came to rest atop hers. He leaned in and wrapped his arm around her waist. Even now, even after what had happened, her body responded as if it wanted more, as if it could take more.

"That depends on the tradition," he said.

"To bare the blade with intent, but deny it blood is to dishonor it. And oneself."

He leaned in closer, drew her in so she was pressed against him. She felt him rise against the silks she'd placed on him. From his eyes, from the hunger on his face, there was no doubt that he was going to take her again, but before he did, she would test if that thread between them worked both ways.

"It would please me," she added, tightening her grip on the dagger. The musk floating around her was making it harder to breathe. Her thighs squeezed together.

It made his nostrils flare and he freed the dagger and placed it in her hand.

She pricked her thumb. The blade was far sharper than she'd have thought possible. She cut much deeper than she'd intended, not just through the skin, but the muscle underneath. Still, the pain was nothing like that which had accompanied the compulsion.

He took her hand and brought it up to his lips, running the blood over them until it dripped down his chin. The amber in his eyes was gone, replaced by something feral.

"Go ahead," she said. "I know you want to."

The cord in her chest was vibrating madly.

"I want you to," she added.

His tongue darted out and swept her finger. She turned it so that he could draw it into his mouth. The pain was gone, and the cord in her chest pulsed with pleasure.

He'd closed his eyes and a growl rose out of his chest, matching the chord's rhythm. He sucked harder, but just for a moment and then pulled away, as if he did not trust himself.

As he swiped the blood off his chin, he watched her with embers in his eyes.

Syteria knew her thumb was healed. She knew that there would be no scar. She didn't have to look to confirm it. She grabbed at his sash, pulled it free, and used it to wipe the blood off the dagger.

"I'm going to need a sheath for this," she said. "One I can wear around my thigh. And you must leave it in place when we couple."

A smile tugged at the edge of his blood-smeared mouth. "Yes, my lady."

CHAPTER FORTY-THREE

*S*yteria could watch the colorful hologram all day. Within a clear shell, cells divided again and again until their number broke through. Nanites swarmed the blastocyst, forming a protective shell of a different kind, like a layer of individual shields coming together. They shepherded it to the implantation site.

From across the chamber, Galen was watching her with an expression that was equal parts humor and curiosity. Anasera beamed, the grin on her face making her look triumphant. Syteria shrugged them both off, settling back into the bio-bed and started the holographic recording again.

"How do you feel?" Anasera asked.

"Surprised," Syteria said. "I thought pregnancies were rare."

"They are," Galen agreed as he approached. "I'm going to have to take a closer look at your alleles."

She quirked a brow at him.

"Your alleles are probably what make you compatible," Anasera explained. "We don't have a complete database aboard the *Edlyn*, and calling for one would rouse suspicion, but once we are on Serigala, we can compare yours to those we have on record. It might help us trace a path back to your ancestry, narrow down where your people are from."

"A way to Kappa?" Syteria asked, dismissing the hologram.

"A way to ancestral migration patterns that might point us in the right direction. Or not." It was Galen, somber once again. She liked him better curious and amused.

He frowned, the look on his face darkening. Anasera nudged him. He put on a smile that didn't quite fit.

Syteria rested her hand on her abdomen again.

"I am happy," she said. She was, truly. The power play with the dagger had erased all vestiges of doubt that what she felt were her own reactions. "Why aren't you? This redeems Darien's honor. You are no longer traitors, are you?"

"The treason is a gray area now. Probably, " Galen said and got a harder nudge from Anasera.

"No, Anasera, let him speak. I would have his honesty, even now."

"It's too easy," he finally blurted out.

"Easy?" Syteria asked. She would not have described it as easy.

"What my father is trying to say is that it usually takes months or years."

"Darien told me how the Right to Claim came about. Did it take months or years then?"

Galen shook his head.

"So it's not without precedent?" Syteria asked.

"No."

"Why are there no children on this ship? There are many couples."

"Because this is a ship of war, despite its comforts," Galen said. "It's an embassy ship—technically—as long as Darien is aboard, but the *Edlyn* is no place for children.

"A claim as politically charged as Darien's invites attack, despite the *donai* pretending it is sacrosanct. The emperor may recognize the claim. The Houses may support House Dobromil's right to make it and take up arms against the emperor should he act against you, but that only means the emperor won't attack us openly.

"It's why we've done everything we could to keep our route a secret. The fact that the Imperium was able to intercept us twice already is a cause for concern."

Fear, cold and dark, wrapped itself around Syteria's heart. It was unlike any fear she'd felt before. It wasn't for herself but for the child she bore.

"How much of a threat is there?" she asked Anasera.

"Enough. You'd be safer on Serigala, but Lord Dobromil knows of the claim and still chose to send us to Gamma Iramana. Darien has no choice but to obey."

Did Lord Dobromil's compulsion reach into Darien's soul and twist it to his purpose as Darien's compulsion had done to her? She could still feel echoes of it sometimes in idle moments, like a wound that ached and would not heal, a constant reminder of what it felt like, truly felt like, to have no will of one's own. She shuddered.

"Are you all right, my lady?" Anasera asked.

"Yes. Tell me every everything I need to know to ensure my child's survival."

IT WASN'T THAT LATE, but like a heavy cloak, fatigue had settled on Syteria's shoulders and refused to lift. She was sitting across from Lowran, the ship's linguist. The dark-haired, statuesque woman that Syteria had sparred with.

Lowran was still standing ramrod straight, surrounded by holographic images. She had some of them stacked in layers. Others were more spread out, often interconnected by color-coded lines. They had been working on filling in the gaps of the Rhoan language matrix. Some of the gaps were from the difference in the level of technology. Others were contextual.

It had provided a wonderful distraction as well as a sense of purpose. To the extent that she could, Syteria would make sketches and they would work on matching words and concepts.

Even with how fuzzy her thinking tended to become this late in the day, her brain was outperforming Lowran's educated guesses and assumptions. The question, "How do you do that?" had been replaced with sharp, but unspoken curiosity, because the only answer Syteria had been able to give her was, "I don't know."

It wasn't that Lowran didn't believe her. Once a connection was made between a sound or a symbol, it cascaded through the matrix, re-ordering it and filling in gaps, like a puzzle solving itself. An incorrect connection would jumble things up, not make order out of chaos.

"Are you all right, my lady?" Lowran asked, the soft skin around her eyes crinkling with concern. She waved the hologram away and approached.

Syteria stifled a yawn. "Yes, I'm fine."

Lowran accepted the answer with a nod, and brought up a new group of symbols. They were Kappan. A few days ago they had started cross-referencing Kappan and Rhoan and Kanthlos. Lowran had been ecstatic to have a language so alien to study.

Syteria's motivations centered more on ensuring that if she didn't survive House Dobromil's political machinations, or her pregnancy, they would still have a way of communicating with her people. The five hundred or so words she'd been able to recall from her childhood seemed far too inadequate, but they would have to suffice.

"Perhaps we should call it a day," Syteria said. She needed to get up and walk or she was surely going to slip right off the chair and end up snoring on the floor.

Lowran bowed. "Yes, my lady. Shall I escort you back?"

"No thank you."

Syteria returned the bow, freeing Lowran to continue. She cast a backward glance as the doors shut. Lowran was already immersed in her work, her brows drawn in tight concentration.

She passed crewmen and officers, returning their bows with a nod and a smile as she made her way to the royal decks. She passed right by the infirmary.

Anasera's first order had been to eat and drink, even if she did not feel particularly hungry or thirsty. Her body was now fueling not just the child's growth, but the nanites' as well. The second order had been to rest. It had proven the harder one to comply with since pair-bonding meant sex.

Syteria had two hours before Darien would join her in their quarters for dinner. Every night they would talk, mostly about the latest information he'd received about the emperor's doings. It was when she brought up more personal matters, about his mother, his father, his childhood, that he'd fall silent and just watch her eat as if he were measuring and tracking every bite.

Afterwards, he'd always start with seduction: a caress; a gentle touch; burying his face in her hair. No longer in doubt of her feelings, she'd responded enthusiastically, but no matter what she tried, he would not make love face to face. She could not judge him for it. She had, after all, made the mistake of playing the dutiful concubine denying her feelings for him.

Now that she knew better, that she knew what he could do, and that he chose not to, she'd realized who he really was.

First and foremost, he was his father's son, one to whom duty came first. She could admire such a man. She could also serve him—as companion, as weapon, as concubine, as anything he needed her to be—for every breath she took, everything that she did for the rest of her life, was because he had rescued her.

Second, he was *donai*. He might step out of that role and take on a human skin, but at his core, he was not human. And she did not want him to be. A human could not protect her, nor her child.

Third, he was the father of her child. Every night he came to bind himself to her, to ensure their child's survival. Whether he did it out of a sense of duty, or because he was an honorable man rather than one who simply loved her, mattered not.

There were worse fates: she had imagined them all.

They were not lovers. She was a spoil of war. One that had chosen her fate, denied that she'd been in love, made an act of passion into one of duty, and then insisted that what she felt could not be real. In the profound solitude of the night, often in his embrace, she had come to understand that within her heart, nothing had changed.

She entered her quarters, stumbling through the main chamber.

Sleep beckoned. She wanted to slip out of the long skirts swishing around her and just succumb to the fatigue. Instead, she just fell into it.

CHAPTER FORTY-FOUR

*a*s House Dobromil's Court physician, the last place Galen should have been was in the *Edlyn's* infirmary, at this late hour, meticulously arranging and re-arranging his lab.

But here he was.

His attempts at sleep had been futile. The perfect remedy, a sleep field, was as abhorrent to him as it was to Syteria, although—given her people's limited technology—probably not for the same reason.

The Imperium used a variant of the sleep field for interrogation. Given an adequate amount of time to map a human's mind, their dreams could be invaded and information implanted or extracted. Other sleep remedies were available, but he'd inoculated himself with countermeasures long ago. It was such countermeasures that had allowed him to survive the emperor.

Nevertheless, there were times like this, times when the calendar rolled to the fateful day that had brought him into Dobromil's service. When the events of that day haunted him, as they did now, he sought refuge in his only escape—work.

It was his work, his success, that had brought him to the emperor's attention.

Emperor Thán Kabrin had been younger then, a *donai* just come to power, still wearing the shorter hair of an imperial heir. He sat atop a throne carved to resemble a dragon. It cradled him in its bosom, its wings extended as if poised to fly off a raised daïs. The emperor looked down on Galen's mistress and her entourage as if he were divine.

Galen remembered the predatory gleam in Kabrin's eyes. It had been a brief glimpse at the new emperor's face, an impetuous dare befitting the young, arrogant physician overwhelmed by the honor of his imperial majesty's interest.

Humans were not supposed to meet the emperor's gaze, but keeping his eyes down had always been a problem, one for which Galen's *donai* mistress had often scolded him.

"Physician, our cousin speaks highly of you," Kabrin had said that fateful day.

As he sat back on his throne, Kabrin's words echoed in the circular audience chamber. Columns ringed the chamber, soaring upward, stabbing into an obsidian dome. House Kabrin's domain had been mapped in jewels that glowed with their own light, just like the stars they represented.

The "imperial" cousin, her ladyship, the honorable Valeria Yedon, master assassin, stood at Galen's side. Regal and smiling, she cradled her infant daughter. She cooed back at the child, a sound so foreign, it drew an astonished look from the emperor.

Galen forced his gaze down again. He bowed once more. It was the only acceptable response. No question had been posed to him. He had not been invited to speak. He'd bitten back the "Yes, Sire," almost too late.

Breathe.

Kneeling on the other side of Lady Yedon was the infant's nanny. Imperial *donai* guards ringed the chamber's perimeter, standing between the columns like sentinels.

A pair of House Yedon's *donai* flanked the lady's entourage. They wore their swords, for all the good they would do in a place where containment fields could drop at the emperor's command. The tiles

447

underneath their feet could transform into utility fog and snare them. Those columns were undoubtedly disguised weapons.

Despite his best effort at calm, Galen's fear made the hairs on the back of his neck stand up. Behind him, one of the guards must've scented it for his breath hitched. The nanny must've heard the guard's reaction too because she touched her forehead to the ground, as though doing so would somehow help.

Lady Yedon seemed oblivious to it all, still entranced by the variety of sounds her daughter was making.

"Who is the father?" the emperor asked.

"One of my *donai*, Sire," Lady Yedon answered, distractedly.

A lie. A dangerous lie. While the *donai* may not be able to read each other as well as they did humans, Lady Yedon's body had not returned to its unaltered state. The emperor might well be able to read her as well as any human and lying to the emperor was treason.

Even for the emperor's favorite assassin. One could even argue, especially for the emperor's favorite.

"His name," the emperor demanded with more than a trace of jealousy.

"Sire, his name was Olier Vidar, and he died protecting me on my last mission for you," she said, imbuing her tone with just the right amount of regret.

Galen's gaze strayed upward to catch the emperor's raised eyebrow, then found the colorful mosaic beneath his own feet again. He counted the tiles.

"You've always worked alone before, Valeria."

"Olier was my pair-bonded mate. It was his right to accompany me, his duty to protect me."

"We knew of no such bonding."

"I had hoped to present him to you, Sire, after our mission, along with the Hevonen traitor's head."

More lies. How often had Lady Yedon told herself this lie so that it would flow so readily off her tongue?

The infant cooed again. Galen's eyes widened—his mistress was using the child as a shield, using the infant's heartbeat to mask her own, using her daughter's scent to dilute the stench of a lie. He looked up out of the corner of his eye.

What kind of woman would use her infant as a shield?

For this, she had risked her life, her dominion, her power? For this, she had killed? Sacrificed?

This is whom I serve.

Galen should've tried harder to talk her out of this audience, or rebelled outright and gotten himself thrown into a cell. She might have brought him anyway, perhaps in chains. They would've been easier to bear. A ready explanation for his fear, and trepidation, both of which were an unwilling feast for the emperor's senses.

"Does she speak the truth, physician?" the emperor asked.

The truth was not his to speak. Caught between his mistress and her master, the truth would only condemn them both. The truth was better forgotten, buried deep, never to resurface.

"The child is the product of two *donai* parents and has only *donai* genetics, Sire," Galen said, his voice steady. It was fact, after all.

"That is not what I asked, human."

"I was not present for the coupling, Sire." This too was fact. The *donai* nobility were adamant about their privacy in such things, and the emperor knew this, but it was something he might accept as a human answer, something that might allay his obvious suspicions.

"Bring her to me, Valeria," the emperor ordered as he stood.

Head held high, as proud as any mother, Lady Yedon approached. The emperor descended the five steps to meet her at the bottom of the daïs. Kabrin was an imposing figure, a perfect *donai* specimen, the full male complement of Galen's mistress, barely a head taller than she.

Galen looked up in time to see Lady Yedon's smile as she held her daughter for him to admire.

"She is *donai*, Sire. The first of a new generation," oblivious maternal pride declared.

The very first. And a daughter no less. No wonder Galen's mistress was so boastful.

The emperor removed a glove and ran a finger across the infant's cheek. The baby grabbed at his finger with tiny hands. A delighted giggle burst out of her at catching her prey. The emperor's face remained as though carved in stone.

"Is she fertile?" the emperor asked over his shoulder, aiming the question at Galen.

"Yes, Sire," Galen said, unable to keep a slight crack out of his voice.

It earned an imperial smirk.

"How is that possible?" Kabrin asked as he crossed the distance between them, thrusting his hand back into the glove as he went.

Too late, Galen realized he'd looked at the emperor directly, so he deepened his bow and aimed his gaze at the tiles once again.

Kabrin's gloved hand grabbed Galen's hair and jerked his head back, unbalancing him. His scalp tore until the emperor tempered his grip. A scalding stream of blood flowed down his scalp and pooled at the back of his neck. Galen stared into the cold, hard glare of hatred.

The emperor's gold and amber eyes narrowed as his lips curved into a sneer, revealing pointed cuspids. "Were you able to reverse the fertility controls?"

"I—"

"Yes or no?"

Galen glanced at his mistress. She had handed the infant off to the nanny and was standing just out of the emperor's reach, holding her breath.

The nanny had attempted to flee through the doors, but Kabrin's *donai* blocked her path.

"We didn't ask her," the emperor said, jerking at Galen's scalp. A fresh flood of liquid scalded the back and sides of Galen's neck. "We asked you."

"Yes, Sire, I can," Galen said miserably.

The emperor let him go.

Galen's knees hit the tiles with a resounding crack. He braced himself with one hand on the floor as the other sought to staunch the flow of blood snaking down the white of his shirt. His gaze trailed the emperor's receding boots.

A cast-off glove landed in his wake, a scrap of bloodied flesh clinging to the seams.

Galen pushed up to stand, but the *donai* behind him slammed a hand between his shoulder blades, shoving him back down. Still clutching his head, he glimpsed Lady Yedon gesturing for him to remain in place.

Lowering himself to the floor, Galen folded, waiting, ignoring the radiating pain. Scalp wounds bled profusely, no matter how shallow. That knowledge, that cold hard fact, did nothing for the pain. Or the fear.

Ignore it. Ignore it and live.

"My lady Valeria, thank you," the emperor said.

Galen turned his head, resting his cheek on the cold tiles. Blood dripped into his eyes. He blinked it away. He was going into shock but he dared not move.

Kabrin extended his right arm in the infant's direction, making an impatient gesture at the nanny.

"Bring me the child," Kabrin insisted.

She had to be jostled forward as she clutched her charge to her chest, pleading silently with her mistress.

Lady Yedon took the child. The nanny fell back with a sob. She lowered herself to the floor, eyes clenched shut, her lips moving in silent prayer.

Cradling her daughter, Lady Yedon faced her master with utmost courage. She could not draw her sword. It dangled at her side, on her left hip, underneath the infant. She could not draw her sidearm—they were forbidden in the imperial presence. Her *donai* armsmen were too few to aid her. They remained in place, frozen either with uncertainty or waiting for an explicit order.

She and Galen had spoken of sacrifice, of what it would take to make her a mother, of the obvious physical tolls, of the *donai* qualities she'd have to surrender, at least temporarily.

They'd spoken of how it would weaken her, make her less *donai* and more human. She'd said she was willing to make the required sacrifices and incur all necessary costs.

Galen had known that she, being *donai*, did not understand what that sacrifice would ultimately entail. He hadn't had the power to show her the meaning of motherhood.

Not until now.

It was in that moment, so long ago, that Lady Yedon had learned the true sacrifice required of a mother—vulnerability.

She could not defend herself. She could not defend her child. She'd miscalculated, and the price for that mistake had been borne by innocents like her daughter and by pawns like Galen.

Kabrin presented Lady Yedon with a choice: the child or the means by which the emperor could reverse the fertility controls imposed on the *donai* by their creators.

Lady Yedon's gaze darted to Galen as she clutched her child closer. The baby's cry pierced the silence as Galen's vision tunneled.

"We accept your generous gift," Kabrin said.

Lady Yedon looked upon Galen for one last time.

Galen never blamed her for choosing her daughter over him.

"GALEN."

Galen blinked, finally seeing the lab he'd been standing in.

Kell stood in front of him. The scarred *donai's* face held fear. Aeda lay across his arms, pale and still like death.

Within seconds they had her in the reconstruction unit. Beams of light swept her from head to toe and side to side.

"What did you do to her?" Galen asked.

"Nothing," Kell said as his hands flexed into fists. "I found her like this. I couldn't wake her."

"Where?"

"In my quarters."

Galen had warned Kell back when he'd brought Aeda flowers. He had not just warned, but threatened. The infirmary had records of Aeda's visits and there was nothing in them to show that Kell's nanites had been adversely affecting her. Kell had been careful.

Galen worked to stabilize her, get her breathing, and raise her temperature. Her heart was barely beating. It looked like it was being cannibalized. Her lungs were breaking down, like something was killing cells and harvesting them for fuel.

More and more interfaces appeared, vying for his attention. Some he sent into oblivion. Others he brought forward. They were all pulsing crimson, screaming at him in the language of data and more data, all telling him the same thing—Aeda was dying and there was nothing he could do to stop it.

The reason appeared in front of him. Within the hologram, a molecular killing machine shed its shroud of human cells and gave off a pulse that caused all the holograms to flicker and power-down.

"What are you doing?" Kell asked.

"I'm putting her in stasis," Galen said. It would take minutes for his diagnostic systems to come back online.

Minutes Aeda didn't have.

The reconstruction unit flooded with nanites. The air in Aeda's lungs barely kept her afloat as the fluid level rose. Kell splayed his hand across her chest and pushed down. He turned away as he held her submerged. Aeda didn't move, didn't thrash, didn't do any of the things her body should've instinctively done.

Galen worked the controls as Anasera rushed in. Fluid was overflowing and spilling over the sides.

"Let go of her," Anasera said. "The canopy can't close until you let her go. Kell, stasis can't start unless the canopy is closed."

Kell growled at her.

"Let her go."

Facing him, Anasera stood her ground.

"Do it now," she said.

He pulled his hand out. The reconstruction unit's canopy solidified over the liquid as Kell let out a roar and took off at *donai* speed.

THE KILLING MACHINES had been able to hide themselves from the beams at first. But only for a brief time. There was no real need for them to shield themselves anymore—the damage they had been sent to inflict was complete enough to meet their mission parameters.

The beams would recognize them eventually, so it was a waste of energy to keep hiding. They had better things on which to spend such energy.

Nanite-enriched fluid—the wrong kind of fluid—filled the host's alveoli. It wasn't like the fluid laced with *donai* nanites. This fluid was the nemesis, a destructive force. Destruction that could only be fought with creation.

Secondary protocol...initiated.

FEAR PERMEATED the infirmary as Palleton carved a path towards Galen's lab. Galen and Anasera were working furiously, rushing between a stasis pod and the lab's consoles. Rovers buzzed angrily around them as if the machines themselves were also afraid.

Bomani had positioned herself on the lab's periphery, keeping out of the way. She had not bothered with her uniform. Her long blonde hair flowed loosely down her back. She clutched her robe shut just below her neck. It wasn't because she was cold or modest. She wasn't just afraid. She was terrified.

"What's going on?" he asked.

"A bio-weapon," Bomani said, tugging the robe tighter as though its presence might shield her somehow.

Nestra burst through, pushing a floating pallet. Kell was behind her, his face dark and unreadable. He gave Palleton an acknowledging nod.

"Cyra," Nestra said, popping the pallet's canopy.

Bomani looked away.

Cyra was struggling to breathe. Her skin looked like it was peeling away from her bones and Palleton would've sworn she'd shrunk. She blinked unseeing eyes that had changed color as if she'd gone blind. Kell picked her up and set her into a stasis pod. He pushed her into the fluid and held her down, all without looking at her, then strode forward and out of the lab, grim jaw set with determination.

"There is another," Nestra whispered as she followed Kell out.

"Another what?" Palleton asked.

"Another victim. Whatever it is, it's only attacking women with *donai* lovers," Bomani said.

"My lady," Palleton said.

Bomani placed her hand on his shoulder. "Galen has been monitoring her. No signs of distress."

"My lord ordered the monitoring stopped."

Bomani gave him an incredulous look and darted a glance at Galen. Her eyebrow rose with an implied, *Really?*

Two of Galen's junior physicians rushed in. Galen shouted orders. The physicians parked themselves behind consoles and worked the interfaces, their brows furrowed in concentration.

Palleton approached a stasis pod, colliding with a rover that beeped at him. He stepped back, right into another pallet.

"Stay out of the way, Colonel or get out," Galen said.

Kell pushed Palleton out of the way. Lowran was on the pallet, writhing in agony. Nestra was busy wiping Lowran's brow. It was beaded with sweat and her tears had a pinkish tinge to them.

"Shh," Nestra said, trying to calm Lowran. "We'll take good care of you."

Lowran closed her eyes and gulped. Nestra's soothing tone had not fooled her any more than it had fooled Palleton. Lowran opened her eyes once more, turning her head to look around her. Clutching her hands to her chest, she let out a scream that ended in a wet gurgle.

A rover headed her way, stopping above her. It sent out pulses that forced her body to go limp. Her eyes closed.

Palleton could still hear her heart beating, but the rhythm was off. A second rover zapped her chest. She convulsed. Her heart beat properly for two beats, then faltered again. Another zap. And then a third.

Kell was there, lifting Lowran into the next stasis pod, that same impotent rage in his eyes.

"That's all of them," Nestra said. "We think."

The lights in the infirmary flickered. The holograms were on for an instant more, then faded again.

The air was so thick with fear-scent that Palleton choked. The holograms came up again, but not as before.

The message, *Forbidden fruit shall never bear proper fruit,* scrolled across them all with agonizing slowness.

THE LATEST INTELLIGENCE reports wrapped around Darien like a multi-layered shield. Resources within the Imperium were mobilizing. The timeline was the most difficult to piece together, since the distance between the *Edlyn's* position and that of the data source continued to be a big factor. It would be days before they'd be able to get additional data.

There was no evidence of military action. House Kabrin had been quite respectful of Dobromil's borders. They had gone through the proper channels to request access through transit points, even turned back when they were denied. It made the hairs on the back of Darien's neck stand up in warning. The emperor's House was being far too passive and compliant.

Meanwhile, he searched for less obvious patterns, minutiae that would betray the building of a wormhole. He had a partial data set, obtained before the *Edlyn* had been dispatched to its exile. He'd been working on it, looking for patterns in logistics and personnel that had been routed to Thertore.

The pattern was laid out in front of him, a complex schema of events that seemed unrelated and would have been easily dismissed had one not known what to look for. But no one built a wormhole generator overnight. And no one, not even the emperor, could build one without leaving evidence.

The Imperium produced humans who were passive, and therefore easily intimidated, or humans who were defiant and put to death. The Imperium took pride in publishing its disciplinary and execution records. There was one name missing, one that should have been there:

Luuedei Kennen. She had been arrested and imprisoned, yet no record of her execution existed. It could very well be that the most up to date records had not reached the *Edlyn*.

Other patterns emerged. Those of couriers. Then of materials. Families of scientists had been relocated to Kanavar, a dubious honor bestowed mostly on hostages.

Darien rubbed his chin and glanced at the door leading to the bedroom. Syteria had been asleep when he'd come to join her for dinner. She'd stirred awake, kissed him, and fallen asleep as he'd removed her clothing. The scent of fatigue had been so strong that he'd let her rest. He'd tucked her into bed, eaten dinner alone, and immersed himself in his duties.

Dismissing the holographic reports, he returned to the dinner table. Atop a clean plate, he piled still-hot food from the tureens. He could hand-feed Syteria in bed and at least make sure she ate something.

The main doors parted.

Galen took a step in.

"My lord, several members of the crew are dying," Galen said as he delivered a precise half-bow.

Galen had taken his words that someone better be dying the next time he overrode the privacy locks more literally than Darien had intended.

As sovereign, your words shall be law. Use them wisely, his father had told him. How many times? Too many. Not enough.

Kell and Palleton emerged from the shadows to stand behind Gallen. Palleton was his usual, stoic self, but there was something about Kell, a darkness that Darien had never seen on his face before.

They had come with Galen for a reason.

Darien dropped the plate and rushed toward the bed chamber. The door opened. The scent of blood hit him as if he'd run into a wall. A scream tore itself from his chest. Palleton's arms wrapped around his torso, lifting him off the rug. Kell rushed past them.

Palleton put him up against a wall and held him there as Galen hurried into the bed chamber.

It was Kell that brought Syteria out, moving as though time had slowed around them. She was pale, her lips blue, and blood dripped off her legs in long, slow rivulets that took forever to twist their way to the rug.

Nestra and Anasera pushed a floating pallet forward, moving with that same unnatural slowness. The air around them filled with the tang of iron and copper and salt. Kell set Syteria atop the pallet. The time distortion allowed Darien's enhanced vision to see that new life no longer burned within her.

There was only the fading light of her own life.

He sank to the floor, falling under Palleton's crushing weight.

CHAPTER FORTY-FIVE

*S*yteria was drowning in blood. It filled her nose and throat. She swallowed it down again and again, until she thought she was going to burst.

But it was better than the emptiness, the hollow, incomplete feeling that had raked her flesh off, burrowed within, and consumed her.

Blood flowed from her mouth, her nose, her eyes, her womb...

The cord in her chest was plucked. By light. By warmth. By love.

It spoke her name and brought the cord to life once again. It felt out of sync, unused, a discordant harmony. Beneath it all, melody lingered, its notes slipping through the threads of consciousness, pulling her upward, out of the sea of blood and pain.

"Syteria."

The cord thrummed again, like a string being tuned, eventually finding its proper harmonies and resonance.

She opened her eyes. Two golden disks shone in the darkness. Gold and amber. They gave off a warmth that fanned over her like flames caressing a corpse, imbuing it once more with life. Floral scents filled the air, fighting the antiseptic undertones that were the trademark smell of the infirmary.

Darien was sitting on a chair and holding her hand. She was on her side, atop what felt like a bio-bed. The hushed sounds of monitors lingered in the background. He lowered his lips to her hand and held them there.

Even in the darkness his hair shone, a glossy black against black. Silver shone at the nape of his neck.

"Our child." Her lips were dry. Her throat hurt.

"Lost." There was so much grief in that one word, that she blinked back tears. Not for the child, who was beyond pain, but for him, because he was not.

Moisture touched her hand, branding her as it flowed down her fingers. She had not known that they could cry. She'd thought she'd be alone, shedding tears for them both.

"How long?" She put her free hand atop his head, parting the silken warmth of his hair with her fingers.

He sighed into her caress. "Two days."

"I'm sorry," she said.

He looked up, his eyes bright in the dark room. "It was not your doing."

She had used the wrong mode, taking blame, but she'd not meant to. "Galen said it had been too easy. That this was to be expected." Her voice was coming back now, stronger, even as a whisper.

He was silent for a long time, simply holding her hand as the lights gradually came on. Flowers had invaded the infirmary compartment, covering every spare surface that the chamber had extruded.

"From the crew," Darien said. "We use flowers for courtship, for celebration, and to mourn."

White robes adorned him, the same type of relics that she'd helped him unpack. The fabric had no pattern embedded in it. Even his boots were white.

Despite the tear that had fallen onto her hand—she could still feel it tingle on her skin. His eyes were clear, without the red she'd expected. He was *donai*. They healed quickly, at least physically.

She drew herself upward. He stood, offering his aid, with a look of intent concern, as if he were expecting her to fall. She allowed him to help her, despite the lack of pain or dizziness.

Someone had dressed her in one of the infirmary gowns, its pale blue shimmer now an old friend.

She rested her hand against her abdomen. Darien wrapped his arms around her and did the same.

She let him hold her like that, leaning into his strength, his scent, the soft silk of his robes. His breath was even, not the excited kind that usually graced her neck and shoulder when he held her like this.

"How long before we can try again?"

His heart thundered against her back. She turned around and looked up at him, laid a hand on his cheek, and stroked the coarse hair of his beard.

"We can try again, can we not?" Fear had entered her voice. She could not bear the hollowness within her. On Kappa the loss of one child might have meant never having one, but here...Surely, it could not be so.

"Yes, we can try again, but first, there is something you must know."

She searched his eyes and they frightened her for she had never seen hopelessness within them. Perhaps because he had lived with the vision of their child far longer than she had, because of everything that was at stake...

"Tell m—"

Galen's entry made them both turn. He too had that hopeless look about him, along with the dark hollows of fatigue framing his grey eyes.

He gave them a deep bow. "My lord. My lady."

"Galen, what's wrong?"

He led them to his lab where three stasis pods waited. Kell and Palleton stood guard, a pair of *donai* statues she could not read. A chill swept through her as she approached them. One of the pods had an opaque canopy. The others, while transparent, were murky with a white liquid.

Galen's voice was distant, cold, detached. He spoke in a pedantic monotone using technical language she didn't understand.

He caught himself, cleared his throat, and added, "I cannot help them. They are in stasis, but they will die. It's only a matter of time."

Her fingers flexed against one of the transparent canopies. "Who are they?"

"Lowran. And Cyra."

"And the third?" Syteria looked towards the opaque pod.

Galen's hesitation drew her gaze to him. He'd raised that clinical façade of his like a shield.

"Aeda," he said, clasping his hands behind him, as if that would make up for the strangled tone.

Syteria's hands formed into fists. Panic flared in her chest and a lump formed in her throat. She swallowed the lump, denied panic its power, and blinked tears away. Darien had remained at the periphery of the lab. She could not blame him. He had no doubt already seen this. Between this, and the child...

"There has to be a way to save them. You healed me. Gave me new life. I was on the verge of death as well. The *grierugon* wounded me worse, did it not?"

He shook his head. "Their chromosomes are being re-tasked. I don't know how or why. Despite all your injuries, your chromosomes were not damaged by the *grierugon*."

"Galen, please, assume I'm not from your world."

"My lady, this weapon. It was designed specifically to kill human women with *donai* lovers."

"Nanites as weapons?"

"Yes, my lady."

Of course. Why not weapons? The nanites were as much a tool as anything else. Fear sent her skin crawling, driving the sensation that something deadly, something invisible could be on her, in her, right now.

"It was meant for me." Her voice was far too controlled.

"Yes," Galen said. "We found a dormant version of the weapon in other women, but only those who had sex with *donai* are dying."

Shudders were threatening. Shudders and tears and screams.

"A punishment?" she asked. "For taking *donai* lovers?"

"For the *donai* taking human lovers."

"The *donai* are *not* dying, Galen."

He cleared his throat and made that deferential half-nod.

"Yes, my lady. The *donai's* nanites make them immune, but it is
punishment nevertheless. Or perhaps 'warning' would be a better word.
Since the women were not pregnant, the *donai* were not pair-bonded to
them."

The words sank deep like fresh stab wounds, evil, bitter little seeds
whose understanding she was just barely beginning to grasp.

"Had they been," Galen was saying, "pair-bonded that is, well..."

He was tugging at his collar again, a slight tremor to his hand.
Galen looked at Darien and said, "Pair-bonded *donai* who lose their
mates can become unstable and very dangerous. For a time."

Syteria pinned him with a glare. "If your wife or your daughter
were dying would you not become unstable? For a time."

Galen had the good grace to look chastised. "I don't have the *Edlyn*
at my command. *I* cannot start a war."

"Why am I still alive?" she asked.

"There was a higher priority target," he said. "Your child."

Syteria placed her hands on her belly and closed her eyes to hold
back the tears. Light seeped through them, like the warm glow of
Kappa's sun, broken only by the leaves of the forest she'd grown
up in.

Before she could stop herself, she gave the child form. He would
have his father's gold and amber eyes. His hair would curl, a dark
shade like his, except when the light hit it to reveal chestnut highlights.
He ran through the trees, leaving laughter in his wake, his bare feet
kicking up the dead leaves of autumn. A figure awaited him, a silhouette she strained to see.

The silhouette held out its arms and scooped him up. As the forest
shadows faded, they revealed her grandfather. Noden had been his
name. Noden Kainda. He was young, a Kappan man in his prime with
the paired knives on his belt. He smiled at her, not that sad smile
behind which he'd hid his pain the last time she'd seen him, but a
warm, happy smile. He kissed her child's cheek and then they both

faded and she swallowed the tears that had flooded the back of her throat and pressed her fist to her chest.

The thread of pair-bond hummed as Darien took her in his arms. She folded into him, determined not to give in to her pain, not to lay it naked before his *donai*. Sobs shook her. As if he understood, as if he knew that she did not want them to see, he placed himself between her and them.

Now that she'd given her dead child form and placed him in her grandfather's care, perhaps she could start filling that hole he'd left in her heart. She had no illusions. Grief and mourning were for the living, not the dead, and it would take time...

She took the grief, the regret, the pain, and the anger that accompanied them and nudged them together like a shepherd gathering a stray flock. She set them in the same direction. If there was to be an opportunity for vengeance she would take it, but until then, she had no desire for more deaths, for war.

But the *donai had* gone to war over a child.

Drawing in a ragged breath, she pushed out of Darien's embrace and looked up at him.

"Are you going to war over this?"

~

"Is it your wish that we go to war, my lady?" Darien asked.

Palleton and Bomani had already taken his command away. Galen had signed off on it, declaring him unfit. But it was only a matter of time before he got it back. And if his father decided to use his grandchild's murder as justification to rally the Houses against the emperor, to challenge Thán Kabrin's primacy, there would be war.

They had been three breaths from war when he'd been exiled. His claim had moved them a breath closer. Now they were just one away.

One innocent, unborn gasp away.

"Not until we have an heir," Syteria said, her face like stone.

He lowered his head slightly, a bow between equals. She understood. Despite who she was, or perhaps because of it, she understood that war could lead to his death and that his life might well be the price for victory. And she was placing their future child's life above his—like a true queen would.

"Galen, why am I not in one of these pods, dying?"

"I don't know, my lady. Perhaps the weapon only had enough energy for the higher priority target."

She drew another deep breath. Darien could feel the pain of it as if he were drawing it himself. He allowed the Cold to slip in a bit, just a touch. The Cold rewarded him with calm. A calm he saw reflected in Syteria as pain fled her body.

Pair-bond. It was real. He hadn't dared believe it. Would it last or was this the last fading residue of it? Would it slip away from them until they shared a child again?

Slowly, Syteria approached the stasis pod with the opaque canopy. Her fingers trembled as they passed over the dark surface.

"Aeda?" she asked, her voice choking on unshed tears. "Dead?"

Galen nodded.

"Can I see her?" It was a soft, ragged whisper filled with pain.

"Wouldn't you rather remember her as she was?" Darien asked.

"No," she said, raising her chin defiantly. "I wish to see her in death, so that when I think of our enemies, it is with absolute clarity. My lord."

"Galen, do as my lady commands."

Galen tugged at his collar as he worked the interface hovering over a nearby console. The canopy faded from opaque to transparent. Liquid swirled, so thick with nanites it was like milk. Gradually, it cleared, but Aeda's body must've sunk to the bottom.

Syteria leaned in, shoulders squared, splaying her hands atop the canopy, as if seeking to touch, to comfort, for one last time. She peered into the pod's depths.

A wail like that of a deeply wounded animal slipped out before Syteria stifled the sound with both hands and stumbled back. Darien heard her heart thunder in panicked flight. It drove the resonance between them into a maddened frenzy as painful as the one he'd felt when he'd realized their child had been murdered.

Darien's instincts kicked in. He placed himself between her and the pod, moved her behind him.

Kell and Palleton were at his side.

The tips of Kell's fingers dug into the canopy. Fractures appeared.

Palleton dragged him away before his grip could lead to a breach in containment. He pushed Kell into a bulkhead that bowed as his weight hit it. Kell's face was frozen in rage, but he stayed where Palleton put him.

The sounds from the healing canopy were like those of freezing liquids, drowning out the warning chime from the pod.

Palleton looked inside the pod and cleared his throat.

"My lord," he said. "You need to see this."

Syteria had placed her fists over her eyes. The thread between them resonated with silent screams that would not pass her lips. Galen pulled her away, took her into his arms and gave Darien a steely look.

Darien moved towards the pod.

Within, Aeda's red hair had transformed to chestnut brown. Her blue eyes were now green, open and staring back at him, even in death. Her face was in the process of morphing, changing from her own...to Syteria's.

Darien's heart skipped a beat. When its pounding resumed, it was with a rage-driven vigor that the Cold he'd drawn upon could not quell.

He saw his mother's stillness in death.

The Imperium burning.

The emperor's head severed by his own sword.

If Galen couldn't save Aeda and the other women, no one could.

All Darien could do was avenge them. He added them to the tally he owed the Imperium. At the top of that tally was his mother.

He could not bear the thought of adding Syteria to it. If he lost her—

Understanding struck him with the power of a lightning bolt. It speared into him, burning, consuming. This was why his father had chosen to—in the emperor's vernacular—"diminish him so."

He'd been told, countless times, that his father's love for his human concubine went beyond the pair-bond, beyond reason. Other *donai* had lost the humans they'd pair-bonded to and recovered. But his father never had.

The Imperium had expected his father to pursue a *donai* once the pair-bond with a human was broken. He had not. His father's devotion, even after his human concubine's death, was seen by the Imperial Court as defiance. But it went beyond defiance of the emperor's desire to maintain pure *donai* bloodlines for its nobility.

Darien saw it now. Saw it for what it really was.

It was a gift.

Father to son.

Another heir, one with a *donai* mother, wouldn't just have displaced him. It would've reinforced the Imperium's ability to control the Houses. Lineages would be controlled through the murder of human concubines.

Through murderous attacks like this one.

The Cold beckoned, inviting, promising to make it all easy, painless, guiltless if only he'd surrender to it and allow it to help him do impossible things.

Hyper-awareness wrapped Darien in its embrace, his senses sharpening to that painful edge that made everything slow down.

Kell and Palleton moving to the other pods, hitting the controls to clear the fluid.

Syteria's tears hitting the floor.

Galen's heart beating out a wretched tune as he tried to cover Syteria's face, denying her a look at the other pods.

Milky, nanite-rich fluid in the center pod faded to reveal Lowran. Her short black hair was more than half chestnut-brown and lengthening. Darien had taken the tall linguist's oath on Tir'Hala-Revir.

In the third pod, Cyra—a botanist responsible for the parkland— lay in the fetal position. The petite blonde was known for her brilliant blue eyes. Now they were open in jade-green death, her hair darkening and curling.

Forbidden fruit shall never bear proper fruit.

CHAPTER FORTY-SIX

*H*ands clasped behind his back, Darien paced the length of his flag cabin.

Stripping Darien of command had been standard procedure. He did not hold it against Palleton or Bomani. And he would never forget himself again. It was too dangerous to have someone with his power succumb to that bit of madness, no matter how brief.

Palleton sat at the breakfast table, a pile of food on his plate. Bomani's seat remained empty.

As Palleton chewed, he watched Darien with the eyes of a predator tracking his prey.

"Commander Bomani's duties prevent her from joining us," he said between bites. He poured himself some tea and stabbed a few sausages.

"How long do the three of you intend on keeping my command from me?" Darien could still hear Palleton shouting overrides to the *Edlyn*. He could still hear Galen speaking his rote script. He could still smell the lifeblood of his child.

"Until we return to Serigala," Palleton said. "Sit. Eat."

"Whose decision was that?" Darien asked.

"We received orders from your father."

"And the mission to Gamma Iramana?"

"Your father's orders didn't include an explanation. I'm sure that whatever is going on with Elva Tavernier's governorship is of a far lower priority than whatever prompted him to order us home."

His father could not know of the bio-weapon. There hadn't been enough time. Something else was happening.

Darien swiped his hand over his desk, bringing the surface to life. A backlog of holographic reports sprouted like sheets of rain flowing upward. He could not make anything of the chaos they showed.

"How did the emperor know what my lady looked like? The Rhoan ship's logs?" Palleton asked.

"No. Those logs would've shown her as she was, as *eniseri*. When we sent that imperial whelp back to his master. The bio-mechanical suits. They would have been recording."

"So they had her image," Palleton said, "but not her genetic code. They *had* to aim their weapon at human women, but couldn't specialize it for her."

Had they been able to...Darien shook his head to banish the thought. Palleton might not be able to read him as well as he could read humans, but read him he could. The elder *donai's* eyes sparkled gold in the dark face.

"Has a weapon like this been used before?" Darien asked.

"I don't think so." Palleton's brows drew together and they stayed that way as he wiped the corners of his mouth. He leaned back in the chair.

Darien crossed the room and poured himself a cup of tea. He took a sip. Like everything that had passed his lips over the last two—going on three—days, it was bitter, tainted by his grief. It had to be the Cold. Traces of it still flowed through him, as though they had never left him, would never leave him. Did Palleton's years of experience allow him to see the Cold when he looked at him?

"Galen has removed the dormant nanites from the rest of the crew," Darien said, setting the cup down. "He's working on countermeasures."

"Kabrin will try again," Palleton said with the certainty of experience. "With something different. Something better. Something that will defeat our countermeasures. Of this, I have no doubt. This is not the first time the emperor has decimated a House for breeding with too many humans. House Hevonen comes to mind."

Darien's hands clenched into fists.

"You think I don't know this?" The Cold had abandoned him, allowed rage into his voice, his blood. "I walked the paving stones that bear the names of Hevonen dead. I saw the Rhoan ship that brought Syteria here, or what was left of it, in the Imperial Gardens. The bones of the Rhoan crew were piled next to it. I know he means to add Syteria's bones to that pile."

"Her skin more likely," Palleton said matter-of-factly. "Makes a better trophy. Evokes a better sense of...understanding."

Shaking away the image, Darien met Palleton's stone-cold gaze with a venomous one. His mentor was testing him, enflaming his desire to order the *Edlyn* into imperial space and destroy Kabrin's trophy garden and the emperor along with it.

He smoothed out the layers of his white mourning robes and gave Palleton his back. The Void's soothing presence beckoned, framed by the viewscreen. Out of all the stars before him, the one halfway down from the middle and off to the left was the sun around which Kanavar orbited. And on it, his enemy, the man that had murdered his child, his mother, and had aimed death at his woman. Thán Kabrin would see House Dobromil destroyed, its worlds turned to ash.

"You would not tell me what happened when you went Cold," Palleton said, his voice gone low and quiet. "I have not asked you since. But I am asking you now. What did you do to provoke the emperor, to make him preemptively strike at your child?"

Darien closed his eyes for a moment, willed the beats of his heart into a steady rhythm, and matched breath to them.

"The emperor threatened to vacate my status as heir."

"Your status as heir never mattered to you before. To your father, yes, but not to you."

"Since my father won't take another mate, my child must be a proper *donai* heir. One with *donai* traits. Not human."

"Again, I ask, what did you do?"

"I let him think that Syteria bore a *donai* heir," Darien said, opening his eyes and turning to face his mentor.

He'd expected a reprimand, a scolding, a curse. Anything but what he got—disbelief, surprise, joy. They chased each other over Palleton's normally stoic face, each one brief, but intense.

Darien's frown elicited one of Palleton's signature huffs. "Did you think us blind?"

"Blind to what?"

"How strongly she affects you. How good of a match she is for you. It was the same with *your* mother. The moment I first saw Ilithyia, I knew. We all did."

"The first time you saw her, she shot you," Darien reminded him.

"Got me right here," Palleton said, splaying his hand over his heart. "Hurt too, even through my armor. No hesitation from her. She thought she was protecting your father. I scented him on her, and her on him, and I *knew*."

Skepticism played over Darien's features.

"What? You think me a monk?" Palleton asked. "I've taken lovers —human and *donai*. Never once was there even the slightest spark, much less the scorching fire I see between you and Syteria. Or that I saw between your parents. Not once."

Palleton was not speaking in metaphor. Not strictly. There were those among the elder *donai*, the ones created by the Ryhmans, that spoke of such things, of actually seeing the energy released when a couple touched. It had not been a trait to select for, but it had also not been a trait to weed out. Only the ghost of some long-dead Ryhman scientist knew for sure.

"When your father sent me to Lady Yedon as consort," Palleton said, "I turned her down. Do you want to know why?"

Darien blinked. His father had turned down Lady Yedon's proposal for an alliance. It had been just one in a long line of similar proposals, all of which had ended without a pregnancy, without pair-bond, and often with dire political consequences. To bond oneself to one of the emperor's closest allies would have cost House Dobromil too much of its autonomy.

"By all means," Darien said. "Tell me."

Palleton tapped the side of his nose. "She was ovulating, driving her *donai* armsmen to a frenzy they did not understand. She kept them in the dark, allowed them to become reckless, undisciplined. All to hide her condition. To hold on to her power.

"But she touched me—struck me actually," he said, rubbing at his cheek, then lowering his hand as if the flavor of the memory had changed. "Her pheromones were on my skin, seeping into my pores. They should have excited me. Instead, her touch made me feel tainted."

"Tainted? You allowed that to—"

"Refuse her. Yes. Why would I allow her to bind me to her for the rest of our lives? I am not some stud animal, something to be bred and discarded. Are you?"

"No," Darien said, understanding. He was not as different from his father, from his full-blooded cohorts, as he'd thought.

"The emperor has initiated many breeding programs," Palleton said, his gaze taking on a faraway look.

"Kabrin's grandfather thought he could command us, turn us all into breeding stock. At first, we obliged willingly enough. It soon lost its appeal, turned bitter. The wounds were too many to count, some never to heal."

"What kind of wounds?" Darien asked.

"Like that wound I saw in your eyes, your soul, when you thought Syteria dead on Tir'Hala-Revir. Has it healed?"

"No." If anything, it had torn open again, deeper and more painful every time he thought of losing her.

"Good. That is as it should be. Not a very useful thing when going into battle though, is it?"

Darien shook his head.

Palleton stood. "With your permission, my lord, I have to dissuade the commander from her renewed obsession with the possibility of a spy aboard the *Edlyn*."

"Do we have a spy aboard?"

Palleton considered that question long enough for Darien to conclude that the answer was a no.

"My lord, if there were any spies—human or *donai*—I would present them to you."

The chill of Palleton's smile made a small part of Darien, the very small human part, shudder. He could imagine it as vividly as any of the real things in front of him.

A gift, presented properly. Alive, but broken.

And he would accept, for they had struck at his heart and at his future.

GALEN WAS busy at an infirmary console when Darien walked into the antechamber. Empty bio-beds were lined up as always, waiting. Rovers nestled in their cradles, dormant. The sense of order gave Galen comfort. It was about the only thing that did.

"She's asleep," Galen said as Darien walked past him.

"I won't wake her."

"A word, my lord," Galen said and stood. He tugged at his collar, then dropped his hand to his side as if one gesture cancelled out the other.

Darien had stopped, a frown on his face.

"This weapon," Galen said. "Like the *grierugon* failsafe, it is beyond my expertise. Beyond the expertise of anyone on this ship. I need Damarin Keight's help."

Darien's frown deepened. "The same Damarin Keight my father sentenced to death?"

"The very same."

A brilliant man, Damarin was nevertheless a criminal in Dobromil's eyes. Even in the emperor's, although for different reasons. But he knew more about these kinds of weapons than Galen ever hoped to learn. Unlike Galen, Damarin had taken Dobromil's trust and abused it.

"Does my father know you helped him escape?" Darien asked.

The boy didn't miss much. He had to give him that.

And he had been a very young boy the last time Damarin had been on Serigala. That Darien remembered him at all was surprising. What else did he remember? The role Damarin had inadvertently played in his mother's death? No, not that. If that, Darien would be seeking vengeance.

"Answer the question, Galen. Does my father know?"

"Probably. He's not chosen to call me to task for it. Not yet, anyway."

"You play a very dangerous game," Darien said. Razor-sharp anger drove those words, making them less a warning and more of a threat.

Galen replied with an as-do-you look.

A bitter mask replaced the frown on Darien's face.

"How many dead women remade in Syteria's image do you want her to see?" Galen asked. "Hundreds? Thousands? Because while I neutralized what I found, I cannot guarantee that the Imperium won't be able to deploy this weapon—or a better version of it—throughout Dobromil's domain. And I really don't know why the weapon didn't kill Syteria. It should have. Killing her would have killed the child as well."

Darien moved over to the pods and for a moment, closed his eyes.

"I can't let you go after Keight."

Galen raised a critical brow. "Why? Because it defies your father?"

"No. Because I cannot guarantee your safety."

"It's a chance I'm willing to take."

Darien heaved a sigh, fatigue descending on him like a cloak. His shoulders remained just as square, his bearing as noble, but something had changed, perhaps in his eyes, or on his face.

"I told the emperor that my claim would bear proper fruit."

Galen slapped his hand down on the console beside him, the smack resonating in the quiet of the compartment.

"Arrogant fool," he muttered, not quite under his breath as his hands trembled with unspent fury.

Darien waited, unmoving.

Galen had no doubt, that in this one moment Darien would allow himself to be struck. Instead, Galen shoved his forefinger right into the center of Darien's chest.

"*You* killed your child. *You* killed these women," Galen said, voice shaking with anger. "*You*. Kabrin is going to think your heir, your *proper* fruit, your *warchild*, was my doing. It will renew his obsession."

Galen took a deeper breath, cut the air with an angry hand, and continued. "All your life, your father and I have worked to destroy this myth, this rumor, and you've...you've...You don't know what you've done."

He stepped away, shaking, running his hands through his hair. Placing his fisted hands atop a console, he let them bear his weight as his shoulders slumped. Fatigue displaced the anger draping over his shoulders like a heavy cloak—right atop the leaden one made of guilt.

"All myths are based in fact," Darien said.

"I've asked you before if you wanted to know why you aren't pure *donai*. You've never cared for an answer of any kind. Has the emperor's obsession now tainted you as well?"

"No. I know my father chose my mother to give me what he could never have."

It might as well have been Dobromil speaking, without a trace of humanity, without the changes Darien's mother had brought to his father. It belied everything Darien was, everything he should have been.

To see the father manifest so fully, even for just a moment, in his half-breed son, chilled the blood in Galen's veins.

"Is that what you are doing now? Choosing a mother to give your child something you cannot have?"

Darien's eyes blazed like twin suns. He was maddeningly silent.

Galen ran his hand through his hair again.

"You do understand, should Syteria give you a *donai* child, it *will* shift the balance of power. Whatever the emperor did to bring that Rhoan ship here, whether intentional or not, he will seek Rho. It will not end well for her people."

"That is why I'm trying to find out how Kabrin brought her here, before he can do it again. We cannot protect her people if the Imperium finds them first."

"We may not be able to protect them regardless," Galen said.

"I gave her my word and I intend to keep it."

"I know. That is why she agreed to risk her life."

"She is Kappan. A Kappan woman risks her life with every child she bears," Darien said, a hint of smug pride in his tone.

"The two of you." Galen let out a frustrated sigh. He shook his head. "A matched set."

"She suits me, Galen. Far more than you could have ever imagined. I never did thank you for that, did I?"

"I'm not sure I want your thanks, and I'm not sure you'll be very thankful if she dies because you put her in the emperor's way."

"She was in his way from the moment that wormhole opened."

"Oh yes, but then you and I," Galen said, his anger deflating, "took that and made it so much worse."

"I don't regret my decision."

"Of course not. You are *donai*. What are a few human deaths to you?"

A sneer formed on Darien's face, and along with it, the shift in vision. Nostrils flared. Hands curled into fists. And then, as if a switch had been flipped, they were all gone, and in their place something far more frightening—that arctic calm of a *donai* gone Cold.

Darien tugged at one of his sleeves and his hand came to rest at the dagger wrapped into the belt of his mourning robes.

"I will have my warchild and a queen to stand beside me. I will avenge every life taken by Thán Kabrin and his proxies, including you."

CHAPTER FORTY-SEVEN

*S*yteria held the position for an extra beat. The sword's tip pointed downward over her left shoulder in a defensive over-head block. Drenched in sweat, she paused to regain her breath.

She moved through the form, cutting the air, fighting an imaginary opponent because she had no tears left to shed.

Her body flowed into another diagonal cut, the blade slicing the air with a hiss. Pivoting into a counterclockwise arc, she raised her sword again.

She was no longer alone.

"Commander Bomani," Syteria said, lowering the sword.

She wanted to blame her grief, the numbness she dared not shake, for her lack of awareness, but couldn't. She had been careless.

"My lady." The judgmental tilt of Bomani's chin and the shallow-ness of her bow belied any respect.

Syteria bought herself some time by clearing imaginary blood from the channel forged down the center of the sword.

The blade's collar clicked into the scabbard's mouth. At her hip, the sheathed sword was a comforting weight.

Their gazes locked.

"Humans are forbidden the sword," Bomani said as though she were announcing that the sky was blue.

"I am aware."

"Are you also aware of the risk my lord is taking in teaching it to you? My lady."

The venom in Bomani's voice was potent. What kind of a threat did Bomani see in her? Was this another enemy—like the emperor—that she had not earned?

Since Darien had rescued her, Bomani had never sought her out. And why would she? She was not crew. Until recently, she had been someone to whom Bomani could barely speak. And she was unlike the other women who'd welcomed her. Who'd befriended her. Died because of her.

Perhaps Bomani was the smart one.

"We are alone, Commander. Be assured, I will not begrudge you the lack of my title."

"You should. You've never been out there in the Imperium, where humans are little more than chattel. This," Bomani said, indicating the *Edlyn* with a sweep of her hand, "is the smallest representation of an ideal, of what should be. But isn't."

Syteria advanced on the sword rack. She unfastened the cords at her waist and jerked the scabbard loose. Her hands were surprisingly steady as she placed the sheathed sword on its rack. She gave herself a few more heartbeats, a few more carefully drawn breaths to test the depth of her calm, and turned.

"Enlighten me," Syteria said.

Bomani's eyes widened.

"Please, Commander, tell me about the Imperium. Tell me about humans. Tell me everything."

Would Bomani comply or would she ration knowledge the way Galen and Anasera had? Probably not.

Bomani's sharp, biting tone hadn't implied that she considered Syteria fragile. She had no reason to protect her. In a way it was a relief, to finally meet another human who didn't see her as a fragile thing ready to shatter.

"It's a dangerous game," Bomani said, "for a human to get too close to the *donai*."

And I've gotten close. As close as anyone can get.

Syteria's nod invited Bomani to continue.

"My brother served as a diplomatic aide to Lord Dobromil. He attracted the attentions, some say the affections, of a female *donai*."

Bomani's face darkened as she approached the sword rack. She ran covetous hands over the curved sheaths.

"My brother was no fool," she continued, her voice shaking as she captured Syteria's gaze with a hard look. "He knew the male *donai* would never allow it, even though he posed no threat to their genome."

"What do you mean, no threat to their genome?"

"A female *donai's* nanites destroy human cells. It's impossible for a female *donai* to conceive a human's child."

"What happened?" Syteria asked, carefully keeping an eye on Bomani's hands and shifting her weight in case they wrapped around the sword's hilt.

"They returned him to Lord Dobromil with apologies and generous 'compensation.' "

Syteria's tongue moistened dry lips as the hair on the back of her neck rose.

Bomani's gaze faded into the distance. "I pieced him back together myself, all dozen perfectly preserved pieces of him."

That blue gaze returned to the here and now, sharpening.

"One part was missing," Bomani said. "Can you guess which one?"

Hand flying to her abdomen, Syteria backed away.

"They castrated him?" Syteria asked.

"Smart girl."

So, this message, this warning to House Dobromil, had been sent before.

"Galen has never seen this kind of weapon," Syteria said, fault lines cracking the calm she was trying to project. "This weapon the emperor aimed at me and used to kill my child."

Bomani's smile thinned to a thread, the ire in her eyes ample contrast to the line of her mouth.

"Have you asked yourself, if Galen has never seen this kind of weapon before, how can he know what else it has done to you?"

Bomani stepped closer, and added, "Once Lord Dobromil learns you bear no heir, he won't blame Galen. He'll blame you. You'll merely be the human who stands in the way of his son's ability to pair-bond with one of his own kind. You'll be the *arrogant* little human who dared cast herself as the fittest mate to his heir."

"I was not the one who cast myself in this role," Syteria said.

"What happens to you when Lord Dobromil finds out that Darien lied, that the child you lost was not the basis for his claim, that he's compromised not only himself but his House's honor?"

Bomani's thin smile turned into a smirk as she went on. "Lying to the emperor was one thing. I would tell a million lies to bring House Kabrin down. But lying to one's own men? That...that is something beyond redemption."

"He did it to save me. To save my life. And I will redeem his word. I will give him an heir."

Bomani laughed. "How naïve are you, child?"

"Go ahead," Syteria said, raising her chin. "Tell me."

"Naïve enough to think you have no options but what he's offered you. Naïve enough to think that his human side is dominant."

"I have seen what the *donai* are capable of."

"That little hunting expedition where they let us humans think we're something more, something worthy? Where they tempered who they are just enough to appeal to us? Do you think that's all there is to them?"

Syteria's heart denied Bomani's words. Bomani may have been with Darien far longer than she had, but she did not understand him.

"What happens the next time he goes cold?" Bomani asked.

There was a burning ache in Syteria's chest.

"Did he not mention going cold to you, his...lover?"

"Galen mentioned it."

"Let me guess," Bomani said, making a careless wave. "He used some clever little euphemism, like 'inhuman,' or some innocuous technicality."

"One does not have to be *donai* to be inhuman," Syteria said. If that's all Bomani had, she knew little of Syteria's past, of what she had been.

"I am being kind to you, girl. Far kinder than the female *donai* you will encounter as part of your 'duties.' "

"Why are you trying to scare me?"

"I am trying to help you. I'm here to offer you a way out, an escape. Away from him. From all of them. From the Imperium. A place where you wouldn't be found. An alternative to being his broodmare."

The doors behind Bomani parted.

"Yes, Commander, by all means. Show my lady the alternatives."

Syteria bore the full brunt of Darien's gaze as Bomani whirled. He walked past Bomani's stiff bow without acknowledging her.

"Commander," Darien said, his gaze locked on Syteria. "Prepare an infiltrator and stand by to launch."

"Destination?" Bomani asked without hesitation.

"The one place in the Outer Regions you think is out of the emperor's reach."

"Yes, my lord. I—" The barest tremor resonated in her voice.

"*You* will be dealt with, later."

He loomed in Syteria's field of vision like a golden-eyed titan with ice running through his veins, obscuring Bomani's retreat.

A potent desire to soothe him welled within Syteria. But he was the embodiment of control. Bomani was wrong. This was *not* his human side.

"Is it true? Are you giving up your pursuit of an ideal mate by claiming me?"

"No," he said sharply and without hesitation. "Have I not made this clear to you?"

"I am not the one who needs clarification."

The coils in his shoulders relaxed. "I had hoped to delay defining your role publicly, for a little longer."

"Why?"

"Bomani is correct. A human will not be welcome. Not by everyone."

"So I can expect more challenges."

"Our loyalty—yours *and* mine—will be tested," he said as amber returned to his eyes. "This too is part of being mine."

"And going cold?"

"It's a response to overwhelming threat directed at those we protect. It allows us to do whatever is needed without remorse or guilt, without emotion of any kind. My men will bring me out of it. It need never concern you."

She closed the gap between them and placed her hand on his chest. He looked down at her.

"What's a broodmare?"

"It's an insult that female *donai* use for women like you."

"That part I understood. Why is it an insult?"

"Because for decades at a time, humans are always fertile."

"Interesting."

He raised a mocking brow. "The comparative biology lesson?"

"No," she said, smiling. "They envy us—us 'broodmares.' "

He cocked his head and frowned.

"The Rhoans 'gifted' me with freedom from the 'curse' of fertility and the 'enslavement' to its results. The *donai* prize me for all the things the Rhoans deemed unnatural, immoral, and wrong."

"Other *donai* see you as a prize. That is not how I see you."

She moved her hand up to his cheek, caressing the coarse hair. Amber eyes studied her. She could see her own reflection in the golden pupils.

"And the Commander?" she asked.

He took her hand, caressed it, and tightening his possessively around hers. "Bomani *is* captain. I cannot afford to undermine her authority on this ship. But she is also my vassal and she is testing the bounds of her oath."

Would telling him that Bomani's offer held no temptation soothe him?

Had she been tempted?

Freedom from the Imperium sounded like an unattainable dream; one Bomani had not grabbed for herself.

Freedom from the *donai*? Something held these humans to these *donai*, drove them to earn a place among them.

Freedom from him would not be freedom. It wasn't just her desire to save her people. It wasn't just the thread that bound them, that resonated in her soul, that loved him. She would not change him despite his faults, and now Bomani had come expecting her to betray him.

Bomani thinks I have no honor.

"Is she lying about the world outside this ship?"

"No."

"Then perhaps it's time you stopped protecting me from the truth, or at least armed me with the knowledge I need to survive it."

It was in that utter silence, the naked need in his eyes, that assured her that she was truly prized. Prized and loved. She had already made her choice and cast her fate alongside his. Because she loved him. As unimaginable as that feeling had been for her most of her life, she loved him. Loved him enough to die for him.

"Darien, you must allow me to prove myself worthy to stand by your side."

DREA ENTERED THE ROYAL DECK. She steeled herself with a deep breath as heavy legs slowed her approach. It would've been easier if Palleton had been sent to arrest and drag her to Darien's flag cabin. It wouldn't have been much of a fight.

She'd always known she'd meet her end at the tip of a *donai's* sword. It might as well be Darien's. He'd be merciful, quick.

At least she'd earned her end. Her death would be unlike her brother's. The so-called autopsy had revealed the degree to which he'd lingered.

Had he begged? Pleaded?

Her death would be different. No pleading. No begging. She had done the right thing. And not just for herself. For House Dobromil. For its master. Even for Syteria.

Darien may not see it now, but eventually he would. His place upon the throne of Serigala rested on a *donai* child, not a human one. He had been fortunate to inherit so many *donai* traits, but whatever child Syteria gave him could not be more *donai* than he was.

The doors parted without a prompt. Her tongue went dry against her palate.

He sat behind his desk, arms wide, hands embracing the edges, attentive to data streaming across the desk's surface.

Within reach, the onyx curves of sheathed swords rested atop the desk. The mourning robes were gone. Traditional robes wrapped him in layers of black and crimson.

Death and blood.

She bowed and came to attention.

"My lord, the infiltrator is prepped and ready. The pilot is standing by to take my lady to a safe outpost in the Outer Regions." There was no shrillness, despite her ardent desire to scream at him.

She waited, eyes straight, gaze over his head. Past him. Right at the bare spot where Darien honored his mother's memory with a public display of her dagger. She looked for it on his desk. It wasn't there.

His silence and the clenched jaw were the only outward sign of struggle. For as long as she'd known him, this is how he'd worn his rage, how he nurtured it, using it as a fuel for other things.

The voice that emerged from that struggle to say, "We gave no such order," was quiet, clear, and colder than the Void.

Her objection died on her lips. It wasn't just his tone. She'd expected him to dress her down for breach of protocol, even exact the price for breaking her oath to him. She was willing to pay the price if it set him on the right course again. Her career, even her life, were worth it.

"This is not the Imperium," he said. She caught a glimpse of her service record.

"We do not require blind obedience," he continued, "but you have sworn fealty to House Dobromil and to me.

"We command your loyalty but your conscience remains your own.

"Your oath as an officer requires more than simple fealty, and our responsibilities to you are increased in turn. Your position as the *Edlyn's* captain places you in our chain of command, but we require officers to retain the ability to think."

His gaze finally rose to hers, and she braced herself in anticipation of rage.

"You. Are. Our. Vassal."

The precision edge of those carefully worded daggers dug into her soul.

"You are not our teacher."

She wished he'd reach for the swords—

"You are no longer our mentor."

—and end it.

"You are most definitely *not* our father's surrogate. You are here to cover our back, not go behind it. When you have concerns, you bring them to us, you do n—"

"And when my concern is *you*?"

She took another breath to brace her riposte. "I have a duty to this command, to everyone aboard this ship.

"We just came off a punishment detail from the ass-end of space as damage control for your last misadventure, yet you couldn't pass up the opportunity to further inflame matters.

"You enter Thertore's exclusion zone to satisfy your curiosity and think you're justified because you managed to steal one of the emperor's *grierugon.*

"And this woman. Another shiny new toy, as much a theft as that creature. I endorse your treason, for her sake, for saving her from the tender mercies of the Imperium, only to find her on a path to the same fate as your mother. At least Ilithyia understood the risks she faced."

She faltered under his gaze, under the look she'd put there. It was unfair, invoking his mother's memory to her cause, but she forged ahead.

"Ilithyia was the best of us. The Imperium ran her to ground, destroyed her, and almost destroyed your father and your House in the process.

"Does Syteria have *any* concept of what you are asking her to do?

Whose mantle you are asking her to don? The consequences of her failure? A responsible man, an honorable man, would mitigate her risks, not increase them by teaching her the sword."

She paused to draw breath.

"Just how large of a target must Syteria become to suit you?" she asked.

Darien leaned back in his chair, his grip on the armrests tight enough to crack the metal.

Drea took a step back, retreating, afraid that he'd gone cold. That fear had been an intimate companion ever since she'd learned that he had inherited that ability.

A member of the peerage stared back at her. Darien was every bit Thán Kabrin's cousin by lineage and nature, an emperor in waiting, willing and able to watch the world burn if it served him. The swords at the edge of her vision remained remarkably untouched.

Her legs faltered, weakening. Had her words destroyed the last vestiges of his humanity, along with whatever remnants of Ilithyia had survived this long?

"None can stand by our side without becoming targets," he said. "The best we can do is harden the target.

"We use damage control so we can live to fight another day, not as an end to itself. We do not take the path that will merely allow us to lose at a slower rate. We do not squander opportunities to gain intelligence because we fear risk. We do not stand idly by while House Kabrin consolidates and expands the power of the Imperium.

"For us, biology is destiny. If we die without issue, our mother's sacrifice is wasted. How large a target must Syteria become to suit us? As large as necessary."

He stood.

"Your concern for my lady's well-being would seem sincere if we hadn't walked in on you treading dangerously close to breaking your oath *and* enticing Syteria to treason. Had she been tempted by—should she ever become tempted by—your offer of 'freedom,' we would be required to treat her as a traitor and punish her."

A sick, roiling turmoil took Drea in its grip.

Unrelenting, Darien continued, "Imagine the satisfaction it would bring the Imperium to watch me carry out her sentence."

"I—"

"Commander, you are correct in that Syteria lacks the background to navigate the hazards of the Court, but you do not. That is why, when we return to Serigala, you will remedy Syteria's education and undo the damage you have done.

"Or you will board that infiltrator and take yourself out of our reach forever. A lifetime of service to House Dobromil has earned you this second chance.

"There will not be another."

CHAPTER FORTY-EIGHT

The chill of the hangar hung around Syteria, as damp and metallic as any graveyard. Her steps echoed despite her best attempt to quietly approach the three coffins.

They had been set in the center of the hangar. House Dobromil's banner was draped across each coffin. Two words blazed above and two below, also in red—blood on death—each one written with symbols that she was still struggling to master.

Black skirts swirled around her bare feet. Her arms were heavy with flowers. She cradled them to her chest as if they were a shield. A simple ribbon tied and held her hair back. Nothing elaborate, nothing glamorous, just the unburdened simplicity of mourning.

Galen walked beside her, wearing a more formal uniform with a black and red sash crossing from shoulder to waist. He came to a stop several steps from the coffins.

Syteria continued without him.

Her fingers were steady as she removed one stem and laid it atop the banner. She added another. And another.

Meticulous. Precise. Something she could control.

So strange, these people. Flowers for love and death. To celebrate and to mourn.

On Kappa, stones were laid out in precise spiraling patterns. Kappans had no time, no resources, for something as frivolous as flowers. Especially flowers designed just for coffins.

Soft white petals shone like stars against the black of the banner. The crisscrossing green of the stems and leaves were a reminder of life, renewal, and rebirth.

"There. Is this correct?" she asked, stepping back from her handiwork.

As if in answer, tears appeared on the petals, each one a perfect, sparkling statement of loss. A shimmer passed over the flowers, the stems, the tears.

Syteria ran her finger across one of the petals. It had turned to stone. Something that would not wither, would not rot, would not die. The tears gracing each of the petals sparkled like diamonds, then turned to rubies, and back again.

Teardrops and blood drops; loss and pain; acceptance and revenge.

Galen came up behind her. He undid his sash and shook it out. It flowed from its confines, flying out across the trio of coffins, to come down like a gossamer veil. It settled like a trail of fog clinging to the ground before sunrise.

It was then that the words "in war" appeared across that gossamer surface. The strokes of the lettering were bold and wide, written in the simpler version of their script—one used only by humans.

Galen backed away, breath shaking, the nervous way he stretched his neck belying the calm countenance he was projecting.

Syteria draped her arm across his shoulders.

"Why?" she asked. "I thought you didn't want this to be seen as an act of war."

"This is for their honor, not mine. Not *his*."

"I understand," she said. "Humans and *donai*. Bound together. One to the other."

He made a strangled sound and nodded. There was moisture in his eyes.

She leaned in and placed a chaste kiss on his cheek.

"Thank you, Galen. Thank you for my new life."

~

Syteria was surrounded by mirrors. They hovered in place around her.

Layers of white silk, at least a dozen of them, had been draped over her. She had expected them to hinder her motion, but they didn't. Their length hid the white slippers on her feet.

Her hair was loose behind her, flowing down almost to her knees. The weight of the dagger at her thigh seemed more prominent than before, an illusion created by the light touch of white finery. Darien had had a sheath made for her. Dobromil's sigil was stamped on every length of supple black and red braid, and etched into each buckle. It was a work of art worthy of a queen. As much of a relic as any of the finery she wore, it gave her a sense of comfort, of connection with her past.

Her lips tugged into an ironic smile. Unlike the sheath, the blade was not a relic and together they made a powerful statement: that her past held the future in its grasp.

She worked the fingers of her right hand through all the folds covering the blade. Syteria had made the cuts herself, much to Anasera's horror at defiling the relics.

They are mine now, are they not? Syteria had asked.

Anasera had nodded and made no further objections.

Syteria pulled the dagger out and re-sheathed it to make sure she could draw it properly. Satisfied, she dismissed all but one of the mirrors with a wave of her fingers. The mirrors changed back into utility fog and flowed away to cling to the chamber's walls. Only a shimmer betrayed their presence and then faded.

The woman in the mirror was no longer an *eniseri* drudge. She was no longer a victim, no longer a slave except maybe to duty and love.

She still saw traces of Aviel in her reflection—in the jade of her eyes, the chestnut hair, for this was the face she would have had, had she not been taken by the Rhoans. She gnawed at her lip with perfect white teeth she would not have had on Kappa. They would have worn down and started rotting by the time she'd have grown into an adult.

490

Her skin was flawless and unchanging and it still begged the question of how much of what she saw was Kappan and how much was Galen's relentless handiwork. She appreciated the quality of the workmanship, but she still would have liked to know how much time had passed.

Darien had said that, wormholes being what they were, they could not know. There were moments she believed him and moments where she did not. Even if ten thousand years had passed on Kappa, ten thousand years had not passed for her. Perhaps she was as much of a relic as her robes. It was just as well. The *donai* seemed to treasure their relics.

She held the swell of her still vacant abdomen in her left hand. Galen had reassured her: she was fertile. She could conceive. He'd also warned her that it could mean her life, as if that would have changed anything.

Her biggest fear was not that the child would kill her. It was that she could not have another, that the emptiness of one death could never be filled by another life. She feared that a spark would not ignite again and four lives had been sacrificed not only to send a message but to enforce it.

On Kappa, people died all the time. On Kappa there was no expectation of living to old age. On Kappa there was no expectation of happiness.

But here, in *his* world, all those things were possible, even for chattel. People here had not just expectations, but potential. It made the loss of those four lives seem heavier somehow, for she could not absolve herself of her part in them.

The cord in her chest trembled. Darien was near. She waved the remaining mirror away and turned as he entered.

Like her, he was wearing white, but his robes were made of a thicker material. Swords were tucked into his belt, a stark contrast with their obsidian shimmer.

He took a breath as if he was seeing her for the first time and a smile passed his lips. He bowed his head. She did the same.

His strides consumed the distance between them and she was looking up into amber eyes burning full of promise.

491

"We shall create new life," he said. "I swear it."

She wrapped her hand around his neck and pulled him down as she rose on her toes.

"Yes, we will," she whispered.

A triumphant smile lit the sharp, masculine angles of his face, but he schooled it into a neutral façade as he held out his arm. She placed hers atop his and allowed him to lead her to the balcony.

Below, the *Edlyn's* parkland was awash with white uniforms and robes. Everyone not on duty was present and waiting below.

The balcony lowered and opened onto a path covered in white petals. At the end of that path, a raised daïs awaited.

Bows preceded them as a breeze stirred the air around them.

So many faces. So many souls. All human.

No matter how sincere their bows, they still made her uncomfortable. She would never get used to them, despite knowing they were meant as a sign of respect. She never wanted to get used to them, whether or not they were for her, or for the man walking at her side.

And then, far too quickly, the moment was upon them. The *donai* waited on the daïs, their black swords prominently standing out against their white robes. They formed a semi-circle around a statue.

A wolf had been carved of obsidian stone that reflected streaks of red when the light hit it just right. The wolf was curled around a crystal bowl, its face in a snarl, its fangs bared. Amber eyes sparkled within all that black.

They stopped in front of it and Darien let go of her arm. He positioned himself by the statue's tail. She took her position by its head. She wanted to reach out and pat its snout. Instead, she stole a glance at Palleton, for if anything, the statue looked like an animal version of him.

"It is our tradition," Darien said, "that when a child is born, the mother yield her dagger to the father, that the father cut the cord connecting child and mother, that he place the dagger in the child's hand so that a weapon is the first thing the child holds."

His voice rose above them, as resonant and commanding as she had ever heard it. It tugged at the invisible thread between them with a power like she'd not felt since he'd compelled her. But instead of pain, a comforting strength embraced her.

"We have no cord to cut," Darien continued, "but we will honor our lost *donai* child"—surprised whispers passed over the crowd—"child with this rite."

Galen had not been able to tell if the child had been human or *donai* or something in between. The nanites that had formed around that nascent form had thwarted his ability to examine it. But *donai* meant heir and Darien had said that he could no longer afford to be just a father in mourning. He had to be both a warrior and prince, his actions no longer personal, but driven by political and military strategy.

He'd been created as a weapon by his father, just as she had been by the Rhoans. And what else would two such as them—cast in those molds—create except another weapon.

Warchild, they called it.

The word itself was like a dagger wielded against her soul. If she could place her hands around it she might pluck it from her chest, but she would not cast it aside. She would fold it against her heart and nurture it, give it such strength that it wouldn't just survive, but thrive. A mother could do no less. And neither could a father. This too was familiar, Kappan.

Syteria reached into the folds of her robes and pulled out the dagger Darien had given her. She held her left arm out, baring it and holding it so her palm faced the crowd.

This time, when she wielded the dagger, she did so knowing its sharpness and made a shallow cut along the upper part of her thumb.

Blood ran down into the bowl.

She passed the dagger to Darien's hand. His blood dripped into the bowl, mixing with hers. He held his cut open with the dagger so it wouldn't heal, holding her gaze the entire time. She saw their child in those eyes again and tears welled. She blinked them away.

When her blood clotted, he pulled the blade out and handed it back to her.

She placed it in the sheath, staining the white of the robes along the way.

Palleton stepped forward, dipped his forefinger into the bowl, and smeared blood across his lips. His eyes went from amber to gold, and he knelt in front of Darien and renewed his fealty oath.

Seventeen other *donai* followed his example. They all cast their augmented vision on her and yet, not once did she feel like she was their prey.

Darien had told her, that it was considered a great honor to be allowed to taste their lord's blood, and an even greater honor to taste hers. Most of them would never know the taste of a pregnant woman's blood. For a few more days her body still had traces of pregnancy in it.

He had another purpose as well. Now they would be able to swear, to the last man, that his claim had been valid, and the word of nineteen *donai* was not without value. The Imperial Court might reject Galen's word, for he was considered a traitor. They might reject Darien's for he was a half-breed, but they would not reject the word of so many *donai*.

It is my gift to them, he had said.

Kell was the last of them. He raised the bowl from its stand, raised it to his lips, and drank the remains as the crowd murmured its surprise. Their voices were drowned out as the *donai* pounded their chests in wordless, synchronized succession. She could feel the power of it pluck at the cord in her chest. Darien had not told her of this.

When Kell had had his fill, he lowered the bowl back to its stand, his eyes still shut, blood dripping down his chin. The pounding of *donai* chests came to an abrupt halt. Kell let out a roar and the pain of it echoed through the parkland, and when the echoes died, the air was still, as if no one dared breathe.

He turned his golden gaze to her and dropped to his knees at her feet.

She looked at Darien, a question on her face. He gave her the barest nod.

The other *donai* knelt, their gazes downcast.

Kell took her hands, drew them between his, and pledged his featly to Syteria Kainda, a Kappan, a human.

He pledged his life, his honor, his service to her.

"Command me," Kell said.

There was lump in her throat, one barely soothed by the proud look on Darien's face.

"Rise."

THE EXCITEMENT on the *Edlyn's* bridge assaulted Darien's senses. It was as if the bridge crew could not contain it, despite their adherence to procedures. The rhythmic whispers of telemetry were not enough to temper it. The familiarity of rote speech wasn't either.

His vision kept shifting, showing him their blood, their joy. Their scent was stronger too. He could see himself feed off of it, use it. Something had changed him. Perhaps the ceremony. Or the pair-bond. Or the Cold. Perhaps all three. Time would tell.

Syteria stood at his side. Her excitement was sweeter than the others. It was alloyed just a bit with trepidation. She would adapt. He had no doubt about it, even if she did.

She took hold of his hand as the *Edlyn* passed through the phase-point.

The main holographic display zoomed in on Serigala. Her eyes went wide at the sight of it, for it was impressive, even by *donai* standards.

It wasn't just the blue of its oceans, the vivid green and ochre of its continents, its sparkling icecaps, or its companion moons that looked like they had been sprinkled with diamonds. It was the honeycomb shell of the defensive grid around Serigala and its moons.

The *Edlyn* was approaching on a course that gave them only the dayside, showing off Serigala's clouds and its widest, deepest ocean. Despite having seen it a thousand times before, he held his breath. Her hand squeezed tight, warm and soothing, her pulse a steady throb. He squeezed back, despite the lack of decorum.

Bomani, and anyone else, was welcome to seethe about having Syteria on the bridge. Until his flag was reinstated, he was Lord

Dobromil's heir, and in that capacity, he could indulge Syteria and Bomani could deal with it.

The only one who didn't seem to care was Kell. He had taken his post at the entry. His gaze was not on Serigala. It was on Bomani. He too could smell the emotion-driven chemicals Bomani was putting out despite the professional demeanor that ignored Syteria's presence.

Bomani's calm, measured voice betrayed nothing as she responded to the hails of the small fleet of ships that had been sent to greet them.

Darien's gaze returned to Kell. The *Edlyn* had been buzzing about what he'd done, for no *donai* had ever given his oath to a human. It was an honor to be chosen to protect a lord's mate, but it had always been an honor bestowed, not taken.

When Darien had asked Kell why he'd done it, the man had been penitent. He had gone to one knee, made as deep of a bow as he could, all to signal that he still considered Darien his lord. Kell had sworn that his actions were not a challenge or a statement that he did not think Darien strong enough to protect Syteria.

Just as Palleton had been given to Darien at his birth to protect him, Kell wanted to be given to their heir in order to give meaning to Aeda's death.

Darien had accepted his explanation even though he knew there was more to it than a need for meaning. There was vengeance, and if Kell was at Syteria's side, then it was the best way to make sure he was there to get it. Darien could not fault him for it. To deny him would have meant taking the man's life, or declaring him outcast, which was the same, and he would not waste one with so much devotion.

Whatever the political fallout from Kell's act, it paled in comparison to what awaited Darien when he faced his father.

It had been almost a year since he'd last spoken to or seen Lord Dobromil. When he'd been exiled, he'd been a petulant young man who had thought he could bend the rules because his cause was just.

Today he was less petulant, less idealistic, and while his fondness for bending the rules had not waned, it had been tempered.

His status as heir had never mattered to him. He'd accepted it with reluctance, first out of obedience, then because he'd seen that it could be used to his purpose. And he'd misused the trust his father had put in him. Now that he'd made his penance, he hoped his father would see fit to trust him once again, for he was no longer merely the prodigal son.

He returned not just with a path to power, but with the future of House Dobromil standing beautifully at his side.

The End

NEWSLETTER SIGNUP

Be in the know! Be the first to know!

Sign up for my newsletter and get the latest news, releases, and maybe some freebies.

Click here to sign up or go to www.monalisafoster.com

ABOUT THE AUTHOR

Monalisa won life's lottery when she escaped communism and became an unhyphenated American citizen. Her works tend to explore themes of freedom, liberty, and personal responsibility. Despite her degree in physics, she's worked in several fields including engineering and medicine. She and her husband are living their happily ever after in Texas.

She learned English by reading and translating books from the juvenile section at the public library. She'd walk to the library with her dictionary and a notebook and start copying sentences and then translating them by hand.

After a few days of this, a kindly librarian took pity on her and offered her a library card and then broke some rules in issuing one to a ten-year-old. This was back in the bad old days when kids were still free range and parents didn't get jailed for letting them go places unsupervised. But, the library was air conditioned, an important thing when the temperature reaches triple digits, so she spent the summer there anyway, and along the way discovered Robert Heinlein and science fiction. It didn't take long to devour the juvenile section and move on to the grown-up books.

www.monalisafoster.com

facebook.com/MonalisaFosterStoryteller

twitter.com/HouseDobromil

amazon.com/Monalisa-Foster/B075Z7SDJ1

pinterest.com/m2foster

bookbub.com/authors/m2foster

goodreads.com/m2foster

instagram.com/monalisa_foster_storyteller

ENEMY BELOVED: A RAVAGES OF HONOR NOVELLA

Ilithyia Dayasagar survives alone, on a distant continent. For her mission to succeed, she must remain hidden.

But the fireball that splits the sky and scorches the earth does not go unnoticed. Neither does the corpse she finds instead of the meteor.

Especially once he turns out to be very much alive. And very much a mystery.

Passion and betrayal collide in "Enemy Beloved," a story of true love and sacrifice.[1]

Available exclusively for newsletter subscribers via www.monalisafoster.com.

---

1. A shorter version of this novella appeared in the Venus Anthology.

FEATHERLIGHT: A RAVAGES OF HONOR NOVELLA

Lady Valeria Yedon, the emperor's favorite assassin, thought herself free.

But in the Imperium, oaths of fealty have no expiration date. The burdens of duty and honor bind everything, and everyone, together.

And freedom always comes at a price.

Part of the **Ravages of Honor** universe, "Featherlight" focuses on one warrior's struggle for her future...and her soul.

DOMINION: A RAVAGES OF HONOR NOVELLA

Part of **Fiction River: Face the Strange**
(edited by Ron and Bridget Collins)

The fading chaos of rebellion gives rise to a new power. Rival Houses compete for precious knowledge essential to the *donai's* survival.

The key to victory and power exists in only one place: Teirani's head. Injured, short on time, she sees failure loom like a shadow across everything she has fought for.

Galeron has chased Teirani across the stars. He knows she will choose death before dishonor.

Now these two rivals must trust each other and work together. Without breaking their oaths. Without betraying themselves.

BONDS OF LOVE AND DUTY: A RAVAGES OF HONOR SHORT STORY

Available April 7, 2020

Mankind made a crucial mistake by creating the *donai*. Now its about to make another—one from which it may never recover.

For fifty years, Calyce has fulfilled the role of mother to the *donai* children under her care. Determined to save as many as possible, she comes up with a plan.

Andret cannot wait to start his formal military training. Calyce has raised him well. He would do anything for her.

Bonds of Love and Duty focuses on the early events leading to the *donai* rebellion against their human creators.[1]

---

1. "Bonds of Duty and Love" is a short story in this anthology edited by Laurell K. Hamilton and William McCaskey.

PRETENDING TO SLEEP: A COMMUNISM SURVIVOR'S SHORT STORY

Based on actual events, this short story provides a quick glimpse into life under Ceaucescu's brutal communist regime. Like so many Romanians, ten-year-old Renata lives in fear of Securitate (Ceaucescu's secret police). They don't always take you in the middle of the night. In a world where the living envy the dead, not all examples are made in the shadows. Some are made in the light of day.

(This book is appropriate for children 10 years and older.)

CATCHING THE DARK

Operation Barbarossa destroyed most of the Tsarina Tatiana Romanova's aircraft.

Sixteen-year-old Natalya loves to fly, to soar. And now she gets to. As the youngest member of the Tsarina's Own Night Bomber regiment.

A story for anyone who loves WW2 alt-history, aviation, and stories about heroism.

Night Witches strike terror in the hearts of darkness.[1]

---

1. "Catching the Dark" is a short story in the anthology, **To Slip the Surly Bonds** (edited by Chris Kennedy and James Young).

THE HERETIC

Ninety-two years of dynastic squabbles have cursed France with war. Men see God's hand in all. Even prophecy.

Jehanne, a peasant girl from Lorraine, aims to fulfill the prophecy by crowning a king.

But crowns do not make a king. Neither does Jehanne's obedience to God.

History tells us that Joan of Arc burned at the stake. What if history is wrong?[1]

---

1. "The Heretic" is part of the alternate history anthology Trouble in the Wind (Phases of Mars, Book 3) edited by Chris Kennedy and James Young

BELLONA'S GIFT

Mitzi Carrera's family hides in the Cochran jungle. Because of her, they face death every day.

They put up a good fight. They have done it for years. Despite her father's leadership, they cannot win.

Then the answer to their prayers drifts in on the evening tide. In order to save her father, she must guide a group of soft, untrained young men across the jungle.

The goddess of war has more than one gift to bestow on Mitzi. If she will only accept it.[1]

---

1. "Bellona's Gift" is part of Terra Nova: The Wars of Liberation, an anthology of the Carreraverse, edited by Tom Kratman.

PROMETHEA INVICTA

Promethea Invicta: A Novella

No longer part of the United States, in 2071 the Sovereign Republic of Texas remains bound by the Outer Space Treaty it inherited.

Theia Rhodos stands ready to free humanity from the shackles that keep lunar resources out of her reach. Done taking "no" for an answer, she acts boldly, ready to sacrifice everything.

Only the gods of scarcity, woe and lament stand in her way.

Everything in life has a cost. And a price.

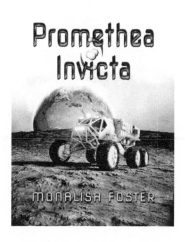

Made in the USA
Coppell, TX
03 January 2021

47392198R00308